SUMMERDAY

CHRISTOPHER ST. JOHN

Harvest Oak Press

Published by Harvest Oak Press, April 2023

First Printing, 2023

ISBN: 978-1-7368857-2-7 (paperback)
ISBN: 978-1-7368857-3-4 (ebook)

Cover art by Belle McClain

For the animals

Chapter 1

"Almighty Yah made the Blessed Ones, not to harm us, but to help us. They take the weakling, the foolish, and the disobedient, so that the Tree of Rabbitkind may grow strong," saith the Loved One.
                                                    —Book of Barley: 2:13–14

ANASTASIA

Anastasia flicked her long brown ears forward as she watched Freddie come racing up the high grassy hill near Warren *Sans Gloire*. It was only a few months since she had said *no* to a Blessed One, launching a tiny revolt that had somehow bumped the world off its axis. Something about the way her stocky black-and-gray friend was running suggested big news. And that usually meant bad news.

Freddie crested the hill and ran straight to her. The two rabbits touched noses. "Wolves are going to come," he said,

1

panting from his long dash. His eyes were wide in his harlequin face.

"What?" said Anastasia, standing up, her ropy muscles sliding under her stiff brown fur. "To the Free Warrens? Now?" A prickly buzz started at the base of her neck and traveled down her spine. She turned and looked northward.

"Don't know when," said Freddie. He sat up tall, and his gyrfalcon talon necklace gleamed in the sun. "But the scouts have come back. They went everywhere, even across the river."

"What did they say?" Anastasia hefted the Dragon Claw strapped to her right front paw, suddenly glad to feel the weight of it.

"They found out something about coyotes," said Freddie. "They work for those golden wolves who live way up north." He glanced over his shoulder.

Nicodemus, an elder rabbit who had been grazing some distance away, hopped toward them. "Yah's teeth," he said, his silver fur shining in the bright afternoon light. "Are you sure?"

"They talked to many warrens," said Freddie, his scent sharp and acrid. "They all said the same thing. Wolves rule. Coyotes serve. Everywhere."

Anastasia pulled down her left ear and cleaned it. "The golden wolf I talked to seemed to think they own everything," she said. She let go of her ear. "Called herself a Landlord."

"They're not going to be happy we killed a coyote," said Freddie, still breathing hard.

"No," said Anastasia. She quietly started touching the pebbles near her in a complex repeating pattern. She spoke thoughtfully. "So as soon as they hear about it, they're going to be—"

"Coming here," said Nicodemus. "If we killed one of their retainers, they *have* to come. They can't *not* do it."

"And that's another reason why this killing was never a good idea," said Freddie. His dark eyes flashed.

"It's not like we *wanted* to do it," bristled Nicodemus. "We were forced into it. And we didn't know they were so chummy with wolves."

"Friends," said Anastasia, raising her right forepaw in the *stop and hush* position. She took a deep breath. "We all did the best we could. The killing was"—she looked down for a moment—"horrendous. But it proved to everyone that things not only *could be* different, they *are* different."

"Yes," said Nicodemus. He sat up tall, though he was still stiff from his injuries. "Warrens are joining. The alliance is growing."

"And now we have to fight for it," said Anastasia.

"We probably have some time," said Nicodemus. "It's a very long way up to the Spires where the wolves live, and they don't come this far south very often. Good chance they haven't heard yet."

"All I ask," said Freddie. "Is that we don't forget who we are." He looked at them fiercely. "We are rabbits. We are lovers of life, earth, grass, water. We will fight to defend ourselves and our warrens, but we are not natural-born killers."

Anastasia rested her golden eyes on his, remembering the Battle of the Gyrfalcon, when Freddie had earned the claw that now hung from his necklace. The laughter of kittens playing drifted up from the field of sunflowers and white foxglove at the foot of the hill. In the distance, the bright blue Shandy River flowed serenely through the Million Acre Wood.

She came near to Freddie and touched noses with him. Her scent was warm and sweet. "We will do many things," she said, "but we won't forget that. I promise."

Then she turned and ran down the hill to the Warren *Sans Gloire*[1] drill yard, where rabbits, squirrels, and warmice were practicing with dummies made of various durable skins stretched over twig frames. There were apple peel weasels, pineapple skin foxes, and coyotes made of the new cactus leather the craftmice at Musmuski Grove had been working on. The warmice were attacking lower areas with their spears, while the rabbits were practicing jumping as high as they could and slashing with bite blades they held in their teeth. Squirrels were leaping from tree branches above like high divers, driving their thorn rapiers down and in.

Anastasia sprinted forward, and her Dragon Claw flashed out as she vaulted over a cactus leather coyote, striking downward as she cleared the shoulders. The bright sunlight picked out the wide, incised letters spelling out the name of the dragon it had come from: "X-ACTO."

Then she landed and rolled forward to where Yasmin and Holly were standing on one side, observing and talking. These two young mothers, both refugees from warrens that had cast them out, had become the administrative backbone that Anastasia relied on to get things done.

"Radish Team, go," called Yasmin, her cinnamon fur glowing in the sun. "Fig Team, fall back." She looked around.

---

[1]   Warren Without Glory.

"Resting teams, practice your paw signs. Silent talking could save your life one day."

As the teams changed places, Anastasia retracted her blade. "How are the teams doing?" she asked.

"Good. They have a lot of heart." Yasmin nuzzled her side. "Thank you again for asking me to be Captain of the Home Guard, Loving Auntie," she said. "Not everyone would be willing to appoint a foreigner." She touched the dark rim of fur around her eyes that showed her Hotot blood.

"No foreigners around here," said Anastasia. "*Sans Gloire* is the home warren of no one. And everyone." She exhaled sharply. "And it's about to get busy." She drew her paw across her throat, making the sign for *enemy*. "Wolves are going to come."

Holly blanched and looked around nervously. "Oh, my stars," she murmured, her amber and white fur quivering.

Yasmin drew a deep breath and stayed focused on Anastasia. "Tell me."

Anastasia quickly explained what the scouts were saying. "It won't be today or tomorrow. But almost certainly within a few weeks. They could have other Blessed Ones with them. Most likely coyotes. Maybe more."

Yasmin rocked back on her heels. "*Ahura Mazda*[2] be with us," she said. "I thought it would just be skirmishes for the next few months at least."

Anastasia shook her head. "It'll be more," she said. "We need to be ready. And we need to be smart. Let's talk it through, Captain."

---

[2]   Wise Lord.

Yasmin nodded and took a few steps to an area of bare earth. "Here's *San Gloire*," she said, drawing in the dirt. "Here's the high hill. Here's Tumble Stone Warren." She drew a small circle. "Here are our other allies." She indicated several other warrens. "First problem. The warrens are scattered. They don't share common perimeters. Each one will be on its own." She looked up at Anastasia.

"Second problem," said Anastasia. "The golden wolves are *much* bigger than coyotes. You remember the one we met. It would take a very lucky hero or some kind of monster rabbit to bring one down." She sucked her teeth. "And we're short on those."

"But a well-drilled team—" began Yasmin, her eyes drifting toward the attack dummies.

"Might do some damage," said Anastasia. "But the wolf would be killing left and right. And as soon as they were pressed, they could leap over everyone's head and take a new position. Or attack in any way that suits them."

"So our first response…" Yasmin rubbed the side of her head. Her scent was beginning to roil. "It's going to have to be a retreat underground," she said. "Keep the squirrels on high alert for early warning." She looked down at her earthsketch. "Widen the perimeters to give us more time. We're almost done gating all the entrances for the new allies." She chewed a foreclaw as she looked back and forth from Anastasia to Holly. "We could hold out for a while."

"We'll need to have supplies in all the warrens," said Holly, the mommy-at-large for the Free Warrens, as she pulled her ear down with her remaining foreleg and cleaned it. "Fruit for water. Greens for food. Rotated often. I can get everyone started on that."

"That's good," said Anastasia. "But that will buy us days, or at most a couple of weeks, before they just dig the warrens out." She sat up and looked at the plant leather dummies, currently surrounded by fierce mice, earnest rabbits, and acrobatic squirrels, eagerly leaping, attacking, shouting. "The thing is," she said, "if they get close to us, we've already lost."

ALIYAH

The muscular and graceful Aliyah Summerday slipped noiselessly through the tall balsam firs and tamarack trees that grew along the base of the Boreal Cliffs. She was just a day's walk north of the Shandy River, and she was scanning for deer. As the Lead Striker for the golden wolves of the Summerday Clan, she was a practiced and methodical killer. And she was hungry.

Her brother, Alaric, trailed sulkily behind her. It seemed like he was always grumpy these days. She decided to ignore him.

Little by little, she became aware of an auditory tickle from the songbird layer in the trees above. Usually, she tuned out songbird chatter as irrelevant, but slowly an odd sound was piercing her consciousness. It was a single syllable, popping forward out of the trills in flickering repetition. A sound she had never heard in the mouth of a songbird.

Coy.

Usually songbirds ignored coyotes, unless it was a meadowlark or some other ground nester. They were concerned about threats from climbers and flyers, not ground-based predators. There it was again, from a blackpoll warbler.

"Look at that big yellow grin
What a state that coyboy's in"

The notes had a frothy sound, almost like a chuckle. Aliyah stopped moving and cocked her ears. "What is it?" asked Alaric, in the studiously bored tone he had been affecting of late.

"Shhh," said Aliyah.

There was a flicker of gray above her. She saw a dark-eyed junco alight on a branch and began to sing.

"Coy is fierce and coy is free
Coy smell like a carrion tree"

The junco popped from branch to branch. It seemed happy, almost giddy. Aliyah squinted. It was a standard coyote insult. But why would this little songbird care so much? Behind her, she heard a northern cardinal open its throat and deliver a mocking couplet.

"Poor lil' coyboy, don't he lie
Cold under the summer sky?"

It seemed like a glimmer of laughter ran through all the songbirds within earshot. Alaric came close to her and nose-bumped her side. "Why are we stopping?"

Aliyah flicked her maple-green eyes toward him. "Don't you hear the songbirds?"

"Songbirds are ninnies," said Alaric. "They'll say anything that rhymes."

Aliyah frowned. "Clan *Paresseux* was having some kind of problem … with rabbits. Maybe it turned into something."

"Always with the coyotes," scoffed Alaric, as he took a moment to sit and groom his golden fur. "Not the sharpest thorns on the bramble."

"Sounds like something happened," said Aliyah. "I'm going to head down to the South Shandy and check it out." She turned and took a few steps southward. "Coming?"

"By all means," smirked Alaric, as he stood and moved toward her. "Mission of mercy. Helping those in need. That's what being a Landlord is all about."

Aiden

Aiden, the Rememberer of Bloody Thorn Warren, felt the sharp tang of thorn trees fill his nostrils as he came up the ramp to the meeting place favored by the Warren Mother. He chewed his lip. As the warren's resident officer of the priestly class, he often found it difficult to juggle Olympia's demands, the dictums of the ecclesiastical hierarchy, and his own goals.

His primary duty was to make the *Word of Yah* available to the rabbits of the warren. This oral text was occasionally corrected by the most senior Rememberers at the faith's governing body, the Known World Symposium. They had been causing problems recently.

And of course, Anastasia had been no end of trouble.

Olympia was pacing and looked distracted. A single sunbeam filtered down through the interlaced branches above and made the slash of white fur across her face gleam against her gray coat. Fufu, her little gray-and-red robin, was feeding on a dead beetle in a nook near her.

"Holy day," he said brightly, putting his game face on.

"Every one a gift," said Olympia. She stopped pacing and looked at him. "I've reached out to every Rememberer in the South Bank Conclave, whether they voted for me or not."

"Excellent," said Aiden. He preened his thick, cream-colored fur nervously, his dark ears flicking.

"I talked to the ones nearby, and sent messages to the others." She leaned down and kissed the robin's head. "Poor little Fufu has been flying so much, haven't you?"

"Yes, Mommy," said Fufu, and went back to cracking the beetle carapace in her strong beak.

"I've been disavowing Anastasia, apologizing for her actions, and calling for unity." Olympia began raking up clawfuls of dirt and tossing them. "She's my disgraced daughter. I can't run away from that. But I can be zealous in my efforts to deal with the problem."

Aiden nodded. "That should at least blunt the initial efforts to get a special election called to replace you," he said. "So your position as Presiding Spirit of the South Bank Conclave is still … safe?"

"Ish," said Olympia. "We need to do more. And I've been implying that we *will* do more." Her scent was brisk and pointy.

Aiden felt a prickle run over him. "Like what?"

"It depends on what my troubled girl child is doing," said Olympia. "Does she need to be helped into the loving arms of Yah as soon as possible? Or maybe she will pull back from the abyss and return to more rabbitlike ways, far from the killing fields of *Sans Gloire*." Olympia came near to Aiden. "You're my Rememberer. Give me counsel."

"Errmm," said Aiden as he did his best to look wise. "Yah always asks us to offer love first. The soft paw, not the sharp claw."

Olympia looked at him for a long moment and then nodded. "Then hop yourself over to Warren *Sans Gloire* and have a chat with our poor excuse for a spy. I don't think we're going to see our boy Coriander again, unless we force him to talk to us. See what there is to learn."

Aiden bowed. "It will be my honor to do so, Warren Mother."

Olympia rose and came close to him and bumped his hip with her own. "Don't forget," she said, "I want you to come by my sleeping chamber tonight."

Aiden nuzzled her fur and closed his eyes for a moment. Their arrangement had seemed so exciting when it started, especially for an ambitious bunny like himself. But Olympia was proving to be quite a handful. He pulled away and smiled warmly as he kissed her forehead. "How could I forget, Honored One?"

GAETAN

Gaetan and his sister Lilou were crouched under a creosote bush, making a very modest meal of a dead animal they had found, and they hoped no one would notice them. It would be another blow to their claim to be the alpha predators of the South Shandy.

"Five days ago we were the proud coyotes of Clan *Paresseux*,"[3] he muttered as he paused to groom his dirty-gray fur. "We were the *gendarmerie*[4] going to arrest a gang of criminal rabbits." He spat out a twig. "And today we're back to eating carrion. What happened?"

Lilou swallowed a mouthful of rotten flesh. "Edouard's murder has everyone spooked. No one knows what to do."

Gaetan finished his portion and turned to face her. "Once again, we're acting like dirty little scavengers instead of the alpha killers we could choose to be. Typical *ploucs*."[5]

Lilou, who had clearly heard this rant before, slowly sucked the remains of her meal off her forepaws. "We got along all right before. We should try to find everyone and bring them back together."

"I think we need to go to the wolves and tell them what's happening," said Gaetan. "We're their *agents*. It's the right thing to do." He crawled out from under the bush and started to pace in a small clearing, limping from the old injury to his foreleg. "And maybe they can help us."

Lilou looked at him. "Maybe." She chewed a foreclaw. "Or maybe we'll get fired as the Summerday agents in the South Shandy. Maybe they'll drive us out of the Million Acre Wood."

Gaetan stopped pacing. "I don't want to be having this conversation with the Summerdays *after* they find out we hid

---

[3]   Lazy.

[4]   Police.

[5]   Hicks.

Edouard's death from them," he said. "Imagine what kind of mood they would be in then."

Lilou sighed. "Mmmm, you're probably right," she said, dragging her claws through the scattered bones. "Why don't you go, and I'll try to round up the others."

Gaetan came over to her and nuzzled the side of her neck. "What I said about coyotes earlier, I didn't mean you."

"I know," she said. She kissed his forehead and offered the canid's parting benediction: "*May Hunger Mother be deaf to your running feet. May Blood Father be blind to your journey.*"

ALIYAH

Aliyah Summerday stood on a lofty bluff overlooking the Shandy River, her golden fur gleaming in the sun. She liked high places and chose them often. Her brother Alaric lay sprawled on a rock, sunning himself while he gazed with heavy-lidded eyes over the flatlands by the river's edge.

It was now well into autumn, and the wild mix of trees in the land the Dead Gods once called *Canada* had created a leafscape that was astonishing in its complexity. The changing climate had created a sylvan free-for-all as trees from every part of the world competed vigorously to establish themselves. Remnants of the old boreal forest stood bark by jowl with temperate woodland newcomers moving north as the winters grew milder and the summers drier. Non-native ornamentals freed from long-vanished suburban yards had found and exploited surprising niches. And a plethora of exotics and subtropicals escaped from city arboretums were finding toeholds in areas with just the right microclimates to help them survive in a land with occasional hard freezes and a light dusting of snow in winter. All of these mixed together in a swirl of un-precedented color palettes.

Alaric grunted as his yellow eyes drifted along the river bank. "Hey," he said, "a scruffy little coyote is coming this way. Looks to be injured. Maybe there *was* some kind of problem."

Aliyah glanced down the bank. "Oh, that one. It's Daetan. He always limps. Born with it or something." She scratched her ear. "But he should be able to tell us what's happening."

The coyote spotted Aliyah and started to jog toward them, awkwardly. As he followed a winding path upward, Aliyah noticed he looked thinner than the last time she had seen him.

"Running with a limp is so sad," said Alaric.

The coyote came within earshot. "So glad I saw you here," he said. "I was coming up north with news for the Summerday Clan, wise and kind stewards of the Million Acre Wood." He arrived at the hillock they were standing on. "My Lady Aliyah Summerday," he said, with a deep bow. "Lead Striker of the Summerday Clan and—"

"You don't need to do the whole thing," said Aliyah, impatiently.

The coyote turned to Alaric and bowed again. "My Lord Alaric—" he began.

"Do I know you?" broke in Alaric.

"Yes, my Lord," said the coyote. "I'm Gaetan. I was at the Shaman's Conclave last year. And as your loyal retainer, I'm coming to tell you. Something terrible has—" He stopped suddenly and then seemed to be struggling for words. He put on a pained smile and began again. "As your agents in the South Shandy, we strive to represent your interests in a way that reflects … appropriately … on your … but we must ask…"

"Out with it," said Alaric.

Gaetan's eyes were darting around. His scent was scattered, panicky. Aliyah held up her paw in a gesture of calm. "Speak, friend," she said. "As long as you haven't broken any of our laws, no harm will come to you."

"Rabbits killed Edouard," blurted Gaetan.

What? Aliyah felt a long prickly burn start at the base of her neck and slowly travel down her back. The two golden wolves stared at Gaetan without speaking. A mosquito hummed past Aliyah's golden ear. Then Alaric abruptly burst out laughing. "You coyotes have the *funniest* sense of humor." He stood up, looming over Gaetan. "What's next? Foxes are flying now?"

Gaetan struggled to stand upright with his injured leg. "It's real," he said, almost in a whisper. Then he ducked his head into his carrying pouch that he usually used for moneystones, and pulled out a shiny new bite blade.

The curved edge gleamed in the sun as Gaetan held the blade between his teeth and turned it this way and that. Alaric was stunned into silence. Aliyah stared at it, her maple-green eyes huge. After many seconds, Gaetan lay the blade down on a nearby rock.

Finally, Aliyah spoke. "A *rabbit* made this?"

"Yes, my Lady."

"How did you get this?"

"We've had skirmishes," said Gaetan. "A weasel brought it out of a warren when they retreated."

"And they killed a coyote with this?" Aliyah was very close to the blade now, her eyes travelling the length of the shiny metal.

"Something like this." Gaetan chewed a foreclaw. "Don't know exactly. We weren't there."

There was a sudden contemptuous exhalation from Alaric. "*Im*possible." He swatted the bite blade with his golden paw and sent it tumbling into the dust. "Look at it. It's no bigger than a mesquite thorn. Any predator that would let themselves be killed with this is an imbecile. Or drunk on dirty apples." His eyes flicked toward Gaetan. "Or weak." The coyote looked down.

Aliyah stared at Gaetan without speaking. In the distant recesses of her mind, an alarm bell was beginning to sound. *The luncheon meat are arming themselves.* The fortunes of many a noble house have turned on whether or not they could hear this bell when it rang.

"And how could rabbits make this?" continued Alaric. "They don't have hands. Probably just found it. Some Dead Gods thing." He started to pace. "And this nonsense can't even be *managed* by our local agents." He looked at Aliyah. "Which is why I've told Daddy *plenty* of times—"

"Hush!" said Aliyah, sharply. Alaric looked shocked, but as he was outranked, he held his tongue. Aliyah came up next to Alaric, pressing her golden muzzle alongside his, and then pushed him away from Gaetan with a quick head toss.

Then she slowly came near to Gaetan, her maple-green eyes fixed on him. He dropped his eyes, and then looked up and held her gaze. "Clan Summerday thanks you for this important information," she said. "With your leave, I will take this weapon and present it to the Clan Mother and Father. They will know what to do."

"Yes. Yes, certainly," said Gaetan, eagerly. "They will know what to do. And Clan *Paresseux* will stand with you. Always." He bowed. "Thank you so much for your kind words, my Lady. It means a lot to a hungry coyote."

Aliyah stepped forward and touched noses with him. Alaric watched stonily. "Thank you, Gaetan," she said. "I'm sure I'll see you again."

Gaetan bowed deeply. "Thank you, Lead Striker of the Summerday Clan and Golden Spirit of the Million—"

"Good *day*, boy," interrupted Alaric.

Gaetan turned to Alaric and bowed again. "And thank *you*, my Lord," he said. Then he headed down the path toward the river.

Alaric lay down and smirked at Aliyah. "Well, aren't you the Landlord every little coyote dreams of," he said. "The golden girl with the common touch."

LOVE BUG

Love Bug was leading a wide patrol along the edge of the wood near Warren *Sans Gloire*. As a hero of many battles, and the possessor of lush white fur, long dark eyelashes, and the gift of gab, he had once been quite popular with the does. But that had taken a left turn in recent weeks. He was mulling it over as he lollopped along.

When the squad came up to a small stream, Love Bug threw the paw sign for *Rest and refresh*. The squad members dropped out of formation to take a drink and have a nibble, leaving four squirrels on lookout in the branches above.

Freddie, on the left flank of the patrol, stood looking out across the half-mile of open meadowlands that covered the floodplains of the Shandy River. With his farblindness, everything more than a few yards away gently faded into a blurry wash of color.

Love Bug plopped down next to Freddie, startling him. He preened his thick fur.

"I had a dream about this place last night," said Freddie. "Golden wolves were coming up out of the water. At first just a few. Then more. There were dozens. Then hundreds, and—" He shuddered, remembering the army of golden blobs coming toward him.

"There's not that many of them," said Love Bug.

Freddie looked at him. "How do we know that?"

"It's a wolf pack. Aren't they usually around ten to fifteen?"

"That's just it. We're not experts on wolves. I've never even seen a wolf. Have you?"

"Some people have. Anastasia talked to one. Sort of."

"Still, we don't know what we're doing, but—" Freddie squinted out across the grass toward the river. "Something about this open space … seems like it holds the secret."

"Mmmm." Love Bug fiddled with his bite blade, making sure he could pull off the agave leather scabbard quickly and cleanly with his front paws. "Speaking of Loving Auntie," he said. "I notice I've seen Coriander visiting her bramble garden a lot lately."

Freddie's dark eyes flicked toward him. "Lots of people go there for meetings."

"He's taking little presents."

Freddie scowled. "All the does think he's so cute, with all the muscles and that shiny agouti fur." He bit vigorously into a seed head. "But Anastasia needs someone who really understands her."

Love Bug looked at him out of the side of his eye. "And who would that be?"

"Someone who's been here since the beginning," said Freddie. "Proved themselves in battle. Useful to the community."

Love Bug grinned at him. "You just described Coriander."

"Pffft," scoffed Freddie. "I mean the *very* beginning."

Love Bug leaned toward Freddie and put a friendly paw on his shoulder. "Buddy," he said. "I used to think I understood does. And then *poof!* it vanished overnight. Somehow, they make me crazy now. That's why I'm taking a vow of *celebrity.*"

"What?" Freddie squinted at him.

"You know, a vow of *celebratory … celerity … celestiality….*" Love Bug shook his head. "You know, that thing. Whatever it is, I'm doing it."

ANASTASIA

As the Loving Auntie visited her teams, trying to wrangle their next steps, she suddenly realized that she should be inspiring them, not just scaring them with bad news. So she nipped back to her chamber and put on the special armored jacket that had been made for her from a Kevlar onesie. She was wearing it with the golden side out, which matched the unbreakable golden ribs. And she was also sporting her shiny *aluminum d'or* circlet on her head. All this crafting had been done for her by Bricabrac, the freelance craftrat from City of Oom who had become the chief weapons maker for the Free Warrens over the last few months.

Now Anastasia was standing at the entryway to the straightstone burrow, which is what the rabbits called the open space among the foundations of the tumbledown cabin near Warren *Sans Gloire*. Bricabrac had taken over this space as a workshop.

She paused. It wasn't so long since her head sickness had required her to sing an entry spell and touch the sides and sill of any entryway she crossed. The need for this had been gradually diminishing in recent weeks, since the alliance of Free Warrens had pushed the local Blessed Ones back and reduced the moment-by-moment fear of death that most rabbits lived with. She took a deep breath and stepped through. There was a twinge, then everything was fine.

Inside, a team of craftmice was using a set of shears rigged with an axe-head as a counterweight. Using this ingenious system, devised by Freddie, they sang to keep time as they raised and lowered the blade to cut sheets of heavy pineapple leather.

>*"Up, mouses! Show your mettle*
>*We are mighty, we are strong*
>*Down, mouses! In fine fettle*
>*Snippy, snappy, goes our song!"*

She touched her paw to her forehead and extended it to the mice in the *respect* gesture, then walked toward the small group waiting for her. Two dark brown rats with copper earrings and a fierce-looking mouse stood as she approached.

By now, everyone had heard about what the scouts had learned, so Anastasia came right to the point. "Come a larger war, what can we make? What's possible?"

Bricabrac sucked in his breath. "You know we've used up all the hardstone and sharpstone. The cans have been cut into bite blades, and we used the nails to make spears."

He looked at his sister, Frippery. "We're using cactus spines as spear tips now," she said. "Not as strong as nails but the burn *will* get your attention." She smiled and her yellow teeth shone in the light of a long, slanting sunbeam.

Death Rage, the only warmouse who had ever been inside a coyote's mouth and lived to tell the tale, stepped up. "I've been testing fishbone rapiers with mushroom leather grips. They take a fine point and they're springy, so they won't break." She flexed a bone rapier with her fine hands. "These would easily be turned by armor, but no one has any." She held the rapier up in front of her face in salute. "Except you, Loving Auntie."

Bricabrac led the small group toward a materials staging area. "We've been having pretty good luck using seashells to make bite blades." He ran his finger along the edge of a shell that had been sharpened with sandstone, then lifted it into the sunbeam. The iridescent colors of the edge gleamed in the bright light. "These are brittle, but they will hold an edge. Not as good as metal, but the craftmice can make an almost infinite number of them. There could be an army of rabbits as large as you like."

Anastasia shuddered. "Which could just be more

slaughter." She nibbled her foreclaw. "The question is: How can we keep the wolves and their army from getting close to us?"

Bricabrac sucked in his breath. "That's ... I don't know." He began to sketch on the dirt floor. "We could build traps, but they could easily avoid them." He brushed his sketch away.

Anastasia's eyes roamed across the many fragments of paper littering the space, most of which had now been pushed into the corners to make more room to work. Have you tried looking at the page pieces?"

Bricabrac shrugged "Ya. It's just junk."

Chapter 2

O, find me a lettuce all moisty and green
And I'll show you something that you've never seen
Find me a mango as sweet as can be
I'll tell you about where the rabbits run free
  —Traditional foraging song of the northern rabbits

AIDEN

As Aiden trekked through the woods toward Warren *Sans Gloire*, his mind turned, as it often did, to the Yah's Flowers and his part in their creation.

A few months ago, Olympia had been elected Presiding Spirit of the South Shandy Conclave. That office had come with significant advantages which were a closely held secret: The Warren Mother who achieved this post was guaranteed a year without attacks on her warren by the local Blessed Ones. In return, she was obliged to propagate corrections to the Word of Yah to all the nearby warrens whenever they were delivered by the local representative of the Known World Symposium, the Lord Harmonizer Tobias.

When Tobias had appeared a few weeks ago with a new correction that suggested true believers would never run from predators, Aiden had come up with a way to make the local warrens accept this impossible teaching: make it aspirational for adult rabbits, and organize the young into troupes of zealots to be inculcated with this new idea.

The Rememberers at the thirty-seven warrens of the South Shandy Conclave had accepted this lawyerly fig leaf, so Olympia had fulfilled her duties and saved her perquisites.

The troupes of young rabbits had been dutifully created, given the new teaching, and dubbed the Yah's Flowers. After that, everyone held their breath. What would it really mean to never run? The Yah's Flowers at Bloody Thorn Warren would be safe, of course, because that warren had the guarantee of no attacks. But what about the other warrens?

The outcome was something of a mystery. As far as Aiden could tell, the number of casualties seemed low, although he had no idea why. Olympia said it was a miracle. It seemed unlikely that it would go on that way.

And his part in it had come to plague him. He had always been the clever rabbit, ever ready to throw out a new plan, his career assured. The idea that a solution he had suggested so glibly had been turned into a real-world policy that had already caused harm, and would almost certainly cause more, dogged him and made him doubt everything he had taken for granted.

Aiden was still lost in thought when he ran across a wide perimeter patrol about four hundred yards from Warren *Sans*

Gloire. First, there was a riffle among the tree branches as the squirrel lookouts swept past over his head, their three-inch thorn rapiers strapped to their backs. Then there was a quiet flurry near the ground as the warmice percolated through the grass, their spears trailing behind them. Last of all, he saw the rabbit fighters, moving across the landscape in a wide wedge formation. Their bite blades were hanging around their necks at the ready, with just a hint of bright sharpstone showing where the bite grip met the agave leather scabbards.

Aiden was unsure whether or not he should say anything. He certainly didn't want to identify himself as being from Bloody Thorn. The young patrol leader looked at him for a moment, then she tossed him a curt nod and passed on without speaking.

Aiden realized he had been holding his breath, and he exhaled quietly as he moved toward the warren in the early morning light. The area seemed unusually busy. He saw a group of rabbits dragging large leaves of kale, holding the stems in their mouths. He nodded and kept walking. A few minutes later, he saw a team of mice cutting off the top of a gourd.

Finally, he saw Coriander's muscular form, pushing a large cantaloupe toward one of the side entrances to Warren *Sans Gloire*. His copper agouti fur shimmered in the sun.

Aiden paused for a moment, unsure how to connect with this young Remembering acolyte he had placed in *Sans Gloire* as a spy, only to have him start losing track of whose side he was really on.

Finally, Aiden stepped forward and put his shoulder to the heavy fruit. "Holy day," he said quietly.

Coriander looked startled. "Every one a gift," he said automatically. After a moment, he leaned toward Aiden and whispered, "What are you doing here?"

"Just wanted to see how you were doing," said Aiden in a friendly tone, as he helped push the cantaloupe along. He gestured at the activity around them. "What is all this?"

Coriander gave him a long look. It seemed like he was going through some internal calculations. Finally, he said, "Wolves are going to be here. Soon, probably."

Aiden blinked. "What?"

Coriander explained what the rabbits of *Sans Gloire* had recently found out as he leaned into the cantaloupe. "We have to be ready for a siege. It could start soon."

Aiden was astonished. "I've never heard of anything like that."

"These are strange times," said Coriander, his back feet slipping in a patch of mud.

Aiden pushed with him in silence for a moment. "You know, you don't have to be here," he said, in a kindly voice. "You've more than earned that posting at the Known World Symposium. You took on a difficult mission and performed a great service to all Rabbitkind."

Coriander grunted as he shoved the cantaloupe up a small rise. He seemed to be muttering, then he exhaled sharply and shook his head. "My place is here."

"Ah," said Aiden. He stopped pushing and laid a paw on Coriander's shoulder. "Are you sure you want to do that?" He patted him. "I know how easy it is to get caught up in these things when you're young. It feels exciting to be part of something. But ... you have your whole life ahead of you." He stepped in front of Coriander and looked into his eyes. "Don't throw it away on a doomed cause."

Coriander shrugged off his paw. "Things can change. I've seen it. It *matters* what we do."

"Of course it matters," said Aiden. "That's why I want you to have a long life. So you can continue making a difference."

"Loving Auntie can do things no one else can," said Coriander as he shoved the heavy melon forward. His scent was dense and sturdy. "And she labors night and day for us. She eats and sleeps next to her earthmap in the bramble garden, trying to work out how to save as many people as possible. When has Olympia ever done anything besides look out for herself?"

"Well," Aiden stumbled and slipped as the cantaloupe rolled over some gravel. "Olympia is a wonderful … person who…" He shook his head and grimaced. "But I'm not here to talk about Olympia. I'm here to talk about you."

Coriander turned to face him. "The world *can* be different," he said. "And I want to help make that happen."

Aiden looked at him searchingly. "Are you sure you're doing the right thing?"

The young acolyte sat up tall. His eyes were steady. "I'm sure."

Aiden gazed at him without speaking.

Coriander wiped a smear of mud off his forehead. "I mean, I'm no murderer. I won't kill for this cause, but…"

"Will you die for it?" asked Aiden.

Coriander started to turn away and then looked back at Aiden. "We'll see."

Lilou

Lilou had spent most of a day tracking down the scattered coyotes of Clan *Paresseux*. She had found just a handful. And now they were gathered together in a stand of balsam firs, far from the tamarind grove where they first heard the terrible news about Edouard's death. Still stunned, they spoke in low tones and quietly groomed each other. It was hard to know what to talk about when every conversation led toward the black hole of recent events: murderous rabbits and the world turned upside down.

So, of course, the coyotes were only too glad for the distraction when a young coyote rushed into the midst of the pack and announced that he had seen a yearling deer just two miles away, upwind, grazing in a grove of jacaranda trees at the foot of the Boreal Cliffs.

This was what a coyote lived for. They looked at each other, glimmerings of hope in their yellow and gray eyes. It felt like a sign. Maybe the old order could return. What if their lives didn't have to revolve around rabbits? Slowly, things began to feel normal again as they proposed plans, dismissed other people's plans, and argued like friends at a sleepover.

Lilou watched all this feelgood chatter with dismay. "Don't even kid yourselves," she said. "You know what Micah Summerday said: No hunting deer unless we're doing it with the wolves."

The coyotes fell silent and looked at her. Benoit, the elder, sat up and glared. His ribs showed plainly through his dirty gray fur in the late afternoon sun. "Can't you just let us … be real hunters again?"

"What do you think's going to happen, *andouille*?"[6] asked Lilou, her scent dark and pointed. "You think rabbits are bad? Try a pack of golden wolves." She moved toward Benoit and looked into his eyes. "It's death. For everyone." Benoit glanced away. Lilou's gaze swept the group. "Or haven't you had enough of that already?"

She tried to nuzzle against Benoit to soften her words. He pulled away. "A coyote who lives in fear is not a coyote," said Benoit. He looked at the few remaining members of the pack, one at a time. "Let the *faibles*[7] do what they want. I'm gonna get me some deer. Just like my *père*[8] taught me."

ANASTASIA

Anastasia found Wendy at the beach, sitting next to a scarred and ancient piece of driftwood. She was chewing a nub of protruding wood as she stared out to sea. A cool, salty breeze blew in off the waves.

As the only lop-eared bunny in the Million Acre Wood, Wendy stood in stark contrast to the other rabbits of *Sans Gloire*. Her face was broad, her muzzle blunt, and her long brown ears hung down by her face. Her wide hips were supported by huge back feet, and her fur hung loose on her like a plush onesie.

When she noticed Anastasia approaching, she frowned

---

[6]   Literally, "blood sausage." Figuratively, "stupid."

[7]   Weak.

[8]   Daddy.

and started chewing with greater ferocity. Her necklace of raptor claws rattled as she moved.

Anastasia sat near her. She gazed at the tumbling gray waves in silence for a few moments. At last, she said, "How are you?"

Wendy sat still, her ears lifting lightly in the wind. Then she spat out a piece of wood. Her scent was dark and sludgy. A seagull swooped low overhead.

Anastasia took a deep breath. "I'm guessing there may have been hurt feelings when some people were asked to be Captain of the Home Guard and other people weren't."

"Geh," said Wendy. She pulled a splinter of wood out from between her teeth with her foreclaw and flicked it away. "Why you think I care?"

"You did amazing things. *Sans Gloire* could not exist without you."

Wendy shrugged. "Hrgggrmmm."

In truth, this sturdy lop-ear from a culture of warrior rabbits had at one point been the only bunny at *Sans Gloire* who had any real idea how to fight predators. Anastasia had armed herself and flung her body into battle, but it was Wendy who had taught the other rabbits real tactics for the first time.

Anastasia moved so she could look Wendy in the eye. "Wolves are going to come," she said. "Soon." She explained what they had learned from the scouts. "And if they get close to the Free Warrens, especially with an army, it will just be a few days before everyone is Glorified. All the mothers. All the kittens. Everyone."

Wendy cocked her head and traced the ancient termite intaglio on the driftwood with her foreclaw.

Anastasia sat up. "We need to somehow push the fight north, up toward the wolves. So we need an Assault Team." Anastasia looked out over the waves for a moment, then back to Wendy's broad face. "And that means we need an Assault Leader."

Wendy's eyes were dark as obsidian. She nodded a few times, then stood up and stretched, letting loose an extravagant fart. She came near to Anastasia and sat down. "I miss world," she said bluntly.

Anastasia nodded. She had thought this might be coming, so she was ready. "I understand. I would miss my home, too." She spread her paws wide. "We know now that you came from an island. If you do this thing for us, here is what we will do for you. We will befriend seagulls and pay them to scout the shoreline. Once we find the island you came from, we will pay a water rat to build an ocean-going vessel large enough to carry you, and then hire the rat and a seagull scout to deliver you safely to your home."

Wendy leaned back against the log. "Why you think you can do this?"

Anastasia brought her paws together. "We know your home island is nearby. We read about it in a piece of newspaper from Warren *Feu de Lune*."[9]

Wendy looked suspicious. "Ehhhh…"

"The newspaper mentioned Elsie MacGowan," said Anastasia.

Hearing the name of her god had an electric effect on

---

[9]   Fire of the Moon.

Wendy. Suddenly, she was very close to Anastasia. "What she say?"

Anastasia did not look away from Wendy's dark and hungry eyes. "She loved her bunnies, and she would fight for them. She was *fierce*."

For just a moment, Wendy looked soft and teary. She sagged against the driftwood and wiped her eyes. Her breath, for once, was not rumbly but high in her throat, like a kitten. Then she abruptly stood upright. "How I know this real?"

Anastasia decided to play her hand as hard as she could, based on what she remembered from the article Nicodemus had read to her. "I know the name of your world," she said. She came close to Wendy's ear and whispered, "MacGowan's Lop Hoppers."

Wendy leaped straight up into the air, landed and bounced in a different direction, then whirled and dashed a few paces before throwing herself sideways and rolling over the marram grass, all the while emitting a series of high-pitched grunts and squeals. Anastasia, astonished at this frolic, suddenly realized she was seeing something she had never seen before: Wendy was *binking*.

"Ya! Ya! Ya!" she was shouting, as she tumbled and rolled. "I going home!"

ALIYAH

Aliyah was late reaching the Summerday family howl since Alaric had been lollygagging along the coast on their journey north, looking for dead sea animals washed up on shore.

As she crested the last rise, she could see the forest of

stone columns called the Spires by animals living in the North Shandy. They were pillars soft sandstone topped with hard caps of basalt, carved by the wind into fantastic shapes. Plants grew in niches in the stone, with long green tendrils hanging down.

The Summerday wolf clan had for many generations made this their home base when they were not roaming.

In the upper reaches of the Spires lived a murder of crows. They swirled among the columns, calling loudly. The strident music of their voices carried far out over the treetops.

In the center of the Spires was a place where several columns had collapsed, many thousands of years before, and the rubble had weathered into a stony hill, now covered with yucca and green and pink bromeliad. The wolves called it the Hill of Voices. They had a long tradition of commemorating the phases of the lunar cycle by gathering here when the sun was low in the sky and lifting their voices to the heavens.

As Aliyah loped forward, she could see most of the Clan was already assembled. So the hill was a mass of golden, partly golden and gray wolves, heads upturned, voices lifted in a sinuous growly howl, holding an empty space in the center of the sound.

She arrived and climbed to her designated spot. As a full-blooded gold, she was huge, larger than many of the males. Her size and bravado had earned her the position of Third She and Lead Striker. It was a dangerous job: The Striker was the wolf who made the move to bring down the prey after a long run. It meant going in close, tearing at the throat or belly, taking a chance on injury from sharp hooves or sweeping horns.

The bite blade was in her carrying pouch. She had wanted

33

to share it privately with her mother first. But since the howl had already begun, she now had to wait for the right moment to present it to the group. The Summerday wolves were sticklers for propriety.

Alaric reached the hill a little behind her. He nipped the Least Wolf, who yelped and rolled onto his back in submission. Then, as Fourth He, Alaric bounded up the hill and took a spot just below Aliyah.

A few moments later, Micah and Sephora Summerday appeared, walking side by side down the wide avenue between the tallest Spires. Their lush golden coats burned like fire in the long low rays of the setting sun.

Micah Summerday was larger than any wolf a Dead God had ever seen. The mutation that made the Summerday clan golden in color had also added heft and muscle. He had the massive canine teeth of a sovereign killer and the aquamarine eyes of an otherworldly lion. Sephora Summerday was larger than most half-gold males. The muscles in her long legs moved with careless power under her tawny skin as she strode. Her leaping ability and the murderous effectiveness of her canines were legendary throughout the Million Acre Wood. And her evergreen eyes shone with a cool intelligence.

They climbed the hill together, and settled onto the flat space on top with easy familiarity. Then they each raised their heads, and with unhurried joy, lifted their voices to join the family howl and weave the many dissonant voices into harmony.

Together the wolves' voices rose and fell, drifted from side to side, developed cascades of harmony, stretched into broad dissonance, returned to intimate consonance, then resolved into slow and tender diminuendo.

At last, they were done. Sephora Summerday looked at Micah, and he gazed out over the many upturned faces and began to speak. "Wolves are a kindly people. When Kiskari Highsummer killed my father and united the two golden packs into the Summerday Clan, he could have killed me and my sister, but he did not." He paused, "Instead, he raised us as his own children, because, as has been known since time immemorial, the wolf is a creature of love."

Several ratifying howls lifted into the warm air.

"We all know hunting has been thin lately," said Sephora kindly. "I look at you here today and see wolves who have been going hungry. How many days has it been since we've seized the gift of a deer's warm self-offering and said, '*Turn your face from me, Hunger Mother*'?"

There was a general groan with a sad, flatted third.

Micah resumed speaking. "But even in these hard times, with hunting hard and threats growing, I ask you, sisters and brothers: Should we act with our hearts and adopt a lone whose pack was attacked by the Municipal Wolves of City of Oom?" With a nod of his head, he indicated a young silver wolf coming out from behind a stone column dotted with fuchsia plumeria blossoms.

The young wolf looked uncertain. Nearby, Aliyah heard Alaric growl, "Why do we need these hangers-on?" Annoyed, she yipped in support of the new wolf.

"I'm Tennyson," said the new wolf. "My clan was destroyed on the orders of the bears in the City, even though we were no threat to them."

There was a general growl at the mention of the bears.

Tennyson's gaze swept across the other wolves as he continued. "The Municipal Wolves tried to chase me off the Boreal Cliffs, but I doubled back and came down the Midsummer Path." Aliyah noticed a keen intelligence in his eyes. "I'm no golden, but I can run, track, and fight."

"So can I," said Alaric. "And I *am*."

Tennyson looked away from him, making eye contact with Aliyah and several other Summerday wolves. "I have nowhere else to go. But I won't trespass on your hunting grounds. Either take me in or send me to the Forever Forest."

"With pleasure," growled Alaric, lips rising to expose his teeth.

"Stop," rumbled Micah. He padded down the hill, claws clicking on the stones. His scent was cool and relaxed. "I know these times have put everyone on edge," he said. He touched noses with Alaric, giving him a meaningful glance, then Tennyson. "Let us hear from the whole clan." There was much yipping in support, and just Alaric and a few of the other young males spoke against.

"I hear you," said Sephora." She turned to Tennyson. "Welcome to Clan Summerday." She returned to her place at the top of the hill. "And now, other business?"

Aliyah bounded up onto an outcropping. "I have news from the south," she said. "One of our agents in Clan *Paresseux* has been killed."

The wolves stared at her in silence. "By who?" said Sephora.

"The bears?" asked another golden wolf.

Aliyah shook her head. "This will sound strange, but it's some kind of uprising. The luncheon meat are organizing—"

Loud guffaws broke out. Aliyah ignored them. "They have weapons." She dipped her nose into her carrying pouch and brought out the bite blade.

The hill quieted as all the wolves leaned forward to look at the weapon held in Aliyah's teeth.

Alaric sat up very tall. "Number one," he harrumphed. "This is why having coyotes as our agents in the South Shandy is not the best idea." He shook his coat. "Not the right sort. Not the best people." His eyes flicked toward Micah.

"We don't want another *wolf* pack in the South Shandy," said Sephora. "They need to be clear subsidiaries—"

"Number two," broke in Alaric. "There's no way rabbits made this."

"Hush!" said Aliyah.

"You can't hush me. We're on the Hill of Voices," said Alaric.

"*Rabbits* killed a coyote?" asked Micah Summerday, very slowly.

"They had help," said Aliyah.

There followed a lengthy conversation about exactly what they did and didn't know, and what to do next. At last, the Clan Mother and Father came to a conclusion.

"We don't want to compromise our dignity as Landlords by flying off the handle," said Micah. "Our reputation is the most powerful thing we have. If we leap into action, we're telling everyone that the Summerdays are *concerned*."

"Which we're not," said Alaric.

"We need to know more," said Sephora. "So we will call on our esteemed friends." She lifted her head and called, "Grammy Kark, may we have a word?"

After a few moments, an ancient black crow came circling down from a nest on one of the stone columns.

"Greetings, mother of my mother," said Sephora, sitting up.

"What is it you need, golden child?" replied the crow in a creaky voice.

"The loving kindness of your murder," said Sephora.

The crow chuckled, making a sound like glass breaking. "The murder is here for you, now and always, delightful one." She flew up onto an outcropping near Sephora. "We will send some fast flyers south to check out these"—her eyes swept across Aliyah—"improbable tales." Then she hopped onto Sephora's back and groomed the fur around her ears. "Until we hear back, I bid you … sweet dreams."

ANASTASIA

Anastasia found Freddie as he was working with a team of rabbits excavating a deep run inside Warren *Sans Gloire*. He was gazing intently at the shiny, craggy surface of a chunk of purple amethyst embedded in the earthen wall of the run. He turned excitedly when he heard her approaching.

"Oh, hey, Loving Auntie. That idea I had about our water supply is working out." He nuzzled her shoulder. "I think we're getting down near the level of the stream. The soil is wet, and we've done some tests." He led Anastasia along the run. "If we dig a hole and let it sit, it gradually fills with water." He splashed up a spray of drops with his paw. "This could give an inside water source if there's a siege. Holly's been talking about how much we need this."

"That's wonderful, Freddie," said Anastasia. "You do so much for us." She double-bumped his flank. "Now I want to ask you something. You know that when it comes to a fight, we need something more than we have now."

"Ya," said Freddie. "I've been thinking about that. Not sure what."

"There are many pages at the straightstone burrow," said Anastasia.

"We've looked at a lot of them," said Freddie. "Mostly it's stuff that doesn't make sense. Or just scraps with a few words on them."

"These pages are the Dead Gods speaking," said Anastasia. "They're our best chance to learn something really new."

Freddie nodded slowly. "That's true."

"So we need to do everything we can to glean something useful." Anastasia nibbled her foreclaw. "You know the straightstone burrow best. I'm thinking you could gather up the Readers and apprentices from our allies and go and search that place from top to bottom. Look at every piece of paper, no matter how small. See if you can put them together." She drew a small design in the earth. "I know it sounds crazy but … we don't really have any other options."

Freddie took a deep breath and sat up tall. "Yes, Loving Auntie," he said. "I won't let you down."

AIDEN

Aiden caught up with Olympia as she was supervising an enlargement of Bloody Thorn warren. The First Born were leading the digging, and the lower-ranking rabbits were pushing the earth out. Her gray fur was covered with a light dusting of fresh dirt, and she looked pleased. Fufu was pecking through the fresh earth, looking for grubs.

"Holy day," she said, smiling, as Aiden approached. "Now that Iris and Pebble have had their kittens, we need more room."

"Every one a gift," said Aiden, trying not to look anxious. "So wonderful, Honored One."

"Yes," said Olympia. "Each one a wonderful gift." She started to walk toward a grove of sugar maples a stone's throw away. Fufu followed after. "We're proving, once again, that you don't need to break the rules to have a successful warren."

"Absolutely not," said Aiden.

When they reached the grove, she bumped him playfully, then turned and faced him. "Now," she said, "What did you learn, smart boy?"

He looked into her eyes. "Wolves are coming."

Olympia looked shocked. "Tell me everything." Aiden poured out all that he had learned from his trip to *Sans Gloire*.

Olympia put her face in her paws. "Yah protect us." Her scent was dark and whirling. "My poor girl is bringing down a new kind of Blessed wrath on Rabbitkind that has never been seen before." She stood abruptly and stamped. Then she stamped again and made as if to nip Aiden. He jumped back. "This is bigger than Bloody Thorn now. Bigger than the South Bank Conclave."

"Yes," said Aiden. "But what should we—"

"I think," said Olympia, her eyes skittering around the maple grove. "This calls for—" She put her paw to her mouth. "This *demands* direct action." She came close to Aiden and fixed him with her ocean-blue eyes. "And you've given us the key." She touched noses with him. "Good work, counselor."

Aiden nodded and forced what he hoped was a brave smile. "Thank you. What—"

She set off briskly for the far side of the warren. "We need help. Time for the Garden of Unmentionables."

ANASTASIA

"Thanks for coming to the brambles," said Anastasia as Coriander entered, his copper agouti fur shining in the last rays of the sun. "Oh, what are these?"

Coriander set down the sprig of bright red berries he had carrying in his jaws. "Lingonberries," he said and sat down next to the patch of clay where Anastasia had been sketching a map of the area.

A crow flew by, calling loudly. Mabel, the acolyte and party girl from Tumble Stone Warren, entered a moment later. Her fur was a lustrous black and white, and the two colors met in a swirl in the middle of her forehead.

Anastasia came close to the berries and sniffed. "I've never seen these before."

"They don't grow around here," said Coriander. "It was a bit of a walk to get them, but I thought you might find them refreshing. They're tart."

"Oooo," said Mabel, nosing among the berries. "Aren't you a sweetheart, just like everybody says."

Coriander shrugged. "Just want to support the Loving Auntie."

"I consider myself supported," said Anastasia, with a

mouth full of berries. "Now let's have a chat." She settled down and let her golden eyes come to rest on them. "How can the Word of Yah help the Free Warrens?"

Mabel and Coriander looked at each other.

"Um, the Yah's Flowers we've been talking to are very receptive," said Mabel. "In six to nine months, when they're yearlings, I think they'll be interested in joining us."

Anastasia nodded and drew a small flower in the earth. "If we're still here."

She thought back to how she had taken Mabel and Coriander, both Remembering acolytes, in the early dawn to have a quiet talk with the very first Yah's Flowers after she had first learned of Olympia's new program. Hearing the baby bunnies sing their hymn about never running from Blessed had been heartbreaking. So Anastasia had improvised some foundational-sounding stories about digging 'huggy holes' so you always could hug your mother, the good earth, when Blessed Ones came by.

When the baby rabbits had asked where this teaching came from, Mabel had invented a source, telling them it was from Newly Beloved, heroine of a little-known part of the Word of Yah, the *Book of Secrets*. It seemed to work, so Anastasia had sent Mabel and Coriander to have secret chats with the baby rabbits at all the warrens in the South Bank Conclave—thus undoing the worst of Olympia's dark work of *realpolitik*.

Anastasia snapped out of her reverie. "Sorry. How can we reach the adults?"

Mabel sat up and placed her paws together. "Warrens who want to join are excited by the idea of freedom, and they only need the thinnest kind of ecclesiastical rationale. I can put that together for them." She picked up a lingonberry and nibbled it. "Even when this story about the wolves coming starts to get out, I think we can still keep attracting new warrens south of the river." She groomed her ear. "Because the wolves are far away, and freedom tastes good *now*."

Anastasia nodded. "So we can keep growing? With all the resources that brings?"

Mabel nodded. "Ya. But if the wolves cross the river, a lot of those sunshine allies are going to disappear. The Free Warrens will shrivel up like an old piece of fruit."

Chapter 3

Two kinds of people in this world: rats and rubes.
—Rat proverb

Lilou

The coyotes of Clan *Paresseux* were running fast and silently through a mixture of pinyon-juniper scrub and old boreal forest. Lilou ran after them, angry and frustrated. "Stop!" she shouted. "Think about what you're doing! Do you want to die for this one meal? Micah Summerday will crack your bones!"

Benoit, the rangy elder, dropped back and ran beside her. "I hear you, *sœur*,"[10] he panted. "You're a good member. You always have a coyote's back."

---

[10]   Sister.

"And I always will," said Lilou, tears leaking from the corners of her eyes.

Benoit glanced at her as he loped along. "If I have to live my life afraid of wolves *and* rabbits, it's not worth living."

"This is just a moment. It doesn't have to be the end of the story," panted Lilou.

Benoit shook his head. "Don't mess this up for us. I wouldn't hurt you, but … I might not be able to stop the others."

The coyotes ahead had come to a stop on a low hilltop. Through the foliage, their sharp eyes could pick out the buck, two hundred yards upwind, in the thick brush under a grove of white birches. With an ease born of long practice, they split up and threw their quiet perimeter around him at two hundred yards out.

Lilou stood on the hill, unable to leave. She watched her pack members creep forward. In a few minutes, the deed was done and they were making their meal.

A young crow flew low overhead, circling several times. "Clan *Paresseux!*" he called. "One, two, three, four, five mighty hunters." Then he was gone.

OLYMPIA

"Thank you, lovey," said Olympia. "Sorry for the short notice."

Darius, the Prime Buck of Bloody Thorn Warren, nodded as he turned and led Olympia and Aiden through his Garden of Unmentionables. His tan fur stippled with brown caused him to merge with the dappled shadows as he moved. Fufu the robin fluttered overhead.

Olympia turned and cast a glance back toward Aiden. "No nibbling."

Darius was peering at the plants as he lollopped among them, muttering to himself. He passed a green, weedy-looking plant with small white flowers. "Hemlock," he murmured.

"Ah, yes," said Olympia.

Darius took a few more steps. "Castor bean," he said, indicating a shrub with many-pointed leaves and poky red flowers. "Not ripe yet."

"Mmmm hmmm," said Olympia. She looked at Aiden. He was staring around with large eyes. The Garden was usually forbidden for all warren members, including officers.

He sidled up to her. "What are these plants, Honored One?"

"These are … tools," said Olympia. "Yah has given them to us to use as needed."

Darius came to a low plant with a spray of large leaves. "Tobacco," he said. "Not quite ready."

"Use for what?" asked Aiden.

"Many things," said Olympia. "Helping people with … transitions that can be difficult."

Aiden frowned. "Like medicine?"

"Spiritual medicine," said Olympia.

"And here we are," said Darius. He stopped before a shrub with purple flowers and shiny black berries. "Nightshade." He peered at the berries, carefully. "I believe some of these are ripe now."

Olympia turned to Aiden. "Tell Fufu where to find the food brought in for Anastasia every day."

Aiden took a step back. "Why?"

Olympia sighed. She had forgotten that Aiden did not know that it was she who had unleashed the coyotes on Anastasia a few weeks ago. *It's so hard for the young ones when it comes time to make their first real decision.*

Aiden

Aiden fidgeted. "I'm really not sure what…"

Olympia smiled and turned her summer-ocean eyes on him. "Honored Rememberer," she said. "You've seen how the sickness in my dear daughter's mind torments her. And now she's upsetting the age-old ways of the world. This can only bring suffering to more rabbits."

"Mmmm," said Aiden, noncommittally.

Darius came forward with a sprig of nightshade berries, being careful not to touch the fruit. He laid it on the earth.

"These sweet holy berries of love will help her fall gently down into the arms of sleep," said Olympia. "And she'll never need to wake up to this sad world again."

Aiden stared at her. His responsibility for the Yah's Flowers idea was already showing up in his nightmares, even though it had been a useful career move. But helping to murder Anastasia, whom he knew well—he had seen her entire childhood—seemed like a leap into the darkness. His stomach flip-flopped.

Olympia came near to him. "This is what's best for *everyone*," she said. "Anastasia can rest in the warm embrace of the Loved One. Her followers will remember her fondly as they gently disperse. The threat will vanish, so the wolves will have no need to come. And you'll be the Rememberer who helped manage the crisis. Today, Bloody Thorn Warren. Tomorrow, Known World Symposium. You could be Lord Harmonizer one day." Fufu came spiraling down from above and perched on a woody stem, gazing at Aiden.

Aiden felt his head spinning. *Steady now. This is the moment for firm action. Don't want to end up a soft little fool like Coriander.* He took a deep breath.

Olympia nuzzled his cheek. "And I'll be your biggest fan," she whispered.

Aiden opened his mouth and found himself talking. "Take the berries to the bramble garden behind the poplar tree that grows over Warren *Sans Gloire*. You'll find fresh fruit and greens near an earthmap. Leave them there."

Olympia kissed his check. "Now there's a smart boy."

ALIYAH

Aliyah, Sephora, and Tennyson were tearing at a dead turtle that had washed up on the beach not far from the Spires.

"Thank you for finding this and sharing it with us," said Sephora, her golden fur dappled by the salt breeze.

Tennyson bowed. "It's the least I can do."

Aliyah noticed the way the bright silver of his coat shone in the summer sun. "Why did the bears order your pack to be attacked?"

"The bears want more and more," he said. "City of Oom is growing. They're now claiming all of the Shandy River valley as their demesne." He glanced in the direction of the Boreal Cliffs. "Used to be plenty for everyone in the uplands. But the more the bears take, the less there is to go around."

"Have you been to the City?" asked Aliyah, as she gripped a decayed flipper with her teeth.

"Yes," said Tennyson. "There's a lot happening there. I could tell you more about it some time."

"Clan Summerday has always had good relations with the bears," said Sephora. She tugged at the lower shell. "At a distance."

Tennyson nodded as he swallowed a lump of flesh. "Distance is good."

"I'm afraid you've found us in reduced circumstances," said Sephora, licking her paw. "Still, we will do what it takes to survive." She gazed for a moment at the mess of carrion between them. "A wolf that only thrives in the fat times is no wolf at all."

Just then, Grammy Kark and a young crow came gliding over the dunes, dark against the white sand. They landed near Sephora. The younger crow looked at Grammy Kark.

"Our fastest flyers have been down in the South Shandy, looking for signs of a rabbit uprising." She pecked at a fragment of turtle flesh and ate it. "That remains undetermined. But we did see some malfeasance that we knew you would want to hear about." She looked at the younger crow. "Tell them, Cacao."

Cacao bobbed his head. "Five coyotes had killed a deer, and they were feasting. It was Clan *Paresseux*."

Sephora's eyes half closed. Her scent was suddenly dark and acidic. She exhaled slowly. "How do you know it was them?"

"I saw many of them at the solstice gathering last year," said Cacao.

Aliyah chewed her lip. "Did one of them … walk with a limp?"

Cacao turned to her. "No."

"Are you sure?" Her maple green eyes were fastened on his.

Cacao and Grammy Kark shared an amused glance. "A crow does not forget," said Grammy Kark. "Have a care not to insult your shadow friends, little one." She took a step toward Sephora. "Shall we summon them?"

"No." Sephora's evergreen eyes were opaque and cool. "We may want to meet with them … onsite."

CORIANDER

Coriander slipped up the ramp into the bramble garden, with some fresh sprigs of dill in his mouth. Anastasia was not there, but he knew she would be back soon, as she had another meeting scheduled with the Home Guard leadership, working on more defense plans.

There were many delightful foodstuffs piled near her earthmap. Everyone knew the Loving Auntie was working hard, so bringing in a little treat for her had become something of a heartfelt pilgrimage for members of the warren. Coriander laid his dill atop the stack, near a sprig of dark berries. As he turned to go, he saw a little gray-and-red robin fluttering through the brambles, singing quietly. He thought nothing of it.

Anastasia came up the entrance ramp as he went down, and the golden circlet on her head shone in a sunbeam angling through the thorns.

He nodded by way of salute. "Loving Auntie."

"Mmmm," she said, lost in thought.

He continued down the ramp and headed back outside for evening feed. The warm day was passing into a long, lovely twilight. A hermit thrush was singing.

From a distance, he could hear Love Bug telling riddles to the kittens. There was a faint ripple of laughter, followed by, "That's stoopid, Uncle Bug!" Coriander smiled and nibbled some carrot tops.

There was a flicker of extra darkness as a crow flew by low overhead, moving silently and fast. Coriander remembered something he had wanted to tell Anastasia. It was an idea about using the Word of Yah as a morale builder. Her meeting wouldn't have started yet. It would take just a moment to mention it.

He turned and headed back to the bramble garden. As he was coming up the ramp, he heard a soft sound. A quiet cry of pain. He could hear the terror in it.

He froze for a moment, and an instant later was racing up the ramp and bursting into Anastasia's meeting chamber.

She was laying on her side, half-eaten greens scattered around her. The sprig of black shiny berries near her head seemed to absorb all the light in the space. Coriander rushed to her face. Her mouth was open, her breath coming fast and ragged. Her eyes were open, and her pupils were huge, as dark and shiny as the berries.

Coriander raced down the passage to the healing hall, yelling about Anastasia and poison. Grégoire was out, but Juniper was there sorting a pile of herbs. She ran back with him, taking a moment to run by the library to find Nicodemus.

The old gray rabbit met them in the passage, eyes wide

and alarmed at the noise, and followed them back to Anastasia. Freddie and some apprentice Readers came trailing after.

In a few seconds, they were by her side, filling the space and scuffling the foodstuffs. Coriander thought he heard Freddie calling out something, but then most of his world went silent. All he could hear was Anastasia's fast thready breath and small sounds of her paws scraping the floor as though she were running.

Nicodemus was shouting at him now. He came awake, pawing around in the mess of scattered food, finally coming up with the sprig of nightshade berries. Nicodemus blanched when he saw it, then immediately sent Juniper to the healing hall to bring back *ipecacuanha* roots. She dashed away.

Nicodemus banged at Coriander with questions about the nightshade berries. He felt bewildered. He knew nothing about them. Then Juniper came back with the bark. Nicodemus seized it and began chewing it, letting the liquid drip from his mouth into Anastasia's throat. Freddie hovered around her head, kissing her ears and stroking her fur as tears ran from his eyes. The area was filled with rabbits, and more were coming into the hallway.

Nicodemus threw the paw sign for *Stop and hush*, and all the shouting stopped. All the rabbits held their breath and listened to her fast, shallow breathing. Only Freddie's stifled sobs could be heard. Coriander's mind was roaring. *How did this happen? How?*

ANASTASIA

In a dreamspace, Anastasia was running fast over meadow-land and scrub, up and down hills of dead fescue and thistle, under a leaden sky. She dashed through a dark wood of lodge-pole pine where no birds sang. And she sprinted along the marshy banks of a river, studded with horsetails and bracken. At last she came to the shore of a dusky red ocean, so large that it could swallow the sun.

She stopped and looked out over the wine-dark sea. And a large, roiling whirl of shapes rose up from the water. It looked as though it were made of parts of many animals, or every animal. And the elements she could see merged, grew together, sank back into the center, and were replaced by other shapes. She saw faces, limbs, ears, tails. Eyes within eyes. Teeth within teeth. But she was not afraid.

The whirling shape spoke in a voice that sounded ancient beyond imagining. "I have been waiting for you, child."

Anastasia felt the voice flow over and around her. It was like being wrapped in the coziest warmth possible. And being known, perfectly. "Who are you?" she asked.

"Anima Mundi[11]," said the tumble of life. The voice was like a thousand animals speaking all at once, somehow melded into a unified whole.

Anastasia bowed deeply and covered her eyes with her paws. "Are you an angel of Yah?"

The vast spirit did not answer. A bright whirl of light came forward and wrapped around her.

"Arise, Anastasia," said the vast spirit.

Anastasia sat up, her forepaws spread apart, facing upwards.

---

[11] Life of the World.

"You are forgiven for your killing," said Anima Mundi.

The little brown bunny felt a tremendous weight being lifted off her shoulders. She wanted to speak, explain, offer thanks, make promises, but she could feel none of that was wanted.

An immense rumble came toward her from the whirling gyre. "But know this: every death is cause for sadness."

A stinging wind, wet with salty spray, blew in off the ocean and hit Anastasia in the face. The salt drew tears from her eyes. She bowed her head. "I understand."

"Your path will not be easy," said Anima Mundi. "So I give you this gift. Nothing is more powerful than the word. The word creates. Everything else follows."

The salt breeze grew stronger. Anastasia wiped her face. "So what should I do?"

There was no answer except the roaring of the wind.

"What should I do?" Anastasia asked again.

The thousand voices spoke for the last time. "You have everything you need."

Then the spirit came near to her. And as the spinning tumble drew close, looming over her, she was afraid.

Suddenly, it seemed as though the turbulent power had entered her, and her own body was now a fierce storm of chaotic energy. She was scared that she would be torn apart. She tried to call out but could make no sound.

NICODEMUS

Anastasia began convulsing. Her abdomen heaved. Then she heaved again. The third time, a stream of liquid poured out, black and stinking. An anxious hubbub rose in the room.

"No, that's good," said Nicodemus. "She's getting the poison out." Anastasia continued to push out the deadly toxins. Freddie gently held her ears and whispered into them fiercely. Rabbits pressed around on every side. "Take her out to the greensward," said Nicodemus. "She needs more air. Bring her water."

Coriander and many other rabbits picked up Anastasia and carried her down the ramp and through the passageways. Her body was terribly limp; there was no fight in her. They lay her on her side on a soft patch of moss and earth near the main entrance. Her two front paws lay lightly together. The metal circlet on her forehead shone in the last rays of the sun. Juniper and the Reading apprentices ran for leaf cups of water. Freddie lay near her head, his paws resting lightly on her side. His tears trickled down her fur. Coriander knelt by her feet and chafed them between his paws.

Dozens of rabbits had gathered by now. Some were even streaming in from nearby warrens as songbirds carried the news outward. Everyone stared, eyes white. Some rabbits prayed. Some sang hymns quietly. Death Rage and the other warmice came and knelt around Anastasia, their spears trailing, the guttural sound of the warrior's visit-to-death chant rolling from their throats.

The squirrels began to gather. At first in the branches, and then they began to come down to the ground. Dingus walked through the crowd and laid his body face down upon the earth. He reached out and laid his hand upon Anastasia's back foot, which was motionless.

Love Bug approached and kissed her front paws. Then he began to draw a protective circle in the earth around her, since she could not do it for herself. Holly came forward, limping. She lay next to Anastasia's ear and whispered, "*You are strong.*"

Yasmin came and knelt by the Loving Auntie, placing her front paws together. She bowed her head and sang quietly,"*Vohu Manah*[12] is in you. Your task awaits. You will not be released today."

Last of all came Wendy. The crowd of animals parted to let her pass through. She stood for a long time, looking down at the Loving Auntie, her face locked in stone. Then she reached up to her necklace of raptor claws and seized one of them. She jerked it, and the necklace snapped, spilling the claws onto the earth. Wendy knelt down and placed the owl claw between Anastasia's two front paws. She kissed the pad of her right front paw and gently touched Anastasia's forehead. A great, sad groan arose from the assembled multitude.

Then Nicodemus waved the other animals back. He knelt beside Anastasia and lay his head upon her chest. He listened with great concentration for a full minute. He rose and looked closely into her eyes. Then he stood and looked around at the rabbits. "Her breathing is good. Her eyes are normal. I think the *ipecacuanha* got the poison out." Juniper started pouring a little water into her mouth from the leaf cups.

A hundred creatures breathed a sigh of relief. Nicodemus silenced them with a wave. "Assassination attempts mean we are winning," he said brusquely. "Your Loving Auntie is now the most dangerous rabbit in the world." His scent carried the

---

[12] Good Purpose.

bright clarity of age. "Protect her with your lives. There cannot be a next time."

ALIYAH

The sun was beaming as Aliyah and Sephora trotted briskly into the Spires. Soon they spotted the enormous golden form of Micah Summerday. He was playing with the gray cubs that had been born last year, after the clan had adopted a pregnant female lone. They were stalking him, hiding inside a large roll of *aluminum d'or* wire stamped with a faded logo, "*Halcyon Ranch – Luxury Rural Living.*" They leaped out on him when he passed by. Micah threw himself on his back in a gesture of play submission, so they could pretend to attack him. Their happy growls echoed off the stone towers overhead.

"My love," said Sephora, "A moment of your time?"

Micah rolled up onto his feet, still chuckling, and followed her as she padded a few feet away. "What?" Then he caught sight of her face. "Bad news?"

Sephora's evergreen eyes were cool and flat. "The *Paresseux* killed a deer. Crows saw it while scouting the rabbits."

Micah frowned and grunted. "Again with them?" His scent became prickly.

Sephora rubbed her muzzle against him. "I know," she said "And bad timing, too."

Aliyah, feeling the wave of their anxiety wash over her, pressed against her mother.

"We've overlooked much in the past with the *Paresseux*," said Sephora.

"Mmmm," said Micah. "They haven't worked out as well as we had hoped…" He let out an exasperated growl. "I really thought they could rise to the opportunity. I thought Benoit—"

"The thing is, we just *can't* have our franchisees ignoring our stated policies," said Sephora. "We made a clear ruling: no deer hunting without wolves." She scratched her ear with her back leg. "If we let this stand, the Summerday word is worth nothing in the Million Acre Wood."

"I know," said Micah. He chewed a foreclaw.

"And that means lawlessness."

"I *know*." He lay down and nosed up an ancient femur from the rickrack of scattered bones that carpeted the area. "This will need to be an onsite visit." He started chewing on the bone meditatively. "It's forty-five miles to the river." The bone cracked in his powerful jaws. "So it will take us two days to get down to the South Shandy and find them."

"They didn't all do it," said Aliyah. "Five did. Others didn't."

Micah nodded as he cracked the femur again. "We'll take the crows with us. They will identify." He stood up abruptly and shook his coat, sending dust and leaves flying. "If we start now, we can be halfway there by end of day." His aquamarine eyes were unreadable.

Sephora nuzzled against his neck. "It's not easy being the Landlords," she said. "Thank you for all you do for us, War Leader."

Micah dipped his muzzle under hers, pressing against her dense golden fur. "Thank *you*, my love."

FREDDIE

While Anastasia recuperated, Freddie and his team of Readers and apprentices from the fifteen members of the Free Warrens were scouring the straightstone burrow with a will. Not only were they in desperate need of some information that might lead to an advantage, they were taking part in the biggest intellectual discovery in the history of rabbits. It was a motivated team of rabbit nerds, and they could not have been more thrilled to be there.

So besides the mostly disintegrated books and magazines, and the scattering of loose page fragments, they investigated every nook and cranny of the collapsed cabin. They dug up the entire earthen layer around the old concrete foundations, seeking out every scrap of paper or any item that could be used. And Freddie drafted teams of craftmice to creep up onto the old wooden floor, now a thick, densely packed jumble of cracked linoleum, rotted furniture, crumbled plaster, rusted pipes, decayed timbers, tangled electrical lines, shreds of insulation, and pieces of roofing tiles, all thickly grown through with vines and roots over the last three hundred years.

They found and collected hastily jotted notes, faded grocery lists, chewed-up birthday cards, snatches of legal documents, scraps of supermarket flyers, and receipts wadded into balls with ancient lint. All of this was brought to a clean, well-lighted place for pages, to be pored over by the best readers, led by Nicodemus himself. He had once been the Reader for Anastasia's home warren, Bloody Thorn, and was widely considered the most knowledgeable Reader in the area.

After the pieces were laid out, flattened, and as much as

possible fitted back together, the rabbits studied them assiduously. The pages were mixed and crumbling. Many turned to dust at a touch. So their knowledge was spotty, arbitrary, and layered with words they did not understand, but their world was exploding with information.

They learned that Mary had a little lamb. That someone once reminded themselves to get "tofu." That a white rabbit was told that "Trix are for kids." And that many bad things seemed to have happened to the Dead Gods all at once, way back in the distant past. Even from a distance, they could recognize the fears about war, disease, and famine that tracked across the pages.

And they found the occasional odd bits of information that they had no idea what to do with. Like the print ad from *HappyHome* magazine that trumpeted "Talk to your pet!" across the top in huge letters. Underneath, a large subhead read: "New CRISPR gene editing tools means the next generation of companion animals can tell you how they feel!" There were photos of Dead Gods engaged in deep conversations with small cuddly animals: puppies, kittens, bunnies. A helpful snipe popped up from the corner: "Choose your favorite fur and eye color!"

Several of the Reading apprentices gathered around Nicodemus as he gazed at it. "What does this mean?" asked one of them.

"Not sure," said Nicodemus. "This must be from right before the Awakening."

"You mean when animals learned to talk?" piped up the youngest apprentice.

"Some animals," said Nicodemus. "Others learned later."

"What is CRISPR?" asked the apprentice from Tumble Stone.

"Dead Gods magic," said Nicodemus. "It's hard to understand. But it seems like they could change living creatures. Then they lost control of it. That's when the Awakening spread to animals outside the Dominion."

The apprentices looked at the page with deep unease. They did not like being reminded that there was a time when they were voiceless, wordless, helpless. Without stories, without plans, without songs, without names.

"I don't like this," said the youngest apprentice firmly. "My Warren Mother says there have always been Readers."

Nicodemus touched noses with her and looked her in the eye. He smiled. "And there always will be."

The next day, one of the craftmice came up to Freddie trailing several crumbling sheets of lined paper covered with handwriting and said, "I think you'll want to see this." Freddie glanced at it briefly and then ran to collect all the best Readers.

Soon, the sheets were spread out on the floor and a ring of Readers and apprentices surrounded them. Together they began to read, murmur, question, argue, hypothesize, and read some more. It was a letter, from a young girl named Magdalenium, who dotted her "i"s with tiny clouds and crossed her "t"s with curlicues. She was writing to her uncle, who lived in the cabin. And as they devoured her words, a distant world appeared.

She was part of a large family, which was frowned on by the other people she knew. It was a family of readers, of tinkerers, with industrious hands. People who appreciated the old ways, read books on paper, and loved tools. They played hymns on musical instruments that they made themselves. The oldest son made wooden toys for his younger siblings. They compared themselves to the 'Swiss Family Robinson.'

They loved history. They looked to the past, when things were better. Before the heat, the floods, the diseases had torn their world apart. They made finely crafted tools of wood and metal. They made beautiful weapons the way their ancestors had made them a thousand years earlier. They filled their long evenings with beautifying their creations. A delicate intaglio grew over the things they made, and the designs flowered in the margins of the little girl's letter.

The last page of Magdalenium's letter made several things clear. They were abandoning their dying farm in Missouri to trek north across the High Plains Desert. They were bringing everything necessary to build a new homestead.

Their plan was to build a 'bunker' to protect themselves and all their tools, books, and weapons. The rabbits weren't totally sure what that word meant, but it seemed like some kind of mostly underground space, with a few holes to let in light. That sounded homey. And, amazingly, this thing was going to be in what the rabbits called the Million Acre Wood, just north of the Shandy River.

At last the rabbits stopped to take a breath. In the distance, crows were calling. Soon it would be time to take the page fragments inside for the night where they could be protected.

"This is what we've been looking for," said Freddie. His scent was bright as he looked around the circle. "This is what Anastasia was hoping to find."

There was some cautious cheering and a bit of back-slapping among the apprentices.

"This letter is three hundred years old," said Nicodemus. "Anything could have happened." He sucked his teeth as he looked at the others. "It's an extreme long shot, but it's the only one we have." He placed his paw on the page with the hand-drawn map. "And if there *is* a treasure trove of weapons here, for Yah's sake, we need to find it before the wolves do."

Chapter 4

Crow is the all-seer. Wolf is the all-doer. Open your eyes and be a crow.

—*Corvid proverb*

ALIYAH

The Summerday Clan flowed over the land like droplets racing down a windowpane. Aliyah and Sephora were the fastest, their long golden legs flying over the ground. And Tennyson proved himself capable of keeping up with them, with the other females close behind. Micah, Alaric, and the other full-golden males, heavier and slower, were in the next wave. And the half-golden and gray males came a few yards after. The crows from the Spires who were not already out scouting flew low and fast behind them, silent and black.

The wolves reached a copse of trees on the top of a hill overlooking a wide expanse of the South Shandy and stood panting. In the last two days, they had run more than fifty miles. The crows settled down on bushes close to the ground, where they would not be noticed from afar. Half a mile away, Aliyah could see several gray coyotes resting near a stream at the foot of the Boreal Cliffs, just as the crow scouts had told them.

Micah faced them all, breathing heavily. "They have done their best for us, although they were perhaps not cut from the finest cloth. It may not be their fault, but it *is* their time. What say you, wolves?"

"Blood Father is awake!" growled the other members of the clan.

Micah raised his head to the sky for a long moment, his eyes closed and his enormous canine teeth shining in the sun as a low rumbling note poured out of his throat, so quiet it could just barely be heard. All the other wolves growled a drone harmony in the same hushed tone, the males sounding the third of the chord and the females singing on the fifth. Aliyah added a long drone on the seventh, which scooped and then slid down past the other voices toward Micah's basso profundo. It was a mark of their sadness at what had to be done.

Then Micah lowered his head, opened his eyes, and whispered, "Summerday, kill."

Gaetan

The day was still. The coyotes of Clan *Paresseux* had been feeding on the carcass of the stag for three days, so they were still in a food stupor, muzzles bloody, bellies swollen. Benoit and Lucien traded insults in a desultory way, mostly dozing, occasionally rising to nose out some tidbit that had been overlooked.

Gaetan and Lilou skulked around the edge of the kill zone like miserable Cassandras, uncomfortable and angry, but still unwilling to part company with the only coyote society they had ever known. Although they were hungry, they did not eat from the body of the deer.

Then, without warning, there was a flash of gold and the Summerday Clan was there, stepping out of the brush, hot and panting. A dark whirling cloud of crows rose above their heads, their harsh voices suddenly loud, echoing off the cliff face. The wolves stood in a semi-circle, trapping the coyotes against the cliffs.

Micah Summerday stood in the center, shining and huge like a canid Apollo. "Cousins," he rumbled. "You have gone against our word. Skimmed the rental payments. Taken advantage of our affection to steal from your Landlords."

Gaetan could not tear his eyes away. It was the thing he had feared, but could scarcely bring himself to believe could really happen. He had hoped for help from the golden ones. And now these demigods were here, teeth bright in the late summer sun.

The coyotes crawled up onto their feet, eyes wide and staring. "Clan Father—" began Benoit, his voice a dry croak.

Sephora stepped forward, her evergreen eyes cool. "For the crime of embezzlement, the penalty is iterated in the by-laws. Your contract will not be renewed."

Gaetan's heart was pounding. Were they really about to—? He could not finish the thought. His eyes flicked over to Aliyah. Could there be some appeal?

The coyotes near him started to back up. Lilou came and stood pressed against him. He could feel her trembling.

A younger crow flew out of the murder and hovered over Gaetan, speaking in his creaky voice. "This one, no."

A wave of relief flooded him, although he wasn't sure what was happening.

Another crow flapped forward and hovered over Lilou. "This one, no." Gaetan nuzzled her neck.

Micah looked at each of them in turn, then gestured for them to leave with a flick of his aquamarine eyes. Gaetan and Lilou hurriedly dashed though the semi-circle of shining killers.

The wolves, golden, half-golden, and gray, took a step forward. The remaining coyotes shrank back.

Micah Summerday looked up at the sun and opened his throat. A mournful cry rose from him and pulsed in alternating octaves, the ugliest sound a wolf can make. A few moments later, Sephora joined him, her voice leaping in dissonant octaves, grinding against Micah's ululation. Then all the wolves joined in, the strident machine-like noise rolling out of their bodies and pinning the coyotes against the cliff wall.

The coyotes were climbing over each other now, scrambling like insects under an overturned stone, desperate to escape the thing which could not be escaped. Gaetan hovered, unsure what to do, unable to look away from his companions in terror for their lives.

The termination howl died away. Micah took a few steps forward and spoke in a voice heavy with sadness. "Benoit, we played together as cubs." His eyes swept the coyote pack. "You are my blood cousins and I love you well. But the lawbreaker brings chaos, and we cannot allow that in our demesne."

Lucien was weeping, and some of the other coyotes also. Benoit stepped forward, his legs shaking. "Clan Father, I led them to this," he said, his voice trembling and breathy. "Take me and let them go."

Micah turned his glowing eyes to Benoit. A sad rumble rolled out of him. "The noble hearts of Clan *Paresseux* will be sung for many a year."

Then he leaped forward. An instant later, the other wolves followed. Gaetan and Lilou turned and ran as fast as they could, but the sound followed them, even into their dreams.

WARREN SANS GLOIRE

Anastasia lay on a bed of green moss on one side of the bramble garden. She was still weak, but she looked alert. The black and shiny owl claw that Wendy had given her hung from a cord around her neck. All the members of her council were gathered around, and their faces were grave and anxious.

Beyond them, members of the *ad hoc* Loving Auntie's Guard that Yasmin had formed were watching all entrances to the meeting space and spread out across Anastasia's living chambers below. The Guard's newly appointed Captain, Love Bug, stood behind Anastasia, his eyes restlessly scanning the area.

"I know it must have seemed to you that I lay still while I was on the other side," Anastasia said, her eyes a little too bright. "But in fact, I went on a journey." Her gaze swept across the chamber. Her scent was bright and airy. "I ran down to a red sea. And there I met"—she paused; the story seemed suddenly private—"a friend."

Freddie caught Nicodemus's eye. "Ummm, Honored One," said Nicodemus, laying his paw on Anastasia's forehead, "Are you, perhaps, tired? It's only been three days since—"

Anastasia smiled sweetly at him. "I'm not tired, old friend. But thank you for asking," she said as she gently pushed his paw off her head. She turned back to the group. "Here is what I learned. First, Yah has forgiven us—well, *me*— for Glorifying the coyote. It was an act undertaken in desperation, to save a friend."

Nicodemus chewed his lip. Wendy frowned and scratched at the earthen floor. Death Rage flexed the Kiss of Death and examined its point.

"Second, every death makes Yah sad. And we don't want to make that happen."

There was a little flurry of exasperated sounds, although they were quickly hushed up. There might have been a growl from Wendy. "We're continuing the patrols, right?" asked Yasmin.

"Of course," said Anastasia. "Defending ourselves is part of sharing the world with the Blessed Ones." She was about to mention what she had been told about words, but decided at the last moment to keep that to herself.

Nicodemus raised his paw. "It has to be said: we don't know who tried to poison you." Anastasia's gaze flickered for a moment. His eyes held her steady. "It can't be the wolves. And any kind of Blessed inside our perimeter would have raised an immediate alarm." His dark eyes tracked across the assembled faces. "It was almost certainly a rabbit or a mouse." There was a sharp intake of breath. No one wanted to think about what that implied about the cozy extended family they were building. "The Loving Auntie's Guard is good and needed. But attacks won't always come from people who look like enemies. I think Anastasia also needs a personal body-guard with her at all times."

"Who?" asked Love Bug. He glanced at Freddie.

Nicodemus groomed his shoulder fur for a moment. "We need someone strong, fast, smart."

"With proven loyalty," said Freddie. "Someone who's been here since—"

"Good fighter," interrupted Wendy.

"Dangerous," nodded Freddie, adjusting his gyrfalcon claw necklace.

"Someone who would fight to the last for her," said Love Bug.

"Yes," said Freddie.

"Someone like Coriander," said Nicodemus.

Coriander looked up. He seemed startled. All eyes turned to him, the can-do bunny, brawny of build, who had fought in major battles and been key in saving Anastasia's life just a few days before. A light breeze ruffled his agouti fur and made it shimmer.

Freddie grimaced and looked down.

Anastasia nodded at Nicodemus and smiled. "You're right, old friend. As usual." There was an immediate triple thump of affirmation. While pretending to thump, Freddie sur-reptitiously kicked dirt on Coriander's backside.

Coriander stood and touched both forepaws to his mouth and then extended them forward. *Thank you all.* "I am so hon-ored by your confidence, comrades. I won't let you down."

"Fine," Wendy waved her paw dismissively. She came near to Anastasia. "What we do about *wooves*?"

Anastasia smiled beatifically. "The bunker of the Dead Gods that our wise Readers have discovered is Yah's gift to our family. We will go north and seize it." She mustered the strength to sit up and her golden eyes shone. "We will use what we find to teach the wolves to respect us."

Wendy let out a long belch. "Good."

Anastasia gently fanned the air around her with her forepaw. "And we need to start probing the wolves themselves. Not just scouting the north bank of the Shandy. I don't know how, but we need to put someone in their lair."

Nicodemus sucked in his breath. "That's going to be dangerous work," he said.

A moment later, a very sharp rapier was raised aloft. "I will go!" said a small, fierce voice.

Nicodemus nodded at Death Rage. "So we'll send a dangerous mouse."

ALIYAH

The destruction of the five coyotes was the work of a few minutes. Then the Summerday wolves gathered white roses and scattered them on the bodies as the crows sat silently in the trees overhead.

Aliyah trembled a little as she held the rose stem in her mouth and lay the flower on the body of Benoit, the old coyote whom she had known since birth.

Micah Summerday climbed up onto a high rock and spoke the funeral words. "The death of any wolf-kin is a sad day for all wolves, but the majesty of the law could not be gainsaid. We were forced to uphold its higher purpose: order."

Sephora stepped up next to him. "In this final moment, we fought as adversaries, but we bid you farewell as cousins. May your hunting be fine in the Forever Forest. "

Aliyah and the other wolves together uttered the final blessing. "Blood Father turns his face from you. Hunger Mother forgets you."

Then Sephora raised her head and let a long, sad howl pour out, gradually climbing by minor thirds. Micah joined her, and their voices entwined in a soaring *pas de deux* of the mourning cry. Every creature within miles knew that wolf-kin had died.

Then the golden wolves left the killing floor and walked away, their heads low. Aliyah walked next to her mother, pressing against her. As the wolves moved away, the crows rose from their branches and quietly descended on the bodies of the coyotes, their only sound a vast fluttering of wings.

The wolves went to a nearby stream and washed the blood from their bodies. Then they lay in the sun to rest. After a deep sleep, filled with restless dreams, they woke in the late afternoon. The sound of the crows making a meal a hundred yards away was still going on and getting more raucous.

"I'm *starving*," said Alaric, lying on his back, looking up at the sun shining through the tree branches overhead. "The crows are feasting. The wolves are wasting away."

Sephora began to speak. "These are dark days for the children of the sun." She breathed out a deep, rumbling growl. "I know you are hungry. We need to keep our strength up. We may need to take … new measures."

There was an anxious groan from the pack and Sephora stopped talking for a moment. She shared a glace with Micah, and then continued. "Creatures of the sea do not easily come to us," said Sephora. "Therefore, we must gaze upon the Tree of Life and see who is most fitting to join with us in this time of need." She stood, looking lean under the bright sun. "We need to expand our rental base. It is with regret that I say that our friends the raccoons recommend themselves."

This time the outcry was much louder. Aliyah felt a harsh burn flicker across her neck and shoulders. She shared an anxious glance with Tennyson, who was next to her.

"But the Truce has stood for a century," said the Second She, Sephora's younger sister.

Sephora's evergreen eyes flicked to Micah, who lay with his chin on his paws. "Listen to the words my love speaks," he growled. "For in her is wisdom."

Aliyah stood, her eyes anguished. "Raccoons are … good people," she said.

Alaric shook the dust out of his coat and rolled up onto his feet. "We can say goodbye to our dirty apples."

The hubbub of voices grew. Sephora raised a paw for quiet. "Allowing our Clan to grow weak is the one thing we may not do. If there is another option, please bring it forward now."

There was silence. Aliyah glanced at each face in turn.

"We make this decision in sorrow, just as we took our action today," said Sephora. "War Leader, tell us how to treat this sacrifice with the utmost respect."

Micah rose to his feet, his large frame spare and angular. He looked thoughtfully at the other wolves. "Raccoon apple orchards are surrounded by dense hedges of thorn trees. These hedges are pierced only by small winding paths." He licked his paw. "The wolf cubs who were born last year are small enough to fit through the pathways."

Aliyah dry heaved suddenly as the implications of this plan became clear.

"The cubs will penetrate the thorn hedges," continued Micah. "They will engage with the raccoons, who will run through the paths to escape. The first group of wolves be outside waiting by the entrances—"

Aliyah began whining. She could not help herself. And several other wolves joined in. Micah spoke over the rising noise. "And we will harvest the life gift *respectfully*—" The whines became a loud screechy tumble, so loud that it was hard to hear. "I said, '*respectfully*'—" continued Micah, raising his voice. The noise grew until it sounded like iron plates grinding. The crows began to appear, looking around curiously, disheveled and bloody from their meal.

Micah stopped talking and carried his huge, rangy form around the group, aquamarine eyes blazing, staring down the wolves one at a time. His breath was damp on their faces, and his scent was hot and roiling. One by one, the wolves fell silent.

He took a deep breath. "It will be quick and painless. A second group of wolves will guard the perimeter so that no raccoons escape and spread the alarm. Panicked raccoons roaming the countryside are unseemly and will reflect poorly on them."

The other wolves were silent. Sephora growled in assent.

Micah continued. "Harvesting the life gift in this

disciplined fashion will prevent any one group of raccoons from alerting others. This will preserve everyone's dignity. It will be our final gift to our ancient allies." He looked around the group. "What say you, wolves?"

Alaric and several other wolves yipped in support. Aliyah laid her muzzle on the cool earth and closed her eyes.

Dingus

Dingus the squirrel, former scold artist and cultural entrepreneur, was becoming a different kind of animal.

After Anastasia's initial clashes with foxes earlier in the year, Dingus had provided tours for the tree-based community, racking up a considerable take in nuts in return for his dramatic renditions of Anastasia's adventures.

Then he had had a close brush with death during a coyote attack on Tumble Stone Warren. After that, he had holed up in his nest in the oak tree, communing with a torn print ad for "...OGA FOR KIDS" that Freddie had given him.

There were many days of arboreal tourists showing up with their nuts, waiting somewhat patiently, and then not-at-all patiently, for Dingus to come out and give his performance of the *Flagellation of Foxes, Hammering of Hawks, and Walloping of Weasels by the Rabbit Without Antecedents*. But he never showed. And eventually his fans gave up and stopped coming.

Squirrels in nearby trees would catch occasional glimpses of Dingus on the highest branches of his oak tree. One day he was standing for hours in a deep lunge with his hands out to the sides, looking like a tiny, tufted warrior. Another day, he was balanced face down on his hands and feet, with his hips in the air, tail curled into the infinity symbol. He did this every day, perfectly still. The only thing that moved were the fluffs in his tail.

No one knew what to make of this. He was famous for his many advertising jingles, so he was still remembered by the local denizens even though they no longer cared to follow his antics—not unlike an influencer gone to seed.

That meant it was only a mild surprise when a beautiful orange-breasted bluebird approached him one day. The bluebird alighted on his branch and sang out a lovely set of liquid notes.

Dingus did not move. Only his tail fluff shimmered in the wind.

The bluebird hopped a few steps closer on his tiny legs. He opened his throat and poured out a stream of poignant syllables that seemed to drift down from on high.

Dingus remained still. Although he noticed the bluebird appeared to be balding.

The bluebird came still closer to Dingus and peered at him with his black eyes. "Hey!" he said suddenly. "I'm talking to you. You think I'm over here singing for my health?"

Dingus opened his eyes. "Hello, brother," he said pleasantly. "What brings you to this branch on this lovely morning?"

The bluebird hawked up a glob of phlegm and spat it into the air, where it narrowly missed taking down a passing dragonfly. "Raptors snatching less squirrel. Raptors snatching less mouse. Raptors snatching less rabbit. You know who they're snatching more of?"

The question hung in the air, accusingly.

After a few seconds, Dingus said, "No."

"Songbirds!" snapped the bluebird, in a very ugly tone.

"I'm sorry to hear that," said Dingus evenly.

"We want more than that," said the bluebird. "Name's Stan, by the way."

"What do you want?" asked Dingus, still unmoving.

"In," said Stan.

"In what?"

"In with youse. All of youse," said Stan. "The whole rabbit-squirrel-mouse murder trifecta. You bring us in, under your protection, and we'll fight for youse. We'll be your air soldiers. Your eyes in the sky."

"Why are you telling me this?" asked Dingus, with just a hint of irritation.

Stan looked surprised. He fluffed his feathers. "Because you're in a tree, stupid," he barked. "And we know you're in tight with the auntie-lady. We don't like going down to the ground. Good way to get killed."

"I hear you, brother," said Dingus thoughtfully. "But I thought the raptors were doing the killing."

"There's a lot of killing going on all over the place," said Stan. "But recently, it's gotten worse, and it's because of what youse been doing with your Free Warrens and what not. We don't want to be left out like chumps. We want in."

"I feel your pain," said Dingus. "But you should know this. On your perches in trees, squirrels can help you…" He reached down beside his leg and suddenly a shining spear materialized in his hand, plucked from a fold in the bark. Stan jumped back with an appreciative growl that suddenly turned into a high trill of praise. "…but in the air, no groundling can be there for you. You must look within."

"Look within what?" snapped Stan. "Raptors are twenty times bigger than we are. If not fifty."

Dingus arose and walked sedately back toward his hole in the trunk of the oak. He reached in and took out two acai berries from his collection of snacks. He came back carrying one in each hand. He looked steadily at the bluebird, who was pacing back and forth on the branch. "Brother Stan," he said. "If I throw these berries in the air, can you pierce them with your beak before they reach the ground?"

"Of course," said Stan. "I catch bugs on the wing all day long."

"Show me," said Dingus, and tossed the berries into the air.

With an annoyed grunt, the bluebird leaped into flight and within a few seconds had turned both berries to mush with his sharp beak. An instant later, he landed near Dingus. "What does that prove?"

"Those two berries are a raptor's eyes."

Stan stared at him for a moment. "Raptor's eyes are attached to beaks and claws as big as my body."

Dingus did not look away. "And there are twenty times more of you than them. If not fifty."

Stan looked like he would have ground his teeth, if he had any. "Will you talk to the auntie-lady or do I have to go down there and do it myself?"

"I will," said Dingus. "Namaste." Then, quick as thought, he skimmed along the branch and down the trunk.

As he was leaving, his sharp ears picked up the bluebird muttering. "Just my luck. I come looking for a *consigliere*[13] and I get Jonathan Livingston Squirrel."

---

[13] Counselor to a powerful boss.

ANASTASIA

Anastasia leaned over her earthmap as she spoke to the principals assembled in the bramble garden for the northern expedition planning meeting. The sunlight filtered through the foliage overhead and bathed her in dappled light. Her black owl claw looked very handsome against her brown fur. Coriander sat nearby.

"Here's where we are, friends. We know the Million Acre Wood is a strip of land between the Boreal Cliffs and the sea." She tapped the map with her Claw. "We know it's seven miles wide where we are. But what we *don't* know is what happens to the north of us." She indicated the wide smear of smooth mud at the top of the map. "So we have to proceed with the information we have. We're assuming a platoon of ten rabbits, twenty mice, and five squirrels who can scout a quarter of a mile of territory while moving through it. So to create a solid line we need twenty-eight platoons, armed and trained. And we have to do that without robbing the Home Guard."

Yasmin and Wendy leaned together and conferred for a moment. Then Wendy sat up and jerked her chin up. "One more week," she said. Anastasia nodded.

Then Bricabrac stood up, wearing his best client-facing demeanor. "I'm proud to report that we're actually ahead on the spears, and making our dates on the squirrel rapiers." He cleared his throat. "Unfortunately, we're a little behind on the bite blades," he said, bowing apologetically. "The quality control takes longer for seashell and fish bone." Then he steepled his fingers. "We could hit two hundred and eighty blades for the expedition teams in a week." He coughed. "Or so."

Freddie stood. "We're continuing to glean what we can from paper fragments at the straightstone burrow," he said. "And we're putting together a Forward Reading Corps to accompany the expedition. They'll deploy if we find the bunker."

Anastasia smiled. "You mean, 'when.'"

Freddie looked embarrassed. "Of course. Sorry, Loving Auntie."

Anastasia raised both her forepaws to her mouth and extended them broadly. *Thank you all.* "Now," she said. "I have some late-breaking news. We've been approached by a songbird who wants to work with us. He may be able to bring in more songbirds. That would obviously be wonderful for scouting."

"Hooah!" rumbled Wendy.

Anastasia nodded. "We're just talking now. I'll let you know if anything solid happens." She nibbled a foreclaw. "And that brings up an important point. We will win or lose this fight, not because of the blades in our mouths, but because of the allies by our sides. Let's make it a point to make friends, not enemies."

Aliyah

It was very late. There was no moon, so the grove of conifers where the wolves were sleeping was quite dark, even though the sky was brilliant with stars.

Aliyah awoke and noticed Micah and Sephora were missing. Casting about with her sharp ears, she heard quiet murmuring fifty yards away at the edge of the trees. She stepped over Tennyson, who was sleeping near her, and crept quietly toward the sound. Soon she came upon her parents. They had broken open a rotting log and were busy licking up the insects within.

"Sure, we could go and investigate this rabbit problem now, since we're already down here," Micah was saying. "But you saw how the pack was today."

"Nobody likes change," said Sephora. She looked up at the stars.

"I think we just need to get everyone home and settled," said Micah. "When the crows make their report, we'll discuss it then, in an orderly way."

There was a moment of silence as they gnawed at the log and tore off more chunks.

Then Sephora spoke. "I'm worried about Aliyah."

Micah grunted. "She's a fighter. It's hard for her if it's not clear who to fight."

"She likes big, easy problems," said Sephora, as she nosed among the leaf litter. "Not small, complicated ones."

"Well," said the War Leader of the Summerday Clan, as he lay on his golden belly licking up splinters and larva. "Maybe our little goldybug just has some growing up to do."

Chapter 5

It was the transgression in the First Days that brought rabbits to their current estate. They disobeyed Yah. They ate the Dillweed of the Lord.

—Tobias Ironstone, Lord Harmonizer
Address to the Known World Symposium

FLYERS

The lone raptor circled lazily in the sky above Warren *Sans Gloire*. Stan, the orange-breasted bluebird, sat on a twig high up in Dingus's oak tree and looked up at the raptor sourly. "I make her to be a northern goshawk. Forty ounces easy. Me, I'm bringing two and half ounces to this fight."

"Weight is a distraction," said the squirrel from a nearby branch, where he stood on his left foot with his right foot tucked against his thigh, and his hands in the prayer position. "You have laid the groundwork. Attention to breath."

Stan muttered something not quite intelligible, and then launched off the twig. He flew out across the open space above the trees, slowly and a little erratically. From five hundred feet up, he would look like a late-life bluebird who was getting tired and slowing down, a sight to warm the cockles of any raptor's heart.

"I'm prolly gonna frickin' croak out here, but at least I'll be a hero to all bluebirdkind," he grumbled. "My poor old mamma and babbo can have that as a comfort in their old age."

He glanced up and saw the goshawk's spiral take a downward turn. He flew on as though he were unaware, his eyes scanning the trees below him. He knew what was coming. The crushing talons, the death strike to the neck, and it made him tremble. "In, two, three, hold. Out, two, three, four," he murmured, in time with his breath.

He cast a surreptitious glance upward and saw the raptor coming down in a steep dive, calculated to intersect with his trajectory in the next hundred feet. "Aw, geez..." His heart started to hammer. He drifted down, past the tops of the trees. The goshawk adjusted accordingly, angling down, claws extending.

Stan stole one more look upward and saw that the raptor was just a few feet above him and dropping like a stone. He flapped hard, thrusting himself to the side as hard as he could, suddenly no longer an old and feeble bluebird but a young and powerful flyer. The goshawk, surprised, did not make a clean strike. One claw missed entirely, but the other claw caught Stan by one wing. He thrashed vigorously, his body flipping back and forth as he fought. The hawk was also struggling to get a grip on her prey, and they were both falling. Now they were well below the tops of the trees.

"Now, youse idiots!" shouted Stan. "Now!" Then he erupted into a piercingly beautiful song as he tried to cover his head with his free wing to ward off the death blow.

All at once, a fusillade of sound and color erupted from the trees around them. More than fifty songbirds came bursting out of the foliage and were arrowing toward them. Bluebirds, cardinals, orioles, meadowlarks, chickadees, mockingbirds, racing together in a swirl of red, blue, orange, and yellow.

The raptor, startled, stopped trying to get a better grip on Stan and instead began a rapid series of heavy downbeats to gain altitude. The bluebird's falling, meandering flight had lured her much lower than raptors would normally go for an airstrike. Now the songbirds were actually intersecting her flight path from above, trapping her in a bowl of trees.

She still held Stan's wing in her claw. The onrush of songbirds had apparently not yet triggered any alarms. Then the leading songbird, a robin, made contact, and drove her beak straight at the goshawk's left eye. The goshawk jerked her head away just in time, and an instant later, a cardinal arrived on her other side and slashed at her right eye.

The goshawk uttered a little shriek and let go of Stan, lashing out with her claws as she climbed. She seized an oriole and tried to hit it with her beak. But the bird squirmed away and the strike became a glancing blow that slid off. So she shook it, then threw it down. It fell for several seconds, stunned, and began flapping again just in time to prevent a crash landing.

The goshawk grabbed a meadowlark as the oriole was

falling. She had no time to land a killing blow, so she just threw it to the side.

But by then half a hundred tiny birds were surrounding her, creating a storm of sharp points, all aimed at her eyes. Each one was dangerous, and each one was theoretically easy to kill, but there were far too many to kill quickly.

Within a few seconds, the goshawk's right eye was swollen shut and her left eye was closing. She swept great arcs with her beak and claws as her wings beat the air. The space around her was so thick with songbirds now that her heavy wings actually hit and pushed off of them, helping her climb. Several songbirds, stunned by the wingbeats, fell from the sky, and most of the rest scattered.

Within a few seconds, the goshawk was climbing quickly, and a brave scarlet tanager who followed landed a final peck before dodging away from the sharp claws. She flew back singing triumphantly.

"Good on youse!" shouted Stan, flying in a circle around the battlefield. "We proved this can work! This is a great day for songbirds everywhere!" He did a barrel roll in celebration. "Let me hear your victory songs, *paisanos*!"[14] As the songbirds burst forth in a laissez faire orchestral celebration of *David v. Goliath* triumph, Stan flew back to the branch in the oak tree, where Dingus was still standing on one foot, as before.

"Did you see that?" he called excitedly, alighting on a twig nearby.

---

[14] Compatriots.

"I did," said Dingus, as he stood on one foot with his eyes closed. "Today is a great day for you, brother. You became your most self."

"We all did!" exclaimed the bluebird, hopping from one foot to the other. "Hey, that stuff you're doing really works. What's it called again?"

"It neither works nor doesn't work," said Dingus. "It simply *is*. It is Oga For Young Goats."

Aliyah

Tennyson had found an ancient peach tree with many windfall peaches scattered beneath it, and he had come and quietly nose-bumped Aliyah. Now they were busily gobbling up the soft peaches in the late twilight. Nearby, a whip-poor-will was beginning to sing.

After they had downed a few peaches, Tennyson said, "We should tell the others."

"In a minute," said Aliyah, starting on her next peach.

Tennyson persisted and finally Aliyah agreed. He put up a short *gather* howl and the rest of the Summerday Clan soon appeared. It was a mark of how hungry they were that they were delighted to see the ripe peaches strewn about, and they fell on them with a will.

"Yips to the mighty hunter of stone fruits," said Sephora. "A strong addition to any pack."

"Just want to do my part, Clan Mother," said Tennyson.

Alaric nodded grudgingly. "Thanks."

Tennyson dipped his muzzle in acknowledgement.

A small group of crows appeared out of the darkening sky.

Aliyah looked up to see Grammy Kark, Cacao, and several others landing. They hopped toward Sephora.

"Welcome, mother of my mother," she said.

"We have the news you seek, golden child," said the ancient crow.

Sephora laid her muzzle on the ground. "Speak, old friend."

Grammy Kark fluttered up onto a nearby boulder. She fixed her black-within-black eyes on Sephora. "The rabbits … are doing things no rabbits have ever done." All the wolves gazed at her in silence. "They are loading food into their warrens. Berries, melons, greenleaf, even gourds filled with water."

There was a long moment of silence.

"Siege preparation," rumbled Micah. "They're expecting us."

"Guilty behavior shows guilty minds," said Alaric.

"How many warrens?" asked Sephora.

"At least eighteen." Grammy Kark took another step nearer to Sephora. "They are amassing great stores of weapons. Spears, rapiers, and blades like the one you showed me. So many they have to stack them outside where we can see them." She blinked. "Hundreds."

Alaric snorted. "A bunch of armed rabbits are still *rabbits*."

"They're proven killers," said Aliyah.

"We won't be taken in a drunken stupor like the coyote was," said Alaric.

Grammy Kark flew down off the rock and came very close to Sephora. "And there's more. Tell them what your group saw, Cacao."

The young crow walked toward Sephora and bowed deeply. "The craftmice have constructed models of hunters with sticks and plant skin. Weasels. Foxes. Coyotes. And they are drilling coordinated attacks." He stopped and looked at Grammy Kark. She nodded at him to continue. "Mice go low. Rabbits go high. Squirrels drop from above."

Alaric chuckled. "They want to be *us*. Why can't they be happy as the gods made them?" Without looking at him, Sephora laid a paw on Alaric's paw.

Cacao was scratching his head and looking uncomfortable. "Is there more?" asked Sephora.

Grammy Kark stepped forward. "Just today, our flyers saw that the craftmice had used the skin of the golden echeveria to build their first..." her eyes tracked across the group "...golden wolf."

Aliyah felt a chill run over her, from her shoulders to her paws. Alaric was blathering, of course, but she could not hear him. She was in a quiet space, and she could see, for the first time, how new this was. How much the world had changed. Now people with whom she had no quarrel had decided they *hated* her. And wanted to kill her. In her mind's eye, she could see the model golden wolf, motionless, helpless, lifeless. She saw the tiny creatures swarming over it and she felt sorry for it. A wave of grief rolled over her.

Then the world was back and her family was continuing its interminable, obvious conversation. Without even stopping to register what they were saying, she burst out. "This is war. We need to go on a war footing *now*."

There was a moment of silence. Then Sephora looked at her and spoke. "War is a contest between equals. War can be righteous. Glorious." She sat up and faced the other wolves. "This is a constabulary action against criminals. We will not dignify it with the name of *war*."

Micah rose and padded over to Aliyah. He nuzzled her neck. "It's clear what needs to happen," he said in a soothing rumble. "We will handle it, and then everything will be like it was before."

Aliyah leaned into him for a moment. "Thank you, Daddy," she said, as she struggled to collect her thoughts. Then she stepped away and faced the others. "Whatever this is, it is new. We should get enhancements. I want to call a craftrat." There was a surprised hubbub among the wolves and crows. She spoke over their rising clamor. "The criminals are enhancing their natural weapons. We should be as well."

Micah got a concerned look on his face and tried to come near her again. "Goldybug…"

Aliyah stepped away from him. "We need to do what is best for this family."

"We already have the best weapons," said Micah. "Wolf teeth and wolf claws, and our pack members by our sides." Alaric and some of the other young males yipped. "Getting … enhancements … just tells everyone we don't think we have what we need." He paced toward her. "It puts us halfway to losing before we even start."

"The world is changing, Daddy," said Aliyah. "We have to keep up."

"What would these enhancements even be?" asked Micah, an edge of irritation beginning to show in his voice.

"They would be things that we—" Aliyah groped for specifics, trying to remember what exactly had been said during her hurried conversation with that craftrat down in the South Shandy weeks ago. "Useful items like…" she trailed off, furious at herself.

"Chain mail, for one thing," said Tennyson, stepping forward. All eyes turned to him. And Aliyah felt an immense wave of gratitude. "The simplest kind protects your throat and chest. Some covers your whole body. There are some canids in the uplands with varying amounts." His silver fur was bright in the twilight. "The bears don't like enhancements, for themselves or others, but there's a black market for it. Nice in a fight." He smiled. "Or you can get something fancier if you have the moneystones."

"All well and good," said Micah gravely. "But the Summerday Clan has always proudly borne the banner of tradition."

Tennyson bowed deeply. "I understand, Clan Father." He paused for a moment. "My family was very traditional." He scuffled the earth at his feet, looking down. "And now they're all in the Forever Forest."

Micah and Sephora shared a glance. The War Leader cleared his throat. "Well," he said slowly. "I don't think I need this for myself, but I guess it would do no harm to … look into it."

Aliyah nodded. "Thank you, Daddy." She approached Grammy Kark and laid her chin on her paws. "Mother of my grandmother. Will you send a fast flyer south?" Aliyah dipped her nose into her neck pouch and came out with a curved piece of broken glass that said, "oca-C" on it. It hung on a braided cord a few inches long. She laid it on the earth. "A mile below the Shandy River, near the beach, there's a hill with a redwood tree that was killed by lightning," she said. "If this diamond necklace is hung on the highest branch where the morning sun will strike it, it will call a craftrat."

Grammy Kark stood on one leg, and then the other. "I have no love for any rat," she said. "They eat our eggs and murder our chicks. "Aliyah looked at her steadily. Finally, Grammy Kark said, "But you are the Summerday to come. In our great love, we will indulge the golden cub."

"Thank you, Honored One," said Aliyah.

Sephora stood and shook out her coat. She came near to Grammy Kark. "Thank you for all you and your murder have related, mother of my mother. We would be blind without your eyes."

The old crow nodded and ruffled her wings.

"Now, I will ask this of our dark friends," said Sephora. "Call your kin. Then send your shadow flyers far and wide. Call all the hunters north of the river. Tell them the Landlords of the Million Acre Wood are having a gathering at the Spires."

Grammy Kark bobbed her head. "It shall be done."

Sephora looked up for a moment. "And we want to gather all the information we can." She leaned toward the old crow. "Send some flyers to the southern banks of the Shandy. Find the remnants of Clan *Paresseux*. Find any others who have fought the criminals, and summon them to the service of their realm."

Grammy Kark fluffed her feathers and scratched her neck with her talons. "It will be our pleasure to serve the bringer of feasts."

CORIANDER

Anastasia wanted to look at the Shandy River near Warren *Sans Gloire*, and see what places would be best for the northern expedition to cross. Of course, under the new protective regime, this meant that Coriander and the Loving Auntie's Guard had to come along, with mice, rabbits, and squirrels creating a travelling perimeter around her. For someone like Anastasia, accustomed to roaming the surrounding lands as she pleased, it was clear that she did not find this an altogether welcome development.

And there were some kinks in the system to be worked out as well. The young squirrels in the Loving Auntie's Guard, excited to be in the presence of their hero, began calling out as they raced through the trees overhead, "Make way! Make way for the Rabbit Without Antecedents! She Who Smites the Meanies and Destabilizes the Fangapalooza!"

"Yah's teeth," said Anastasia. "Tell them to stop that." And before Love Bug could say anything, she called out to the squirrels. "I know you mean well but that's not helping."

So Captain Love Bug had to go and have a chat with his over-enthusiastic charges.

As they paused, Coriander chuckled and said, "Of course, it's totally wrong-headed, but … it's just because of their great affection for you, Loving Auntie."

"Eh," said Anastasia. "That's sweet, but I don't want them to love me to death."

"Me neither," said Coriander.

Love Bug raised his right paw, swirled it, and pointed ahead. *Advance.* The unit moved off through the meadows filled with bladderwort and nettles, heading for the groves of red maple and river birch that grew near the Shandy River floodplain.

"It must be hard sometimes," said Coriander as they

lolloped long. "Managing all this emotion coming at you. So much love, hate, everything in between."

"Ya, it's weird," said Anastasia. "I just remind myself that it's not really about me. Most of the people having these strong feelings don't even *know* me."

"The people who do know you seem to have a great fondness for you," said Coriander.

"Well," said Anastasia, grabbing a quick bite of a seed head as she went by. "They love the person they hope I am. That's not exactly the same thing."

"What was it like for you at Bloody Thorn?"

Anastasia pursed her lips and cocked her head. "Mmmm, I was a difficult kit, always asking questions and running off to touch distant objects because of my head sickness." She exhaled and shrugged. "I was part of the founding bloodline, otherwise I would have been run out a lot earlier."

Two hours later, they were at the river and stood in the shade of a weeping willow, looking across to the other side. At this point, the Shandy was a hundred yards wide, blue and placid. Brilliant turquoise dragonflies zigzagged over the surface.

Anastasia sucked in her breath. "We have to put over three hundred rabbits across this," she said. "And seven hundred mice and squirrels."

"There's a place just around the bend where there's an island in the middle," said Love Bug. "Probably a better spot for crossing."

Anastasia nodded. "Which means the wolves will probably try to cross there, too," she said. "We should try and fortify it, in case..." She trailed off. Coriander finished the sentence in his own head. *In case we're overrun by the army of Blessed Ones and they come down and murder everyone we love.*

In a few minutes they were on the riverbank near the island. "I was originally thinking we could do something with boats, but it would take way too long," said Love Bug. "We just have Bricabrac's catamaran. We've made some inquiries, and couldn't find any other craftrats with boats on the Shandy below the waterfall."

"Ya, I don't think craftrats come down here much," said Coriander.

Anastasia squinted across the river. "Maybe we could put some agave cords across to the island. It's just about thirty yards away here. Bricabrac could carry the free ends across on his boat, then we could tie the cords to tree trunks. Mice and squirrels could cross on those. Then do the same on the other side."

"Not rabbits, though," said Coriander.

"No," said Anastasia. "It will have to be lower cords for us, just above the water. We can hang onto them while we swim."

Love Bug scratched his ear with his hind foot. "We won't like it, but we'll do it."

It was a warm day. Love Bug put the Auntie's Guard into relaxed watch mode, with squirrel lookouts in the sago palms, while the others rested and nibbled.

Anastasia and Coriander found themselves a little ways away from the others. Coriander nosed around and turned up some watercress. He munched it thoughtfully.

Coriander was the kind of bunny who liked to know where he stood. And what he stood for. Being a spy and a

Rememberer had been easy when he was helping the forces of goodness and order investigate a heretic. Then, as he had slowly become convinced of the righteousness of Anastasia's cause, he had little by little slipped across the line of orthodoxy, and now was definitely in uncharted territory. That did not feel good, but he was prepared to do it, because the lives they were saving were in the forefront of his daily experience, which trumped lingering concerns about abstractions.

But when he had been named Anastasia's bodyguard, that had begun an immediate grind between who the *Sans Gloire* rabbits thought he was, and who he thought he was. And he couldn't come clean, because that would mean exile from his new community. Surely, they would not stand to have a spy sent by Olympia living in the heart of the Free Warrens, laudable conversion story or no.

And there was the matter of the poisoning. *Was* it Olympia? She had never asked him to do anything like that, although at one point she had hinted at it. Still, as Nicodemus said, it didn't make sense for the *wolves* to do this. And who else would it be? He had seen a little robin in the bramble garden just before the nightshade berries appeared. That could have been Olympia's weird little pet. He grunted to himself. Olympia just didn't seem like a killer. She struck him more as a smooth-talking gaslighter, someone who preferred to—

"You're awfully quiet," said Anastasia.

Startled, Coriander jumped and blurted out, "Oh, just thinking about the … poisoning ... attempt."

"Ya, we haven't figured that out," said the Loving Auntie. She looked down at her foreclaws for a moment. "Guess that's one for the haters."

"It must feel so bad," said Coriander. "Knowing some-one who looks like us"—of course, he couldn't mention the robin—"tried to hurt you so profoundly."

"It's creepy," said Anastasia, glancing out across the river. "It makes me feel like there are only a few people I can trust." She turned and looked at him. "I'm glad one of them is you."

CROWS

Grammy Kark and her children had called their kin. And their far-flung families had answered, happy to be in the good graces of the Summerday Clan. So now the crows were winging southward, covering all of the northern Million Acre Wood between the Boreal Cliffs and the sea. "Come! Come! Come! Hunters one and all, come to the Spires. Your realm has need of you. Your Landlords command you. Come join the throng. Come! Come! Come!"

After an initial rush of questions, Sephora had added some explanatory text to the call: "Nursing mothers, stay. Half-grown cubs, leave. Yearlings, bring. Come!"

And in the southern Million Acre Wood, south of the Shandy River, crows were landing, chatting up foxes, gab-bing with weasels. Asking, looking, remembering, and finding their way to those who had seen the criminals up close.

So it was that the foxes Isadore and Juliet, who had just weaned their three cubs, found themselves talking with a young crow who was so excited to meet them, anxious for them to receive their due regard as early heroes in the fight against the lunchmeat crime wave, and insistently inviting them to come meet the Landlords whom they had heard about but never seen.

And the white weasel Saskatoon found herself trading tips on the tenderest meats with a silky-voiced crow who told her the golden wolves were desperate to receive her wisdom as one of the first crime-stoppers, and promised VIP access to the best parts of the Spires, where the truly elite killers hobnobbed.

At last, even the coyotes Gaetan and Lilou, who had run far to the south and were eking out a living in the southern marshes, found themselves approached by a trio of crows who addressed the two of them respectfully as the leaders of Clan *Paresseux* and delivered an invitation to a meeting with the golden bosses in the home office, where the stone columns pierced the sky. In fear and trembling, their nights still haunted by the terrible punishment the Summerdays had inflicted on their colleagues, they accepted.

BRICABRAC

Bricabrac was nosing about near the straightstone burrow, scaring up some breakfast, when he decided to shinny up a nearby pine and check on developments. In a couple of minutes, he was fifty feet up the straight trunk, high enough to see out over tops of the lesser trees to where the huge, blackened hulk of the old redwood stood, dark against the early morning sky. And there, on the highest remaining branch, there was a flash of light the same color as the sun. A few seconds later, he saw it again, as the curved piece of broken glass on a string that he had given to Aliyah Summerday weeks earlier now twisted back and forth in the gentle morning breeze.

A huge grin broke out on Bricabrac's face, and he ran quickly down the trunk of the tree to the spot in the straight-stone burrow that Frippery had chosen as her sleeping place. "Baby sister! Baby sister!" he called softly, not wanting to wake everyone up.

Frippery sat up and rubbed her eyes with her small knuckles. "What? What is it?" she said sleepily in a *this-better-be-good* kind of voice.

Bricabrac knelt down next to her and took her hands in his. He was beaming. "I got you a client!"

Chapter 6

If it's not dirty, is it even an apple, bruh?
—Traditional raccoon toast

Hunters

In a small glade among the Spires, the eleven foxes, five weasels, and two coyotes who had personal experience with the criminals were having a private audience with Sephora Summerday.

Five stone columns rose around them in a circle, giving the place the feel of a classical temple dedicated to an earth goddess. A small brook flowed through the glade, the water clear and pure over a white sandy bottom, with specks of quartzite catching the sun's rays. It was an audience chamber calculated to inspire awe, which was exactly why Sephora had chosen it. Aliyah sat upright behind and to the right of her mother, serving as her honor guard.

They had just spent a long morning sharing their stories, as Sephora solicitously interviewed each one, drawing out the details, probing for actionable information.

Gaetan and Lilou lay with their chins on their forepaws, their eyes round and restless. Sephora was very courteous to them, and addressed them with respect. But just being so near the animals who had killed their packmates was generating an ongoing fight-or-flight response that the coyotes struggled to control. With all the adrenaline in their veins, it was hard not to flinch when Sephora came near.

Isadore and Juliet sat very erect, nestled in with the other foxes. Isadore looked tired. Juliet sat quite still, the long diagonal slash of a scar running across her neck and chest. The scar tissue was months old now, still a light pink, with a few areas knotted with proudflesh. She looked like a tightly wrapped bundle of rage ready to explode. Her cubs had been half-relieved to see her go when she and Isadore had received the special message from the crow, and they had been bundled off to stay with Isadore's sisters and other kin.

Most of the weasels were lounging by the stream, looking sleepy and a little bored. Saskatoon lay sprawled on her back, her short legs sticking up. She was playing with a sunbeam, moving her paw around to cast shadows shaped like small creatures on the floor, all the while singing a little song to herself.

> *"Hi, Mister Two Legs, I'm going to kill you,*
> *Hi, Mister Three Legs, O! You're dead,*
> *Hi, Mister Four Legs, run into my mouth now,*
> *Hi, Mister Five Legs, where's your head?"*

When all the animals had given their reports. Sephora paced slowly back and forth. "Hunters," she said, her voice low and modulated like a kind but fierce mommy. "Thank you all for sharing what you have seen. I know the journey has been a long one."

"Ya rilly," said Saskatoon, as she pattycaked her front left paw against her right rear paw in a casual samba rhythm.

Aliyah cast a sidelong glance at her mother. Sephora generally tolerated a certain amount of indecorous behavior, and then suddenly, the toleration would be over.

Sephora ignored the weasel. "I know we've all been confronted with things we've never seen before, and it's important that we speak to one another in love, so I'll just say this once: this is no way to run a wood."

The coyotes looked glum. Juliet stepped forward. "Clan Mother, I agree with you. We have tried. And we have failed. So we are here now, ready to fight, ready to die, for the honor of foxes." Isadore looked alarmed, then he frowned and stared resolutely at a patch of sky between the columns.

"Say what, now?" said Saskatoon, propping herself up on one squatty elbow. "*I'm* not ready to die. I'm here to make *other* people die. That's what I do."

Stung, Gaetan could not stop himself from replying. "It's not always that easy."

"Poor coyotes," said Saskatoon in a singsong voice as she put her forepaws behind her head and peddled an invisible upside-down bicycle. "Bullied by rabbitsss. Should we put you on suicide watch?"

In a flash, Gaetan was across the glade, jaws wide and homing in on Saskatoon, his growl sizzling like a close-range lighting strike. The weasel darted up one of the small trees and clung to a low branch, spitting insults at the coyote.

"Stop it!" roared Sephora, lunging toward the two. "This is a new problem. A dangerous problem. And we'll beat it by working together." She paused, not even breathing heavily. "Next incident like this, I'll do something you won't like. Do you hear me, cousins?"

Gaetan turned and moved away. Saskatoon fell silent and climbed down from the tree.

Sephora sat down. "We're all familiar with the occasional rent strike. And I daresay we know how to deal with them." She licked her lips. "But this goes far beyond that. There has been violence toward legitimate authority. Our agents." She looked at Gaetan and Lilou. "Our loyal friends."

The two coyotes exchanged a look. Saskatoon quietly splashed a rear paw in the brook, and then sucked on it.

Sephora went on. "After the unprovoked violence directed toward the lawful hunters of this wood, I don't wonder that you feel on edge. *You* are the real victims here."

Isadore nodded and nuzzled Juliette. She leaned into him.

"But you're so much more," said Sephora. "You have firsthand experience with these criminals, and no one else does. I want you to brief your counterparts here in the North Shandy. They need to know what it feels like when you're suddenly attacked, by luncheon meat gone bad."

Death Rage

Death Rage, Bricabrac, and Nicodemus had gathered for one of the many meetings that were coming to dominate their lives.

They were producing weapons that had to be transported to eighteen different warrens. And now the talk of going north made everything even more complicated. Nicodemus had taught everyone in the warren a new word recently: *logistics*.

Since they were a few minutes early, that had fallen into conversation. Nicodemus started talking about what they had been learning from the scouts pushing up into the North Shandy.

"The stories say something about the wolves living around big pointy rocks," said Nicodemus. "Our scouts have gone several miles north now, and they've been talking with the local bunnies, too." He started sketching on a bare patch of earth as he spoke. "They've been observing that the land between the cliffs and the water gets narrower, but no one's heard of any tall rocks like that. I'd guess the range of gossip between warrens might be ten or fifteen miles, so that suggests the wolves' lair is very far north." He smoothed out a large blank space with his paw.

Death Rage was walking her fingers around the map. "Just one step from here to the river," she said.

"Yes, about two miles," said Nicodemus.

She walked her fingers north. "And already ten times that far to the wolves."

"At least," said the old bunny.

"Long way for a mouse to walk," said Death Rage. "It'll be winter by the time I get there."

"If not next summer," said Bricabrac. "What about Raptor Air? There are a couple of local ospreys that will still come down for me." He patted a spot on the map. "If I'm in the special spot, they know it's safe."

"I'm not jumping into any raptor talons," said Death Rage, flexing her needle. "I'm a swordfighter. I don't plan on becoming a mouse kebab."

"They wouldn't hurt you," said the rat. "It's just about moneystones."

"Everything's not about moneystones," said Death Rage.

"Can't trust them anyway," said Nicodemus. "They are Blessed. Lines are being drawn."

"Lines were *already* drawn," said Death Rage.

"Maybe the songbirds can help youse," said a raspy voice above their heads. They looked up to see a beautiful orange-breasted bluebird, sitting on the lowest branch of the oak tree. "It's Stan," said the bluebird. "Since we're in talks to join with youse, we'd be happy to offer this favor."

"Could you carry a mouse?" asked Death Rage doubtfully.

Stan laughed, which sounded like a cross between a trill and a sneeze. "No," he said. "You're as big as we are. But maybe a mob of us could. We could all grab your legs, fur, ears, whatever. We're strong like that." He cocked his head. "Might be a little uncomfortable."

"Ugh," said Death Rage.

Bricabrac chewed a forepaw absent-mindedly. "We've been making a lot of cord lately. We could weave it into a net. Make a kind of hammock."

"Mmm," said Nicodemus. "Death Rage probably weighs about three-quarters of an ounce. Songbirds usually weigh a few ounces—"

"Two and a half ounces of fightin' birdflesh right here," said Stan.

"So a squad of eight could probably carry her," said

Nicodemus, scratching some rapid notes in the dirt. "Take along some extra escorts to rotate in for relief. Four should do it. How far can you fly?"

Stan snorted. "When we migrate, we go two thousand miles," he said. "You need flying done, songbird is who you call." He stepped off the oak branch and fluttered down to land on a juniper bush near the map. "Not some lazy raptor who always wants to take five."

Nicodemus looked at him appraisingly. "This could be a real solution."

"Thanks." Stan fluffed his feathers "Everyone says you're the big brain," he said. "You're very *logistical*." He puffed out his chest sang a short, lyrical trill. "People say songbirds ain't too smart cuz we got birdbrains. I don't buy that. I'm pretty *logistical* myself."

"Thank you so much, friend," said Nicodemus.

"Yeah, yeah," said the bluebird. "Just lemme know when it's time to get this party started."

ANASTASIA

The practice models were cut to ribbons after Yasmin, Captain of the Home Guard, had been training the platoons on them all day. Now everyone was at evening feed, and the late-hour sun was coming in from the side and burnishing the plant leather surfaces to a bright gold. The night shift of craftmice would be here soon, repairing some sections, replacing others, preparing for another long day of training tomorrow.

In this brief interlude of quiet, Anastasia was practicing with a bite blade for once, instead of her Claw. She wanted to be ready if she lost the Claw in a battle and had to pick up whatever weapon she could find. Her Guard was silently positioned in the bushes around the clearing.

Anastasia's lean, compact body was made for acrobatics, and the months of practicing with the Claw had given her a good feel for the leap-and-thrust required by this kind of fighting. Lost in thought, she took to the air with elegance and grace, plunging her bite blade home again and again.

"Pretty fierce for someone who doesn't want to make Yah sad," said Coriander, returning from grabbing a quick bite. His agouti fur blazed in the golden sun as he lollopped forward.

Snapped out of her leaping, tumbling reverie, Anastasia turned to look at him. "We owe it to Yah to be exact," she said. "Shoulder, not throat. Ribs, not belly." She scratched her ear. "It's a conversation. We're saying 'go away.' Not 'I want to kill you.'"

Coriander shook his head. "If I'm that close to a golden wolf, it's hard to believe I'll have the presence of mind to do anything more than flail and pray."

Anastasia came near to him, her golden eyes focused on his. "Here's what I've learned," she said. "Even when you're terrified, *you're still there*. You can still choose what you want to do."

Coriander smiled. "I hope, when my moment comes, I'll be as brave as you are."

"Practice hard and you don't need to be brave," said the Loving Auntie. "I'm not."

She raised her right paw, pads inward. *Follow my lead.*

He raised his left paw, pads inward. *I will follow.*

Anastasia turned and took three steps, then pushed off

with her powerful back legs and became airborne. A moment later, she planted her blade in the shoulder of the cactus skin coyote, then pushed off with her back feet and landed several feet away.

Coriander took a running start, lifted off, and ended up with the flat of his blade bouncing off the chin as he went under it. This threw him off, so that he flipped and fell on his side. He got up sheepishly. "Sorry I'm so clumsy. It's hard to do something exact—"

Anastasia raised her right paw, pads forward. *Stop and hush.*

He smiled and patted the side of his head with his left paw. *Understood.*

She turned her paw so that it faced inward. *Follow my lead.*

Without waiting for an answer, she took off at a run, then slid under the pineapple fox, striking at the ribs. Without pausing, she leaped over the apple peel weasel, dragging her weapon along the back. A few more steps took her to the cactus skin coyote, where she launched into the air and struck at the legs as she passed behind it.

She looked back and saw Coriander close behind her, bite blade clenched in his teeth. So she took several flying leaps toward the golden echeveria wolf. A vertical bounce took her up and her momentum carried her forward. An instant later, her bite blade found a place near the shoulder. On landing, she slipped and fell on her side and lay there, surprised to find herself laughing.

Coriander skidded to a stop and lay down a little ways away, looking pleased with himself for having kept up.

Anastasia touched her forehead with her left paw and extended it forward. *Respect.*

He touched his mouth with his left paw and held it out. *Thank you.*

Their paws brushed together briefly. Coriander looked as though he were about to speak. Then Anastasia suddenly noticed a familiar lumpy brown shape standing in the shadow of a mulberry bush some yards away. It was Wendy, who saluted with a short upward jerk of her head.

Feeling embarrassed, Anastasia rolled up onto her feet and headed for a nearby dandelion patch. Coriander started to call after her, but she reached out with her right paw and made a pressing-down gesture. *Done.*

Olympia

Darius, the Prime Buck of Bloody Thorn Warren, had invited Olympia to his Garden of Unmentionables to inspect the first harvest of the tobacco plants. So she had just returned to her working chambers with a fresh piece of tobacco leaf in her cheek and was feeling the jittery buzz. Now she was pacing through her thorn maze, the series of twisting paths among the thorn trees that grew above Bloody Thorn Warren, moving quickly among the sharp points. Walking through it was a kind of game. How fast could she go without getting pricked?

As she passed through a particularly pointy stretch, she made a misstep and a sharp tip pierced her gray fur near her ribs and pricked a hole in her skin, calling forth a drop of blood. She stopped and inspected the injury for a moment. *I deserve that.* Then she was off again.

A few minutes later, Aiden the Rememberer arrived. She saw his smooth creamy fur moving through the thorn maze from yards away. He approached her cautiously, dark ears down, his posture telling her the news was not good.

"Holy day," she barked.

"Every one a gift," returned Aiden.

"What happened?" asked Olympia.

Aiden looked pained. "It is as we thought. There were many days when she was on the brink of Glory, but she did not successfully complete her journey to be with the Loved One."

Olympia covered her face with her paws. "My poor, poor baby. Suffering still." Aiden watched in uncomfortable silence. "Why not?" she asked suddenly.

"Coriander raised an alarm. Nicodemus interfered."

Olympia stamped. "Coriander? We've created a *monster*." She touched the fresh spot of blood on her side and then looked at the red on her paw. "We may need to organize a new Coriander to take care of the old Coriander." She sucked her paw thoughtfully. "And Nicodemus, that old busybody," she growled. "We should have had him Glorified for stealing when we found out about it the first time." She batted irritably at a low-hanging thorn cluster near her. "Let's put him on our list."

"Honored One," said Aiden. "We can't just … Glorify … everyone we don't agree with. That's not going to help you stay Presiding Spirit."

Olympia stopped moving and looked at him. "Of course not," she said soothingly. "We only do what's needed to keep our warren safe." Her blue eyes were big and kindly. "These lists are just … possibilities … to be considered at a later time. As needed."

"Okay," said Aiden.

Olympia began to lollop, and soon was pacing though the thorns again. "The whole team around Anastasia is going to be very careful about unknown foods now. We can't use that trick again."

"True," said Aiden, feeling a burst of relief.

Olympia hummed tunelessly for a moment. "How is the Mark of Blessing on the Yah's Flowers going?"

"As well as can be expected," said Aiden, trailing after her. "The Flowers don't love the pain, of course, but I think we'll have good, clear marks in another week or so. We reinforce them daily."

"Good," said Olympia. "We need to show Tobias we are doing all we can to implement his correction." She turned and looked at Aiden. "The safety of our warren is something we *earn*," she said, quoting the Lord Harmonizer. Aiden nodded and shuffled his feet. She touched noses with him. "Safety above all."

"Yes, Warren Mother," said Aiden.

"Now," said Olympia, taking off at a brisk pace. "I know more warrens are joining their misguided enterprise, and they are gearing up for something big."

"Yes," said Aiden as he trotted after her. "Everyone can see they're making weapons. Clearly, they're imagining they're going to fight the wolves."

"Poor lost children," called Olympia over her shoulder as she raced ahead. "How can they not see? It's not the wolves they're fighting, it's Yah."

"You're right, Honored One," huffed Aiden as he put on a burst of speed to keep up. "But what can we do?"

"We must help them understand," said Olympia as she jogged down the twisting path. "Here's an idea that won't hurt anyone. Get Briar and some of our other stalwarts to go out and circulate among their convert warrens. Let them present themselves as worried members of this unholy alliance. And have them spread this idea: *If only we will confess to being criminals, and lay down our arms, the wolves will be merciful.*"

Olympia's back feet were throwing up clods of earth. "Ouch!" She stopped to disengage herself from a thorn that had penetrated the skin on her foreleg. She rubbed the bloody spot with her other paw, then touched her forehead, leaving a roseate smear.

Aiden came to a halt, panting hard. "Yes, Presiding Spirit. I'm ever your counselor."

Olympia turned and fixed him with her bright blue eyes. Her ears flicked forward. "And a handsome creamy one at that. Perfect for these cool fall nights."

SEPHORA

Sephora Summerday had been arranging meetings all week, with Aliyah as her assistant. First, the briefings with the South Shandy visitors, who told their tales over and over. Foxes with foxes, coyotes with coyotes, the weasel group wiggle.

Then she started working out how the hunters should be organized: creating a command structure, assigning roles, developing policies. As Peace Leader, this is the kind of thing she liked to do. As War Leader, Micah Summerday had a more focused skill set. He was very good at scaring people. And also killing them.

Now Sephora stood on the top of the Hill of Voices, looking out at all the hunters who ranged over the Million Acre Wood north of the Shandy River. Altogether, there were several hundred. It was a sea of reddish brown foxes, interspersed with the undulating forms of mostly tawny weasels. The dirty-gray coyotes of the North Shandy clan, *Bâtard*,[15] moved like clipper ships through the rolling mass of lesser predators. Around the edges stood the specially called hunters from the South Shandy, still unsure what to make of all this. Aliyah stood just below her mother. Several murders of crows wheeled overhead. None of the other Summerdays were visible.

Sephora opened her throat and a low howl, dropping by thirds, rolled out of her throat. In a few seconds, all the animals had gone silent. Even the crows had settled onto the tops of the stone columns.

"Friends," said Sephora, shining like a beacon in the late afternoon sun. "I am Clan Mother of the Summerdays, and the loving mother of everyone in the Million Acre Wood. I have met many of you during these past days. Your realm is in need of you. Thank you for hearing the call."

There was a mild cheer and a bit of yipping from some of the canids.

"Crime is a kind of filth," said Sephora. "Soon we will

---

[15] Bastard.

begin the cleansing of our Wood. And I just want to remind you of something very important. The natural rabbit is not our enemy. The natural mouse or squirrel is not our enemy. We treat them with respect and affection. And we invite them, as needed, to join with our bodies to make us stronger. We are the Landlords. They are the Tenants. We share a bond that is as old as time. And that is the way of love."

There was a loud roar of approval from the northern coyotes and foxes. The weasels smirked.

Sephora scanned the crowd. "But these unnatural creatures from the southern banks of the Shandy River—*our* river—know only hate. They hate their lives. They hate the world. They hate you."

Some of the younger foxes booed at this, and then were shushed.

"We have given them everything," said Sephora. "And all we ask is that they engage in the circle of life with us. But they refuse. They are perverting everything that is right and good. And they are coming to kill you. They are coming to kill me. Their works are death."

"Death! Death! Death!" shouted the crows.

"They will try to pass as their ordinary kin. You must be vigilant. Look for the different. Look for the strange. A mouse carrying a wooden sword is a natural mouse. Our little friends duel each other all the time. A mouse with a metal blade is a criminal. Any rabbit or a squirrel carrying weapons is a lawbreaker."

There was a loud round of boisterous booing from the hunters. Sephora indulgently let it continue for a few seconds before raising her paw for silence.

"Look for fortifications," she continued. "Look for structures. Look for maps. These are not part of the *accoutrement*[16] of our honest and innocent luncheon meat friends." Sephora's gaze swept the hundreds of pairs of binocular eyes fixed on her. "And look for these rabbits. We want them alive. *Wendy. Nicodemus. Freddie. Love Bug.*" She paused. "*Anastasia.*"

At the name of Anastasia, the coyote-killer, all the coyotes raised their voices together in a climbing, grinding stairstep of fourths that rose two octaves and then devolved into cries of "Murderer!"

"When you see something, your first duty is to alert the tactical team. This will be a group of wolves and coyotes that gathers all the information in one place and turns it into actionable intelligence. Every crow you see north of the Shandy has valiantly joined the fight. Flag one down and they will tell us."

The crows swooped low over the assembled animals, and there was a great outpouring of collegial affection from the quadrupeds.

"Now," said Sephora, "You have been formed into a lawful body for the defense of this community. By the power vested in me by Hunger Mother and Blood Father, I deputize you as members of the *Posse Comitatus*.[17] Your goal is to restore order and protect the innocent."

There was a swelling noise from the hunters. The Clan Mother stood tall, her golden coat gleaming. "Hunters, you have your assignments," she called. "Soon you will take your

---

[16] Equipment.

[17] Community Force.

place on a single unbroken line that reaches from the cliffs to the sea. Nothing can get by you. Nothing will escape you. You will sweep south like a shining wave, cleaning the wood as you go. We wolves will scout out in front of the line, and we will also be part of tactical team behind the line. But you will be the backbone of the *Posse*. All legitimate power rides with you." She paused and cocked an ear. "Do you hear Micah Summerday coming?"

A great guttural rumble burst from the throats of the assembled animals, rising, falling and then rising again. The Hill of Voices was suddenly peopled with wolves. They opened their mouths and joined the rolling thrum of noise. Even the weasels, until now immune to patriotic inducements, wound themselves up into a collective glissando whine, indulging their penchant for chromatic progressions. And the crows, whipped into a hyperkinetic mass, hammered at the air with a rapid series of staccato shrieks.

At that moment, Micah Summerday appeared on the Hill of Voices. He dwarfed all the other wolves, and the low, slanting rays of the sun played over his body as he mounted the hill. His newly lean form enabled the light to show every curve of his musculature in high relief. With his aquamarine eyes and massive shoulders gleaming like burnished gold, he looked like a god. Just as Sephora intended.

He raked the crowd with his alien eyes. "I am with you," he rumbled. Then he raised his head, opened his massive jaws, and rolled out a throbbing bass note that seemed to make the Spires themselves vibrate. All the canids joined in with their voices and beat their paws upon the ground. The crows rasped out a backbeat accent with their claws upon their beaks. The weasels' long bodies swayed, and they raised their forelegs like they were at a revival meeting. Some were seen doing a few steps of the *paso doble*.

Then the Summerday Clan Father ended his thrumming ululation and roared, "*Go!*" The hunters poured out of the Spires and into the surrounding woodland like leaves before a gale. In less than a minute, the area was cleared, except for the wolves.

Micah looked at Sephora. "How'd I do?"

She nuzzled under his chin. "You killed."

Chapter 7

Scratch a warmouse, find a craftmouse.
—Musmuski Grove proverb

Aliyah

Near the Spires, the Million Acre Wood spanned twenty miles from the Boreal Cliffs to the sea. The many members of the *Posse Comitatus* were working on forming a single line that stretched all the way across the wood, organized per Sephora's detailed instructions. The crows kept a vigilant eye on things and also delivered a steady stream of messages between the squads and the tactical team.

Getting the line in place was turning out to be a multiday operation, and the Summerday Clan didn't need to be in the line every moment while this was happening, so they took a moment to harvest the new resource they had arranged and reserved for themselves alone.

Raiding the fortified raccoon orchard closest to the Spires had gone swiftly and according to plan. None of the raccoons had escaped to spread the word of the new regime. And the remains were rapidly disappearing down a dozen wolfish throats.

Aliyah had been there at the beginning of the raid, but a few minutes in, she had abruptly left. Now she was returning.

"She's back," said Alaric as Aliyah came around the side of the thorn hedge. "And someone looks a little green."

She shoved past him. "Get out of my way."

Alaric snickered. "Welcome to your first war crime." Then he put his paw to his mouth. "Oops! Sorry, not supposed to call it a call it a 'war.' What is it? A 'constable's picnic?' That makes it all better, right?"

Aliyah's lips came up off her teeth. "Hush!"

Alaric followed after her. "I saved you a little piece of your friend."

Aliyah turned on him in an instant, white-hot snarl lancing out of her throat as she bowled him over onto his back, her teeth closing around his throat. He fought at first, but his snarls turned to whimpers as her powerful jaws crushed his airway and turned his breath into a panicky wheeze.

"Stop that!" shouted Sephora, nipping Aliyah's shoulder, hard, making her yelp with pain. Aliyah let go of Alaric and walked away, head down, breathing hard.

Sephora fell into step with her and nuzzled behind her ear. "Where did you go, darling? Aren't you hungry?"

"No," said Aliyah. She kept walking.

"But why not, my love? We've all been hungry lately. Come and get your share."

Aliyah turned away. "I'm good."

"But why—"

"*I knew them, mother.*" Aliyah turned, her green eyes filled with tears and rage. "When we were cubs we *played* together." An anguished groan escaped from her. "We bought apples from them for *years*."

Sephora's eyebrows rose in concern. "You have such a loving heart," she said. "You are a wonderful wolf." She pressed close against Aliyah's side. "Sometimes being a Landlord means you have to make hard choices." She licked Aliyah's muzzle. "We have to avoid sentimentality. That's the truest form of love."

Aliyah leaned against her mother. "I know," she said. "I'm weak. I'm sorry."

"You're not weak," said Sephora. "You're just young." She kissed Aliyah tenderly. "This is the world the gods have made. It's not always an easy place to be a wolf."

A dark shape flickered by overhead. Then a crow banked steeply and dropped down near Aliyah.

"Honored friend of the murder," said the crow. "This osprey was looking for you."

The osprey alighted and a young female water rat wearing a copper earring scampered free from his claws, dragging a heavy bag behind her. Then she turned and said, "You are a friend to small animals everywhere," and tossed the osprey a dime. He caught it expertly and secreted it in a pocket near his arm pit. Then he grunted, beat his wings and took to the air.

The rat, who had dark brown fur on her head and back and a reddish-brown underbelly, approached the wolves confidently. The crow nodded sideways toward Aliyah.

"You must be Aliyah," said the rat with a winning smile. "I was told you need technical assistance. I'm Frippery, certified craftrat." She flicked her earring, "All the way from Oom."

Aliyah was still breathing hard and looking down, so Sephora stepped forward. "Sorry about the mess," she said, indicating the carnage around her. "We've had to rethink one of our relationships recently."

"I'm sure you took action … as needed," said Frippery blandly, looking away from the worst of it.

Sephora nodded, and bowed to the rat. "I'm the Clan Mother," she said. "We welcome your expertise. Not that the Summerdays have ever gone technical before." Her mouth curved into a rueful moue. "But these are new times for all of us."

Aliyah noticed that Tennyson was licking some blood off a stone nearby. As the newest clan member, he had gotten the least to eat, so he was still hungry. She could tell he was following the conversation, but he said nothing.

Alaric sauntered up, looking a little worse for the wear. He kept his distance from Aliyah. When he caught sight of Frippery, he said, "The *hors d'oeuvres* are late. We already had the main course."

Frippery's amiable expression did not change, but her eyes started darting around.

Sephora glared at Alaric. "We do not speak to guests this way. Keep a civil tongue in your head." She nodded at Frippery. "We're talking potential enhancements."

Alaric nodded solemnly, and then belched suddenly. "The day I need enhancements to fight a rabbit is the day I turn in my wolf card."

Free Warrens

The planning and preparations had taken many weeks, but the moment was finally here. It was the last night before the big push north across the Shandy River, and the bright harvest moon would soon be shining. Anastasia was going to address the many small animals who were going into unknown territory in the cause of freedom.

There had been rumors circulating among the twenty-one allied warrens that if the rabbits would lay down their arms and repent for their criminal activities, the wolves would be happy to offer mercy and lenient treatment.

This is the kind of thing you might try to make yourself believe if you were scared to death. Anastasia understood being terrified, but she also understood that there was no way back to the place where they had started. The wolves in the past might have offered a kind of casually benevolent negligence. But there would be no mercy now.

She had been trying to work out how she should respond to this. Her dream conversation with Anima Mundi came to her mind, as it often did.

The word creates. Everything else follows.

She nibbled her forepaw as she watched the rabbits, squirrels, mice, and songbirds come streaming in. She would need to have the answer soon.

In the meantime, there were party guests to attend to. Representatives of many warrens had arrived with treats to share. The Warren *Orleans* bunnies had recently appeared, rolling their big stomp drum. And a load of fermented apples had shown up at the warren that afternoon.

The gift came from Wellbutrin and Lorazepam, the well-known raccoon power couple in the local dirty apple trade. The note on the apples read, in Lorazepam's neat handwriting, "To the new sheriff in town." And the fermented apples were already being served, along with the treats, to the bold warriors who were heading north on the morrow.

Coriander, as the bodyguard, was on high alert. If there was one assassination attempt, there could easily be a second. He scanned the boisterous company, looking for what, he was not sure. Of course, the Loving Auntie's Guard was also deployed discreetly in the crowd.

Anastasia took a big bite of dirty apple to help her get in the mood and then leaped nimbly up onto the flat-topped boulder that commanded the area. The crowd roared. The songbirds zoomed excitedly from branch to branch.

Freddie looked up at her, and he felt tears coming to his eyes. He was so proud of her and what they had done together. Starting from a bare hole, and now living at the center of an alliance of Free Warrens, standing up to all the teeth and claws in the world. He took a bite of fermented apple and felt the warmth burn down to his belly.

Anastasia sat up tall. "*Citoyens*!"[18] she called. "Free peoples!" The roar became louder, and the songbirds began to circle the crowd of rabbits. "Let me welcome you with words you have never heard before." She flicked open the Claw and raised it over her head, where it shone brightly in the late afternoon sun. "*You were born a prey animal, but you don't have to die as one.*" A huge cheer rose up from the more than one

---

[18] Citizens!

thousand members of the northern expeditionary force, some on the ground, some in the trees. The warmice clashed their spears. The rabbits triple-stamped in affirmation. The squirrels shook their branches. The songbirds trilled a rousing melody.

"Look around you," she called. "You are part of an army of free animals, marching to take our place in the world. *Bienvenue dans l'Armée Libre.*"[19] A massive cheer spiked upwards and slowly faded. "We have already done more than we could ever have imagined possible," continued the Loving Auntie. "And we wield our power within the love that Yah has for us and all living creatures." There was more cheering, leavened with somersaulting binks.

Coriander noticed a small bunny, young, on the edge of the crowd. It was a doe with golden fur, green eyes, and a strange marking on her forehead. She stood out because she seemed uncertain of her surroundings, unlike the other rabbits, who had visited enough to know the area.

"Tomorrow we go north," proclaimed Anastasia. "With three hundred mighty rabbits."

Suddenly, a shining array of bite blades sparkled everywhere in the crowd, showing bright surfaces of both sharpstone and iridescent seashell. And the triple thump of ratification sounded.

"Hooah!" rumbled Wendy. "Elsie MacGowan wills it!"

Love Bug noticed Coriander focusing on something, then followed his line of sight and saw the little golden doe, who was momentarily standing by herself in a cleared area on the opposite side of the boulder.

---

[19]   Welcome to the Free Army.

"And five hundred and sixty fearsome warmice," called Anastasia. A forest of spears appeared, followed by a clarion-bright roar of mousey power.

"It is our honor to fight for freedom!" shouted Death Rage, her bottlecap helmet shining brightly.

Coriander started edging toward the golden doe through the packed mass of bunnies. To him, she had the look of a zealot. Bright-eyed, wandering through strange territory, but somehow confident at the same time. Love Bug moved toward the doe as well. He left the Guard members in place, so as not to disrupt their well-planned perimeter.

"With one hundred and forty strapping squirrels," shouted Anastasia. The trees around them resounded with a cacophony of, "Ah, chek chek chek chek chek chek chek." And the squirrels leaped from one branch to the next in an arboreal version of the wave that swept completely around the gathering.

"Our new allies, a hundred and ninety keen-eyed songbirds," called Anastasia. The songbirds whirled in close about her for a few seconds, then spun away in a dizzying mix of speed and color.

The doe disappeared from Coriander's line of sight. He started pushing through the crowd. Love Bug couldn't see her either. He caught the eye of two of his guard members and signaled them to discreetly flank Anastasia.

"Fifty brilliant craftmice!" shouted the Loving Auntie. A small band of mice raised their shiny tools in salute, then clashed them together in an intricate murine rhythm.

"And our Forward Reading Corps!" called Anastasia, indicating Freddie and his fifty Readers and apprentices. They began to chant the alphabet, but it quickly devolved into general cheering.

"Now," she said, raising her forepaws for silence. It took a goodly number of seconds for the boisterous crowd to settle down. "We know the wolves call themselves Landlords. They and their agents have collected rents made of our bodies for far too long. But I tell you this, sisters and brothers. We are not Renters. We are *Owners*. The ground we stand on belongs to us." Anastasia realized she had found the right words. "*Our lives belong to us*," she shouted.

A great outpouring of *yes* rose up, a sob mixed with a laugh and a cry of recognition from deep in the gut. They had been waiting their whole lives to hear this. One rabbit binked, and suddenly every rabbit was in the air, and the greensward exploded with motion.

Any chance of finding the golden doe disappeared in the chaos. Coriander and Love Bug shared a glance. *Probably nothing, but let's keep our eyes open.* Coriander headed back toward Anastasia and continued to scan the crowd.

The Warren *Orleans* drum team took the mass binky as their cue, and they began to pound their big stomp drum with their powerful legs. Immediately, everyone was moving to the beat, fueled by dirty apples and the communal high and shipping-out-tomorrow jitters.

Some Musmuski Grove mice had set up a small wind orchestra featuring wooden flutes and pipes of all sizes, carved into fantastical shapes. Seizing this moment, they leaped into action and added a wild, sensuous melody to the mix, as mice are wont to do.

Anastasia was beside Coriander now, nuzzling his

muscular shoulder. "Sing us a song," she shouted over the noise. She took a big bite of dirty apple.

He turned, distracted. "What?"

She was playful, riding high on the energy of the crowd. "You were an acolyte, so you've been trained as a cantor. Sing us something. Happy, I mean." She bumped him with her flank. "Or are you afraid?" Coriander looked once more at where the golden doe had been, then turned to her.

"Okay, Loving Auntie," he said, producing the agreeable smile that all the does loved. "Um, there was a song we used to sing at the springtime festival in my old warren."

"Do it," she said, holding out a chunk of fermented apple. They both took a bite.

All the rabbits triple-stamped as Coriander jumped up onto the flat-topped boulder. The warm burn from the dirty apple traveled down to his toes as he lifted his voice, a warm baritone, and began a cheerful song with a catchy melody. The band members listened for a moment, then joined in with a rousing rockabunny accompaniment, accenting the last three syllables of the second and fourth lines with a triple beat.

> "*Sweet little buck, bright little doe*
> *Going to the dance where the big folk go*
> *Hop to the drum, jig to the flute*
> *Two little bunnies and ain't they cute?*"

Most of the animals had not heard this song, so Mabel, the second Remembering acolyte and cantor from Tumble Stone Warren, improvised some moves and got Juniper to do them with her. Soon, Yasmin and Holly joined in. And a few moments later, many of the small animals were dancing. Freddie, not pleased by Coriander's star turn, stood off to one side, glaring.

"*Down comes the dark, out comes the moon*
Lighting up a dance on a night in June
She dances close, he dances near
Two little bunnies just oh so dear"

By the end of the second verse, most of the animals on the ground were either dancing or stamping along with the triple accent beat. The squirrels found the triple beat suited their classic stampy dance perfectly, so they were stamping on their branches with alternating feet. And the songbirds were pitching in with multiple harmonies. Anastasia watched Coriander's copper agouti fur shimmer in the sunlight, creating an almost iridescent effect. She was surprised to find herself beaming.

"*They share a smile, they share a kiss*
They share a moment of endless bliss
She dances wild, he dances free
Two little bunnies like you and me"

There was a large cheer as Coriander jumped down. Then Mabel, the priestly party girl, hopped up on the rock and began one of her familiar songs. Anastasia leaned toward Coriander. "Some of our folks are pretty jittery tonight. You brought them a bit of joy. Thank you."

"Oh, it's just a little tune," said Coriander, smiling. "Happy to help."

The golden harvest moon was rising as they set off into the crowd, snacking, sampling the fermented apples, and offering boisterous cheers to those marching with the *Armée Libre* tomorrow.

They clapped for squirrels engaging in an impromptu contest to see who could crack the toughest nuts with their mighty jaws. They marveled at the songbirds as they one-upped each other in their usual go-to game, polysyllabic reiteration, in which the goal was to learn and repeat the longest and most complex song patterns. As the evening progressed, the competition developed into doing this while flying upside down.

At one point, Anastasia, Love Bug, and Wendy joined a competition to see who could balance the most blueberries on their noses. With her broad, flat face, Wendy won this one handily. "Bah," she said good-naturedly as she tucked into the first prize, a veritable mountain of berries of all kinds.

A little later, Freddie challenged Coriander to a friendly boxing match. He immediately started getting the worst of it, even though Coriander was pulling his punches. At the first sign of a scratch, Anastasia immediately stopped the fight. Coriander offered a hug, but Freddie said they would have to hug later, as he had just remembered a pressing engagement elsewhere. The tipsy Coriander slapped him on the back anyway and assured him he was a capital fellow.

After several hours of small-animal carousing, when Anastasia and Coriander were heading toward the main entrance of the warren, walking closely together, the Loving Auntie's Guard was nowhere to be seen. The *aluminum d'or* circlet on Anastasia's forehead was askew, her golden coat was rumpled, and Coriander was stumbling a little.

Anastasia and Coriander zigzagged down the main hallway, engaging in a little frank canoodling on the way. Finally,
they made it to the entrance of her sleeping chamber.

"I don't know where the Guard is," said Coriander, looking around. "I'll stay here in the hall tonight." He started set-
tling himself down directly in front of her doorway.

Anastasia looked at him for a long moment. "Why don't
you come inside? It'll be more comfortable."

Coriander dropped his eyes to the ground for a moment,
then raised them and looked at her searchingly. "Are you sure,
Loving Auntie?"

Anastasia nuzzled his shoulder. "Call me Anastasia," she
said.

As he looked at her, the sound of a nightbird calling
drifted in from outside. He smiled. "Yes, Anastasia."

They walked tipsily into the sleeping chamber together
and stood near the leaves and moss that made up Anastasia's
bedding. As Coriander nuzzled her flank, a movement in the
passage outside caught his eye. It was a flash of golden fur. In
an instant he was in the doorway, and he saw the golden doe
a few steps away. He threw himself forward and pressed her
against the wall, holding her there with his body. From close
up, he could see that the curious marking on her forehead was
a scar on in the shape of a 'Y.'

"Looking for someone?" he growled.

The little doe squealed. Anastasia, who was right behind
him, shoved him out of the way. "Sunbeam!" she exclaimed.
"How did you get here?"

Startled, Coriander looked back and forth between the
two rabbits, and grudgingly took a step backwards.

"What are you doing here, baby sister?" she asked, covering her with kisses.

"I just wanted to be with you because … I love you," said Sunbeam, licking her forehead.

"You can't just … come at me like that," said Anastasia.

Sunbeam blinked her bright green eyes. "Why not?"

Anastasia quickly sorted through a series of possible answers, then decided to ignore the question. "What happened to your forehead?"

"It's the mark of Yah's Flowers. They scratched our foreheads with a thorn every day until we bled. After awhile, it made this scar."

"Oh, for Yah's sake," muttered Anastasia angrily, kissing her. "And they call *us* criminals." She sat back and looked at her little sister searchingly. "You're too good for them, precious girl." After a moment, another thought popped into her head. "Does Mother know you're here?"

"No," said Sunbeam.

Anastasia looked around as she embraced her. "Well, by the time she finds out, we'll be gone."

GAETAN

Aliyah must have decided there was something interesting about Gaetan, but he wasn't sure what it could be. She had decided to attach him to her entourage instead of sending him out with the *Posse Comitatus* along with his sister Lilou. So now he was tagging along with her as she went about her wolfy junior manager business.

At this moment, Aliyah, Gaetan, and Tennyson were

standing around Frippery and watching closely as she picked up a hook she had made from the spool of 9-gauge *aluminum d'or* wire in the Spires. The bright harvest moon made the wire shine as she fit it carefully around a small sapling.

"Thanks for doing this experiment with me tonight," said Frippery. "I've gotta keep moving if I'm going to get this gear figured out and into production in time for you to use it." She picked up one end of a rope of agave fiber she had braided over the last two days and threaded it through a loop in the hook. "This should help defeat the wooden gratings that you described," said Frippery to Gaetan.

"Too bad you can't just ask their craftrat exactly how their defenses work," said Gaetan, an edge of suspicion creeping into his voice. "Then we'd know exactly what to do."

"Ya, that'd be great," said Frippery blandly. "But you know, that would be against the *Rattus Rattus High Code of Craft & Ethics.* Can't share information about clients. Not ethical."

"You've never sold information about a client?" said Gaetan. "I'd think it would command a pretty moneystone."

Frippery stood up and walked backward, stretching out the rope. "It's bad for business." She glanced up at him. "You may not love rats," she said. "But you know we mean business."

Gaetan looked at Aliyah. "If I may, Third She," he bowed low. "When you told me this story, the craftrat you talked to in the South Shandy was travelling with a rabbit. Then that rat sent *this* rat. Seems a little too ... cozy."

"That job request went to the central posting board for freelance craftrats in City of Oom," said Frippery, as she started tying knots in the rope, four feet apart. Her scent was cool and undisturbed. "Just business as usual."

Tennyson cleared his throat. "I believe that *is* how it's done," he said, his silver fur shining in the cool moonlight. "Craftrats come and go, visiting clients all over the uplands all the time."

"Let's remember to practice courtesy with all living creatures," said Aliyah, giving Gaetan a sharp glance.

Gaetan bowed to the rat. "My apologies," he murmured. "I guess we're a bit out of the swing of things down here in the Million Acre Wood."

Frippery smiled. "No problem, sir," she said. "I *love* getting out to the countryside." She threw her arms wide. "All the fresh air!"

Tennyson chuckled and then nodded his head. "Country people are good people," he said seriously.

Frippery finished her knots and tugged the rope to pull it taut. "Now," she said. "Here's the test. "You three grab the cord in your mouths. I have three spaced-out knots for you to bite on, so you can keep a grip without slipping. If you can jerk this sapling out of the ground, I think you can pull out those rabbit gratings."

The three canids each took up the cord, and at a signal from Frippery, they trotted ahead to take up the slack, then turned around so they were facing backwards in their best pulling stance. They strained for a few seconds against the sapling. Nothing happened.

"Need to pull and release together in a rhythm," said Frippery. "Try it on my count. One … two … pull … one … two … pull…"

After three pulls, there was a small tearing sound. On the fifth pull, the roots began to lift on one side of the tree. And on the eighth pull, the whole thing came loose and they dragged it, roots and all for a few feet.

Frippery whooped.

"Now what?" asked Aliyah.

"Now," Frippery gestured grandly, "Weasels go in. Bunnies come out. Problem solved."

Chapter 8

Sleep now, sweet and tiny wolfy,
You will grow up kind and strong,
Noble and courageous Landlord,
Brave and loving is your song.
                              —Traditional wolf lullaby

ARMÉE LIBRE

There was a good deal of argument on the council about whether or not Anastasia herself should march with the *Armée Libre*. This was not resolved until the last minute. Freddie wanted her to stay at Warren *Sans Gloire*. And Love Bug said he also thought *Sans Gloire* would be a safer place for her. Coriander said it would be harder to guard effectively in changing circumstances, but that he would follow her anywhere.

Anastasia had learned by now to couch things in a way that would be easier for her council to hear, so she said that staying in one place just made her a more convenient target for the next assassin, and moving around would make her harder to find. She did not say, *I'm not going to ask all these people to march into danger and then sit home because I'm afraid. What kind of person would that make me?*

Nicodemus surprised everyone by agreeing with her assassin rationale. He said, "Unless you have very good communications, just having your target move a mile away will effectively make it disappear ... for awhile. A Loving Auntie on the move will be mostly invisible to long-range plotters." And so it was decided.

On the morning of the launch day, the team of songbirds carrying Death Rage took off for the north. They had wanted to start earlier, but it took longer than expected to learn how to fly together in a coordinated way, holding the netting that would carry Death Rage like a hammock. They still looked a little shaky as they took off and circled once around the greensward, Death Rage clinging to the rough mesh.

"Everything okay?" called Anastasia.

"*Timent muram!*"[20] shouted Death Rage as they rose over the tree line.

Wendy sent fifty of the songbird scouts, captained by Stan the bluebird, out to the area around the planned river crossing. That would be the northern assault's most visible moment, and the goal was to discover if there were crows nearby who could report them to the wolves.

Wendy came from a culture that had long studied the

---

[20] Fear the mouse!

habits of birds. So she gave the songbirds strict orders not to approach the crows aggressively, since attacking the crows would only draw attention to the area. Rather, they should present themselves as injured or old. By masquerading as believable victims, they could lure the crows away from the river crossing, then drop down through the treeline to lose their pursuers and stealthily make their way back.

Then Wendy gave the sign for the platoons to form up and start drifting through the woods toward the crossing point, moving slowly and keeping under cover. The squirrels were very firmly instructed that there would be no cheering, but normal chatter about nuts and bugs was encouraged.

Grégoire the Healer and his apprentice Juniper ran among the troops, fussing over the rabbit and mouse medic teams they had trained, one for each platoon. Juniper was doing last-minute checks on their backpacks of supplies, and Grégoire was answering questions and dispensing generous doses of encouragement.

At last, it was time for Team Auntie, the command group, to leave. Love Bug threw out his traveling perimeter as Nicodemus, Wendy, Coriander and other members of the team gathered. Anastasia noticed Sunbeam wandering around and added her to Team Auntie so she could keep an eye on her. Holly, the newly appointed Home Steward of the Free Warrens, gave Anastasia a long and tearful hug, followed by Yasmin and a dozen other bunnies. Wendy picked her teeth with a bramble thorn and rapped out orders to a constant stream of songbird messengers. At last, all the embraces were done, and they were off.

It was nightfall by the time they all reached the river

crossing, which was exactly the plan. They went across in shifts. Anastasia and the other members of Team Auntie swam with the rest, clinging to the agave cords strung across earlier. Bricabrac had offered to ferry the command group members across in his catamaran, but Anastasia had declined. Not everyone on Team Auntie was happy about that. Ultimately, Bricabrac did end up carrying Nicodemus, since he was an elder bunny and more likely to get sick from being wet.

On the far side, Anastasia ran into Dingus. After his great success bringing the songbirds into the fold, Anastasia had had a long talk with him about vision and community-building. She was hoping he would recruit northern squirrels, but she wasn't really sure what he was going to do. She noticed him setting off alone into the northern wood, flowing along the branches like quicksilver.

"Yahspeed, brother," she called to him. Dingus glanced back at her. She waved and smiled. "May the seeds of your wisdom fall on fertile ground."

Dingus raised a coolly elegant hand. "Talking about seeds only reveals your desire." His tail flicked. "I go. What happens, happens."

"Take care—" she began, but he was already gone.

When everyone had reconvened on the north bank, Wendy sent out the twenty-eight platoons to form a continuous line between the cliffs and the sea. Now that they were across the river, and under cover of night, they could move more quickly. Which was good, since some teams would have to cover several miles. The goal was to have the line completely formed by end of the next day.

Once in place, each platoon's songbirds would sweep

back and forth, looking for warrens and keeping the line orderly. The squirrels would stay with the platoons and act as scouts. The platoons would approach any warrens that they discovered and invite them to join. And of course, everyone would be looking for the bunker.

AIDEN

It was always a little strange waking up in Olympia's soft moss bed. Aiden yawned and stretched. He rolled away from the Warren Mother's sleeping form and realized with a start that Darius was sitting in the entryway to the royal chambers looking right at him, his dappled tan and brown fur wet from the morning dew.

"Greetings, um, Prime Buck … sir," he stuttered. "I was just … uh…"

Darius gazed at him with an unreadable expression. "It's not easy to make lovey happy," he said, finally. "You've managed to hold her attention for almost two months."

"Sorry to … be in the way…" Aiden began, then trailed off.

"No reason to be," said Darius cheerfully. He turned and gestured. "I've asked Briar to bring in a nice fresh breakfast."

Briar bustled in with a golden fall pear in his mouth and set it down near the bed.

"Oh, nice," said Aiden faintly. Briar bowed and left.

Olympia began to stir. "Lovey, don't you think this fine Rememberer is a big smarty?" she asked.

"That's what everyone says," murmured Darius. "He has fine shoulders. He carries himself like a smart rabbit." His scent was oily and cool.

Aiden was starting to feel a little creeped out. "Mind on Yah, heart on the warren," he murmured, trying to claw his way back to his official identity.

"So riddle me this," said Olympia, as she rose from her cool moss bed and sidled up alongside Aiden. "What revelation would call earnest Yah-loving rabbits forth to take part in a spiritual war?"

CORIANDER

The command group was moving into the northern woods at something like strolling speed. They were surrounded by the multiple moving perimeters of the *Armée Libre* and the Loving Auntie's Guard, so the effect was rather cozy, something like a walking picnic.

Anastasia was wearing her Claw, and her Kevlar jacket with the camouflage side out. After wrangling the launch of the whole operation, she looked exhausted. She seemed only too happy to meander along, sometimes leaning against Coriander's muscular form. This intimate hobnobbery with her bodyguard would certainly have raised a few bunny eyebrows, if they had had any to raise, but it seemed that Anastasia was too tired to care. She sighed deeply and nuzzled into his agouti fur as they ambled along.

At a sign from Love Bug, the Guard withdrew to a discreet distance to offer her some privacy. Freddie stomped up to the leading edge of the group and engaged in a loud conversation with Nicodemus about the difficult aerodynamics of lichen.

At one point, the command group crossed a small stream,

hopping across on stepping stones. Anastasia stopped partway across, looking down into the clear bright water.

"Oooo," she said. "Look."

Coriander came up behind her. "What?"

Anastasia pointed with her forepaw. "Tadpoles."

Coriander wrinkled his nose. "So slimy."

Anastasia elbowed him. "They're not slimy, they're … well, okay, they *are* slimy. But in a beautiful way."

"Mmmm." Coriander playfully pretended to be considering this very carefully. "What's beautiful about them?"

"Everything they might ever do is inside of them right now, waiting to happen. I love just being near so much … life."

As others came up behind them, she turned and hopped off the steppingstones. Coriander caught up with her as they walked on. "What do you want to do when this is all … over?"

Anastasia leaned into him as they ducked under some hanging ferns. "I'd like to have a burrow by a little waterfall. The sound is so soothing."

"Sounds wonderful."

"And I do love little baby creatures of all kinds. Tadpoles, baby spiders, caterpillars. And bunny kits, of course. Maybe I'll start a tinytown were babies can play together."

Coriander nuzzled her and they walked in silence for a few moments. After a while, he said, "Do you want to start a family?"

Anastasia pulled away from him as she hopped over a patch of mud. "I'm not going to have kits. My body doesn't do that."

"Sorry, didn't mean to pry," said Coriander.

Anastasia waved a paw. "No, it's fine. I went through all that at Bloody Thorn. Once it became clear I would never create children, the bucks tossed me." She shrugged. "Didn't have much to offer. Just a plain brown bunny."

"You are beautiful—" began Coriander.

Anastasia laughed. "You don't have to make up crap to tell me." She turned to glare at him. "And do *not* tell me I am beautiful inside. I will smack you."

Coriander smiled. "Understood, Loving Auntie." He nuzzled her long, elegant ear. "I will say that I'm honored to be your romping buddy."

"Ehh," Anastasia made a dismissive sound and glanced at him out of the side of her eye. "The Free Warrens thank you for supporting the cause." She chuckled and nipped his midsection playfully, which made him jump. "Now *you* are beautiful. The does never stop talking about you. Thanks for bunking with me."

"You changed my life," said Coriander, suddenly earnest. "When I first met you, I—" he stopped abruptly. This was dangerous ground. It was no time to blurt out a hasty confession. *I was a spy. I fell for you. Let's hug it out.* "I knew you were different," he finished lamely.

Anastasia nodded. "You mean crazy."

Coriander chewed his lip. "Well, okay, everyone says that." He turned to face her. "But … I didn't realize how much goodness you could bring into the world." He pressed his cheek against hers, so his lips were close to her ear. "My question for you is this. Are you getting some goodness for yourself, Anastasia?"

Death Rage

It was a day and half since the songbird air transport team had left *Sans Gloire*, armed with only the direction to go north and rumors about the wolves living among tall stone columns. After much flying, following the coast, they had seen a line of Blessed Ones stretched out across the Wood, with crows wheeling above. So they had made a long detour out to sea, then pushed north past the line of Blessed. Now the Spires loomed in the distance, their ancient forms jutting above the surrounding forest of cedar and white birch.

Death Rage was still riding in the net made of braided agave cord. She had darkened her bottlecap helmet with mud, so that its shine would not give her away when she reached the wolves' area.

The closer they got to the Spires, the harder it was to avoid the crows. After the songbirds saw their third dark flyer, they dropped down and started flying low, whizzing though the space between the lower tree branches and the ground in the gray twilight.

"Go, go, go," hissed the songbird captain, a handsome white-throated robin. "We don't want that crow to drop and see what we're doing."

Death Rage clung to the net with all her might. She would have looked green if she weren't covered in thick brown fur. The leaves, stones, and branches that were rushing toward her now were almost more terrifying than zooming across the forest at two hundred feet in the air.

"Just … get me there alive," she managed to croak.

"The crow's probably *already* wondering what we're

doing," said an evening grosbeak, yellow and white wings flapping furiously. "A dozen birds flying right together in some kind of clusterflap. Gotta look weird."

"Attention to breath," said the robin, as they swerved around an ocotillo cactus. Death Rage's stomach gave up its battle for control and she threw up her lunch, which trailed away in a thick mess with chunks of sunflower seed.

"Feh! Blim-blammit!" barked the varied thrush flying at the back edge of the netting, shaking her left foot. Her orange breast feathers looked splattered.

"Sorry," gasped Death Rage.

"You're lucky I didn't just drop my edge," said the thrush.

"Almost there," said the robin captain as they wound through a grove of aspens. "We'll put you down by those white lilies."

The songbirds caromed in for a hasty landing, and Death Rage spilled out of the net, rolling over and over. She grabbed the Kiss of Death and held it tightly as she tumbled. Her little backpack took up some of the impact, with the piece of broken glass for signaling and the dime that Bricabrac had given her as 'mad money' jangling together. As she rolled to a halt, she took a deep breath and wrinkled her nose as she got a whiff of the purple fruits rotting under a nearby carrion bush.

"You good?" asked the robin.

"Yeah," said Death Rage, shakily.

"Remember, when you want pickup, hang your diamond on a dead branch on the highest tree you can find. We'll stay in this area until we hear from you."

"Let's go! Let's go!" hissed the varied thrush. Some of the other songbirds were already taking to air.

The white-throated robin turned her head and gave Death Rage a long look. "We're with you, brave one. Come home safe." She kissed her wingtip and threw the kiss to the Death Rage. Then she rose in the air and was gone.

Death Rage knelt down for a moment in the gathering darkness. She took out her rapier and held it in both hands, taking comfort from the feel of the strong flexible steel. The easy part was over. Now for the wolves.

ANASTASIA

The *Armée Libre* was slowly pushing up into the North Shandy. Their days were long. Finding and talking to local warrens, scouring the woodlands for a 'bunker' that might look like nothing more than a lumpy hill after three hundred years, and doing it all under cover so as to be unseen by the crows was tiring labor.

Anastasia moved Team Auntie up and down the line as they went, so she could be offering constant contact and encouragement to the platoons. She and Nicodemus talked through possible scenarios all day long as they marched. What might they find? How best to use it? The possibilities were great, and definite answers were few. Coriander offered occasional pithy comments, since he was usually within earshot as he orbited her position, scanning the area. And he was always available for moral support.

The area they were moving through was studded with outcroppings of chalcopyrite, and its glittery purple surface kept activating Anastasia's need to dart off and touch distant shiny stones. This meant Coriander had to run after her.

"Why do you do this, Loving Auntie?" he panted after one foray.

Anastasia grimaced. "Once I see it, I have to touch it," she said irritably. "If I don't, something bad will happen. And if I wait, it starts to hurt." She shrugged. "It's part of my head sickness."

This didn't make Love Bug's job any easier. As captain of the Loving Auntie's Guard, his responsibility had expanded to maintaining a protective perimeter for Team Auntie as a whole, so the Guard had grown significantly in size.

He was turning out to be a popular commander. Anastasia observed that the same talent that had once delivered an endless stream of pickup lines enabled him to easily dispense attaboys, productivity tips, compliment sandwiches and other middle management patter. She smiled as she listened to him artfully conceal a request for greater punctuality inside a warm fluffy serving of *great job, buddy*.

At Anastasia's request, Freddie's Forward Reading Corps stayed a few hundred yards behind the front line. As the Free Warrens' brain trust, she did not want to risk them getting engaged in combat. The training of a Reader takes years, and if the Reading Corps was decimated in a fight, the Free Warrens would be crippled for a generation. Which was much longer than this war was likely to last. She knew they chafed at this restriction, and wanted to stand shoulder-to-shoulder with their comrades, but she had been firm.

And of course, it was a way to remove Freddie from the day-to-day operations of the command group. Even Anastasia had finally noticed how much he sniped and glared at Coriander, and creating some distance helped to keep the peace.

Wendy mostly travelled with Team Auntie. She was in constant communication with the *Armée Libre* as a whole via a steady stream of songbird messengers from the platoons and another stream of songbirds reporting scouting information, all flying in on carefully varied, casual-looking flight paths. The last thing they wanted was to reveal Team Auntie as an epicenter of songbird travel.

The songbirds would often stand or sit on Wendy's flat head while they were talking to her. So on busy days it looked as though she was wearing an ever-changing assortment of brightly colored feathered fascinators.

One thing they noticed almost immediately was how scarce Blessed Ones were. In the local area, there were only cubs, elders, and the occasional exhausted nursing mother, easy to fight off. They weren't sure what to make of it. Surely the Blessed weren't running in fear of an army of prey animals? It was a seductive thought, but Anastasia knew it couldn't really be the answer, not when an army led by wolves was on the way south.

Wendy, who had grown up on an island, offered this comment. "Sometime water go away. Gone long time. Then come back bigger." It was a sobering assessment. If the wolves had really drained the area of local killers in order to build up their army, that suggested the wave coming at them could be much larger than they had thought.

On the fifth day, Stan came meandering through the foliage, singing a classic bluebird folk tune about the beauty of grubs. Then he dropped into the midst of Team Auntie, currently camped under a shrubby cinquefoil, and said, "Found something weird. Could be it."

Anastasia felt her heart beat faster. "What is it?" she asked as the team gathered around her.

"Strange hill. Some kind of flat slits in the surface. Just half a mile from here." He looked around the group. "All grown over, of course. Gonna take some work to get in." He scratched his balding head with his foot. "Glad we got these rabbits with their fancy choppers."

Anastasia nuzzled his side. "Thank you so much."

"Wasn't me," said Stan, taking up his accustomed perch on Wendy's head. "These two gals in our scouting group, Acadian Flycatchers. They found it for youse."

"Give them a kiss for me," said Anastasia, as she gathered up her gear and prepared to move.

"Soon as I get lips, I'll get right on that," said Stan.

"Maybe just a peck," said Nicodemus.

Wendy sent songbird messengers to bring the main line forward. Then Team Auntie and the Loving Auntie's Guard percolated through the loblolly pines in a kind of rushed saunter, doing their best to be inconspicuous.

An hour later, they were rewarded by the sight of a small, squarish hill, covered with a dense mat of vines and scrub, nestled in an ancient grove of sinewy yew trees. Dark horizontal strokes could be grown-over windows. And a shadowed smudge behind a dense wall of kudzu vines might be a doorway that led into the side of the hill. A few dozen yards to the north, a broad stream bubbled over gray stones.

Anastasia immediately sent a songbird to Freddie to bring up the Forward Reading Corps.

After a quick consultation with Wendy, Love Bug threw a cordon around the bunker with a mouse picket line hidden under foliage at fifty yards and the squirrel sentries patrolling a hundred yard perimeter at lower tree-branch level, moving slowly so as not to attract any attention. The rabbits in the Guard took up positions close at hand.

Wendy had Stan put his fifty songbirds in casual groups arranged on a perimeter a mile out from the bunker, just chirping, looking for seeds, and singing brightly, as they might on any day of the year.

Then the rabbits in Team Auntie swarmed over the hill, chewing, tugging, pulling off detritus and throwing it down. Soon the Forward Readers and several nearby platoons showed up and there were more than a hundred rabbits at work, gnawing away the vines, roots, and even tree branches that blocked the windows and doorway.

Anastasia and many other rabbits were attacking the thick ropes of kudzu that covered the door that led into the earth. It looked to be all hardstone, heavily rusted.

Her breath came fast, but she strove to appear calm. Could this be it? A gift from Yah that would change the balance of power and give them a fighting chance? For the Readers to learn about this relic of the Dead Gods, and then for the songbirds of the Free Warrens to find it, was beyond anything she had ever heard of. She heard the voice of Anima Mundi in her ear. *You have everything you need.*

Rabbits were coming down from the somewhat uncovered slit windows now. They were long rectangular apertures set into the side of the small hill, covered with thick slabs of diamond. Inside it was too dark to see.

Anastasia wanted to get through that door. Now. Before this amazing miracle vanished into a puff of nothing-here-for-you.

She bit ferociously at the root she had her jaws around, and Freddie, who was next to her, helped her pull it back and away from the door. A large section of kudzu came down and revealed the door to be standing open a few inches. Nicodemus, Coriander and some other rabbits seized the kudzu and dragged it away.

Anastasia stood at the doorway and sniffed the darkness. It smelled like a cave, damp and dusty. And there was a strong scent of ancient straightstone, beloved of the Dead Gods. She had smelled this before among the foundations of the collapsed cabin near Warren *Sans Gloire.*

She paused. This was the most significant threshold she had ever passed. Suddenly diffident, she gently touched one side three times, then the other, then touched the doorsill twice.

Coriander came up beside her, looking concerned. "Are you sure you want to go in first, Loving Auntie?"

She looked at him as she sang her couplet.

"A thousand hearts have come to see
If Yah will set his little ones free"

Then she squeezed through the gap into the darkness.

Aliyah

The *Posse Comitatus* line was now five miles below the Spires, moving south at a rate of about a mile a day. It was still close enough that it was easy to lope back and forth from home base to the front line for a check in.

At this moment, Aliyah and Tennyson were about a mile out in front of the *Posse Comitatus* line. Technically, they were scouting for criminal elements. But since the line of hungry hunters behind them was scouring the landscape as they passed over it, the two wolves were more focused on nosing up anything edible than on bringing the righteous wrath of justice to malcontents.

It had rained earlier in the day, so many earthworms had come to the surface. And now the once-proud Lead Striker of the Summerday Clan was snapping them up eagerly. As the day wore on and the ground dried out, both Aliyah and Tennyson started turning over stones and pushing aside old logs in an attempt to extend the meal.

At last, they rested, sitting side by side on the high cliffs looking out over the ocean.

Aliyah rolled on her back and sunned her underside. "If I ask you a question, will you tell me the truth?" she asked.

Tennyson lay down a few feet away, gazing up toward the sun peeking out from behind the gray clouds scudding across the sky. "Of course."

"Are we a bunch of hicks?"

Tennyson laughed and then turned to look at her. "Why would you even ask that question?"

Aliyah rolled on her side and gazed at him with her maple-green eyes. After a pause, she said, "I notice you didn't say 'no.'"

"Your family has run the Million Acre Wood for time out of mind," said Tennyson. "You've got a pretty sweet deal here." He scratched his ear with his foot. "Sure, you've never been to City of Oom but so what? I've been there, and it's not so great. The bears are doing things no animals have ever done. They don't even hunt now. They live off fish from the Shandy. The Civil Raccoons have a whole operation with nets to keep the City fed." Tennyson licked his paw. "So they have lots of time to think about ways to harass freelance hunters." He smiled ruefully. "That's why I'm here."

Aliyah touched noses with him. "I'm so sorry."

"Thank you ... again," he said. "Your family's awesome. I would *never* call you hicks. You're honest, working wolves who hunt for a living as Hunger Mother intended."

Aliyah sat up and looked at the distant waves. "The thing is," she said. "I've realized in talking with you and these craftrats that there's a lot of stuff to know. And we don't know it." She glanced down toward the rocks. "Like those things Gaetan was asking ... I wouldn't even have thought to ask questions like that. And he's a *coyote*." She glanced at him. "You seem to know a lot."

Tennyson cocked his head. "You're used to being the lords of your world." He rolled up onto his feet, his silver fur shining in the sun. "And that *can* make you a little dumb." Aliyah blinked. He looked at her seriously. "When the answer to every question is 'yes, my lord,' you don't know what you don't know."

Aliyah was a little shocked, but tried to play if off as nothing. "Oh, ouch."

Tennyson smiled. "Myself, I know a little," he said. "From what I've seen, the main thing isn't knowing or not knowing, it's whether you're willing to learn." He idly flicked against a piece of broken shale with his forepaw and sent it clattering down to the rocks below. "Not everyone is. You are."

Chapter 9

We loved the Dead Gods. We learned from them. We kissed their faces while they slept. And what did we get for it? Blind hatred.
                    —*Rattus Rattus, Book of Gnawledge*

ANASTASIA

Anastasia could smell that there were no Blessed Ones inside the bunker. Mostly, it was just a musty, fusty smell. She also got just a whiff of ancient sharpstone. She took a step into the darkness and felt a point prick her forepaw.

Coriander squeezed in right after her, followed by Love Bug and other members of the Loving Auntie's Guard, all with weapons ready. She stood over the sharp point so no one else stepped on it. They fanned out in front of her, half-feeling their way into the darkness, calling out to each other as they went.

The surprise sharpstone buoyed her spirits. Who knew what treasure might lay within this ancient fortress they had been led to? *Let your love be mighty, Lord*, she prayed. *Make it fearsome. Make it hurt.*

She could hear Wendy outside, organizing the platoons to line up against the door and push.

"Hooah," she growled.

"Hooah!" grunted the rabbit soldiers as they heaved together against the heavy weight.

Slowly the door began to move inward, letting in the light of day.

Anastasia absent-mindedly raised her paw to her mouth and licked her injury. *Let it somehow touch Blessed who are far away.*

As the door opened, she could see the point she was standing over. It was sharpstone, as she had imagined, about half an inch across, a simple triangle.

As the light crept in from the slowly opening door, she could see, cut into the surface, the same delicate intaglio that she had first seen in the margins of the letter from Magdalenium that the Readers had turned up at the straightstone burrow all those weeks ago.

Now the door was half open, and rabbits and mice were streaming past her as they fanned out into the interior. Nicodemus came in and nose-bumped her quickly as he went by, eyes bright. Rabbits outside were continuing to strip vegetation from the high slit windows, which brought in more light.

Freddie and the Forward Readers poured in. So proud of what they had done in leading their people to this windfall, they were eager to see what might be discovered.

Anastasia turned to Coriander, who had stationed himself nearby. "What do you think this is?"

He blew out a breath between pursed lips. "Some kind of weapon?"

She frowned. "It's beautiful, but … so small."

Coriander shrugged. "It's a mystery."

Anastasia let herself get swept along in the swarm of eager animals. There were six rooms in all. And the high, narrow, horizontal windows set into the outer walls brought in more and more light as the rabbits outside worked to clean the debris off them. The bunker itself was much better preserved than the cabin foundation near *Sans Gloire* that they had been using for a workspace, but the interior was a wreck. Everything had been thoroughly ransacked, probably many times. Most of the furniture had been smashed to bits.

There was so much clutter, it took the animals some time to realize that most items of value had long been taken. The workshop and storage rooms were mostly bare, with a scattering of empty food containers and broken tools. Almost all the books were gone.

Slowly, they brought the best items into the main space. Several dozen random-sized nails and screws, some toymaker's tools, part of Magdalenium's diary, a few torn pages from a book on ancient weaponry, a disintegrating box of complicated metal parts, a rusty saw blade, several dozen empty cans that could be cut into bite blades, and the tiny point.

Clearly, the bunker had been thoroughly pillaged, and their dream of a rich hoard of Dead Gods weapons was not to be. Anastasia felt the mood sinking as this realization set in. The little animals, so joyful an hour before, were slowly drooping as they realized they were facing an army of killers with nothing more than the weapons they already had. No miraculous new tool of destruction was coming to save them.

They had hoped, they had labored, they had rushed to do the unthinkable thing and had thrown an army across the river to find and seize the gift of Yah or the Dead Gods or anyone who might be willing to help them. Now they had found, as little animals always did, that their lot was the leavings and afterthoughts of the world.

No, thought Anastasia. She paced, muttering. *No. We have—*

She jumped up on a broken stool. "The gifts of Yah are a mystery for us to solve. Now is the time for our Forward Readers, led by Freddie ... and ... and .. Nicodemus ... whom you all know have amazing Readerly powers, to solve this puzzle left for us by our loving Lord, Almighty Yah, Creator of Heaven and Earth."

A small voice rose out of the group. She could not see who it was in the half light. "What if there isn't anything?"

Anastasia sat up tall and spread her forepaws in her best approximation of the Rememberer's blessing gesture. "*We have everything we need.*"

DEATH RAGE

The musky smell of wolves was overpowering. Wolf scent glands. Wolf urine. Wolf scat. Freshly killed animals. Fragments of recently killed animals. All mingled with bones from kills stretching back years.

All this burned into Death Rage's nerves and brain and

triggered her amygdala to send out a frantic high-volume internal alarm that screamed *danger, danger, danger*. As a mouse, the number of seconds of life she would have between discovery and death could be counted on one paw. So crawling into a wolf den felt to her body like she was committing suicide.

It had taken her most of a day to creep from her drop-off point into the area close around the Spires. Now she was resting under a dead palm leaf, pressing her face into the soil. Her lips fluttered as she quietly whispered a hymn in communion with The One Who Makes The World.

> *"Close by me,*
> *You I see,*
> *Never far*
> *Ever free.*
>
> *What shall we do*
> *I and you,*
> *This day to*
> *Make the world?"*

Up above her, stone columns reached up into the late afternoon sky. Ahead, she could hear a mix of snarls, yips, growls, rumbling breaths, and conversations. There seemed to be at least three or four different groups of wolves scattered about in this space.

Best not to get surrounded, and avoid the pathways at all costs. Death Rage took a deep breath and crawled forward into a messy mixture of hydrangea, deer grass, and viburnum.

The cluttery space felt good. Felt safe. Just ahead, she could hear several voices talking.

She drew the Kiss of Death from its scabbard and held it in her front right paw. If she was discovered, she reckoned that plunging her rapier deep into the nose of the first wolven head that came her way might buy her a few seconds to scramble away into the shadows and clutter. Might.

She inched forward until she could see what was happening. There was a flat, sandy place between several stone columns. A long, roughly rectangular shape had been drawn in the sand, and many small pebbles of different colors were scattered about within it. A young golden wolf stood, looking at the stones with maple-green eyes, talking to a smaller tawny-gray coyote who had just entered.

"Thank you so much for showing me this," said the coyote.

The wolf took a few steps forward. "It's forty-five miles from here to the Shandy River," she said. "This helps us keep track of where everyone is."

"Do you think the *Posse Comitatus* discipline is good?" asked the coyote. "They could be cleaning out every warren of natural rabbits."

"Clan Mother made it clear that they cannot do that, since we will be relying on the natural rabbits for food over the long run. The teams have been told they can do short-ration Glorifying, but the natural warrens must be left intact. We're noting the locations here."

All of a sudden, Death Rage realized she was looking at a map of the Million Acre Wood. She could see the long strip of land between the cliffs and the sea. At the north end, there were tiny versions of the tall stone columns that surrounded her. Two thirds of the way down, a curving line of blue stones indicated the Shandy River. A few miles north of the river, she could see an area where the sea had eroded the land and reduced the Wood to just a thin strip against the cliffs. At the southern end, a swath of wet moss represented the Southern Swamps. A ragged red line of pebbles across the map showed the Blessed armies, moving south.

The coyote got up and walked around the edge of the map. Death Rage noticed that he was limping. "What's keeping the teams in check?" he asked.

The golden wolf sat down and licked her paw. "Mummy told them that Daddy would eat them alive if they disobeyed." She snickered quietly. "Daddy is the nicest wolf in the whole world, but he makes a great boogeyman."

The coyote shuddered and looked down. "Yes, he is … nice." His voice sounded whispery.

The golden wolf looked over at him, then padded toward him and nuzzled his neck. "I'm sorry that had to happen to your Clan."

The coyote looked like he was trying to speak, but could not. Finally, he coughed and said, "Me, too."

"We love our little cousins," said the wolf. "I'm thinking maybe you could gather a new coyote pack to manage the South Shandy after this is all over."

The coyote looked stunned. He took a few paces away and stood looking down at the pebble map. "Me?" he said.

The wolf gazed at him without moving. "We would do it differently this time. Put someone in charge. You're the natural candidate."

The coyote licked his injured leg and turned to face her. "Why me?"

"You're different than the others. You make it a point to find out new things." She came toward him. "And you acted with honor when those about you did not."

Just then, a crow flew into the space, landed, and then walked out onto the map.

"Here," said the crow. "Natural warren."

A female rat with dark brown fur and a reddish underbelly appeared from behind a philodendron leaf and ran out onto the map carrying a white pebble. She placed it where the crow was standing. "A hundred and twenty-seven natural warrens so far," she said briskly. "They're getting denser as we move south."

With a start, Death Rage realized she recognized her.

It was Frippery, Bricabrac's sister, who had worked on the *Sans Gloire* fortifications and weaponry. Her eyes bugged out, and she almost yelped in surprise. *What?* The wheels in her mind turned furiously. She remembered Bricabrac telling Frippery he had found a client for her.

Death Rage, student of honor, felt her mouth twist in a sour grimace as she quietly spat out the ugliest word she could think of. "*Mercenary.*"

ANASTASIA

Anastasia sat in a big circle with Freddie, Nicodemus and all the Forward Readers gathered from the warrens who had joined the alliance. All the items they had found in the bunker were spread out in the middle of the circle. A breeze ruffled the torn pages of the damaged books and clanked two of the empty cans together. Many anxious faces were looking at her.

"Friends," she said. "Many of you know I have a soft spot for Readers." Her eyes rested for a moment on Nicodemus, then swept around the circle. She touched both paws to her heart and then extended them, paws upward. *I love you all.* Nicodemus and many others nodded gravely. "The word creates. And Readers know that."

Some of the apprentices cheered quietly.

"It's important to speak the truth among friends." She rubbed a forepaw over the dry earth. "We are engaged in a heavy labor, and we all share in it. Sometimes the weight falls heaviest on the fighters. Sometimes it falls heaviest on the builders." Her eyes tracked across the group. "Today it falls heaviest on you."

Freddie sat up, his black-and-gray face very serious. "We are seizing this task, Loving Auntie."

Anastasia nodded. "The gifts of Yah are not easy to discern. I know that." Her gaze roamed the group. "If you come to me and say, 'there is no gift,' I will continue to love you. And we will go out and fight as fiercely as we can against the wave of teeth and claws that is bearing down on us. And we know how that story is likely to end."

A just barely audible groan swept the group.

Anastasia let it trail off and vanish. "But if you come to me and say, 'here is the way we can take the fight to the Blessed Ones'"—her golden eyes blazed—"'here is the way we can change the balance of power,' you will be loved, not just by me, but by every rabbit who lives, for the rest of time. It will be the Readers who saved the day." Her scent was suddenly clarion bright. "Friends, *this is your battlefield.*"

Many of the Readers nodded, looking fierce and determined. Some of the apprentices glanced at each other, excited and wide-eyed. Others were looking around anxiously. Nicodemus was still as a stone.

Anastasia stood up. "We haven't heard back yet from our forward scouts, so we don't know exactly what lies to the north. The rest of the army is moving north today. You'll stay here, with guard platoons and scouts. Our lives are in your hands."

Freddie stood up. "We hear you, Loving Auntie," he said, with a slight quaver in his voice. "We accept your great charge. We are not just the Forward Readers, we are the Free Readers, and we will not fail." He looked around the circle, from one face to the next. When he spoke again, his voice was solid and determined. "For the first time in history, the poets will sing about not just the warriors, not just the builders, but *us.*" He sat up tall and spread his forepaws. "What do you say, Readers?"

There was a moment of uncertain silence.

"Hooah!" said Nicodemus, suddenly.

"Hooah!" shouted all the Readers together.

Anastasia stood and threw the *respect* sign. "Good hunting, Readers."

Armée Libre

As the *Armée Libre* pushed further into new territory, the platoons continued to discover many warrens and did their best to invite them to join the alliance. Just having an armed group of rabbits, mice, squirrels, and songbirds show up was often persuasive, because no rabbits had ever before seen such a concentrated display of small animal power.

But many warrens were afraid of the ramifications of going against the Word of Yah. The recent correction that suggested that all animals should love the Blessed more, followed by the teachings about Yah's Flowers, which were percolating up from the South Bank Conclave, had muddied the waters. For animals who had turned to the Word of Yah for solace and meaning for a hundred and fifty generations, it was not easy to walk away.

As they went north, the space between the cliffs and the sea continued to get narrower. A mile north of the bunker, they were surprised to discover a spot where millennia of erosion against a section of soft limestone had compressed the Million Acre Wood to a strip just eighty yards wide. This area was about two hundred yards long, mostly meadowland, with just a few scrubby trees growing along the base of the Boreal Cliffs, and some bushes clinging to the edge overlooking the sea.

The *Armée Libre* had to break up into its platoon elements and filter along the sides under the cover of the bushes and trees. After Team Auntie had crossed, Wendy stood on the edge of the exposed terrain, looking back over the meadow. "Don't want cross all time," she growled. "Hawk. Owl."

"Plus, it's easy for crows to see us," said Coriander.

Anastasia nodded. "What's our best option?"

Love Bug sucked his teeth. "We could dig a forward base. Like a warren, but it would just be for us, no kits or families."

Wendy frowned. "Many Blessed come. Send many weasel."

"We'll have the gratings in place," said Love Bug.

"As many Blessed as they have, they will almost certainly figure out a way to dig those out," said Anastasia.

Love Bug exhaled. "True."

"But I've been thinking about that," said the Loving Auntie. "The thing that makes a warren so vulnerable to weasel attack is that it's a maze of tunnels. So there usually isn't space for more than two or three rabbits to fight back, at most. When that weasel got into *Sans Gloire*, we were lucky that the fight happened at a large intersection, so many bunnies could fight together."

Wendy grunted and nodded approvingly. "So … few entrance run … big space in middle."

"Could that work?" said Anastasia.

Love Bug looked thoughtful. "That would mean when they come down the ramp, they don't find two or three rabbits—"

"—they find two or three hundred," said Anastasia.

"Oh, my Yah," said Love Bug. "That would totally change everything for underground fights."

"Good," said Wendy.

"Let's start on this today," said the Loving Auntie. "With all the diggers we have, we should be able to do this in a couple of days." The others nodded. "Find a place with plenty of roots to support the big central space."

Just then, Stan and another songbird appeared, doing their usual surreptitious approach. Stan alighted on a low branch on a black chokeberry. In spite of himself, he let out a loud burst of brilliant song. Then he spoke. "We haven't heard back from the birds that took Death Rage. They're waiting to find her before they come back. But we did get some scouts very far north. It's worse than we thought. A line of Blessed squads strung across the whole Wood. Organized. Not hunting. Marching. They're coming south, and they're searching every inch of ground."

The other songbird, a green leaf warbler, teetered on her branch. "I saw the line first, and I was able to fly a long way along it before they noticed me and I had to turn back." She looked from face to face, her eyes large and dark. "Putting everyone's report's together, we're guessing fifteen wolves and thirty coyotes, those are the officers. And two hundred weasels, five hundred foxes, and crows for days."

"This ain't no mob. This ain't no rabble," said Stan. "What's coming at youse is an *army*."

DEATH RAGE

Death Rage had been in the wolves' area for almost two days, and she was exhausted. She had seen much, learned much, but didn't feel that she had yet learned anything truly useful. She needed something that would give the Free Warrens an edge when the Blessed collided with them, in what was sure to be an orgy of destruction, now just a few weeks away.

She drank from a small muddy puddle and chewed a few seeds she had managed to find. Glancing up warily at the gray and white raptor she had seen overhead earlier, she crawled slowly toward the next open area. When she reached the edge of the space, she peered out from a comforting jumble of agave plants, flowering hibiscus, and several stands of thistles. This space looked different from any others she had seen.

The stone columns stood close together, and dead undergrowth had been pushed into many of the spaces between the columns to make it even more closed off from the elements. Inside the chamber, there were many stacks of wrinkled white rectangles with dark lines crawling across them. After all her time at the straightstone burrow near *Sans Gloire*, she knew immediately what these were: pages.

But why would wolves have pages? Everyone knew wolves had no Readers. Most people assumed they couldn't read at all. And their Shamans memorized a mixture of hunting lore and astronomical factoids.

As she lay there, puzzling this out, the young golden female wolf she had seen in the map room entered, followed by an older golden female. They were in mid-conversation.

"It's good that you're trying new ways, darling," said the older wolf. "But we shouldn't forget the old ways. Remember, unless proven different, old ways are best."

"That's what Daddy says," said the younger wolf. "Is that what you say?"

The older wolf regarded the younger wolf steadily. "It's the old ways that made you a Landlord of this wood," she said. "Don't forget that."

The younger wolf looked suitably chastened. "Yes, Clan Mother."

The mother continued. "Now, we know the luncheon meat are in North Shandy, but we don't know exactly where. It's hard for the crows to see what's going on. We think they may be criminalizing natural warrens." She scratched her ear.

"Anything that can be done must be done. It's not just us. The whole hunter way of life depends on it." The mother came near to the daughter and looked in her maple-leaf green eyes. "I want you to be Clan Mother one day. And I want there to be a Clan for you to be Mother of."

Without waiting for a response, the golden mother lifted her head and rolled out a low howl, starting in the mid-range and descending by semi-tones. Half a minute later, an ancient crow fluttered through the space between two spires.

The crow landed on the floor and fluffed her wings. "My favorite granddaughter cries out during her afternoon nap?"

The mother wolf bowed, "To your claw and eye, I turn once again, Grammy Kark."

"What may I do for you, golden child?"

"The luncheon meat are pursuing their unholy lust for weapons. We need a new correction or … revelation."

Death Rage blinked several times at this. Were they talking about the Word of Yah? The rabbits were always talking about Yah, and whatever they thought usually filtered down to the mice. Death Rage had cast off Yah long ago, along with the ancestor worship most mice still adhered to. She clasped her forepaws together anxiously.

The old crow hopped over to the stacks of pages. "Tell me more."

"What does the Word of Yah say about weapons?"

The old crow groomed herself under her wing for a moment as she thought. "Erm. Let's see. There's a proverb somewhere."

Death Rage's mouth fell open. These wolves and crows knew about—*cared* about—the Word of Yah? *Why?*

The mother wolf paced among the stacks of pages. "Then there can be a correction. We just need to find it."

"Right, right." The crow began to hop from stack to stack, picking up pages and looking at them.

"Maybe the Book of Banyan?" said the young wolf. "That has lots of proverbs."

"Mmmm. Mmm hmm," said the crow, fluttering to another stack and quickly picking up pages in her beak and restacking them. "I think we ... yes. Here it is. "*The weapons of my Blessed Ones are for the Glorification of the world. The tooth, the claw, and the beak are my gift of love.*' Book of Banyan, 4:17. We could add something here."

Were the wolves *writing* the Word of Yah? Death Rage felt dizzy. Her heart began to race. Was this just some weird wolfy crowy fantasy? Surely it couldn't have anything to do with the real religion? That was controlled by Conclaves, Symposiums, Presiding Spirits, Lord Harmonizers, all the structures of an established faith. It couldn't just be edited by a couple of wolves and a crow in a room somewhere. Death Rage edged forward a little to see better.

The crow hopped over to a nook, picked up a smudgy quill pen, sharpened it with her beak, and dipped it in a puddle of ink inside a small gourd. Then she fluttered back to the page, holding the pen in her claw, poised over the blank bottom half. "What shall our correction be?"

"Oh, something about the Lucky Fields, apples, the usual luncheon meat yearnings," said the mother wolf. She looked at her daughter and chuckled. "You're pretty good at getting in other people's business. What do you think?"

Death Rage, heart pounding, held her breath as the younger

wolf sat down and looked upwards. "Ummm, okaaay." She blew out a long breath and the began to speak. "'*The tooth, the claw, and the beak are my gift of love. They are perfect ... Let there be no others ... Any who would create weapons ... shall never see the Lucky Fields ... never taste the Apple of Joy ... and never sleep in the bosom of the Loved One ... in the endless golden afternoon.*'"

The crow cackled loudly, "Very niiice, impetuous one. Perhaps you are ready for a seat at council." She wrote neatly on the page, holding the pen delicately in her claws.

"You have made my daughter happy with your kind words," said the mother wolf. "The Clan thanks you."

Death Rage felt that she might faint. Did this mean that the whole Book of Yah was a creation of the Blessed? The ramifications of this idea multiplied exponentially until she felt that she was at the edge of a yawning chasm.

"This will be a big change," said the younger wolf. "The Symposium will really have their work cut out for them."

"Oh, they'll find a 'lost version' from an island or something," said the mother breezily. "If they push back, we'll just remind them that the safety of their warrens is something they *earn*."

The old crow finished writing, then rapidly wrote out a copy of the new text. When that was done, she cawed loudly several times. In a few seconds, a sturdy young crow fluttered into the room from the far reaches above. "Yes, Grammy Kark?"

The crow handed him the newly amended page. "Take this to the Known World Symposium. Be sure to give it to Tobias."

Tobias. That was the final proof. It struck Death Rage like a thunderbolt. Yah was a lie made up by killers. *This changes everything*. She had to get this information back to the rabbits as soon as possible. She turned to go back the way she had come.

But in her haste to carry the news, she moved a little too fast. Her movement caught the younger wolf's eye. In a well-fed season, the sight of a mouse would have meant nothing. In these lean times, it caused even a golden wolf to make a quick lunge.

The huge golden head was darting toward her, jaws opening as it came. Death Rage let out a tiny terror shriek as she scrambled away. An instant later, the wolf's face was smashing into the dense, prickly foliage of the thistles. She yelped as the needles stung her lips and eyelids. Death Rage seized the moment to scurry away through the thick underbrush.

At first, it seemed as though the threat had passed. She could get out of the Spires, find a tree, and hang her diamond to bring the songbirds. Then she heard a large animal crashing through the brush behind her. The wolf, now clearly angry, was in no mood to let her escape.

Death Rage zigged and zagged, careening away at unexpected angles, trying all the mouse tricks. At one point, she was well ahead, and darted to the left to cross a clear area. She heard an ancient creaking voice above her cry. "There goes your lunch!" and looked up to see the crow flying just a few feet above the tops of the bushes, cackling.

The wolf made a hard turn, and it sounded like another wolf had joined in. Death Rage felt her heart go into overdrive as the plant stalks and clods of earth flew past her. In her panic, she was uncertain which direction was the way out of this terrible maze of stone columns, brush, wolves, and crows.

The wolf was on her scent now. She could tell by the way she followed her twists and turns. The adrenaline burn was so painful, it felt as though she was on fire. And it wasn't just the terror. It was the information that thrummed in her mind like an electric charge. The rabbits must know. *Loving Auntie must know.*

Death Rage came to a small, fast flowing stream, only a yard wide. The brush had grown thickly over it, and she began to dart up a fat plant stem to make her way across. Then she changed her mind and leaped into the water, swimming downstream as hard as she could. Ten seconds later, she was already thirty feet away. She heard the wolf arrive at the place where she had jumped into the water. It sounded like the wolf simply bounded over the stream and continued running, sweeping from side to side to pick up the scent.

Of course, there was no scent for her to find.

The stream came out from under the densely packed brush and Death Rage found herself being carried out into an open meadow. How long until the wolf realized she had lost the scent and started backtracking? And how long would it take her to realize her quarry had gone down the stream? Precious seconds were flying by.

Death Rage looked up and saw the raptor she had seen earlier. She recognized the checkered gray and white undercarriage of a peregrine falcon, the fastest raptor in the known world. With death behind and death above, her heart slowed. It was all too much. No mouse, no matter how brave, no matter how honorable, could stand against these endless waves of killers.

Her limbs felt leaden. Her head was heavy. She had done her best. She slipped below the surface, and fought her way back up. She coughed and seized a breath. Then she was pulled down again by her heavy backpack. Her precious diamond signaler was useless now. Her dime was just so much dead weight. Her *dime*. From *Bricabrac*.

Suddenly, she was swimming hard for the bank. In a few seconds, she was out, shaking the water off her fur, and heading out across a slab of light yellow sandstone where she would stand out in high relief. Then she was struggling, limping. She could hear at least two wolves crashing around in the brush now. It sounded like they were coming her way.

She rose and fell, staggering, moving erratically. Everything about her said *injured mouse*. And the stream had washed the mud off her helmet, so it gleamed brightly in the sunlight, further calling attention to her. The golden wolf broke out of the brush and stood for a moment looking. A few seconds later, another wolf appeared.

Death Rage whispered prayer.

"This we will do
I and you,
This day to
Make the world."

Death Rage rolled over on her back and saw the peregrine falcon diving toward her at two hundred miles an hour, now just starting to beat his wings to slow his approach. When the talons were just seconds away from piercing her tiny body,

Death Rage cried out the special phrase she had learned form Bricabrac. "*Olly olly oxen free!*"

The wolves were noticing her now. The falcon veered off and landed clumsily. "What?" he snapped.

"You heard me! Let's go!" shouted Death Rage. "I got a dime in my backpack."

"Where's your earring?"

"New kind of craftmouse. Stealth mode," barked Death Rage. She willed herself not to look at the wolves racing toward her as she dredged up phrases she had heard Bricabrac say. She assumed the most imperious tone she could muster. "Protected status. Ursine Law. City of Oom business. Now, *move it*. Unless you want the bears on your tail."

The falcon looked once at the wolves, grunted, then snatched Death Rage and soared skyward. Three seconds later, the two golden wolves reached the spot where she had been standing and launched themselves ragefully, uselessly, into the air.

As the falcon beat his way upward, Death Rage stared down at the snarling mass of shiny teeth and golden fur and felt waves of warmth rolling through her body. *This changes everything.*

Chapter 10

It was the craftmice, with their earthrooms topped with slabs of chewy diamond, who first grew pineapples in the Million Acre Wood.
    —Thimble Thimbalian, History of the Known World

FREDDIE

Freddie was taking a dill break outside the bunker, trying to collect his thoughts. He noticed an ant's nest and sat down near it. With his farblindness, he was often attracted to detailed objects and creatures that he could view up close. And the repetitive, random motion of scurrying ants was something he found particularly soothing. It led him to drift into a gently dissociative state that helped calm his anxiety, which had been climbing ever since the news of the wolves.

He noticed an ant that had become lost and nudged it back toward its fellows. "There you go, little buddy," he murmured.

Now the fate of the Free Warrens seemed to be resting on the Readers and what they were able to glean from poor treasure they had found. Freddie himself had been trained as a Remembering acolyte but had then abandoned it. Later, he had scraped together some training in Reading, but he was not a real Reader.

He had the mind of a builder, an engineer who can see things that don't yet exist—and how to get there. Freddie had played a key part of designing the bite blades the rabbits fought with and the moveable wooden gratings that protected the entries of all the warrens in the Alliance.

He stared at the ants bringing in morsels of food and tried to soften his gaze. Then he let his mind drift, angling toward the friendly trance state that was familiar and welcoming. The Forward Readers had found something today. A drawing. It could be useful. Very useful. Now it was up to him to make it a reality. He let the shiny silver complexity of dissociation take him.

ANASTASIA

A quarter moon was shining brightly over the Million Acre Wood. The nightjars were calling. Anastasia lay snuggled next to Coriander in her sleeping chamber in the forward base the rabbits had just finished digging at the north end of the Narrows. They had dubbed it Warren *du Nord*.[21]

As usual, she was rerunning recent conversations in her

---

[21] Warren North.

head as she lay awake while Coriander slept. Reassessing, second guessing, looking for mistakes and what could be learned from them. She chewed her foreclaw as she raked over her day. This could go on for hours, and often did.

Beside her, Coriander stirred a little and stretched, so she could tell he was waking up.

"Do you think I scared the Readers when I talked to them?" asked Anastasia quietly.

He turned over and nuzzled the back of her neck. "No," he said. "I mean … yes … but appropriately."

She could feel his breath on her long brown ears. "I just wanted to get across that this is now or never. Readers can tend to wander. I wanted to get them focused on now."

"They are focused," murmured Coriander sleepily. "You are the focuser-in-chief." He kissed the back of her head.

She chattered her teeth with pleasure and then lay in silence. After a few moments, she began again, "Do you think I—"

"Loving Auntie," interrupted Coriander kindly. "You are doing a wonderful job." He put his foreleg around her. "Be kind to your body and give it the sleep it needs."

She turned over to face him and kissed his forehead. "Always guarding me, even from myself," she said. "You're good at your job, too."

As they were touching noses, they heard a ruckus in the large central chamber. Someone was shouting. It sounded like a mouse. Now other voices were adding to the noise.

Coriander rolled off the sleeping moss and went to the doorway of the chamber, looking out between the two armed rabbits stationed as door guards.

Death Rage appeared suddenly, eyes wide. The door guards knew her and did not resist as she squirmed past them. "Loving Auntie!" she shouted. "Yah is a lie!"

"What?' said Anastasia, sitting up.

"The Blessed are writing the Word of Yah!" cried Death Rage. "I saw it with my own eyes."

"Huh?" Coriander grunted. He wiped the sleep from his eyes with the back of his paw. "The Word of Yah is hundreds of years old."

"That's what they want you to think," said Death Rage, shivering.

Anastasia stared at her, covered with damp mud, her eyes wild. "Are you all right?" she asked. "How did you get back? The songbirds sent a message saying they couldn't find you."

"Raptor Air," said Death Rage. Anastasia's eyes widened at this. "But that doesn't matter," continued the mouse. "The wolves wanted to change the Word of Yah, so a crow wrote it down on a page—"

"I'm sure you've been though a lot," Coriander broke in, looking at her skeptically. He moved toward her, making a placating gesture. "Let's get you clean and settled first, little one—"

Death Rage had the Kiss of Death out in a flash, the tip quivering less than an inch from Coriander's throat. "Don't call me that."

Coriander stopped moving and looked over Death Rage's head at the guard rabbits coming up behind her. He pressed his left forepaw downward. *Stand down.*

"My apologies, honored warrior—"

"Everyone *hush*," said Anastasia. The guard rabbits began

to back out into the larger space. "No one leave this room."
The two guards took up positions just inside the door. Death
Rage sheathed her rapier and knelt before Anastasia.

"Loving Auntie—" she began.

"Wait," said Anastasia. Slowly, she washed her face. A
hum was starting in the back of her head and she felt a buzz
run down her forepaws. *What was Death Rage even saying?*
It didn't make any sense. She had expected her to come back
with intelligence about Blessed army size or plans, not some
theological revelation. Anastasia was getting a nasty feeling
that she was standing at the edge of an abyss and struggling
with a case of vertigo.

She dropped her paws and looked at Death Rage. "You
know my respect for you is deep." Death Rage nodded.
Anastasia settled down and became very still. "Start from the
beginning. Tell me everything."

Death Rage launched into her story. When she talked
about the map of the Million Acre Wood with the pebbles on
it tracking the movements of the Blessed, Anastasia said, "We
need to set up one of those." Coriander and the guards nodded.

When Death Rage mentioned seeing Bricabrac's sister
Frippery working for the wolves, Anastasia's face became
very dark and she thumped angrily. "I treated Bricabrac like
family. I offered him—"

"Rats are scum," blurted Death Rage. "*Mercenaries*."

Coriander raked his claws through the earth. "We'll need
to deal with that." The guard rabbits whispered together.

But when Death Rage started talking about seeing the two
wolves and the old crow discussing the Word of Yah, writing
down new verses, and laughing as they did it, Anastasia felt a

hot, prickling sensation crawling over her skin. She reached down and placed her paw on her Claw as it lay in its usual place by her bed. The cool sharpstone felt good. Felt normal.

A few moments later, Death Rage was quoting the verse, "*'The weapons of my Blessed Ones are for the Glorification of the world. The tooth, the claw, and the beak are my gift of love.*' Book of Banyan, 4:17."

Anastasia looked at Coriander. He said, "Yes, I know that verse. Every Rememberer does."

"But they weren't Remembering," said Anastasia. "They had it written down." The abyss was yawning open behind her.

Then Death Rage added the correction. "*'They are perfect. Let there be no others. Any who would create weapons shall never see the Lucky Fields, never taste the Apple of Joy, and never sleep in the bosom of the Loved One in the golden afternoon.*'"

In Anastasia's mind, images were flashing of herself as a kit, learning from older brothers and sisters, learning from the Rememberer, learning from her mother, that the world was the way it was because Yah had made it so. And it was good. And rabbits knew that it was good because the Word of Yah told them so. And every time a rabbit was Glorified, there should be no tears. It was a good thing, because Yah said so. And he said so in his Word, the Word of Yah, the holy verses that gave comfort to everyone.

And then she saw an image of crows and wolves making up new words. New words that would go into the Word of Yah and rule countless lives of rabbits and other creatures. New words that would cause more deaths among all those who are small and live in fear and trembling, and whose greatest hope is that they would just make it alive to the end of the day. The holy day. Every one a gift.

And the Blessed Ones laughed as they did it. They *laughed*.

Anastasia felt her stomach heave and she tasted bile in her mouth. Death Rage stopped and looked at her, and Anastasia gestured for her to go on. Then Death Rage repeated what the old crow had said as she handed the page of new words to a young crow: "Take this to the Known World Symposium. Be sure to give it to Tobias."

And that was it. The deed was done.

The chasm behind Anastasia was *so* wide now, and a terrible current was pulling her down. Then she was falling, dropping into a pit of darkness with no bottom, and seeing the sky above her become a tiny, shrinking window as she fell and fell, her mouth open but making no sound.

A deep, visceral groan forced its way up out of her abdomen. It sounded like the sobbing, grinding shriek of stone blocks sliding over each other when tabernacles fall.

Anastasia somehow got to her feet and pushed past the guards, making for the nearest entrance ramp. Coriander was on her heels. As she reached the ramp, she turned and gave him a look that froze him in his tracks. It was tearful and confused, and filled with killing rage.

"*Leave me alone*," she whispered in a voice that brooked no opposition. He stopped and looked down and away, anywhere but at those wounded, murderous eyes. Anastasia staggered up the entrance ramp and froze for a moment at the sight of the exit threshold. She took a deep breath, quickly touched one side three times, then the other side, and touched the floor twice. Breathily, she sang her spell.

> *"Run, sister, fast as you can today*
> *Over the hills and far away."*

Then, just as she had so many months ago at Bloody Thorn Warren, she tumbled out into the night.

FRIPPERY

Frippery was hard at work cutting and bending one-inch lengths of the 9-gauge *aluminum d'or* wire that Aliyah had played with as a cub. In front of her lay hundreds of loops of the wire, interlocked to make a flexible sheet. There was much to be done, so she was working far into the night. The bright moonlight made the shiny wire loops gleam as it slanted into Frippery's workspace between three of the stone columns.

Aliyah bounded in. "Thanks for working late. *Posse Comitatus* is twelve miles south now. I want to head out soon."

Frippery banged the ring closed with her heavy iron pyrite hammer and said, "The eviction tools aren't quite done."

"Why not?"

"I'm having a little trouble finding materials."

"Even from the City? Mummy said we would spend—"

"These parts are rare. Even in the City." Frippery smoothed out the jumble of shiny rings. "I finally got this finished. You want to try it on?"

"Yes," said Aliyah, her breath quickening.

"Put your head through here, and your front legs here," said Frippery.

Aliyah pushed her nose under the strip of links and then stood up, shrugging the links into place across her shoulders. A cap of mail fit snugly on her head, with holes for her ears. And a curtain of interlocked rings hung down in front of her chest. Then she put her front legs through two lower loops, and the sheet of rings hugged her lower neck and chest, wrapping around to the sides.

"Now stand up on your back legs," said Frippery.

Aliyah did so, and a long sheet of mail hung down her back.

"Step through those holes," directed the rat.

Aliyah stepped into the leg holes and dropped forward onto her forepaws. She now had a coat of mail covering her back and sides, and reaching partway down her legs.

She shrugged and bounced, trying to wriggle into a comfortable fit. "This feels weird."

"It *is* weird," said Frippery. "You're the only person in the Million Acre Wood wearing chain mail."

Aliyah passed near a pool of clear water at the edge of the workspace. In the reflection, she saw a shiny wolf wearing shiny armor, and she was entranced. "It's beautiful." She looked closer at an area on her chest where the rings were assembled in a different pattern. "What's that thing in the center?"

"I took the liberty of adding a noonday sun design," said Frippery. "Let's call it the sigil of the Summerday Clan." It was a bright circle surrounded by rays streaming outward.

Aliyah was turning at different angles, fascinated by her reflection. "What's a sigil?"

Frippery came and stood next to Aliyah. "It's your family's symbol. Do you like it?"

Aliyah smiled. "I love it."

Frippery shook out her tired hands and then rubbed them together. "I like to think of myself as an artist, not a mechanic."

"You are both." Aliyah licked Frippery, which covered her whole body in drool.

"Pthah! Thanks," she said as she scraped off the saliva and wiped it on the pebbles.

"I'm going to take off on a scouting trip," said Aliyah. "I'm tired of waiting, no matter what Mummy says. I'll take this with me."

The rat smiled and bowed. "So glad you like it, madame," she said. "Remember to tell everyone, it's *Couture de Guerre,*[22] by Frippery."

CORIANDER

Coriander stood on the entrance ramp of Warren *du Nord* in an agony of indecision. Should he go after Anastasia? The news he had just heard from Death Rage made him feel like his own brain had torn a seam somewhere in the back, and he was afraid it might split open. He was pretty sure Death Rage had had some kind of traumatic experience at the hands of the wolves and was now back telling impossible stories, the

---

[22]   War Wear.

way some animals did when they came very close to being Glorified. When you talked to them after that, you always saw the fear of Glory in their eyes.

But what if Death Rage was saying something real? She didn't seem like the type to get scared and wander into a panicky fog. What if she had seen something actually happen, but misunderstood what it was? Or what it meant? A crow wrote on a page. That didn't mean that everything he had been taught, his whole life, the entire edifice of Yah, was tumbling down. Maybe it was just a fantasy that the wolves and crows indulged in? *Maybe they knew Death Rage was there.* They had chased her afterwards, right? Maybe the whole thing was a trick to tear the rabbits down. Confuse them. Demoralize them. Take away the most precious thing they had.

That was a good idea. It took some of the pressure off. He felt less like the back of his head was going to tear apart now. Gradually, he became aware of a hubbub rolling through the warren. It was the sound of rabbits and mice spilling out of their bunking chambers around the perimeter of the big central space as Death Rage ran among the tree roots shouting about what she had seen.

Everyone was talking, and the noise of the talking got louder and more excited as more people joined the throng, with everyone saying the same thing. *What? What? What?* The central space was jammed.

Everyone had a question. Everyone had an answer. Everyone had a theory. Everyone had a story.

Coriander caught sight of Mabel in the crowd, and she ran up to him and stood nose to nose, Rememberer to Rememberer.

There was a wild, fierce light in her eyes. She said something to Coriander, but he couldn't hear her.

Mabel put her mouth close to his ear and shouted. "Do you know what this means?" He shook his head. Her face was radiant. "It means Yah is much bigger than we thought!" she yelled. She looked like an explorer at the edge of an undiscovered country. "Yah is not just what we can *remember*." The words rolled out of her like stars. "Yah is what we can *imagine*."

This was making the seam in the back of his head feel like it was starting to split open again. "No," he said. "Yah is real." Not just a story. *Not just a dream.*

Coriander was a good boy. He learned all his verses. He learned how to talk about them. He learned how to care for tender hearts. He did everything he was asked to do. And when he found one who was bringing more love into the world, he recognized her as a new avatar of the Loved One and clung to her with all his might. And that mattered because Yah was a living god.

Mabel kept yelling at him. Her scent was wild and aggressive. She was pummeling him with her joy. He felt like he could actually hear his skull creaking under the weight of her blows. He started backing away from her, looked down and away from those glittering eyes.

Wendy came bulling her way through the crowd, tossing rabbits left and right like ragdolls. When she reached Coriander, she shouted something, but he could not understand it. He just looked at her and shook his head. She put her lips next to his ear, and he winced, afraid of the bellow that would smash his already beleaguered head wide open.

Instead, the voice that came into him was as deep and comforting as waves on a distant shore. It seemed that she hardly made any noise at all, but he heard the deep thrum of her voice perfectly clearly. *"Where she go?"* It felt so good, he leaned against her, hoping she would speak again. She did. *"Where Anastasia?"* He nodded, then he pulled away from her and looked at the nearest entrance ramp.

Wendy frowned. Then she stamped. Again. And again. Even with all the noise, everyone could feel it. As rabbits do, they picked up the stamp and joined in, repeating it. The talking faded until there was nothing left but stamping. Then Wendy stopped and everyone stopped. She sat up tall. Her eyes swept the crowd.

"Loving Auntie outside," she rumbled. "Alone." Her voice rolled across the warren like distant thunder. "We find her." No longer soothing, it was now electric. *"Go out. Two by two. Now!"*

And so they went, out into the darkness, and looked for their mad queen.

ALARIC

It was early morning. Alaric, the golden bully, had loped for more than twenty-five miles. At some point, he and Aliyah had quarreled, so he had split off from her and run on alone. He was a wolf. He liked to run. He was made for it.

Now he was within a few miles of the Shandy. The Wood was narrowing. He knew from Aliyah's map that he was down near the area where the criminal infestation was rampant. But he had a hard time imagining them as dangerous. So little. So juicy. Refusing to pay rent? Believable. Super-smart rabbits with hate in their hearts and world-shattering plans? Whatever.

A little *zzz!* drifted by his nose. Rabbit. He sniffed again. Rabbit and ... something else. Raccoon? Rat? Nah. He licked his lips. Whatever it was, it was probably delicious. He had worked up quite an appetite and hadn't fed in two days. He slipped along by a wall of boulders. The *zzz!* was louder. He could tell he was downwind, so they couldn't smell him. He crept along, silent as any cat, plotting the smellscape in his mind's eye.

He saw a big golden ninebark bush and bellied down to creep under it. The yellow leaves made perfect cover for a big golden killer. Then he saw the luncheon meat. About fifty feet away, in amongst the boulders. One was a fluffy white rabbit who looked as lovely as a dandelion. The other was an earthy lump with no ears who seemed melted into the ground. It was just a brown tube with no feet visible. Alaric decided it looked like a turd.

They were resting and talking, a little careless. Alaric could see that there was a pathway leading among the boulders behind them. If he came at them now, the Fluff and the Turd would dash into the pathway. And if it led to a blind alley? He licked his chops.

Were they criminals or natural rabbits? Should he find their warren? Make an assessment? Determine the correct amount of rent to be collected? He grunted dismissively. Assessments and rules were for the little people. He was golden. He was owed.

To think was to act. Alaric's rear claws bit into the ground and propelled his massive golden body forward. The Fluff and the Turd bolted into the boulders, just as he had predicted, kicking up a small storm of leaf litter. Their small bodies vanished.

But he was faster than they were, and in the confined passage among the stones, their zigzagging ability had no value. Alaric pelted down the trail, the sweet smell of luncheon meat sprawling lavishly across his nose. In less than half a minute, he rounded a corner and saw that the passageway among the boulders had dead ended, and the Fluff and the Turd were racing around looking for crevices between the stones they could squeeze into. The Turd was snuffling around a scree of fallen stones on one side. On the other, the Fluff had just run into a short pathway between several boulders. It was a blind alley.

The Fluff froze as the wolf came on the scene. Then Alaric sat down at the entrance to the short passage where the Fluff was trapped, positioning himself so that the Turd could not run out the same way they had just come in.

He gazed at the Turd, frankly curious. "What are you?" he snickered. "Tell me and I'll make it quick."

The Turd just twisted in on itself and made a weird, unrabbit-like rumbling noise.

The Fluff sat up straight. It was wearing a little necklace with some kind of pendant on it. So these must be some of the little haters. The list of names Sephora told everyone to look for drifted through Alaric's mind. He batted it away lazily. "I hope all that hate makes you extra spicy," he said.

The Fluff looked terrified. It had no way out. It started talking, as some lunchmeat do, at the end, hoping to stretch out their lives by a few seconds. "We have no quarrel with you. Leave us be and we'll leave you be."

Alaric guffawed at this show of bravado. When they did talk at the end, it was always nonsense. The Turd took a couple of steps closer to him, then squashed itself against the nearest boulder. "What made you decide to become a criminal?" said Alaric.

"Just want to live," said the Fluff. "Just like you."

Alaric noticed movement out of the corner if his eye. Was the Turd inching closer to him? He smirked and rolled his eyes. Then he was tired of this unamusing banter. "You look crunchy," he said to the Fluff. "Let's start with you." Without even stopping to take a breath, he launched himself through the air, jaws opening to catch and crush this little white snack. Perfect for a gourmand like himself.

Just he left the ground, he saw the Turd suddenly uncoil, lumpy body reshaping itself into a torpedo, wide back feet pushing off against the boulder at its back. The front end was no longer blunt and featureless, but had somehow become a sharpy-stabby thing on a trajectory toward his face.

Alaric spent valuable microseconds thinking, *That looks like one of those things that little coyote—* An instant later, as he continued hurtling forward, the Turd arrived, sweeping its head in a wide arc, dragging the sharp blade down the length of his muzzle, setting thousands of nerve endings on fire. Then its baggy body struck his shoulder, pushing his airborne body to the side. A moment later, it was falling backwards.

Thrown off course, a yell of rage burst out of him as he smashed into a boulder. The Fluff momentarily forgotten, he clawed at the stones and pulled his upper body around, then managed to push off with his rear legs and hurl himself back toward the Turd, now tumbling in the dust. Two steps and he was on it. The stumpy back legs were working like pistons, racing out of the blind alley into the larger space. But there was no place to dodge to. Within seconds, his jaws were coming down and closing around the baggy brown body.

He was just starting to feel the bones take shape against his teeth, just starting to hear the creature's final squeal of terror, when a fiery pain he had never felt before exploded into his cerebral cortex. It was coming from underneath him. His jaws stopped closing in order to open in a roar of rage. The Turd staggered away from his mouth. As he ducked his head down to look under his body, he saw where the pain was coming from.

The Fluff's necklace was now magically transformed into a sharpy-stabby, and it was driving into the soft flesh of his underside as the Fluff leaped upwards. In another instant, it found an artery. As the Fluff fell back, a dark stream came forth.

The white rabbit slipped and fell onto his side, then struggled to get up and run. Alaric scrambled into a turn, and took a step after the floundering rabbit.

He plunged ahead, eyes on the Fluff. That one would die, at least. But after a dozen paces, his blood pressure was plummeting. The ground felt soft, and he couldn't seem to make any headway. The day was darkening. The pain was receding. He could still hear the rabbit's nails scraping on the ground, and his own claws tearing at the earth, but he couldn't see them.

And when the world came up and hit him in the face, he didn't feel it at all.

LOVE BUG

Love Bug heard the sound of a great weight hitting the earth close behind him. He cast a hasty glance over his shoulder and saw the unthinkable. The huge golden wolf lay sprawled across the dusty ground like a fallen god. Like a dragon brought low by a single lucky arrow.

The white bunny turned and stared at the great head, breathing hard, the blazing adrenaline spike still coursing through his veins. Was this real? The world-shaking colossus in an instant torn down. The shining teeth that had ended thousands of lives now coated with dust, never again to slam shut on a small body. Love Bug tried to clean some of the blood off his face. It was hard to believe that he was still alive, and this massive killing machine was dead. He started shaking.

A few yards away, he saw Wendy come hobbling toward him, walking slowly and in great pain over the bloody sand. Her breath was fast and ragged, and her eyes were different than he had ever seen them before. She had been close to death before he pulled the wolf off of her.

He stumbled toward her, giving the dead wolf a wide berth. In a few seconds, they were very close.

They looked at each other, and the air between them became suddenly very cozy, the way it does when you're looking into the eyes of someone who was just fighting for your life. Someone who made the rest of your life possible. They sat nose to nose without speaking for a very long moment. Hearts still pounding, breathing each other's breath.

At last, Wendy broke the spell, her voice shaky. "You save my life."

A wave of prickly fire washed over Love Bug from head to toe. He tried to speak and found he could only whisper. "You almost died … for me."

"You fight golden woof … and win," said Wendy. She sounded dazed.

"*We* fight," said Love Bug. He nuzzled her cheek.

She kissed his forehead. "You … Bug of War. You Goldkiller."

Love Bug stared at her, almost without breathing. Then he took a deep shuddering breath and shivered.

Wendy's obsidian eyes shone with a dark fire. She did not speak. She kissed him again. Then she raised one of her great ears, which had always hung straight down. Love Bug turned to be nearer to her, and snuggled under the broad, velvety ear. For the first time since he had been run out of Moonfall Warren many months ago, he felt warm, safe, seen, protected. *Home.*

FREDDIE

Freddie was still puzzling out the new kind of Dead Gods weapon that was almost within reach. He had gotten stuck at his last gateway into dissociation, so he had been hunting all morning, and felt very lucky to find the pink Latticed Stinkhorn mushroom. It looked something like a miniature self-contained coral reef, a marvel of complex surfaces created by a network of holes of varying shapes.

He put one paw over his nose to dry and dampen the rich smell of rotting flesh that emanated from the mushroom. Of course, it was surrounded by flies, but that was a good thing, as their flickering, chaotic, intersecting flight paths added to the complexity.

As he gazed at the shimmering whirl of motion, he felt his eyes start to defocus. Then he began to slip into the silvery dreamspace, where he could see three-dimensional forms in his mind. Here he could rotate them, disassemble them, change them, and then put them back together. He could even move some things and see the effects they would have on other things.

He took a deep breath and brought forth the shapes he had seen on the crumbling page from the bunker titled, "My First Crossbow."

CHAPTER 11

You and me gots shiny teefies
Me and you gots poky claws
Us and we gots hungry bellies
Time for softy, sneaky paws
                    —Weasel love song, archaic period

ANASTASIA

Anastasia could not stop moving. It was now more than a day since she had left Warren *du Nord*, but still she continued to drive headlong. Running until she was exhausted, then walking until she had gathered her strength and the cold spur in her ribs drove her to run again.

She could not find a place or a posture or even a moment where she felt safe. Or even comfortable. The world felt deadly cold. She had been fed the stories of Yah along with her mother's milk. And she had drunk in the whole world that came with that.

Somehow, even though there was so much suffering, the truth was that world was overseen by a wise and kind and powerful friend, who would make sure everything turned out all right in the end. Everything happened for a reason. You didn't have to understand. Just put your head down and do as you were told by those who were wiser than you. One day your life would be as good and sweet as a ripe golden pear on a sunny fall afternoon.

And on that day, you would know that all the pain and death had been not just necessary but *good*. All part of a plan. And you would be happy and all your friends would be there and you would embrace each other and feel so grateful that you had all made it through and the hard part was finally over.

Now all that had been stripped away. There was no certainty. About anything. The people who loved you lied to you. Killers told you sweet stories and then killed you. There would be no reckoning. You would never be rewarded for laying down your life. There was no paradise waiting at the end of a hard journey.

There were no magical creatures. No Loved One. No Anima Mundi giving you wise counsel. She felt an extra stab of grief as she realized that.

Anima Mundi is just me talking to myself.

And so she ran and walked and crept and ran again. Now she was scrambling along the base of the Boreal Cliffs. A cool wind was blowing. She came to a small waterfall. An upland stream tumbled off the cliff edge high above and fell eighty feet into a small clear pool, surrounded by ferns and cottonwoods. A dead tree had fallen across the basin, its surface covered with emerald moss.

She stepped out onto the tree trunk and began to cross. The moss was slippery. Halfway across, a squall blew up suddenly. She stopped moving and tucked herself into the nook formed by a dead branch. She shivered as the cold air whipped past her. And then she began to have a new thought.

The coldness of the world without Yah also meant something else. Yes, the protective walls had come down, leaving her feeling terribly exposed, but they also left her free to do as *she* wished. Not as she was told. It was the winds of freedom she was feeling.

The world was colder, but it was also much bigger. She could go anywhere. Do anything. Make any choices. Answerable to herself and herself alone.

A gust of wind mixed with rain struck her, and she lost her footing. In another instant, she was slipping off the trunk and falling toward the clear water below. When she hit, the coldness of it shocked her. It penetrated her fur and set her synapses firing. She gasped as she broke the surface, breathing in great lungfuls of the cool moist air, feeling the raindrops pelting her face.

Then she was swimming for the stream's gravelly edge. Her mind felt clear and strong. *I have everything I need.* She climbed out on the streambank and shook herself. She could feel the raindrops, but they no longer felt cold. *I know, because I heard it from myself.*

Posse Comitatus

The most visible aspect of the line of hunters moving south was the crows. All the murders north of the Shandy River had joined in the fight at the behest of the Summerdays. Initially they were scattered over the nine hundred square miles of the North Shandy, scouting for criminals, but as the *Posse* had pushed south, they had become more and more tightly packed in the shrinking area of forest that remained in front of the predators. Now that the *Posse* line was fifteen miles south of the Spires, it had covered a third of the distance to the Shandy. And there were hundreds of crows reeling back and forth across the front lines, filling the skies with their harsh, beautiful music.

The *Posse* had been finding plenty of warrens. More than three hundred had been mapped. All natural. As directed by Sephora Summerday, the *Posse* members took just a few rental payments and left the rest of the rabbits unharmed, even though they were hungry. No one even wanted to think about Micah Summerday's huge jaws closing around their skulls.

But everyone hoped they would start to find criminal warrens soon. If they were new enough, they might not have their fortifications finished, in which case they could be weaseled, even without the eviction tools. And that would mean full bellies for the squad that found them. Every squad wanted to be that squad.

FREDDIE

"We are on our own," said Freddie to the members of the Free Warrens council. They were gathered inside the bunker, so as to be less visible to a passing crow. All the travelling craftmice and Forward Readers, many of the songbird scouts, and several platoons were also in attendance.

It was a tight squeeze, especially since the largest room had now been given over to creating a living map, similar to the one Death Rage had described, so they could combine what they were learning from songbird reports to try and keep track of the Blessed Army.

Freddie took a deep breath and washed his black-and-gray face. "We don't know where Loving Auntie is. Wendy, Love Bug, and many others are still out looking for her. And Yah may be nothing but a lie forced on us by our enemies." He sat up very tall. "But none of that matters. Because the wolves are going to *be here*." He looked around the crowd. "*Soon*." There was a nervous shuffling among the rabbits. "So the Forward Readers have been pressing on."

He looked from face to face. "Many days ago, Loving Auntie gave us this charge: find the thing that will change the outcome of this war. We believe we may have done so." He picked up a torn sheet of paper from the partial book that had been discovered in the bunker and laid it before the assembled rabbits. It showed a technical drawing of a small curved bow with a taut bowstring attached to a wooden stock. Inset images showed details of the trigger mechanism. Across the top, large text read: "My First Crossbow."

Everyone in the audience craned forward. "What does it do?" asked a squirrel.

Freddie gestured with one forepaw. "We couldn't figure that out ourselves at first. But Magdalenium, who brought us to this place through her letter, drew a sketch of this in her diary." Freddie picked up another page and laid it beside the first. It was a handmade drawing of an object with writing all around it. At one end was a simple point attached to a shaft about seven inches long. At the other end were neat rows of feathers along the sides of the shaft. A caption nearby identified the object as a "quarrel."

Freddie tapped the paper. "I spent some dreamtime with these shapes, and I *think* I understand them now." He looked around. "This machine will allow us to throw sharpstone points at the Blessed from eighty yards away." A gasp ran through the group, followed by an immediate hubbub. No one had ever heard of a weapon like this.

"If it works," said Coriander.

"You're right," said Nicodemus, the elder Reader. "This is our best hope. Not a certainty."

There was some anxious chatter. Freddie raised his forepaw in the *stop and hush* sign. "It won't be easy. These are too big for us to carry as the Dead Gods did, so we'll have to mount them on travois and drag them." He groomed his shoulder for a moment. "We've been learning. The yew trees that grow above this bunker were planted because they are the best wood for bows. We found a box of hardstone parts that seem to be a trigger mechanism, so we have a model to make copies of. We even found what we are pretty sure is a point for one of these quarrels, so we know what they look like."

"It was the first thing Anastasia stepped on when she went inside," said Nicodemus.

Freddie looked around the group. "With the tools we have, we can probably make a number of these in the next three weeks or so before the Blessed Army arrives." He chewed a foreclaw. "Ten would be good. Probably need to have around thirty to really make a difference."

Nicodemus nodded. "There's a huge amount to be done.

We'll need to bring an army of craftmice up from Musmuski Grove. We can probably find a thousand willing artisans there."

There was a loud buzz of excitement. One of the craftmice in the audience called out the craftmouse motto. "*Our fingers sing for freedom!*"

Nicodemus threw the *respect* sign. "Thank you, friend. But that won't be enough. These are too big for mice to build by themselves. Or even rats. If we're going to do this, we need the biggest animals in the Known World with hands." Nicodemus peered out across the group. "We need the raccoons."

Coriander stood up. "With all respect to you and the Forward Readers," he said, "isn't the first problem that these will kill Blessed? Is Loving Auntie going to be willing to do that?"

Freddie nodded. "I'm with you, brother," he said. "We've thought about it." He started drawing shapes in the earth with his foreclaw. "We're thinking we could use different kinds of points. Some would do more damage. Others less. We don't have to kill Blessed to make them take a step back." He stopped drawing and looked up. "If you're getting peppered with small injuries, that would make you want to leave."

"Anyway, Yah is dead," called a rabbit in the audience.

"One mouse says that," said Coriander. "Where's the proof?"

"If I said it, I saw it," snapped Death Rage, hand falling on the hilt of her rapier.

A nervous buzz started to rise among the animals.

"Not dead, living," said Mabel. "Yah is for us to discover."

"Yah is inside you and me," said Sunbeam in a small voice from the back rows of the meeting.

"We can't be bound by lies created by killers," said Death Rage. "This is our moment to seize our freedom and run. Let's *go*."

"But how do we go forward without the Word of Yah?" asked an orange-and-white rabbit.

"I've known Yah longer than any of you," said Nicodemus. "Maybe the kindest thing Yah could have done for us is bow out right now."

The hubbub increased as the power vacuum caused by the absence of Yah and Anastasia pulled conflicts into the open.

"The bigger point is this," called out another rabbit. "You think you're going to invent a new weapon in three weeks? You're dreaming."

"We're not inventing, we're copying," said Freddie. "It already exists."

"But Loving Auntie—" began another rabbit.

"There hasn't been a sign of the godmother," said Stan. "None of youse have seen her, or the songbirds either. Is she in charge here or what?"

"Should we even be here?" called another voice. "Are we throwing our lives way?"

The rapid-fire exchange was quickly escalating into a free-ranging fracas.

"We all have to agree on our next steps," said Nicodemus, speaking over the rising voices. His silver fur shone in the gathering gloom. "So let's talk it through. Loving Auntie would want us to work together."

"But what's our basis for deciding?" called another voice in the crowd. "What are the rules?"

There was a small commotion among the packed rows of animals on one side of the room, then they parted and suddenly Anastasia was standing in the center of the space. Everyone stared at her without speaking. Freddie felt a knot in his belly unclench at the sight of her. He breathed out slowly as a wave of warmth swept over him.

She stood on her back legs and raised her forepaws, pads facing upward. Her bright eyes swept the crowd of animals. Her scent was bold and crisp. There was a long moment of silence. Then she spoke. "No … more … rules."

Olympia

Olympia was playing with some of her many grand-kits in the slanting sunlight of early fall. It was Sweet Leaf's new litter, now just two months old. They lollopped about in the shade of the flame azalea that grew not far from Bloody Thorn Warren's main entrance. Most of them were blue and white like their mother, and one was a dappled brown.

She wanted to clear her mind of all the hurly-burly of dealing with Anastasia's war, and just go back to being the mother and protector of her children and warren for a few minutes. The warm sun felt good on her gray fur.

Fufu, her pet robin, came fluttering through a nearby mountain laurel holding a twig in her claws. "Look what a big stick I got, Mommy!" she shouted. "I can carry a heavy weight."

Olympia smiled. "Your training is going very well. Go

get yourself some grubs, darling. And remember, if you want to bring me a gift, make it a … cherry or something. Mommy doesn't like grubs."

"Okay, mommy." The robin spread her beige-and-white wings and flew up through the azalea toward the blue sky above.

Briar appeared from behind a black chokeberry bush and cleared his throat. "Warren Mother, the Lord Harmonizer Tobias is here to see you."

Tobias came close behind him, his scarred face weary. "Presiding Spirit," he nodded to her. "Holy day." The bright sun picked out the notch in one of his large ears, and his muscles were taut and rangy under his stiff brown fur flecked with gray.

"Every one a gift," said Olympia, gesturing for Briar to go and get some treats suitable for company. "What brings you here, Lord Harmonizer?"

"There's a new correction to the Word. It's one of those very unusual occurrences that I've never seen in my lifetime. Several lines have been completely forgotten by the Known World Symposium and then recovered."

"What?" Olympia frowned. "How could that … happen?"

Tobias sat up and folded his paws and looked very wise. "The process by which it happens, a kind of attenuation, can take decades, even centuries to occur. What is miraculous is the method of recovery." He paused for a moment to wash his face. "Recently, one of our spiritual scouts came into contact with a warren that had been living on an island off the coast of the South Shandy, down by the Southern Swamps. They've been living there, totally cut off from the world, for more than a hundred years."

Olympia stared at him. She'd never heard of anything like this. Was the Known World Symposium testing her? Did they know about the nightshade berries? Had Coriander blabbed about it?

"Of course, we rejoiced," said Tobias.

"Absolutely," said Olympia. "Every soul a gift."

"And when we compared notes, we discovered the text that we had lost. It was truly a gift from Yah."

The next question burst out of Olympia before she could stop herself. "How do you know that their version is right?"

The Lord Harmonizer pulled down his notched ear and cleaned it. "We use a technique called textual criticism," he said evenly. "Very abstruse. You see, at the Known World Symposium, we have specialist rabbits who remember earlier versions of the Word of Yah. Using them, we were able to theorize that there was a hypothetical version of the Word, unknown to us. That version appears to be the source of both our modern version and this antique version containing the correction. I know this is all very difficult for one not trained in the Remembering arts to understand."

Tobias smiled benignly. Olympia noticed a ropy muscle in his shoulder was twitching.

"What is the correction?" she asked, finally.

"It is the completion to this verse in the Book of Banyan, 4:17. *'The weapons of my Blessed Ones are for the Glorification of the world. The tooth, the claw, and the beak are my gift of love.'*"

The Lord Harmonizer placed his paws on his temples, and his eyes rolled up until only the whites were visible. "Here is the correction. *'They are perfect. Let there be no others. Any who would create weapons shall never see the Lucky Fields, never taste the Apple of Joy, and never sleep in the bosom of the Loved One in the endless golden afternoon.'"*

Olympia stared at him, blinking. A deep current of rage was welling up within her, and keeping it pushed down below the level of consciousness was making her feel ill.

"That's a lot of correction," she said, finally, sounding more snappish than she intended. "We're still dealing with the *rapture* revelation. And it's been no end of trouble." She fought down the urge to rake her claws across the old rabbit's face. "How much do we have to do to keep the Blessed Ones away from our warren?"

Briar entered carrying a leaf with huckleberries on it. "It's often said that those whom Yah loves the most, he tests the most," said Tobias, his eyes resting on her, unblinking. He picked up a huckleberry. "Yah's love for us is without end."

"And our love for Yah?" asked Olympia. Her scent swirled around her, dense and cold. "Is there an end to that?"

Tobias flicked away a fragment of huckleberry. "Because of my great love for you," he said. "I'm going to pretend I didn't hear that."

FREE RABBITS

Anastasia spent her first hours back nuzzling and kissing all the little animals gathered around the bunker. The thinkers. The fighters. The builders. The lieutenants. She realized, looking into their faces, how much she had scared them all by leaving. And she promised over and over that she would never again leave them without a word.

Everyone wanted their moment of snuggle with the Loving Auntie, from Nicodemus to the smallest craftmouse. And so she gave it to them, gladly. In her newly wide and breezy world, there was no warmth coming from the benevolent sureties of Yah and tradition, so the best place to find a comforting glow was in an intimate moment with friends. Once, she had felt crowded and harassed by all those who wanted to be near her. Now she was hungry for it.

Later, Anastasia called a meeting with just her privy council under a dense juniper bush. Coriander took up his post as bodyguard, sitting with his flank touching hers. And the Loving Auntie's Guard reformed around her, even though their commander, Love Bug, was still missing.

Freddie was sitting on one side, where he had been showing some baby squirrels the principle of the seesaw with a sturdy poplar shoot placed across a fallen log. They giggled as they clung to the shaft with their tiny hands while he gently helped them with the seesaw motion. "Yay, Uncle Freddie!" they shouted. "You the up-and-downiest of all the bunnies!"

Freddie chuckled. It felt good to be using his spatial talents for something besides war machines. Then the Loving Auntie stood to speak, and he quietly shushed them and kissed their heads.

Anastasia looked at the pages with the crossbow diagram and the target quarrel drawing that lay before them. In the distance, the sounds of a trio of squirrels practicing with their percussion instruments came drifting on the crisp air, while a mouse flautist reeled out intricate melodies in mixolydian mode.

"Thank you, again, dear Readers," she said, looking at Freddie and Nicodemus. "This gift you have pulled from the thin air of dust and history may change the lives of every small animal in the Million Acre Wood." They nodded. "Now," she said. "I can see why we need the raccoons, but this will be a big ask."

"Yes," said Nicodemus. "They've benefitted from a Truce with the canids that has lasted for over a century."

"But that old world is crumbling now," said Anastasia.

"Not by their choice," said Freddie.

"And we can't guarantee that the world will change," said Nicodemus. "If the war goes badly..." He shrugged and grimaced.

"The world has *already* changed," said Mabel, the black-and-white swirl on her forehead bright in the sunlight. "As the news about Yah spreads, rabbits will be realizing that Yah can be who *we* want Yah to be."

"Or maybe no Yah at all," said Death Rage.

"All the teachings about submitting to Glorification will be fading," said Mabel.

"Yes, but that won't happen overnight," said Coriander. "It takes time for people's eyes to open. And more time for them to change."

"Raccoons love moneystones," said Freddie. "We could offer exclusive trading rights with the Free Warrens."

"That's good," said Nicodemus. "But the problem is we're asking them to lose their protected status with the wolves. And they have no reason to think we're going to win this fight."

There was a pause. The words of Nicodemus hung heavily in the air.

Anastasia looked away from their faces and out into the middle distance. She saw two rabbits coming toward her, and her first thought was, *those are the happiest two bunnies I've seen a long time.*

Then she realized it was Love Bug and Wendy. Love Bug was prancing along in a light-footed saunter, almost dancing to the percussion track the squirrels were laying down. Wendy, instead of her usual graceless shamble, was sashaying like a proud kit who just found her first ripe blackberry. And they were walking close together and indulging in occasional micronuzzles as they came.

The other creatures under the juniper noticed Anastasia staring and followed her line of sight. Soon they were all watching as the jaunty white bunny and the shaggy brown lop came strolling up to the juniper bush.

"Sorry we're late," said Love Bug.

The other animals exchanged glances. "Dare we ask what you've been up to?" asked Mabel, smiling.

Wendy and Love Bug looked at each other. Then Wendy reached into the backpack Love Bug was wearing and pulled out a golden claw. She smacked it down on the pages in the center of the group and said, "Everything change. *Today.*"

Anastasia and the other animals clustered around the claw. Anastasia picked it up. It had the smell of death on it. "What is this?"

Wendy sat up tall on her back feet and then leaned forward, her right paw sweeping slowly cross the group as she spoke. "Woof try hurt my boy Love Bug," she growled. She balanced her bite blade on the pads of her left paw and raised it up like an offering. "We … say … *no.*"

Anastasia's eyes flicked back and forth from Wendy's face to the golden claw laying on the ancient paper. "This is a

Summerday…?" she could not finish the sentence. Love Bug's eyes were fastened on hers, teary, proud, grateful, joyful.

"We did it, *Dangereuse*,"[23] he said, his voice breaking. "We did it for you." His eyes tracked around the group. "For *us*. For everyone." Tears rolled onto his cheeks. The animals stared, their mouths hanging open.

"Goldkiller!" shouted Wendy, pointing at Love Bug as she moved in a circle around the space in the slow, high-stepping ceremonial walk of her ancestors. "Goldkiller … here … *now*."

Suddenly, everyone was talking at once.

Anastasia felt a little dizzy. *We kill wolves now.* She lay down and let the hubbub carry on above her head. She felt as though they had crossed over a serious threshold at a moment she had not been prepared for. *Maybe…* She exhaled slowly and pressed her cheek against the soft earth. *Maybe we can really win this.*

WELLBUTRIN

Wellbutrin the raccoon was sorting apple seeds when the brown rabbit hopped up to the edge of his thorn maze. His mate Lorazepam was pruning the trees in their ancient apple grove, climbing from branch to branch, biting off unwanted shoots with her teeth.

He knew who the rabbit was, of course. She was wearing her camouflage jacket, which made her harder to see but easier to recognize. And she was travelling with a full guard, which meant a complement of rabbits, mice, and squirrels,

---

[23] Dangerous One.

with songbirds distributed through the trees and brush nearby. They were in stealth mode, so an untutored eye would have noticed nothing. But Wellbutrin's eye was not untutored.

"Opportunity knocking," said the brown bunny.

"Hey," said Wellbutrin, threading his way through the narrow path among the thorns to show her the way in.

Lorazepam hopped down from her tree and sidled forward. "Whazzup, honey?" she said.

A few moments later, they were sitting comfortably in the shade of an ancient apple tree, munching on strawberries from the vines that grew among the thorn hedge.

"How's business?" asked Anastasia.

"Ah, it's … down," said Lorazepam. "Clan *Paresseux* were our biggest customers. Summerdays got real aggro with them. So…" She shrugged.

"What was it like selling dirty apples to them?" asked Anastasia.

"Coyotes are hella fierce," said Wellbutrin. "It's good to be friends with the fierce ones. Gotta watch your back, of course. Even with the Truce." He eyed Anastasia for a moment. "You're pretty fierce."

"I know they killed your people," said Lorazepam softly. "I'm sorry. For us, it's just business, you know?"

"I know," said Anastasia.

"Now foxes, they don't do dirty apples much," said Wellbutrin, leaning back. "Most of them too uptight."

"Weasels mostly like mushrooms," said Lorazepam. "But sometimes a boogle will order a half a travois."

Wellbutrin glanced upwards. "Raptors buy an apple once in awhile," he said. "Gotta stay under the bushes after that."

Lorazepam nudged a particularly nice ripe strawberry toward Anastasia and turned on her sweet snaggle-toothed smile. "But I know the killer queen didn't walk ten miles to talk about the dirty apple business."

Anastasia pulled down an ear and cleaned it. "Actually, I did." She stood up and swept her forepaw toward the river. "What would you think about exclusive trading rights with all the Free Warrens on the south bank of the Shandy?"

The raccoons exchanged a glance. "We'd be stoked, of course," said Lorazepam, carefully.

Wellbutrin leaned forward. "You know what would be radical? If rabbits came to see how dirty apples can really … add something to your life." He gestured expansively. "Not just for getting toasted at big parties. But just part of a nice meal, you know?" He rubbed his fingers together. "It's not just the burn. It's the *flavor*."

Anastasia mirrored his excitement. "Fifty-one warrens now," she said. "This could be huge."

"Yeah!" Wellbutrin looked at his mate, eyes bright.

Lorazepam was gazing at Anastasia, smiling and slowly nodding her head. "And why would you offer us this?"

Anastasia shrugged off her backpack and put in on the ground beside her. "You know what's coming down from the north."

The raccoons became very still and looked at her seriously. Wellbutrin rested his hand on Lorazepam's back. "We wish you the best of luck with that," said Lorazepam.

Anastasia sat up and spoke earnestly. "We don't need luck. We know how to build a weapon that can drop a Blessed One at eighty yards," she said. "It's called a crossbow."

Wellbutrin scoffed. "What does that even mean?"

"We can kill a coyote. We can kill a wolf."

Both raccoons guffawed. "Good on ya, sister," said Lorazepam with a wheezy laugh. "Call me when it's over. We'll cater *that* party."

Anastasia thumped. "I'm serious," she said.

Wellbutrin leaned forward, "If you can do that, why are you here?"

"We need your hands," Anastasia said bluntly. She held up her two front feet. "Rabbits have paws. All we can do is dig, fight, and run. You're the largest animal with hands in the Known World. A mouse cannot build a large weapon. Neither can a rat. Or a squirrel. You can. Every animal should be scared of you. The *bears* should be scared of you." Her scent was bright and aggressive.

Lorazapam and Wellbutrin exchanged a glance. "Whoa, dude," said Lorazepam. "Don't even talk about the bears. That's bad luck."

Anastasia nodded. "Okay, here's the real question. Why should the golden wolves be the Landlords of the Million Acre Wood?" she asked. "*Why do they get to eat us and no one eats them?*"

The words hung in the air. Some questions just don't ever get asked. Wellbutrin felt the fabric of his world stretch and tear for a moment. It was painful. He and Lorazepam stared at each other. They each put a hand out, and their palms met.

"I don't know if we should continue this conversation," he whispered.

"Let's just hear her out, hun," said Lorazepam softly.

Wellbutrin splashed imaginary water on his face and

murmured a prayer to the Womb of Ocean. Lorazepam turned to face Anastasia. "What do you want us to do *exactly*?"

Anastasia sat up tall and still. "Come to the North Shandy, talk to the local raccoons, and show them why it makes sense for them to join our cause and build crossbows." Her scent was brisk. "You know I'm reliable so you can vouch for me. And you can speak to them in a way that I can't."

Wellbutrin exhaled sharply and sat back on his haunches. Lorazepam put her hand on Wellbutrin's shoulder and stood up. "It's all very easy for us to sit here and talk about killing hunters and running off the Landlords and making fat deals," she said. "You haven't even killed *one* wolf, honey."

Anastasia stood and upended her backpack on the earth between them. A pile of golden claws fell out, and a strong smell of death rose up. The raccoons recoiled. "One wolf down," said Anastasia.

Wellbutrin felt like he was about to throw up. Lorazepam stepped past him. She stood over Anastasia and spoke fiercely. "If we build your weapons, that means *every* raccoon in the Million Acre Wood is at war with the wolves. And *every* other hunter. We'd be throwing away a hundred years of Truce."

Wellbutrin stood up and leaned against an ancient apple tree. He felt dizzy. "No trade deal is worth a thousand of our people dead," he said.

Lorazepam knelt in front of Anastasia. "You want to be free. I respect that, homegirl." She took Anastasia's forepaws between her hands and kissed them. "You do you. But we can't be part of it." She turned away.

"Now take this death out of here," said Wellbutrin. "Please."

Chapter 12

Contrapuntal coloratura or get your beak out of my face.

—Classic songbird challenge, traditionally issued after three rounds of fermented berries

ANASTASIA

Evening feed at Bloody Thorn Warren was long over. Anastasia sat in the shadows, her guards deployed around her in stealth mode, watching Olympia as she dawdled over a fallen apple under the old apple tree fifty yards west of Bloody Thorn. She seemed oblivious to their presence, chewing rapidly, muttering, gesturing. She seemed to be having an argument with someone who was not there. The moon was rising early, and it lit the area under the apple tree as a ragged patchwork of black and white. A sweet and dirty reek drifted over from a nearby carrion tree.

Anastasia was furious. The refusal from the two raccoons whom she knew best had put her in a bad position. Now she would have to make her pitch to increasingly hostile raccoon audiences. And time was growing short.

Since she had travelled down to the South Shandy to meet with Wellbutrin and Lorazepam, she was quite near her old home warren. And even though Coriander and Love Bug had argued against it, she had decided to make a surprise visit to Bloody Thorn.

Abruptly, Anastasia stepped out of the shadows and spoke, "You lied to me, mother."

Olympia jumped and caught her breath. After a moment, she said, "Beloved daughter, you honor me with your presence." She sat perfectly still.

"Yah is a lie," said Anastasia flatly. The sentence hung in the cool air.

"What?" said Olympia. "Why would you even say that?" Her eyes darted around the chiaroscuro patchwork under the tree.

Anastasia took a step forward. "One of my spies saw a wolf dictating the next correction to a crow, who wrote it down and sent it to the Lord Harmonizer."

"Spies? What are you talking about?" said Olympia

"I sent a mouse into the Spires. She saw it."

Olympia stared at her. "Mice have tiny brains, darling. No one listens to mice."

Anastasia looked up at the bright moon, and slowly let her gaze drift down toward her mother's face. Quietly, she said: "*The weapons of my Blessed Ones are for the Glorification of the world.*" Olympia looked stunned and took a step back.

Anastasia's voice rolled on, getting louder. "'*The tooth, the claw, and the beak are my gift of love. They are perfect. Let there be no others. Any who would create weapons shall never see the Lucky Fields, never taste the Apple of Joy, and never sleep in the bosom of the Loved One in the endless golden afternoon.*'"

Olympia sat as still as a statue. There was a long silence. Then she said, "How did you—?"

"I'm free now," interrupted Anastasia. "No more rules for me." She held up her right foreleg, and the Claw appeared. The *zhing*! was very loud in the quiet night. The blade shone like white fire in the moonlight. Olympia's stared at it, and her eyes became huge. Then she turned as if to bolt back to the safety of Bloody Thorn. Instantly, noiselessly, twenty spears rose out of the grass, surrounding her, metal tips catching the light. Ten rabbits appeared from the dappled shadows, steel bite blades glimmering white.

Olympia froze. "Baby girl is a queen," she whispered, her blue eyes shining. "I'm so proud of you."

Anastasia crept closer to her. "Were there ever any rules for you, mother?"

Olympia kept her eyes locked on Anastasia. "I don't know by what magic you know the correction to the Word. I only know that I have always done the best I can for our family in a dangerous world." She pressed her forepaw to her heart. "And I always loved you best."

Anastasia leapt forward, her eyes were fierce and sad. "I may lose this war that *you* forced me into when you cast me out, but I will *never* be a willing tool of the killers. Like you."

She lifted the bright blade. It hung shining in the moonlight over her head. Her mother appeared to be trying to speak, but no words came out. A nightjar began singing and then fell silent. The moment stretched out.

At last Olympia spoke. "It's not because I *want* to," she whispered, her blue eyes huge. "It's because I *have* to."

Anastasia came near to Olympia. "Sunbeam loves you," she said. Her eyes travelled the length of the bright blade. "If anything happened to you, it would break her heart." She dropped her paw and the Claw hung at her side. "Go," she said.

Coriander and the Auntie's Guard melted into the darkness, and Olympia darted away toward the warren. Anastasia stood looking after her. Her voice dropped to a murmur. "Holy day."

Stan

Stan the bluebird had been busy recruiting songbirds in the North Shandy. He was getting better at his recruitment stunt of luring a raptor low so that it could be ambushed by songbirds. And once these tiny flyers had felt the power of collective action against a larger enemy, they were hooked on the buzz of victory and excited to join. In the last week, he had recruited over a hundred songbirds for the cause, so the *Armée Libre*'s scouting and message-carrying capabilities were expanding by leaps and bounds.

It was still hard to know what was going on behind the enemy line, though. The songbirds who had flown Death Rage up to the Spires had stayed near the coast and out of sight, keeping a low profile, so they hadn't returned with much general information.

And the flying part of the Blessed Army was getting more and more organized every day. Murders of crows were thick along the line of squads, making it virtually suicidal for any songbird to approach. And now the big raptors were haunting the wings of the approaching army, extending the line well out to sea on one side, and far into the uplands on the other.

Stan's new scouts were a little shy about running this blockade, so he decided to give it a go himself. After giving it some thought, he had come up with a way to get past the raptors.

As he came within half a mile of the Blessed Army, he could both hear and see the crows flying near the ground and the dark shapes of the raptors circling above. He came in close to the cliffs and then angled downward. As he came upon a grape vine, he stopped and picked up a large brown grape leaf from the leaf litter around it.

Then he coasted down to the rocky beach and held the stem of the leaf so that it shielded his body from above. Then every time the wind blew, he ran along the stony clutter, occasionally taking flight and coasting for a few yards. When the wind stopped, he stopped. It took awhile, but in less than an hour, he had come up even with the Blessed Army line, passed under the raptors, and then fluttered and wafted another quarter-mile down the shoreline. After carefully peeking out from under his leaf, he took to the air and climbed, hugging the cliffs.

Soon he was travelling freely over the area behind the lines, skimming the treetops. It felt strangely deserted. After a few minutes of flying, he spotted an apple orchard. These were easily identified from the air because of their unusual formation: a grove of apple trees surrounded by a dense hedge of thorns.

Stan noticed some golden wolves around the thorn hedge but thought nothing of it. Everyone knew canids bought dirty apples. Then he noticed a raccoon come bursting out of a pathway through the thorns, closely pursued by a gray wolf cub. The raccoon was running as fast as its burly body would allow, but the wolf cub was catching up easily. Now the golden wolves were converging and—

Stan was so startled he stopped flapping and started to fall. *The wolves are attacking raccoons now?*

Then he caught himself and turned back toward the cliffs, flying fast and low, casting just one more glance over his shoulder. His heart was pounding, his breath coming fast. *The whole frickin' world is coming apart.* He flapped ferociously for a few moments. *And they don't want anybody to know.*

FREDDIE

Freddie was out at evening feed near the bunker, meditating on quarrel point shapes while gazing at a late-season dandelion seed head. Suddenly, a whirling, liquid shape descended from a tree branch overhead and came to rest on a sturdy twig near him. Then the spinning motion suddenly stopped, and he could see that it was Dingus. He stood with one leg forward and one back, his hands out on each side like a tiny surfer. And he was very still.

"Dingus!" exclaimed Freddie, dropping his endive in mid-bite. "What happened? We lost you after we crossed the river."

"We are far from the world now," said Dingus. His silvery voice was not unfriendly, but neither was it friendly. It was very different from the sound of the tiny carnival barker who used to deliver proclamations from the oak tree near Warren *Sans Gloire.*

"'We?'" asked Freddie. Dingus looked up and spread his paws. Freddie followed his gaze and saw the blurry shapes of dozens of squirrels standing in the same position as Dingus, on branches all over the tree.

"Your fight is no longer our fight," said Dingus, his voice cool and crisp. "We came to tell the Rabbit Without Antecedents."

"She's in South Shandy," said Freddie. "What are you saying? Are you giving up?"

"The squirrel that was Dingus cared deeply," said Dingus. "*I* cannot."

"But *you're* Dingus—" began Freddie.

"The squirrel that was Dingus sought to leave fear behind," said Dingus. "Desire causes attachment to outcomes. Attachment to outcomes causes fear. The squirrel that was Dingus chose non-attachment." He raised his left hand, middle finger and thumb meeting in the sign of the eternal zero.

"We are not attached to outcomes," said all the squirrels at once, each raising their own left hands with thumb and middle finger joined.

"So you're still doing Oga For Young Goats?" asked Freddie.

Dingus glanced at the other Ascending squirrels, and a slight chuckle ran through their number. "You do not *do* Oga For Young Goats," said Dingus, with the small smile of an amused yogi. "Oga For Young Goats does *you.*"

"Did you hear that we found out the wolves wrote the Book of Yah?" asked Freddie.

"What?" Dingus sounded like his old self for a moment. "That's *crazy*." Then he quickly recomposed himself. A flutter riffled through the other Ascending squirrels, then they settled down. "Gods have always been created by those who look for them," said Dingus, in his silvery voice. With his right hand, he made a mystical gesture and then touched his forehead. "Inquire within." His tail flicked into the shape of an infinity symbol.

"Well, sorry to lose ya," said Freddie with a small, rueful smile. "Even if you did get on my nerves once in a while."

Dingus flicked through the air and was suddenly standing right next to Freddie's ear. "The squirrel that was Dingus is fading, but not yet gone," he said. "He has a message for Anastasia."

"What?' asked Freddie.

The voice that came spinning out of Dingus was quiet, but the silvery shine made every word bright and clear. "*I send you the love of the Infinite.*"

ANASTASIA

Anastasia and the Loving Auntie's Guard were swimming across the Shandy River, hanging on to the cords that had been strung across when the *Armée Libre* crossed many days earlier. She had just pulled out onto the northern shore and was shivering in the early autumn air when a balding blue bird came down at a steep angle, making a stumbling crash-landing.

It was Stan. "Thought I might find you here," he said. "Jeez, you guys are easy to spot from the air."

"That's why we sent our songbirds ahead to scout," said Anastasia irritably.

"Anyway, forget about it," said Stan. "I'm here because I got news. Wolves are attacking *raccoons*." He quickly related what he had seen north of the enemy lines a few hours earlier.

Anastasia stared at him. She could feel her heart rate increasing. "Are you dead certain, brother?"

Stan stretched his aching wing muscles. "With my own eyes, I saw it," he said. "I nearly fell out of the sky."

The Loving Auntie's Guard was re-forming its perimeter. "Let's get off this exposed riverbank," said Love Bug, shepherding the group toward the trees.

Anastasia nibbled a foreclaw. "This is so bad for the raccoons," she said, looking at Coriander as they lollopped toward cover. "And ... this is definitely going to bring them into the fight." She leaned near him. "I feel bad for saying this..." she said, almost whispering in his ear. "But this is good news for us."

Coriander pressed into her as they moved along. "You didn't cause this to happen. The wolves are breaking every rule." He nuzzled her ear. "And yes, we need this bad. No shame in that."

She nodded. "Right. I just ... feel so conflicted." Then she shook herself and called out to one of the Guard's songbird messengers. "Take this news down to Pam and Welly. Ask them to set up a meeting with the North Shandy raccoons."

"When?" asked the messenger, a young oriole.

Anastasia's eyes flicked over to Coriander. "Yesterday."

NICODEMUS

Death Rage dashed out of the central space in Warren *du Nord*, across the Narrows, and into the bunker. There she found Nicodemus, the Reading apprentices, and the craft-mice, working on preparing the materials and plans for the crossbows. They had heard via songbird messenger the news about wolves and raccoons, so they were getting ready for a hoped-for influx of raccoon builders.

"Nicodemus," she said, breathing hard. "He's back."

The elderly rabbit looked up from the page he was studying. "Who?"

"Bricabrac."

"Ah," said Nicodemus, putting down the page and looking seriously at Death Rage.

"We talked about this," said Death Rage. "We have to do this."

"Yes, well…" said Nicodemus. "He has been very helpful to the Free Warrens. He's the one who first showed us how to make weapons."

Suddenly, Death Rage was standing very close to him. "Don't you think I know that?" she said, looking at him fiercely. "It was from him that I got the Kiss of Death." She laid her hand on the hilt. "But I saw his sister with the wolves. And he brought her to *Sans Gloire*."

"I know," said Nicodemus.

"He may be clever. He may be a hard worker. He may … give you a dime when you need one…" she trailed off, looking at her toes. She looked back at Nicodemus, and he could see her eyes were red. "But he's a traitor. Even if he saves your life, he can't be trusted. The Free Warrens must come first."

Nicodemus nodded, feeling suddenly very old. "You're right, honored warrior," he said quietly. "Loving Auntie's not here. We'll need to keep Bricabrac until she returns."

One of the Reading apprentices approached shyly. "We found a Chamber of Reflection this morning," he said. "In the far corner, by those page fragments from *Ça Va Quebecois.*" He led them over to a fat gallon jar with an ancient Vegenaise label that was just barely legible. Some of the apprentices and craftmice followed along.

Nicodemus inspected it, with Death Rage sitting on his shoulder. "Okay," he said, heavily. "Punch some air holes in the top and put in food and water. Then we'll send a platoon to pick up Bricabrac. We can keep him in here."

Death Rage nodded, then buried her face in his fur and burst into tears.

WELLY & PAM

When Wellbutrin and Lorazepam heard the news about what Stan had seen, they immediately began an anxious discussion which lasted all night and included them symbolically sprinkling each other with water while singing prayers to the Womb of Ocean. And as good Rochefarians, they spent long hours gazing at the full moon and turning in slow circles with forelegs outstretched while communing with the spirit of Roche.

Should they push for this merger with the Free Warrens? Should the raccoons attempt to get out in front of this hostile takeover by the wolves by launching a counterattack with rabbits as white knights? The questions were many, and the round white tablet in the sky smiled down benignly but in silence.

Finally, they knelt facing each other, foreheads pressed together, and little by little came to an agreement to join the effort. Once they had crossed that momentous threshold, they used songbird messengers provided by the *Armée Libre* to set up a meeting with the leading citizens among the raccoons in the North Shandy.

ANASTASIA

Anastasia and her team were at one of the favorite meeting places of the North Shandy raccoons, a clearing nestled in a grove of cedars, several miles north of the Narrows. Seventy-odd raccoons were lolling in the open space. The Loving Auntie's Guard was dispersed around the perimeter. And Love Bug and Wendy were both patrolling the line, occasionally taking time out for a quick nuzzle.

The two raccoons were standing near Anastasia, having a hasty confab.

"We got them here," said Wellbutrin. "But lots of people aren't convinced."

"Kind of a gnarly crowd," said Lorazepam. "*We* know you're reliable, but … ehhh, not going to be easy," she muttered.

Anastasia nodded. "Ya, it's a tough sell. I get it." She raked her foreclaws through the earth. "We sent off some songbird teams for extra confirmation. Thought they'd be back by now, but haven't seen them."

Lorazepam leaned down to whisper in her ear. "You're gonna be great, hon."

"I better be," murmured Anastasia.

Anastasia took a few steps away, her breath coming fast. If the raccoons would join them, they had a chance. The crossbows the raccoons could build might turn the tide. If not, all was lost. The killer army would roll over them and it would be as though they had never existed.

Anastasia's scent was bright and flickery. She crouched down behind a boulder and touched her face in complex patterns while she sang a little soothing song.

"Safe, my baby, safe
You are safe right here
Safe, my bunny, safe
All is well, my dear"

Wendy and Love Bug watched Anastasia doing her ritual, then shared a concerned glance. Coriander sat close beside her and nuzzled her ear. Freddie came over and pressed into her side. She leaned against them.

A raccoon called from the audience area. "Can we get this thing started?"

"Someone needs to announce me," said Anastasia.

"I'll do it," said Freddie quickly.

"No," said Anastasia. "Needs to be a raccoon."

Lorazepam and Wellbutrin looked at each other. "That's you, bruh," she said.

Wellbutrin murmured, "Right, right," and heaved himself to his feet. Freddie leaned toward him and rapidly whispered a list of titles. Then Wellbutrin stepped out in front of the crowd of raccoons.

"Hey, dudes," he said, waving his right fist with thumb and pinky extended in the ancient raccoon gesture of greeting. "Thanks for hanging today, in these gnarly times. Give it up for Anastasia Bloody Thorn, Rabbit Without Antiperspirant, Protector of the Excellent, Loving Auntie of the Free Peoples." Freddie hissed another phrase at him, so he quickly added, "Beloved of the Indefinite."

Anastasia stepped out from behind the boulder, looking splendid in her Kevlar jacket with the golden side out and her *aluminum d'or* circlet on her head. The claw gleamed brightly on her forepaw. And the owl talon necklace Wendy had given her looked very handsome.

There was a smattering of applause, but overall, the raccoons seemed underwhelmed.

Anastasia leaped up into a middle-sized boulder and stood there. "Friends," she said. "Our lives are in our hands. In three weeks, the killer army will be here. We can choose to fight them. Or we can choose to give our bodies to them." There was silence. Anastasia's golden eyes raked the crowd. "Always they have kept my people in submission, with a false religion that taught us that our bodies were owned by killers whom we called 'Blessed.' Now we know the truth. *We own ourselves*." She jumped down off the boulder and walked among them. "And we have a common cause, you and I, now that the wolves are breaking the hundred-year-old Truce to kill raccoons."

A raccoon near her, with a jagged white scar that cut vertically through his black mask near his right eye, said lazily, "Stories."

Anastasia turned to him. "I can see why you would say that, but our people have seen this happening."

"I haven't," said the raccoon, who turned and addressed the others. "Have you?" He gestured. "You?" They shook their heads. He looked back at Anastasia. "This is *your* fight, not ours."

"Let her speak, Adderall," said Lorazepam.

Adderall leaned back and folded his arms across his chest. "What is it you want from us anyway?"

Anastasia spread her forepaws. "We have discovered a weapon, first made by the Dead Gods, that will enable us to hit killers at a distance. They called it a 'crossbow.' With these, we can stop the killer army at the Narrows. We can change the Million Acre Wood forever."

Adderall yawned and stretched ostentatiously. "Sounds like it's all slammatocious for you, dude. Why do you need us?"

Anastasia turned to face him. "To build the crossbows."

The raccoons erupted in a chorus of groans and chaffing. Calls of "there it is" and "love ya when they need ya" riffled across the crowd.

"Right, *right*," said Adderall. "Always the raccoons have to do other people's work."

"It's not like that," said Anastasia. "The Free Peoples will all fight together."

"The Free *Lunchmeat*, you mean," said Adderall.

Everyone was silent at the use of this very offensive term.

Anastasia felt a trickle of anger burn through her muscles. Then she saw a whirl of songbirds coming toward the clearing, flying low through the trees, struggling with a heavy burden encased in netting. They arrived at a high stump on the far side of the clearing and set down together to rest.

Doing her best to keep a pleasant expression on her face, Anastasia started to move toward the much bigger raccoon, with Coriander following close behind. As she walked, she looked at the cluster of songbirds and threw two paw signs. *Come. Now.*

The songbirds took off from the stump, still laboring with their netting and flying erratically. Love Bug signaled the Loving Auntie's Guard to move inward and go on alert.

Anastasia kept her eyes focused on Adderall as she walked. "You think it's all good for you, *bruh*?" she said. "You think you're a mini-Blessed? You think the golden wolves are gonna come down here and give you a big hug?" Wendy started to drift through the crowd toward the Loving Auntie.

Adderall leaned back and put his hands behind his head. "Hundred years of Truce, homegirl," he said, with a lazy grin. There were murmurings of assent from the crowd around him. "Killers love dirty apples more than they love raccoon meat. We got skills. What *you* got?"

Anastasia stood near Adderall's face. "I got truth." Her golden eyes swept the crowd of raccoons. "I know what's happening behind the killer army line." She looked back at Adderall. "Do you?" The cluster of songbirds was getting nearer. Coriander stood with his back to Anastasia, scanning the crowd.

"No one knows for sure," said Adderall. "But I know this:

raccoons tucked in all snuggy behind their thorn hedges." He cracked his knuckles. "We're good."

The group of songbirds was now almost overhead, with the outlines of a round, heavy object starting to become visible through the netting.

Anastasia turned and faced the rest of the raccoons. "My dear friends," she said. Her eyes flicked toward Adderall, "Including you, bruh. I'm sorry you have to see this."

The songbirds were descending now, a little too fast, their net spilling out of control. A raucous flurry of birdsong surrounded them as they yelled orders at each other. The people immediately under the birds started to back up. Then some of songbirds lost their grip on the net, and it fell down on one side. A moment later, a yellow and brown object was rolling out of the net, slowly turning, tumbling, dropping. It was a heavily gnawed raccoon skull.

The raccoons stared at it in dead silence for the eternity that it took to fall. Then it hit the ground and went bouncing into the crowd.

That broke the spell. The raccoons shrieked and climbed over each other to get away from the skull as it tumbled. The sound of a hundred-year-old certainty being shredded was agonizing and guttural. And the raccoons' eyes were bright white within their dark masks.

Anastasia stood without moving as the battered skull flew past her and the raccoons melted away from it like sand before a rainstorm.

"I'm so sorry," said Anastasia, her golden eyes tracking over the scrambling crowd. "But now you know. Your lives are on the line. Just like ours." She sat up tall, spreading her forepaws. "Welcome to the Free Peoples."

OLYMPIA

What to do? What to do? Olympia was walking in her thorn garden above the warren, her mind awhirl. She felt there was some sickness growing in her. Ever since Tobias has given her the new correction to the Word, there had been a darkness growing in her guts. And it scared her.

She saw a handsome thorn that she knew well and pressed her left forepaw on it. Not too hard. Just enough to make the slightest prick. She felt the tiny *plink!* of pain and looked down to see a small red rose blossoming on her paw pad. She stopped to savor the moment. *A little gift for you, my spiky friend.* Then she moved on.

Of course, she had told no one about Anastasia's visit and her magical recitation of the correction that she could not have known. But it did make one thing perfectly clear. Her daughter was not an apostate. Not a heretic. She was a sorceress. With powerful demons whispering secrets in her ear. Probably engaging in Yah-knows-what hideous ceremonies featuring mouse brains and ecstatic drugs with her strange, species-mixing coven right now.

Or maybe she was being granted revelations by some new god. Maybe bright furry angels were traversing the aether at this very moment, coming with new wisdom from a shiny new sovereign sprit.

Olympia put her paw to head. Was there no end to these overlords and their demands? She swatted the idea away. Her job was to keep her warren safe by executing her tasks as Presiding Spirit so ably that everyone could see that she was a good and valuable soldier and must be preserved.

So back to her duties in the South Bank Conclave. Not that people were lining up to come to Conclave meetings. She tapped several thorn tips as she walked past. The Rememberers at warrens that fell under the cloud of darkness had mostly stopped attending Conclave functions anyway. Or if they did come, they had radical ideas.

There was still a faithful core, though. Almost half of the South Bank warrens were hanging on. She had an idea about what she wanted to say to them, but she hadn't fully worked it out yet.

This new correction must be dealt with. *Don't use weapons*. This had to get out beyond the faithful remnant, who wouldn't dream of making weapons. She had been setting up Local Harmonizer teams to take this new gospel directly to all the warrens in her Conclave, faithful or not, with plans to reach out to warrens beyond her area.

Her daughter Sweet Leaf was leading the charge—she had a relentless, oily charm—and Briar and the other First and Second Born were providing the muscle as needed. They had been going out on training trips with bunnies from several of the faithful warrens and were now sending out teams in earnest. That should be a suitable showing for the moment.

But there was no getting away from her more intimate problem. Dear, smart, hardworking Anastasia. What a wonderful Warren Mother she would have made. If only she wasn't so prone to run off in strange directions. *She will not listen.* Now she was turning the world upside down.

Olympia felt another surge of the sickness and the bad thoughts that came with it. She distracted herself with a cute baby thorn that had just begun growing out of the bramble stalk. It was so beautiful. Filled with so much promise. She pressed the right side of her face against it and felt the small kiss of pain. The small hot touch felt so good. It blotted out the dark thoughts.

What should she do? If the Blessed army marched across the Shandy and down to the southern end of the Million Acre Wood, her warren might be—mostly—spared, since it was not part of the rebellion. But there would be plenty of death, and the righteous, Yah-fearing social structure that granted her family protections would likely be destroyed.

If the majority of warrens in the South Shandy were wiped out, there would be some kind of desperate free-for-all among the survivors. The new order would be different, it would be ugly, and there would be no place for her. If the threat to the Blessed ceased, everything would, could, maybe go back to normal. But how?

What was needed was a way to attack the darkness of un-reason quickly, before any more warrens fell under the baleful influence. She had dithered too long, uncertain of what to do. And Anastasia's recent visit and display of magical powers had her spooked. Any attacks must be indirect. She could not risk calling down the ire of a powerful, spiritual criminal on Bloody Thorn directly.

What was needed now was a revelation. And a promise.

Chapter 13

If you were born a mouse, you'd be mad, too.

—Fox proverb

Love Bug

It was quiet at the bunker. After a frenetic morning preparing for the raccoon builders to arrive, most of the small animals were taking their usual midday snooze. Love Bug and Wendy drifted away from the communal sleeping chamber and toward a snug spot in a hollow log they had found.

Although they were drawn to spend time together, it was not always clear how to do it. Love Bug, Captain-Casual-Humpty-Hump, and Wendy, Warrior-Who-Walks-By-Herself, did not really fit together neatly. But they had discovered one way to meet in the middle: the afternoon snuggle.

The inside of the hollow log was lined with soft, crumbling punk and velvety green moss. Wendy lay on her side with Love Bug curled into her. It was warm and cozy and felt very safe.

"What you do after?" asked Wendy, rubbing her big paw along the edge of his long white ear.

"After what?" asked Love Bug.

Wendy jerked her head toward the flurry of activity going on outside their log. "War."

Love Bug looked up at a tiny aloe vera growing on the inside rim of the log and said, "I'm not sure." He ran his paw over the moss. "I never really realized before how big the Million Acre Wood is. I'd like to see more of it."

Wendy rumbled, "Mmmm."

He turned over and looked at her. "How about you?"

Wendy stretched. "I go home. On boat."

Love Bug rubbed the broad expanse of her furry belly. "What's it like on your island?"

Wendy sucked her teeth. "Many hawk. Fight much." She touched her claw necklace. "Win some."

Love Bug nodded. "Is everyone like you?"

"No," said Wendy. "Mostly big. Good fighters." She grinned at Love Bug. "I weakling."

He could not tell if she was joking or not. "What?" he said. "No way."

Wendy shrugged. "They call me 'Yip-Yap,' since I talk so good."

Love Bug giggled, then buried his face in the soft fur of her undercarriage. "Yes, you do. You talk very good."

Wendy rolled over on her back and gazed out at the bright blue autumn sky. "Maybe you want visit. Everyone think you handsome."

Love Bug scoffed. "That's me. The cute guy with a soft spot for weaklings. What a prince." He stretched and then nuzzled under her chin. "Actually, that sounds fun."

"Good," rumbled Wendy.

"Now," said Love Bug, sitting up and looking out at a troop of raccoons just arriving at the bunker. "All we have to do is survive this."

SHANDY VALE

Olympia's Local Harmonizer teams were fanning out and working fast, spreading news of the latest correction to the Word of Yah to warrens on both sides of the Shandy River. *Making weapons grieves Father Yah.*

Rabbits from the Free Peoples were also travelling among the warrens, spreading their news about what Death Rage had seen. *Yah is a lie created by our enemies.*

Like many arguments, these zoomed past each other and left the hearers initially confused.

Most North Shandy warrens that had recently joined the Free Peoples still accepted Olympia's Harmonizers and heard their news. So they were shocked and skeptical when rabbits sent by Anastasia told them Death Rage's story. At heart, they were still believers. Signing up to fight a defensive war is not the same thing as turning your back on Yah. Or calling Yah a liar, a trickster, a hoaxer. The Word of Yah had been the guiding force in the rabbits' lives for three centuries, ever since the fall of the Dead Gods. That was easily three hundred generations, and stories with roots this deep in a people do not vanish before the pinprick of an alternate yarn.

But they would at least hear. And after the messengers of both sides had left, they would argue, long into the night. Of course, with war at their doorstep, fortifications in place, and weapons at the ready, proponents of disarming faced a steeply uphill battle. So these warrens dithered, they fretted, they engaged in dramatic marathons of exegesis with their Rememberers, but they stayed armed to the teeth.

North Shandy warrens that had not yet become part of the Free Peoples were already at their wit's end, terrified of the coming Blessed army, crouched with one foot out the door, trying to decide whether they should leave everything they had built and make a desperate run for survival, joining the flood of refugees pouring across the river into the South Shandy. For them, these stories of unheard-of corrections to the Word or devious wolves and crows fabricating stories were just another part of their world falling apart. They could hardly hear them. Or spare a moment to care.

Eighty-seven warrens on both sides of the river had now joined the Free Peoples. But the growth had happened so fast that organization was poor. Holly, the Home Steward, and Yasmin, Captain of the Home Guard, struggled to keep up. But they worked mightily and with mostly good cheer at this world-changing labor. With most of the senior players now gone to the north side of the river to prepare for war, the actual governance of the world they were fighting for was in the hands of these two young mothers.

The technology of defense spread from one warren to the next via conversations and sketches drawn in the dirt, followed by a scramble for raw materials and artisanal expertise. Holly sent out the craftmice, two by two, and they instructed their information-hungry rabbit students in how to build bite blades, spears, and gratings. After these tasks were underway, the mice would initiate a second round of instruction in bringing in food and water to prepare for siege and digging down to the water table to create seepage wells.

The craftmice were closely followed by their warmice compadres, sent by Yasmin, who led warren after warren in drills on the finer points of using their new weapons. She sent no rabbits, because any rabbit with proficiency in weapons was needed at the front lines to the north, or by the Home Guard.

The warmice were usually accompanied by rabbits trained by Grégoire and Juniper in the arts of medicine. The bunny medics brought little starter kits of useful herbs and bark to share, together with best practices when setting up a Healing Hall. It turned out that Juniper had a knack for encoding medical information in easily remembered jingles, so the medics were armed with a brainload of snappy couplets like this:

"If pain keeps you up at night
Willow bark will set you right"

An entire efflorescence of culture was happening across the southern part of the Million Acre Wood, created and driven by the pressures of war.

And, of course, there were refugees. At first, the warrens of South Shandy were welcoming. Their hearts went out to rabbits who had become the thing they most feared to be themselves, homeless wanderers with no friendly nearby hole to bolt toward.

When the first refugees came in their dozens, a whole warren on the run, pregnant mothers, two-month-old kits, anxious fathers, dragging their possessions in makeshift travois, they were taken in with open arms. Brought into underhalls to sleep, shown where the good feed was, advised as to the best place to site a new warren.

But as the dozens became hundreds, and then thousands, rabbits blown south before the winds of war, all with sameysame stories of horrors seen and loved ones killed, the good will began to wear thin. The best feed was long gone, and best new warren sites already taken with rabbits arrived just ten days ago. So the newcomers were pushed further south, toward the less desirable places, the swamps, the rocky badlands near the cliffs, the beaches where bitter marram grass grew.

All the coyotes in the South Shandy were gone. But many foxes remained, and more than a few weasels, learning to fear the weapons of the Free Peoples and focusing more and more on the unaffiliated warrens. They skulked in the hollows, the waste places, hungrier every day, only too happy to come across a tribe of refugees caught above ground, their youngest and their oldest laid out for the sullen remaining Blessed as a buffet that they claimed by divine right.

The future was balanced on a knife tip.

ANASTASIA

The grove of yew trees that grew over the bunker was the perfect source of wood for the bows. Beloved of the Dead Gods, yew heartwood absorbs and stores tremendous power in compression, and yew sapwood controls and drives that power when under tension.

The Reading apprentices had read about the yew trees in Magdalenium's diary, and a large group of raccoons was now walking through the very grove her family had planted three centuries earlier. They were scouting for the best cuts, in consultation with Freddie and some of the lead craftmice.

The large rusty saw blade the rabbits had found at the bunker had now been oiled and sharpened and fitted with handles at each end to make it a two-person saw, and with some practice, the raccoons had gained the knack for using it. Many of the toymaker's tools found at the bunker were also well-suited for raccoon hands because of their scaled-down size. These included a keyhole saw, a coping saw, two small planes, and several sets of calipers. They had all been refurbished by the industrious craftmice, and the raccoons were carrying them as they walked.

The goal was thirty crossbows in three weeks.

Anastasia was there, anxiously hovering, with Coriander nearby. She wasn't wearing her Kevlar, since the day was so hot. Love Bug and her guard were maintaining a thirty-yard perimeter. And Wendy was keeping a close eye on the raccoons, of whom she was inclined to be suspicious.

The songbird scouts watching the far perimeter were in motion because shift change was happening. Some were flying in. Some were late getting started flying out because of an argument among lieutenants.

As the raccoons walked and talked, Adderall said, apropos of nothing, "I'm not sure I'm happy with the terms."

Lorazepam and Wellbutrin exchanged a glance. "You're

getting the same deal as everyone else, bruh," said Lorazepam soothingly.

"Why can't I make my own deals with the Free Warrens near my orchard?" said Adderall, as he pulled on a springy yew bough. "Why do I have to go through this consortium?"

"You'll have access to more warrens like this, dude," said Wellbutrin. "You won't be stuck with the ups and downs of local demand."

"Your grafts are totally yummalicious, and unique to you," said Lorazepam. "After ... this ... is all over, people up and down the Million Acre Wood are going to be begging for them."

Adderall leaned his saw against a tree and turned to face the other raccoons. "The bigger question," he said. "Is why do we let some twitchy rabbit dictate to us? And not even just a rabbit, a *doe*."

Love Bug threw two paw signs out to the Loving Auntie's Guard. *Move in. Look casual.*

Adderall leaned close to another raccoon to whisper a joke, and they both laughed. "Bros before does, amirite?" said Adderall, fist bumping with several chuckling raccoons near him.

Wendy growled, "Bah," and stalked away.

Anastasia said, "I'm not dictating to you."

Adderall turned back to Anastasia. "The thing is, you *are*, honey," he said. "And I don't love it."

"We're offering a trading opportunity that you can take or leave," said Anastasia, doing her best to maintain a pleasant tone. "In terms of the war, the *world* is dictating to you. And the world is bigger than you or me. Or the killers."

"Your deal is good, Addy," said Lorazepam. "Just chill, bruh."

"My deal?" said Adderall, washing his face, which brought his scar into high relief. "My family has been running our orchard of premier Freckled Tawnies and Red Bellies for *twenty-six* generations. I don't need some Janey-come-lately barging in and telling me how to run my world."

Anastasia stood up. "That world is over," she said flatly, and took a step toward him. "I don't know what's going to happen, but I know things will never be like they were." Coriander was close beside Anastasia now. She could feel him trying to subtly push her away from Adderall with his hip.

"Why did you start this?" burst out Adderall. He picked up his saw and threw it. "Things were *good* before."

"Not for *us*. Not for lots of people." said Anastasia. "And you were sucking up to the killers to stay alive. You see how much your 'Truce' is worth now." She was very near to Adderall, chin out, ears back. "You should be thanking me for a chance at freedom, you *bean counter.*"

Adderall made a contemptuous sound and raised his fore-paw as though to slap her. She flinched, and then, angry with herself for drawing back, shouldered into him.

The much larger raccoon was on her in an instant, bowling her over with his size and weight, teeth bared. In the next moment, Anastasia, laying on her back, had the Claw out, with the shining point pressed against his throat.

Immediately, Coriander threw his muscular body between the raccoon and the Loving Auntie, knocking the Claw out of the way. Twenty spears rose out of the grass around Adderall, while ten rabbits with bite blades in their teeth rushed forward.

"Whoa, whoa, whoa!" cried Wellbutrin and several other raccoons. "Cool out, cool out, cool out, people!"

Anastasia sheathed her claw and walked away, stiff-legged from the adrenaline burn. Coriander walked close beside her, pressing against her left flank. "Shhhhh, Honored Love," he murmured. "We can't risk you in fights like that."

Lorazepam, Wellbutrin, and several other raccoons surrounded Adderall, placing soothing hands on him, talking him down.

Love Bug came after Anastasia and Coriander and put his mouth to her right ear. She started to pull away in annoyance, but he followed closely. "Loving Auntie, a word?"

He gestured at a spot a few yards away with a jerk of his head. She left Coriander and walked a few paces with Love Bug.

"Don't look," he whispered. "But there's a wolf at the edge of that meadow, about two hundred yards from here."

Anastasia held perfectly still. "What?" she murmured.

"Wendy saw it," whispered Love Bug. "No one else has. She called in the songbird perimeter scouts. She's going to go lead it over here."

Anastasia turned her head and stared at him. "*What*? Why?"

Love Bug looked at her earnestly. "We can't have the raccoons peeling off every other day. We're their best chance. She's going to remind them of that."

"That's *crazy*," hissed Anastasia.

"Just to scare them a little. They can all climb trees," whispered Love Bug. "I told her it was a risky idea, but..." He shrugged helplessly. "...She went anyway. I'm going to warn the rabbits and mice," he whispered, and left her.

Anastasia allowed herself a glance toward the meadow. It took her a few seconds to see the golden form slipping through the yellowing foliage. It must be upwind from the rabbits. A few seconds later, she saw, a squat brown shape emerge from a patch of weeds and run right across the wolf's line of vision, about fifty yards from it.

The wolf took off like a shot, and Wendy turned and bolted back toward the yew trees. Anastasia stared with her eyes bugging out. In just a few seconds, it was clear that Wendy had misjudged the wolf's ability to run.

Wendy's wide, sturdy body was not built for speed. Even with her stumpy legs going as fast as she could, the wolf was outpacing her, closing the distance between them. Anastasia, started to drift forward to do ... what? She had no idea. She was just pulled toward the running animals as though by an invisible cord. Wendy, the Assault Leader of the Free Peoples, could not die today.

Coriander approached, muttering something about Adderall. He seemed not to have noticed the drama happening two hundred yards away. Anastasia felt annoyed by his presence. "Leave me," she said brusquely. "Go help Love Bug."

Coriander looked surprised.

"Go," she said. He bowed and left. In the next instant, Anastasia began to run. As she dashed through the scrub, she began to assemble a plan. Unlike Wendy, Anastasia was lean and fast, a born sprinter. She could—probably—outrun the wolf, at least for a hundred yards. Up ahead was a dense thicket of weeds. She knew Wendy would run for it. The spindly weeds didn't offer the protection of brambles, but for a few seconds, she would be out of sight. Anastasia made for the thicket, arriving a few seconds before Wendy.

ALIYAH

Aliyah saw the brown rabbit she was chasing run into a dense thicket of weeds. And a few moments later, she saw a brown shape run out the opposite side, so she swerved around the thicket and kept going.

It took her a few seconds to realize that the rabbit looked different now, leaner and running with her ears fanned back instead of flopping at the sides of her head, but that wasn't a reason to stop running. She was hungry. A meal was in front of her. And she wanted it. She was scouting far out in front of the *Posse Comitatus* line in hopes of finding just this kind of opportunity. And she had stowed her chain mail in her backpack so it wouldn't get in the way if some fast sprinting was needed.

After they had run another thirty yards, Aliyah realized she wasn't gaining on the rabbit as fast as she had before. Frustrated, she kicked on an extra burst of speed. They were headed for a grove of ancient yew trees. As they drew near, she could see a number of dark and light shapes moving around under the trees. Raccoons? That was strange. Why were there so many, and why were they outside their thorn fortresses?

Aliyah had been horrified when her family had killed and eaten the raccoons near the Spires who had been her childhood friends. But now, many days and many missed meals later, her feelings about the new policy were not so clear cut. Some raccoons were friends. Some raccoons were not. Some she loved. Most she did not. Was she responsible for every raccoon in the world?

She was hungry. She realized she was starting to salivate as she ran. A raccoon would be a solid meal, much more than a rabbit. Still, the dark eyes of her cherished young friends haunted her.

As she drew near the grove, the lean brown rabbit veered away to the right suddenly, headed for a patch of bramble. She let it go and ran straight on toward the raccoons, still undecided as to what she would do exactly.

When she was twenty five yards away, a smallish white rabbit popped up near a tree root and yelled, "Wolf! Run for your lives!" then vanished. The raccoons, startled, turned to see her and then hurled themselves toward the trunks of the yew trees. An instant later, their claws were tearing at the rough bark as they pulled themselves upwards to safety.

Aliyah sprinted forward, eyes scanning the chaotic jumble of moving targets. Deciding she would claim her prerogative, she picked a male who was a little slower than the others and made a beeline for him as he raced toward a nearby yew. His short legs were pumping frantically, and as he threw a hasty glance over his shoulder, his eyes were huge and terrified in his black mask. The look in his eyes—the terror at the wolf as a *betrayer*—struck at her heart and slowed her steps.

Now he was scrabbling up the trunk. Aliyah was almost there, forcing herself ahead. But she found she was still uncertain and her next step was a stumble. The raccoon was shredding bark as he clawed his way upwards. Her leap at his back legs was half-hearted, and she was not surprised when her teeth snapped shut on empty space.

Her momentum carried her forward, and she hit the ground in angry snarling tumble, already second-guessing her decision. She had missed her meal—and cemented an alliance that aimed to build the first ranged weapons on the planet in three hundred years.

AIDEN

Aiden fidgeted while Olympia faced the South Bank Conclave in a late-afternoon session in their usual bramble patch meeting spot. More than half the warrens in their territory had gone over to the radicals, who were now claiming that there was no Yah, and that Yah was a fiction invented by the Blessed Ones. And with the army of Blessed descending from the north in a solid wave, some people were whispering that it was the end of the world. Aiden did his best to quash that kind of talk, but he was beginning to wonder himself.

There was a line from a new text he kept hearing about, the *Book of Secrets*, that the Rememberers in the breakaway warrens were fond of quoting. He found that it rang often in his ears: *"The end of the world and the beginning of the world are one and the same."*

Bad, heretical thoughts kept poking at the edge of his consciousness. *What if we're on the wrong side?* What if he wasn't waging a heroic spiritual battle to preserve absolute truth received from a fierce but loving creator god? What if he was a foolish drone laboring to preserve a centuries-old rabbit hierarchy that was mostly focused on maintaining its own perquisites? Or worse, what if he was a pathetic toady, slavishly serving the will of the killers of his own people long after more nimble minds had seen the truth?

He pushed away the jumble of conflicting anxieties. *Think later. Let's just get this done.* He focused resolutely on the Presiding Spirit.

Olympia gazed out bright-eyed at the fifteen or so Rememberers who had come, each representing a true-hearted, Yah-fearing warren on the South Bank of the Shandy. In order to keep the numbers up, she had suggested they bring their acolytes as well, so there was a crowd of almost forty rabbits in attendance.

Olympia's ears were twined about with lovely tiny red flowers, and her back was dusted with golden pollen. "The recent correction to the Word that our dedicated teams of young folks have been carrying to every corner of our Conclave is just so beautiful, isn't it? No weapons. Now that's a message that brings knowledge to both the believer and the apostate alike. Wouldn't this world be wonderful if there were fewer weapons?"

Aiden, recognizing this as his cue, began a triple stamp and called out, "Thanks be to Yah." Some of the other Rememberers joined in.

"And like so many corrections from our Lord, we may be afraid there will be a price to pay. But you know?" Olympia clasped her forepaws together and smiled benignly. "There never is." She started to stroll through the assembled rabbits. "Like with Yah's Flowers. Some dark clouds among us predicted it would lead to a rash of Glorifications. But I have not heard of a single one. *Not one.*" She clapped her paws together. "Thanks be to who?"

"Yah!" called Aiden. The other congregants echoed him.

"Now," she bowed slightly. "Our Lord Yah has granted his unworthy daughter a revelation, a command, a promise."

There was an uneasy stirring in the group. Olympia raised her forepaws. "It is time for us to make our personal stands against the godless. That means me, you, my people, your people, need to do everything we can to usher this mistake into the ash heap of memory." She smiled benignly. "'Sabotage' is an ugly word, but it can be a beautiful act, when taken against those who are bringing the world into ruin. So let us send our faithful against the misguided ones at every place in their system." Her eyes tracked around the group. Some were nodding, others were murmuring. "Every structure. Every woven grating. Every stockpile." She lifted her forepaws to the heavens as she spoke over the anxious side chatter. "Let their foodstuffs be spoiled. Let their wells be poisoned. *Let their pages be destroyed.*"

"Let it be so!" roared Aiden, right on cue. It was important to guide the response.

Several more joined in, and soon the whole group was chanting together. "Let it be so!"

Olympia clasped her paws together in front of her face and looked skyward. "And the revelation contained such a wonderful, generous promise, that it could only have come to us because the Loved One asked for it on our behalf. So whichever of your people is drawn to consummate the will of our Lord will be granted direct passage to the Loved One in Paradise, without Glorification." She stopped and rested her paw on the shoulder of a young acolyte, who gazed at her earnestly. "No journey through the jaws of the Blessed, those fearsome angels of the Lord, but simply a happy lollop to the Lucky Fields."

There was an audible sigh, mixed with a quiet groan, that came forth from many throats. No rabbit was far from the terror of death.

"Yes," said Aiden, raising one paw. *Don't think about it. Just do it.* "Yes, Presiding Spirit."

"Yes," said the earnest young acolyte.

The yearning spirits there spoke as one. "Yes. Yes. *Yes.*"

ANASTASIA

It was evening at the bunker. Cicadas were singing. The raccoons were working with total focus. Some were busy cutting sections of yew, using the big two-person saw they had put together. They had to climb high into the ancient yew trees to find branches of the right size, and then they would cling to nearby branches as they worked. Others were shaping the wood using the planes, small saws, and other toymaker's tools. They worked using logs and small boulders as sawhorses.

It was hard. They had never done this before. There were many mistakes, false starts, dead ends. They just set the problem pieces aside and moved on to the next attempt as they labored diligently to create pieces of wood that matched the schematic the Readers had found.

Anastasia made one more circle of the perimeter. It had taken her hours to sort out what had happened, how the wolf had gotten so close without triggering alarms. And it required a lot of fancy talking to get the now highly motivated raccoons back into the workflow without them realizing they had been set up for an attack.

Also, now that the wolves had seen the bunker, they would certainly be back. So the crossbow construction would have to be moved inside as much as possible. She had put Freddie in charge of figuring out how the bunker doorway could be modified so that animals as large as raccoons could pass in and out, without leaving it wide open for attacks from predators. Their initial idea was a large version of the gratings system the Freddie had helped develop for the warrens, now scaled up for the larger raccoons.

Anastasia caught sight of Wendy munching dandelion leaves at the foot of an apple tree about fifty yards from the yew grove, and lolloped over to her. On the way, she sent Coriander and her guard off to a discreet distance. He was reluctant to leave her side, but she gave him the *go now* look and he nodded and moved away.

As Anastasia came near her Assault Leader, she started grazing, taking a moment to collect her thoughts. At last she said, "I know why you did what you did today, but we can't treat our allies like this."

Wendy glanced over at the busy swirl around the door of the bunker area and then back at Anastasia. Her scent was lumpy and unconcerned. "Raccoons working," she said. "All good."

"No," said Anastasia. "A raccoon could have died. That would have been a tragedy. And not just for them. It could have broken our alliance before we even got started."

Wendy gazed at her, dark obsidian eyes drinking in all the light. "*You* led woof on raccoons."

Anastasia took a deep breath. "Yes," she said quietly. "*After* I saved your life." She cocked her head. "You're welcome."

Wendy scoffed.

Anastasia looked over at the raccoons. "It was wrong of me to do that. I was mad, just like you." She nosed up a piece of windfall apple from under the leaf litter. "If I'd had time to think about what I was doing, I wouldn't have done it." She came close to Wendy and nose-bumped her flank. "Which is why you can't go off and do these things on the spur of the moment. We have to talk about it."

Wendy pulled up another dandelion leaf and bit it off. "I do what needed," she said with her mouth full.

"No," said Anastasia striving to keep her voice warm and conciliatory. "*You* could have died. *I* could have died."

"Everyone dies," said Wendy, and belched loudly.

Anastasia could not bite back her exasperated retort. "This isn't low-stakes brawling on an island of Readerless thugs. This is the big world." Her long brown ears flicked. "We might be able to bring freedom to the Million Acre Wood. But not if our Assault Leader is dead."

Wendy's eyes tracked into the middle distance where two nightjars were fluttering.

Anastasia lay down next to Wendy, pressing against her flank. It was the first time she had made such an intimate gesture. "You matter," she said. "And not just because you're a fighter with special skills." She nudged a fragment of apple toward Wendy's mouth. "There's a lot of affection for you here. You're not an outsider. You're a leader. You're a *friend*. People want to be near you. And not just Love Bug."

Wendy gave Anastasia a sideways glance, then waved her

big front paw. "Bah," she said, with a good-natured chuckle. Then she took a bite of the apple.

"I know," said Anastasia. "You're too tough to hear that. But maybe you can hear this. There will be so much killing needed when the golden army arrives. You will get all the fighting you want, I promise you, if you work *with* me."

Wendy looked at her without speaking.

Anastasia turned to face her. "I see you, Wendy Wendarian," she said. "Bringer of Death. Turner of Tables." Her scent was warm and bright. "You're my shadow. We're two halves of the same rabbit. Only you can make me strong enough to build a nation. Only I can lift you high enough to do all the killing you desire."

Wendy was still as stone.

"The only rules we have now are the ones we make for ourselves," said the Loving Auntie. "We can do this, you and me." She touched noses with Wendy. "But you must be with me. With me. *With me*." For a moment, she pressed her cheek against the side of Wendy's blunt face, her mouth tucked under the other's long left ear. "I will unleash you. Will you come with me and be my murder lord?"

Wendy's obsidian eyes glittered in the light of the early rising moon. She stared at Anastasia for a long moment, then jerked her head upwards in an aggressive affirming nod.

Anastasia felt a warm jangle run over her shoulders. "Then let us go forth, shadow sister," she said. "And be the destroying angels we were always meant to be."

Wendy's growl of affirmation silenced the nearby cicadas and wrapped around Anastasia like the warmest, coziest blanket in the whole world.

Chapter 14

The only real wolf is a hungry wolf.

—*Canid proverb*

DINGUS

Dawn was breaking. Dingus and the Ascending Squirrels had roamed far to the north and were now fifteen miles above the Narrows. It was now several weeks since the last time Dingus had referred to his torn print ad touting "...OGA FOR KIDS," since it was far too large to carry. So he was starting to get a little fuzzy on the details. But in the spirit of his new practice, he was moving forward with what bubbled up from within.

"Ah ... *ommm ... is where the heart is,*" intoned Dingus, as he began to flow through the poses of the sun salutation.

"*There's no place like ommm,*" responded the Ascending Squirrels as they followed him through the morning ceremony.

Dingus breathed slowly and deeply as he moved, but his

eyes tracked rapidly around the landscape. It was one of his natural squirrel behaviors that he had not yet been able to eradicate. From his perch high in a sugar maple, he was looking north at a series of rolling hills. Occasional lone crows were visible above the hilltops, which might mean the killer army was approaching. Dingus was unconcerned.

Then he shifted positions into downward dog. Far below, he could see members of a rabbit warren making frenzied last-minute preparations, rolling in melons and dragging in gourds of water from a nearby muddy stream. It looked like they hadn't been able to decide whether to stay and fortify or leave and become refugees, and were now hastily rushing through a lot of compromise measures.

And hanging on a branch above their warren, his sharp eyes made out the austere gray of a hornet's nest attached to a long, slender branch.

Dingus shifted into warrior pose and noticed that he could see elements of the killer army coming over the hill. The whirl of crows up and down the line was the most visible, and soon he could see ground animals as well, moving quietly through the trees, investigating likely spots where small creatures might have sited a nest or burrow.

At the sight of this, the rabbits below abandoned their gourds and melons and fell to filling in their entry holes with new earth, stamping it to make it is tight as possible.

Dingus felt a riffle of concern run through the Ascending Squirrels around him. He considered moving, but then thought better of it. Non-attachment to outcomes was the goal. There was no escaping the harsh realities of the world.

He moved into plank pose. Now he could see a boogle

of weasels slipping through the brush, pushing out ahead of the killer line. Among them was a white female who looked familiar. His eyes flicked down. There were no rabbits visible. They must be inside, racing to force more loose earth into their entryways. Soon, there would be nothing between them and half a dozen weasels but a few feet of soft earth.

Dingus grimaced. He felt the wave of unease disturbing the squirrels around him. A moment later, his youngest acolyte, Boing, was standing behind him. Her mouth came close to his ear. "Namaste," she whispered. "I'm feeling a little attached to this outcome."

"Caring is erring," said Dingus, irritably, as he made the sign of the eternal zero with both hands.

"I know," murmured Boing. "I'm your worst student." She leaned around so she could look him in the eyes. "I'm feeling very weak today," she said, as she balanced on one foot, arms outstretched. "I'm sorry, Ogarishi."

Dingus closed his eyes. "You will do what you must."

She turned and flowed down the trunk of the tree like quicksilver. Dingus intended to rest his eyes on the treetops in the middle distance, but instead he found himself sneaking glances downward.

Boing zipped down the tree trunk and toward the soggy streambank, keeping the scrub around the base of the maple between herself and the approaching weasels. Then she dashed to the stream and rolled along the edge of it, picking up a thick coating of clay and mud. Moments later, as the weasels drew near, she was scurrying back toward the trunk of the maple.

The weasels arrived at the warren and noticed the holes filled with soft earth. They flicked the soft dirt with their paws, and suddenly Dingus could see many grinning mouths filled with white spikes. The weasels fell into a jolly high-stepping dance, undulating their long bodies as they improvised this song.

> *"Many little bunnies, hey, where are they?*
> *I see bunnies in the cold, cold clay*
> *Tell me now, sister, what do you see?*
> *Bunnies in the earth for you and me"*

Now the weasels were strutting in a circle, engaging in a group high-five on the offbeat. Their forepaws flashed in and out of the center of the ring. As the rest continued with the next verse, the white weasel began singing "yummy yummy yummy bunny," in a sprightly counterpoint.

> *"Many little bunnies so warm and sweet*
> *I see bunnies laying at my feet*
> *Tell me now, sister, what shall we do?*
> *Dig up pretty bunnies for me and you"*

With all the noise they were making, the weasels didn't notice Boing scampering up the far side of the maple tree. They didn't hear her gnawing away at the slender limb that the hornet's nest was attached to. And they didn't see a few of the hornets come out to investigate the vibration, briefly swarming Boing's body, before being stymied by her mud and clay coating.

But when the limb cracked and the hornet's nest fell down on top of them, they noticed that *immediately*. The hornets swarmed out in a great rage and instantly laid into the first living creatures they saw. The weasels shrieked and bolted away in all directions, as fast as their stubby little legs would carry them. With his finely tuned ears, Dingus noticed the Doppler effect dropping the pitch of the weasels' continuous "*Eeeeeeeeeeeeeeeeeeeeeee!*" as they ran, each in their own cloud of hornets.

Boing came gliding up the tree trunk still wearing her clay armor. Dingus gazed at her, musing as she climbed. This was what was so seductive about getting invested in outcomes. Helping create a good outcome made you feel ... glorious.

He welcomed her back with a nod as she took her place with the other Ascending Squirrels, assuming the lotus position and resting the forefinger of her right paw on the living wood.

And when the main line of the killer army arrived, an hour later, it parted like the Red Sea had once parted in the dreams of the Dead Gods, and flowed around the hornet's nest at a *very* respectful distance.

As the old rabbit proverb had it: *Even the wolf bows to the wasp.*

Aliyah

Aliyah found Sephora with the tactical team. They were in a field of sunflowers just behind the *Posse Comitatus* line, which was now about twelve miles north of the Narrows, still moving at about a mile a day. It was a busy command post. Crows were flying in from all directions, bringing news, scouting reports, questions, messages.

Grammy Kark was triaging incoming communications, sending crows to several different wolf and coyote administrators as they came in. Sephora was surrounded by eager black shapes, flapping and cawing as she listened and fired off responses.

"Where's Alaric?" snapped Sephora, as soon as she saw Aliyah. "He's supposed to be helping with this."

"I don't know," said Aliyah, nuzzling against her mother's golden fur.

Sephora paused and looked at her for a moment. "I thought he was with you."

"I'm sure he's doing something helpful," said Aliyah primly.

Grammy Kark scoffed. Sephora looked irritated.

"I saw something interesting," said Aliyah. "Down below the Narrows. The raccoons are definitely working with the criminal elements now."

Sephora frowned and looked down for a moment. "I guess the news got out about the new policy."

"I guess it did," said Aliyah, keeping her voice carefully neutral.

Sephora looked disgusted. "Might have thought they'd be more grateful after all we did for them for the last hundred years." She blew out a sharp breath between pursed lips and cocked her head. "What are they doing?"

"Not sure. But they had a lot of Dead Gods stuff scattered around," said Aliyah. "The raccoons treed up when I got close. Then the rabbits and mice ran into this weird square hill." She shrugged. "I couldn't get in. The opening was too small."

A new wave of crows was arriving, all with messages to share. Sephora looked through them at Aliyah. "Take a team. See what you can find out," she said, over the rising hubbub. "The raccoons joining the criminals isn't *necessarily* a problem, but…" She glanced at the *Posse Comitatus* line a few hundred yards away. "It is an escalation."

"Can I take the eviction tools Frippery has been working on?"

"Yes, yes," said Sephora, already distracted. "When you get a chance to try them out, send a crow. I'll join you."

"Okay." Aliyah turned away, thinking about who she should take with her.

"Oh, and darling," Sephora called after her.

Aliyah turned to see the Peace Leader framed in a perfect cyclone of crows. "Yes?"

"I love you."

NICODEMUS

The raccoons worked away at the crossbows with a will. They had discovered that, by working in teams, they could use larger woodworking implements as well as the smaller ones.

So Nicodemus arranged for several tools from the straightstone burrow, which had been set aside as useless because of their size, to be hauled across the river and many miles north to the bunker. Once the raccoons had these tools in hand, the rabbits and mice were amazed at how fast they worked.

Most of the inside of the bunker was now given over to the workshop, with just one room reserved for the living map, and another room where everyone slept. Freddie had the pages with the original drawings laid out on a large flat stone. And there was a constant stream of raccoons, consulting and adjusting.

Freddie received the newly created parts and checked them against the idealized forms that lived in his mind. Then he sent them to the craftmice, who smoothed the surfaces with sandstone pieces from a nearby outcropping. They made many fine corrections as they fit the pieces together.

Since the rabbit Readers lacked the hands to help during all this crafting, Nicodemus sent them out in teams with squirrels to hunt for the stickiest resins. Together, they looked high and low and finally figured out that cedar was the best resin for the crossbows. It was sticky enough to hold parts in place but would allow pieces to be repositioned if sufficiently warmed with body heat.

The crossbows themselves would be far too large for any small animal to wield. They would be carried on travois and dragged into place like artillery. Freddie had worked out a way to have the stock of each crossbow mounted on a large coconut, balanced so that it was level when sitting on flat ground, but easily turned side to side and rocked forward and back. This would enable a racoon kneeling behind it to aim it easily without having to support the weight.

Nicodemus hoped the raccoons would be able to use these weapons. The raccoons seemed feisty but capable. If they would just stick to their work and learn what was needed, everything would go well.

The quarrels gave some trouble. Initially, Freddie had tried creating points based on the sharpstone point Anastasia had found, using seashell. But it was not heavy enough. When they tried early tests, with two muscular young raccoons whipping quarrels down the length of a wooden channel using agave twine, they found that the quarrels did not fly straight. Even with the feathers volunteered by songbirds attached with resin to make fins at the back end, the quarrels had a marked tendency to tumble in flight. In desperation, Freddie cannibalized some of their precious steel bite blades and turned them into quarrel points, but the thin metal did not have enough weight and still the quarrels travelled in a chaotic flurry.

One sunny afternoon, as Nicodemus was obsessively raking over the quarrel problem during afternoon feed, his mind wandered back to simpler times. In the old days, when he had been the Reader at Bloody Thorn Warren, he would often sit outside in the sun and play the ancient game of the northern rabbits, *Terre Soleil.* Daydreaming, he recalled the solid, heavy weight of the mineral game pieces as he picked them up and placed them in holes on the earthboard.

Every warren had at least one game set. There were even regional tournaments. So there were already supply lines set up to extract and deliver these mineral fragments. They were one of the few things the warrens had trade routes for, because the sources were rare and widely spread out.

He felt a tickly buzz at the base of his skull as he ran through the list of pieces in his mind: amethyst, pyrite, anthracite, jade. Maybe some of these could be useful? He took a deep breath and tried to relax into an impressionistic cross-referencing of game piece names with a lifetime of information morsels: fragments of Dead Gods lore, scraps of crumbling pages, snatches of jumbled songs, and scrambled bits of mythology from half a dozen religions.

Which of these were weapons? *Marble?* No. *Granite?* No. He tried many more. At last, an answer clicked into place. *Flint.* Yes. He felt a little light-headed as he stood up. Heavy. Sharp. The Dead Gods loved it. The numbers they had slain with it were beyond counting. *Pumice?* No. *Lignite?* No. *Chert.* Yes. Endless kisses of death, thrown from afar. Nicodemus found himself running back toward the songbird messenger post. *Agate*? No. *Limestone?* No. He felt another click. *Obsidian. Yes.* Edge like diamond. Destructor of empires. Maybe it could do it one more time. His heart was beating fast.

He found the messengers and sent out a stream of messages immediately, to *Sans Gloire* and many other warrens that he knew. *Send these stones now. Our lives depend on it.*

Dingus

Dingus sat in the lotus position on a low, wide branch of a spreading oak. The backs of his hands rested on his knees. Scattered around him were the Ascending Squirrels. After the close encounter with the killer army, Dingus had taken his students back toward the south. Now they were in the territory between the two enemy lines.

At the foot of the tree lay a dead raptor in an advanced state of decay. Dingus had chosen this tree because maintaining neutrality toward the objectionable smell would be good training in equanimity.

A few dozen yards away, six kits came out of the entrance of a warren he had not noticed previously. They were beautiful. One was orange tortoiseshell, her coat bright in the afternoon sun. The young buck behind her was all black with a splash of white on his forepaws. The third had an agouti coat that sparkled with silver fur tips. Two had honey-colored splashes over soft white bellies. And one was a stippled brown.

Even from a distance, Dingus could see the new, pink scars in the shape of a "Y" on their foreheads. The tight new skin reflected the sun and made the scars shine. No other rabbits came out. The warren looked as though it were largely deserted. Dingus knew that these must be Yah's Flowers, baby rabbits convinced to sacrifice themselves. He had heard that some *Sans Gloire* rabbits had been visiting these groups and putting some kind of tricky survival plan in place involving huggy holes. This far north, it was very unlikely these rabbits had been visited. They didn't look like they had a plan. They looked like they were in a trance. They were probably outliers. Swept up in a half-baked idea and now left at the mercy of the winds of war. Just another tragedy waiting to happen.

Dingus grimaced. Outcomes. Outcomes. Outcomes. Would they never stop calling out to him? He wanted to enter a calm place without fear. Without care. Why was that so hard?

The kits began to crop the leafage around them. After a quick meal, they formed a circle on the grass. The tortoise-shell doe sat up tall and spread her paws. "Holy day," she said.

"Every one a gift," said the others.

The tortoiseshell doe nodded to the black-and-white buck, who sang in a sweet boyish voice.

"Oh, how I love my Blessed One
My Blessed One loves me
Together we shall live in love
And I will never flee."

Aliyah

Aliyah stood hidden in a scrubby grove on a small hill, two hundred yards north of the singing kittens. She was wearing a backpack carrying her eviction tools and her armor. And she was surrounded by the team of hunters she had brought with her to investigate the raccoons: Tennyson, Gaetan, and the two foxes from the South Shandy who had been the criminals' first victims, Juliette and Isadore. With her sharp ears, she could easily hear the singing, carried on the breeze.

> *"As Flowers of our loving Yah,*
> *We shine bright like the sun,*
> *Yah holds us in his heart with love,*
> *And we will never run."*

"What *is* that?" asked Gaetan, peering through the foliage.

"Just a little Summerday magic," said Aliyah, with a small smile.

Tennyson, who had been initiated into the mysteries of the editable Word of Yah a few weeks before, smirked a bit.

Gaetan squinted. "What does that even mean?"

Aliyah ignored him. "Watch this." She turned and stepped out of the cover into the sun. The others followed her. Aliyah's golden coat caught the sunlight and burned like a beacon. The rabbits stopped singing suddenly. She chuckled, "A little shine always shuts them up."

The singing slowly picked up again. The kittens did not run, did not move.

"Well, smack me," said Juliette. She turned to Aliyah. "*You're* making this happen?"

"As the Landlords, we do our best to serve everyone," said Aliyah.

Juliette scoffed and snickered at the same time. "Girl," she said. "I'll have whatever you're having."

"That's Lady Aliyah Summerday to you—" began Gaetan, but Aliyah waved him off.

"What's really amazing," she said, "is that as we get closer, they still won't run."

"We're only harvesting criminal warrens," said Isadore. "Naturals we have to leave." He whined with hunger and excitement. "These seem unusual. Are they criminal?"

"They look like criminals to me," said Juliette, as she explored the gaps between her teeth with her tongue. "Shifty. Loitering. Walking on the grass."

"We haven't seen the evidence," said Isadore. "No weapons, no fortifications."

"Natural rabbits would never sit like that after they've seen us," said Juliette.

There was a pause. Aliyah knew they were all waiting for her to make a ruling. She enjoyed making them fidget. After a moment, she said, "This is a new teaching from Yah. What a wonderful god he is."

"How do you know that?" asked Gaetan.

"I prayed about it," said Aliyah.

Tennyson giggled.

"Six half-grown lunchmeat. That's a reasonable rent payment, whether they're natural or criminal," said Juliette.

"Let's see if they have any other hymns for us," said Aliyah, sitting down and yawning ostentatiously.

Juliette took a few steps toward Aliyah and murmured into her ear. "You know what happened to me." She rubbed the long white scar across her neck. "I deserve this payment."

Aliyah turned her head and looked at Juliette with her leaf-green eyes. "The wolf is a creature of love," she said, smiling. "When the time comes, why don't you take two, cousin?"

DINGUS

Dingus sat still as a stone on his wide oak branch gazing at the band of killers in the middle distance as the kittens sang below. He had heard the *Sans Gloire* rabbits talking about Yah's Flowers many times over the past few months. He knew what was coming next.

Out of the corner of his eye, he could see Boing squirming as she sat in the lotus position. A few moments later, he saw her come slipping along the branch toward him.

"Ogarishi… " she said.

Dingus gazed at her in silence. His scent was bright and shimmery. At last, he said, "I'm feeling a little weak today." Then he arced to his feet, quicksilvered around her on the branch, and flickered himself down to the base of the tree. He knew the Blessed Ones would be here soon. The window of opportunity was narrow.

Dingus cast about for tools and his eye fell upon the body of the dead raptor. Inspiration came quickly. He scraped his hand along the front of the body, picking up a generous handful of maggots. He hesitated for a fraction of a second, then smeared them across his face and chest. The remaining few he wiped along the length of his tail.

Then he dashed toward the baby rabbits, and in a matter of seconds he was a few feet from them. They sat like statues. Only their mouths moved as they sang. In their eyes, Dingus could see that special glaze that comes when you are working as hard as you can to make yourself believe something. He knew that glaze.

He took a deep breath and flung himself in the middle of them, reeking of death, his voice twisting into the high whine of nails being dragged across slate. *"I am the Infernal Face Eater Shart From The Seventh Arse Of The Dread God Yah,"* he screeched. *"You have offended me. Leave me at once or I shall tear your faces from your living skulls."*

The rabbits stared in shock. He extended a single shaking finger, pointing south. Then he flew among them, nipping their cheeks and noses, flinging maggots in all directions.

The young rabbits had been prepared for an abstract experience ushering them into the presence of a loving god. They were not prepared for a highly specific monstrosity shrieking credible threats while he peppered their faces with flecks of spittle.

An instant later, they took to their heels, heading south toward the Shandy and the relative safety of the Free Peoples.

Dingus stood, breathing hard, with a sound like a chuckle and a sob fighting its way out of his throat. There was no place nearby to wash. He threw a glance toward the hunters. They were milling around a little looking confused. They must be wondering where the rabbits had disappeared to. Which meant they would likely be covering the intervening two hundred yards in the next few tens of seconds.

Dingus dashed back to the tree and stood on the wide low branch, scraping off his maggot passengers. Several of the Ascending Squirrels came toward him, including Boing. She began the gesture of respect, but he stopped her.

The sound of snarling hunters arose from below the tree, as the canids beat the bushes looking for the vanished rabbits.

"On some days, the student is the master," he said. He turned and looked down at the killers below. "Ah, chek."

ANASTASIA

The stakes were high, the deadline was short, and there was a steady increase in the carping and infighting happening among the work teams. Anastasia decided it would be good to have a night of chatting and bonding, so she had arranged with the raccoons to have several travois of the finest fermented apples brought in.

The rabbits, raccoons, mice, squirrels, and songbirds all tucked in with a will. After some noshing on treats and sampling the very fine Black Gaias and Hokutos this part of the Wood was known for, the conversation began to be a little less about banter and a little more about people finding out what they really wanted to know.

"You know, I don't get rabbit names," said Lorazepam, as she leaned back against Wellbutrin, licking boozy Hokuto mush off her fingers. "Why is your name 'Anastasia Bloody Thorn' even though you live at Warren *Sans Gloire*?"

Anastasia laughed. "I guess that does seem weird," she said. "For rabbits, your last name is the warren where you were born. You have it for life."

Wellbutrin leaned forward. "Even if you're, like, on the outs with that warren?"

"Yup," said the Loving Auntie.

"Okay, okay," said Death Rage, leaning on a walnut with her helmet a little askew. "Why do raccoons have such strange names, instead something normal like 'Throat Punch' or 'Skull Crusher?'"

"Or 'Fluffy?'" asked Love Bug.

"Or 'Steve?'" added Freddie.

Wellbutrin put his hand over his heart. "You read me, dude. Every morning I wake up with a tear in my eye because my dear old mam didn't name me 'Murderizer.'"

All the raccoons chuckled. Lorazepam broke off a hefty chunk of Black Gaia and slurped it. "It's because of our history, honey," she said. "Back during the Dominion, when the Dead Gods were crushing everyone else, they *loved* raccoons."

Wendy scoffed and belched a hefty cloud of Gaia mist. "Bah."

"No, it's true," said Wellbutrin. "They would put out food for them every night, in these special chewystone containers. And when the raccoons came to the feast, they would play music for them."

"I haven't heard that," said Nicodemus.

"I'm serious, bruh," said Wellbutrin. "It was mostly *a capella* with a rhythm accompaniment. They would improvise nonsense lyrics like 'Scat' and 'Gwanbeatit' and do these awesome polyrhythmic solos on small metal drums. A very hip dining experience."

"I have no idea what you're talking about," said Anastasia.

"Those were peak raccoon times," said Lorazepam,

throwing back another handful of Hokuto. "They were living their best lives. We still tell stories about it. And the thing is, in with the food, there was always candy. And some of it was very special: mind candy."

"It was totally radical," said Wellbutrin. "Not just for your belly. It would make your whole mind and body feel different. Kinda like dirty apple, but much more so."

"After the Winnowing, all that stopped," said Lorazepam. "The Dead Gods were gone. No more candy. But some of the best ones became family names."

"There has been a 'Wellbutrin' in my family for a hundred and sixty-three generations," said Wellbutrin proudly, leaning back and lacing his fingers behind his head.

Lorazepam patted his leg. "And when we have cubs, one of our girls will be a new little 'Lorazepam.'" She smiled. "Since I go by 'Pam,' we'll call her 'Azzie.'"

FREDDIE

A steady stream of flint, chert, and obsidian was flowing north from the ninety-six Free Warrens near the Shandy River. Holly and Yasmin were making the gathering and transportation of these minerals their management priority. And the mouse artisans from Musmuski Grove reached out to their kinfolk who lived at the base of the Boreal Cliffs and were known for working with stone. They had never heard of arrowheads, of course, but making sharp edges through the art of knapping was a skill they had practiced for many generations. Freddie had figured out that at least six hundred quarrels would be needed in order for each crossbow to be able to fire twenty times. The stone-crafting mice came in their hundreds, biceps bulging, bringing their heavy tools with them.

Now an entire room in the bunker was given over to making arrowheads, all modelled on the example they had found. The stone mice sang in a lusty, rumbly baritone as they worked on their points, striking their heavy hammers in time to the music. The wood mice provided a graceful tenor and alto counterpoint as they shaped the quarrel shafts and attached feathers volunteered by songbirds to create the fletching. In the nearby rooms, they could hear the raccoons engaging in their own kind of music as they worked: a light riffle of sniping over a foundation of testy banter.

Now, after eleven days, they had a working prototype, with its coconut base resting on a patch of flat earth.

Freddie gathered all the team members outside at the firing range they had set up to watch the first test. A raccoon lay down on each side of the crossbow, rested their feet on the bow, and used their forepaws to pull the string back and cock it. A small cheer arose as they dropped a brand new quarrel into the slot.

Freddie made a short speech, thanking everyone. Then Wellbutrin approached the weapon and gingerly put his right hand on the stock with his finger on the trigger. His left hand lightly held the foregrip. He leaned forward and squinted at the watermelon they had set up as a practice target. The crossbow moved easily, supported by the coconut.

Wellbutrin took a deep breath, held it, and squeezed the trigger. The quarrel, guided by its feather fletching, leaped forward when the trigger was released and sank deeply into the earthen backstop several feet above the watermelon.

"Good, solid shot!" called Freddie. "This machine *works*." All the animals cheered and clapped. They cocked the crossbow a second time, and Wellbutrin took another shot. Again the quarrel missed the watermelon and sank into the dirt behind it. The cheers were a little lighter this time. "Totally normal," said Freddie. "We're just getting the hang of this."

Then Adderall stepped up, offered a bit of jovial "lemme-show-you-how-it's-done" bluster, and sank a quarrel into the earth. Then another. Then another.

Then Lorazepam tried, followed by a string of other raccoons.

Over the course of the morning, as they fired deadly quarrels at the watermelon from thirty yards away and the plump fruit sat in perfect innocence and health, they slowly realized the flaw in their plan. The raccoons were terrible shots.

Chapter 15

We love the little animals of the Million Acre Wood.
They are just as delicious as the big animals.
                                        —Sephora Summerday

YASMIN

Now that almost a hundred warrens had joined the alliance,
the Free Warrens Council meeting had far outgrown the meeting chamber in *Sans Gloire*, so Yasmin and Holly were sitting
with the bunny representatives in a big circle in the shade of a
large elm. A small team of Reading acolytes were taking it in
turns to make notes on large pieces of bark from a paperbark
tree.

There had been a number of disturbing incidents.
Everyone looked very serious.

"For us, it was spoilage," said the representative from
Green Ivy Warren. "We discovered at least fifteen of our

melons had been chewed open and left to rot. And this late in the season, those can't be replaced."

"Seems like we may have had poisoning in our seepage well," said the delegate from Warren *Feu de Lune*. "A number of bunnies got sick after drinking. We're not dependent on it yet, so we were able to drain it and refill, but…" he grimaced. "It's scary."

"Two days ago, we discovered the lashings in one of our side door gratings had been weakened," said the rabbit from Bright Shoal Warren. "Chewed almost through, and then the damage concealed with torn pieces of agave twine." She looked around the circle, her long honey-colored ears flicking. "We're close to the river, so we're on the front lines of the South Shandy. If the killer army does cross, Bright Shoal is one of the first places they'll hit. With weasels."

The black-and-beige bunny from Warren *Orléans* stood. "The scariest thing about this is that no one ever sees anyone suspicious. That means it's almost certainly being done by rabbits."

"Yes, our own people are doing this to us," said the delegate from Burnt Rose Warren. "That's the worst."

Yasmin and Holly shared a glance. Then the Captain of the Home Guard took a deep breath and stood. "*Angra Mainyu*[24] is upon us," she said. "These are not our own people. They may look like us, but they are *not* us."

"Why would rabbits do this to rabbits?" asked the bunny from Stone Pile Warren.

---

[24] Destructive Spirit.

Yasmin shrugged and lifted her left forepaw. "They probably believe attacking us is the best way to help themselves. Or maybe killers are whispering in their ears that they'll be spared if they fight on the side of the big teeth." She chewed a foreclaw. "We have no way of knowing for sure."

"But we can take action to protect our people," said Holly, Steward of the Free Peoples. "And here's what we propose: A password that changes daily. Door Wardens will challenge everyone going in or out. How does that sound?" The idea passed by a voice vote.

"Next item," said Holly, stepping forward. "We need to work as a group to keep the flint, chert, and obsidian moving north as fast as possible." She thumped her left forepaw onto her right as she spoke. "Stars above, we need to make this clear to everyone. More pointystone going north means fewer killers coming south. It's that simple."

CORIANDER

Coriander was taking a rare nap away from Anastasia in one of the many side chambers of Warren *du Nord* when he heard someone enter. He looked up and saw Sunbeam, her green eyes bright in the gloom. "You're a Rememberer, right?"

Coriander sat up and wiped sleep from his eyes. "Yes," he said.

Sunbeam sat down next to him. "Anastasia says that Yah is dead now, but my Mommy says that Yah loves us."

Coriander touched noses with her and kissed her forehead where her scar tissue 'Y' was still bright pink. "Yah is not dead," he said softly. "Our understanding of Yah can change, and sometimes people make mistakes, but Yah himself can never die."

"Okay," said Sunbeam doubtfully. "But why does Anastasia say that?"

Coriander pulled his left ear down and cleaned it. Then he looked at Sunbeam. "Your sister is a very special bunny. She is on a journey, and not everyone can see she where she's going."

"Can *you* see where she's going?" asked Sunbeam.

Coriander looked at her for a long moment. "Sometimes I think I can, but other times…" He trailed off. "I do know this: I will do my best to keep her safe as long as there's life in me." He stood up and smiled. "And every day, we should take every chance to serve our Lord." He nuzzled her cheek. "Now, are you all packed up? You know we're leaving soon. The killer army is getting close. Soon it won't be safe here anymore."

"I know," said Sunbeam.

"Go find Mabel and ask her to sing one of her new songs about Yah for you," said Coriander, as he started gathering items for his backpack. "She'll like that."

"Do you have any new songs?" asked Sunbeam.

"No," smiled Coriander.

"Why not?"

He cocked his head and looked up at the earthen ceiling. "I haven't decided what I'm going to say yet."

FREDDIE

A storm was blowing up over the crossbow firing range. The sacrificial watermelon still sat, green and sassy, almost unscathed. One quarrel had succeeded in delivering a glancing blow which had cut a chip out of one side.

Freddie, Wellbutrin, and Lorazepam sat watching the different raccoons come up to the prototype crossbow that had been set up and try their luck. Freddie was frowning and resting his chin on his front paws.

"See, for me a least," said Wellbutrin, "when I'm holding the stock, I'm thinking about all those gnarly killers racing toward me. And if I miss, it's going to take them about ten seconds to cover the ground between us and sink their teeth into my throat."

Lorazepam reached out and patted his hand, then she turned to Freddie. "I think I'm trying too hard," she said. "My hand jerks right when I'm pulling the trigger. I guess I'm just scared, bruh."

A welter of leaves blew by. There was a cool breath of fall in the air. A bright flicker in the tree above him caught Freddie's eye, and he looked up to see Dingus shining as he stood on the tip of a branch just above Freddie's head, balanced on one foot, leaning forward. His other foot was stretched out behind him, his tail high and swept back, and his arms spread wide. He looked not unlike the hood ornaments once loved by the Dead Gods.

The rising wind blew hard, rocking the branches. But no matter how the tree moved, Dingus remained in his position, steady as a gyroscope. There was a quicksilver twinkle, and the tree was filled with squirrels, each standing just like Dingus in perfect stances while the tree thrashed beneath them.

"Hi, squirrel formerly known as Dingus," said Freddie.

"Greetings, fellow traveler," said all the squirrels in

unison, in beautiful shiny voices, as their bodies rode the gale without being affected by it.

"The *was-ness* of Dingus is now more *is-ness*," said the squirrel who was perhaps currently Dingus.

"The journey from *was-ness* to *is-ness* arrives at the mystery of *now-ness*," intoned the squirrels, their unison smoothly dividing into drone harmony, their graceful poses serene and unchanged while gusty blasts of cool air swirled dead leaves around them.

By now, all the raccoons were staring at the squirrels with their mouths open. "Whazzat?" said Adderall. "Either these squirrels are freaking me out or I'm tripping nards."

"Between the ice dream of equanimity and the hot fire of intention," said the probable Dingus. "We find life." He gestured to the other squirrels. "These wise ones, my teachers, have led me."

The squirrels continued their harmonies. "*We ... choose ... life.*"

"What are you saying?" asked Freddie, his breath coming faster.

"Ask, friend, and it shall be done," said Dingus.

Freddie felt a buzzing in the back of his head. "Could you balance on that crossbow and hit a target?"

The flickering happened again, and three of the quicksilver squirrels appeared on the crossbow. Two stood on the arms of the bow, while Dingus stood on the track where the quarrel lay, not far from the trigger. He reached down and touched the quarrel's obsidian point. Then the squirrels all took up wide stances with bent knees, arms outflung. Gracefully, they shifted their weight, causing the crossbow nose to fall, rotate to the left, then sweep back to the center. They shared a glance and began to surf the crossbow as a team, moving it smoothly in graceful arcs.

Dingus called to the others in a language Freddie did not recognize. A moment later, the nose of the crossbow began to rise as Dingus stepped backwards. Then he did a backwards somersault off the crossbow track. Without his weight, the nose fell swiftly, and he flicked the trigger as he fell past it.

The arms of the bow snapped forward, and the quarrel raced through the air, burying itself in the thick belly of the watermelon. The rabbits, raccoons, and mice all cheered. The air flickered again, and Dingus was standing in front of Freddie. He sank into the lotus position and closed his eyes.

"Ah, chek."

CORIANDER

Coriander was on the greensward in front of Warren *du Nord*'s main entrance practicing bite blade lunges when he heard the songbird sentries who were maintaining the far perimeter come racing toward the warren. "Killers! Killers! Killers! Five canids. Five weasels. Coming now!"

A group of that size sounded like a probe. Their fortifications should handle this with no problem.

As Coriander started to fall back toward the nearest warren entry hole, the squirrels on the near perimeter took up the call, amplifying it. Within seconds, every creature within a hundred yards of the warren had heard the alarm and was moving toward safety.

He reached the main entrance just as Anastasia came up

the passageway from inside. She was looking around, just making a quick visual check before retreating behind the wooden gratings and pulling them up into position. Coriander touched noses with her and was about to start moving down the ramp, when he heard Anastasia's sharp intake of breath. "Look!"

Coriander turned to see Sunbeam sitting quietly on the grass, fifty yards from the entrance. She was looking in the direction of the killers. He was confused. How did she not hear? He started yelling, then he heard Anastasia groan, "She's one of Yah's Flowers. She's doing that thing. Not running."

"But she knows that's over," said Coriander. "I mean, right? We told everyone." A bad tickle crept up his spine. "I'm sure she—" His stomach clenched. What had he said to her the day before, as part of the youth-group patter that he kept doing out of habit? *Every day, we should take every chance to serve our Lord.*

"Oh, my Yah," he murmured.

"Sunbeam!" shouted Anastasia. "Come in, honey! You don't have to do that now!"

Sunbeam did not move. Other rabbits were shouting from other holes, and the squirrels as well, creating a cacophony of noise. Anastasia tried to dart out the doorway, but Coriander threw himself in front of her. Shocked and frantic, she bit his right shoulder. He yelped but would not move. "You can't go," he said, pushing against her. "Too dangerous."

"Let me by!" shouted Anastasia. "I have to get her!"

"Not you," said Coriander, struggling to maintain his position. "Can't be you."

Anastasia continued to call out to Sunbeam, Wendy, Love

Bug, anyone, but her voice was lost in the general outcry. Some other rabbits were coming out of the holes and running part of the way toward Sunbeam, calling to her. But they were afraid to go too far when canids were so close.

Just then, a golden wolf stepped out of the bushes a hundred and eighty yards away, followed a second later by another golden wolf. They were just walking. They hadn't seen anything yet. Sunbeam was still as death. Anastasia threw herself against Coriander, scratching and biting. He absorbed the punishment without fighting back for a few seconds, gritting his teeth. He felt the blood trickling down his right side. Then he said quietly, "It's my fault."

"What?" shouted Anastasia.

He turned and locked eyes with her for an instant. "I'll be right back."

Then he was racing across the meadow, calling out Sunbeam's name. In a few seconds, he reached her and saw that she was half-gone, holding herself in place in spite of her terror, using the only tool she had, the Giving.

She was seven months old now, far too big for him to seize and drag. He forced himself to turn his back on the wolves that were moving toward him over the grass—maybe walking, maybe running—and planted himself right in her field of vision.

As he did, he heard a few familiar words coming from her mouth in a dreamy singsong.

*"Together we shall live in love
And I will never flee."*

"Sunbeam!" he shouted. "Run!"

Her golden fur shone in the bright sun, a perfect match for the golden wolves coming toward her. Her eyelids were almost closed, reducing her bright green eyes to mere slits of awareness. In a tiny voice, she said, "Father Yah wants me to stay."

Coriander's skin crawled with the urge to flee. He forced himself to sit still. How could he reach her? A heartbeat later, he was amazed to hear himself saying, in a shiny voice of great and loving authority, "*My child, don't you know who I am?*"

"No," she said. And he could see, through the slits of her eyes, that she was tracking some movement behind him. He knew what it must be but did not turn his head. He sat up straight and spread his front paws wide.

Sunbeam's eyes began to open. He could see the fear in them, the nearness of the wolves behind him, and the Giving overtaking her. He fought for her attention. "*I am the Loved One,*" he said. Her eyes tracked away from the wolves and locked onto him. His eyes burned. "Father Yah isn't calling you home now. You have too much to learn."

Her eyes were widening. Maybe she was coming out of her trance.

"Take this chance to serve your Lord. *Go,*" he said, with all the authority he could muster.

Sunbeam looked uncertain.

An idea came into his head. "*Anastasia needs you. Run!*"

That was the key that unlocked the lock. Sunbeam turned and bolted for the safety of the warren. An instant later, just as Coriander's back feet were just clawing the grass to launch his body forward, the jaws of a golden wolf closed around his body, lifted him in the air, and shook the life from him.

LOVE BUG

Love Bug heard the commotion and ran to the entryway nearest him. Looking out, he could see Sunbeam bolting toward the main entrance, with two golden wolves a few paces behind, one of whom held a dead rabbit in her jaws. And thirty yards further off, a mix of foxes, weasels, and a coyote. The weasels had some kind of bright jangle trailing after them.

He heard a terrible, guttural scream. It sounded like a doe, but he had no idea who it was. Inside the large central chamber of the warren, there was a storm of running and shouting rabbits and warmice.

Love Bug ran back into the underhall and saw Wendy barking orders to him and the other officers. For just a moment, he was struck by how strong and beautiful she looked, and how utterly calm and focused. If the free world was going to be depending on someone, he was glad it was her.

He gathered his entryway defense group, and they each grabbed a wooden spear tipped with flint, long ones for the mice and shorter staves fitted with bite grips for the rabbits. Then they ran to the wooden grating which lay flat in the tunnel. Love Bug and two other rabbits grabbed the cords attached to the grating with their teeth, and shuffled backwards, pulling the grating upright. When it was in place and blocking the passage, they wrapped the cords around stakes driven deep into the earth and then ran forward to help guard the grating. If all went according to plan, they would soon see weasels come down the entrance ramp, looking for easy kills.

Love Bug and his crew pushed their spears through the grating and waited, breathing hard, jaws clenched tight around the wooden shafts. Around the warren, the same scene was playing out at other entryways, Wendy at the main gate, and other officers at the others. The moment stretched out. Love Bug noticed a splinter on the spear he was holding sticking into his gums. He shifted his bite on the spear. The sound of the doe sobbing in the central space went on and on.

Then a strange sound came down the entry ramp. Not a softly padding weasel singing a killing song, but rather a clang and a shuffle, then the sound of loose earth being shoved forward. All the rabbits peered through the grating in the dim light. The clang, shuffle and scrunch came again. And again.

Then Love Bug saw a battered steel can heave into sight, filling most of the tunnel. He glanced at the other entryways, and saw cans creeping into sight in several others as well. The rabbits stared, eyes flicking from each other to the cans and back. Love Bug, Wendy, and any rabbits who had been at the straightstone burrow or the bunker recognized them as artifacts of the Dead Gods. The other rabbits had no idea what they were looking at.

The cans moved forward again, then again. They could hear hard breathing. Then Love Bug caught sight of a flash of fur behind the can near him and recognized it. *Weasel.* His heart rate jumped. What new terror were these slinky killers about to inflict?

Love Bug watched the can bang up to the wooden grating, and then there was a fumbling sound, and a piece of bent shinystone was pushed through a hole in the bottom of the can. It flailed around. Love Bug squinted. It was a hook, attached to a cord. The hook tapped against the grating. The rabbits and mice, all waking as though from a trance, started yelling and attacking the can with their spears. The stone points bounced off harmlessly.

The hook dropped for a few seconds, then suddenly leaped back into position. It was pushed through the grating, quickly slipped around one of the uprights, and then pulled tight. Love Bug and the other rabbits took turns attacking the hook with their teeth, but the cord attached to the hook was now pulling it hard. They could not move it, and they could not harm it.

For several seconds, the commotion quieted down. There was a deathly silence. Even the crying doe had stopped. Love Bug felt a dark hand squeezing his stomach. *What is this thing?* "Wendy," he shouted. "What do you think?"

"Killers are learning," rumbled Wendy.

Love Bug, trying to peer around the can, saw a flash of fur in motion. It looked like the weasel was retreating back up the tunnel. *Why leave now?*

Then there was a powerful jerk on the hook, and the wooden grating was pulled away from them, the heavy wooden staples fastening it to the floor slipping partway out of the ground. Instantly, the commotion started again, rabbits and mice yelling and biting furiously at the hook.

"Bite blades up now!" shouted Wendy. "Warmice, spear defense!"

ALIYAH

Aliyah strained against the cord she held in her teeth, pulling backwards away from the rabbit hole. Near her, she could see Sephora, Tennyson, and Gaetan pulling at their own cords. Further off, the smaller foxes, Isadore and Juliette, were pulling on a cord together. Each of the cords led into one of the entry holes of this criminal warren they had discovered.

Five weasels were prancing and leaping beside the holes they had just exited, and Frippery, the craftrat mercenary, was scampering among the holes, calling out instructions. No one even blinked an eye at the sight of a rat giving orders to Sephora, the Summerday Clan Mother, one of the most powerful creatures in the Million Acre Wood.

"Pull!" shouted Frippery. The canids inched backwards, paws pushing against the earth. Aliyah fell backward suddenly, losing her balance. After she had stumbled back a few feet, everyone could see the broken remains of the rabbits' wooden grating being dragged out of the hole, with the can hanging on the cord banging as it dragged over the ground.

A few moments later, Sephora's grating was torn free, and she took a few quick steps backward, dragging the broken mess of wooden staves up out of the ground. She turned and nuzzled Aliyah. "You were wise, child. New enemies demand new ideas."

"Just trying to keep the pack up to date," said Aliyah, laughing lightly. But inside she felt a cozy warmth at her mother's words.

"Help the others, please," called Frippery. "Timing is important." Aliyah and Sephora helped the foxes pull their grating out, then Tennyson and Gaetan pulled theirs free.

The weasels were spinning now and gradually coalescing around a killing song, in five-part harmony.

"Clever little bunnies, down in the dirt
Clever little bunnies in a world of hurt
Scared little babies, down in the gloom
Terrified babies in the murdering room."

Aliyah called to the weasels, "This is no natural warren. The evidence lies before us. The criminals are doing all they can to upend the peace of the realm." She looked at Sephora, who nodded. Aliyah stood tall, her golden armor shining in the afternoon light. "Go, and execute our judgement."

Frippery cleared her throat. "Sorry to butt in. Please take the end of the cord with you. There may be other items we want to pull out that would be too heavy for you. When you're ready for a pull, just give the cord three sharp jerks." Frippery bowed to Aliyah. "Third She."

Aliyah nodded, and then looked at the weasels. Two of them were swinging a cord like a jump rope, while the other three weasels were doing crisscross double-unders. "Don't forget to ask about the leaders," she said. "You know the names. Go on, cousins."

The weasels bowed. Then they each picked up the melody of their killing song and slinkied down the entry holes, humming quietly

The canids and the craftrat chatted for a moment about crime and punishment, and shared an unkind joke or two about the creepiness of weasels.

And then Aliyah heard what she had been waiting to hear: the distant sound of snarls and fighting, muffled by the carapace of earth. She looked at her mother and nodded, and Sephora smiled. They shared a moment. *Team Summerday, rising to meet new challenges.* Warren by warren, they were dealing with this contagion. Soon, it would all be taken care of.

The noise from underground went on for a bit. The canids lay down and yawned. This could easily go on for an hour with a large warren, with all the mopping up required. Juliette snapped at a passing butterfly. Sephora rolled on her back and lay in the sun.

Then the sound from the warren stopped. Aliyah looked at Frippery, who shrugged apologetically. This was not expected. Then she looked at the other canids. They had all heard the silence and were looking at her quizzically. It was an awkward moment.

Just then one of the cords was shaken by several twitches. Aliyah got up quickly. She seized the cord in her teeth and pulled. Whatever it was, it was surprisingly light. She jerked at the cord again, walking backwards. In a few seconds, the thing came into sight.

It was a large piece of paperbark, with lines of dark blood striped across it. They peered at it and realized the lines formed letters, smeared from being dragged up through the earth. Frippery, the best reader among them, spoke the words aloud: "'*Run while you still can.*'"

OLYMPIA

Olympia was out with the rabbits of Bloody Thorn Warren at evening feed. Bunnies of all colors were feeding and playing in the grassy meadow near the warren. She was lolloping among them, chatting, doing her best to ignore the dark lump in her guts that had been plaguing her since the visit with Tobias.

Aiden appeared and came near her. "Warren Mother? A word?"

She followed him to a secluded spot a few yards away. "Yes?"

"I've just been speaking with our eyes and ears at other warrens," said Aiden. "Your revelation has been successful in causing damage. Many answered the call."

Olympia nodded. "Yah is with us." She was smiling but her blue eyes were guarded. "And?"

Aiden groomed his shoulder. "It's been successful enough that the Yah-deniers have now started using passwords. That will seriously hamper our efforts."

Olympia frowned. Aiden interrupted her before she could speak. "One more thing." He blew out a long breath and looked at the ground. "I had a dream about Coriander last night. I think it was a *visite de décès*."[25]

Olympia's eyes widened for a moment, then she looked away. "That's just a superstition. It doesn't really happen."

Aiden continued as though he hadn't heard her. "He asked me if I was sure I was doing the right thing."

Olympia felt an ugly prickle start at the base of her skull. "Don't even start with that kind of defeatist talk." She leaned against his shoulder and pushed him behind a holly bush a few yards farther away from the feeding bunnies.

Aiden gazed at her. "It's only defeatist if we're not sure, right?"

Olympia felt the darkness rising within her. She fixed her blue eyes on him. "I'm sure."

Aiden looked away. "I'm not." He chewed a foreclaw. "We've done things ... that some people ... many people ... would consider bad." Olympia was silent. "We've attacked

---

[25] Death visit.

good rabbits who are just trying to help themselves. We've tried to kill innocent people." Aiden took a deep breath. "And we gave baby rabbits to killers to help our own warren."

"None of the Yah's Flowers have died," said Olympia quickly, eyes blinking. "It's a miracle. And that proves how much Yah loves us."

"You know that can't be true, Olympia," said Aiden softly. "And yes, even though by some amazing intervention deaths have been surprisingly low, that didn't happen *because* of us, it happened in *spite* of us." He took a few steps away from her. "For Yah's sake, we can't even imagine a world in which our god isn't ordering us to give our lives to the predators? What is the *matter* with us?"

The prickle was now climbing all over Olympia's back. Her breath was getting short. "Why now, Honored Rememberer? You were happy to whisper your clever ideas into my ears before—"

"I wanted to believe it was good," burst out Aiden. "I wanted to believe that our enemy was so terrible that anything we did was righteous. But after awhile, I just couldn't keep it up anymore." He stamped. "And this last 'correction' from Tobias. '*Don't make weapons*'? It might as well have been signed, '*With Love, The Wolves.*'" He put his face in his paws. "I became a Rememberer because I wanted to learn, I wanted to teach, I wanted to help." He blew out a breath. "I don't know what happened to that. I don't know how to get back to it, but it's not by doing this."

The cold gloom in Olympia's gut was making her shudder as Aiden spoke. She yearned to say, *Yes, I also am afraid I'm being swallowed by darkness*, but revealing that much about herself seemed dangerous. She had made a lifelong practice of presenting an impenetrable façade. So she said, "What are you saying?"

"I'm leaving Bloody Thorn," said Aiden, looking surprised at himself as he was speaking. And without another word, he turned and walked into the brush.

Olympia stared after him. She had thought her anger was at Tobias, and his relentless, ridiculous demands for his 'corrections' to be propagated through the South Bank Conclave. But now she realized her anger was at the whole system, reaching all the way up to the god who sat at the top and spoke the words that created their world.

She had never thought to sit in judgement on Yah, only to study Yah's creation in order to eke out any advantage she could use to keep her warren safe.

Finally, she murmured, "If Yah is the god of rabbits, we deserve better." The next thought was too awful to be spoken at all. *And if Yah is the god of wolves, we need a new god.*

The prickle shimmered across her entire body. *And Anastasia needs to live.*

Suddenly, she was running back toward the main entrance to Bloody Thorn, calling out, "Fufu! Fufu!"

Within a few moments, her red-and-gray robin appeared, fluttering through the thorns. "Yes, Mommy?"

"Darling, go find Sunbeam right now," panted Olympia. "And give her this message: Don't do it. *Don't do it.* Gather your special tools and come home."

Chapter 16

Big sky, little bird
Share that lovely song you heard
Big bird, little sky
Punch a raptor in the eye!
                    —Free Songbirds party chant

FREDDIE

The survivors of the Warren *du Nord* attack, together with
the other Free Peoples leadership, most of the raccoons,
several *Armée Libre* units, and hundreds of craftmice were
gathered on a gently sloping hillside near the bunker. The
songbirds hovered in branches overhead. Freddie was sitting in the front row, with Nicodemus, Wendy, Mabel, and
the Forward Readers. Love Bug and the Loving Auntie's
Guard were maintaining a wide perimeter. Lorazepam
and Wellbutrin were standing near a large Vegenaise jar

they had brought, keeping it carefully tucked under some bushes.

Anastasia stepped out in front of the crowd, resplendent in her golden Kevlar jacket and her *aluminum d'or* circlet on her head. Freddie could see that she had been crying.

"Seven heroes of the revolution gave their lives yesterday," she said. She paused for a long moment, then named them. "Coriander, Violeta, Half Moon, Yarrow, Blue Vine, Vere, Emilien." Anastasia bowed her head in silence, and the other animals followed suit.

The songbirds floated out a sweet, sad melody. There was some weeping from scattered rabbits in the crowd, and Anastasia let them be heard. After a few moments, she raised her head, a soft glow in her golden eyes. "These rabbits are our sisters and brothers. And they wanted to live." She looked down and dragged her claws through the cool earth. "We will memorialize them in the main underhall at Warren *Sans Gloire*. They are weasel killers, they gave their lives for freedom, and their names will never be forgotten."

Freddie felt so proud, watching her. So grand, so sad, so perfectly the rabbit for this moment.

She spread her forepaws and looked up at the sun. "Tell me who they are," she said quietly.

"Weasel killers!" cried the little animals.

"Tell me again," said Anastasia.

"Weasel killers!" shouted the crowd.

Anastasia thumped. "Let them hear you!"

"*Weasel killers!*" roared the assembly, all of whom had lost loved ones to the teeth and claws of hunters. And the outpouring tumbled into a wordless cry of victory, rage, and grief that went on for a full minute.

When it was over, Anastasia hopped up close to the edge of the crowd. "The pressing question now is: *What did we learn?* Weasels came down our tunnels, protected by hard-stone armor, and destroyed our fortifications with the help of wolves. What did we buy with the lives of our friends?" She leaned forward. "What did we buy with the most precious currency we have?"

There was confused shouting from the throng. The songbirds started to whirl. Freddie squirmed anxiously, unsure where this was going. Love Bug and Wendy shared a questioning glance.

Anastasia lifted her forepaw and quieted the animals. "When we started this, we were young. All we had was fear, and a tiny bit of hope." She shrugged. "And some dillweed." There was a chuckle from the rabbits in the audience. "And we—I—knew nothing."

Anastasia turned and looked at Wellbutrin and Lorazepam and threw a paw sign at them. *Come.* The two raccoons picked up the big *Vegenaise* jar and carried it out onto the turf near Anastasia. Bricabrac the craftrat was inside, along with a bedding of leaves and moss, and a small gourd of water. They set the jar on the ground a few feet from Anastasia. Bricabrac put his paws up on the glass, speaking quickly, earnestly, desperately. But the air holes in the lid of the jar let out only a muted sound.

Anastasia put a paw on the jar and looked out at the crowd. "I found a friend. He made this for me." She flicked out the Claw, and the blade shone in the sun. "He made me a killer, before I even knew I was a killer. And I loved him for that."

Bricabrac was darting around the jar now. He pressed against the glass, trying to speak to Anastasia. Freddie felt sick to his stomach watching him. He remembered the brash little creature who had come into their lives and armed the fragile fighting spirit of Anastasia.

The Loving Auntie of the Free Peoples looked out over the assembled throng as she tapped on the glass with her Dragon Claw. "There aren't any craftrats left in the Million Acre Wood now. They've all gone off to bigger and better things, in City of Oom, where little things like friendship don't matter." Her scent was dark and bitter.

Anastasia walked away from the jar. "So this rat sends his sister, who has full working knowledge of our fortifications, to work for the wolves. Which makes perfect sense, right? The Summerdays have moneystones like anyone else." Anastasia bellied down and for the first time looked at Bricabrac. "And we know how the world works. *Rats is for rats.*"

She stood and looked at the audience. "This treason cost the lives of seven of our friends yesterday. Good friends. Intimate … friends. Every one of them loved, and was loved, by someone. And this treason will cost countless more deaths in the days to come." She pushed against the jar. "What should we do with this traitor, Free Peoples of the Million Acre Wood?" She dragged her X-ACTO blade across the glass, creating a high, grating, whine.

A deep sound arose from the crowd of animals: a long descending groan that fell slowly down toward silence. No one had ever heard a rabbit talk like this. Bricabrac shrank back, the terror clear on his face.

Freddie was just a few feet from Anastasia. He sat up tall

to get her attention and raised his left paw, pads forward. *Stop.* Then he pressed both forepaws together. *Please.*

"What's the right thing to do here?" asked Anastasia, the claw slicing through the air as she talked. "For Coriander? For Violeta? For the others?" Freddie glanced at the shocked and saddened eyes of the animals around him and felt sick. He threw a rapid series of paw signs at Anastasia. *No. Stop. Stand down.*

"Open this jar," said Anastasia.

Wellbutrin ran toward her and unscrewed the top. Immediately, Bricabrac's voice could be heard, protesting, imploring. "Please, Honored One, I beg you. I didn't mean for it to happen like this—"

Freddie could not sit still any longer. He rose and moved toward Anastasia. "No," he said softly. "This isn't who we are, Loving Auntie."

Anastasia waved the raccoon away and leaned against the jar, the Claw scraping against the rim. Bricabrac was suddenly quiet.

The crowd of small animals, exquisitely attuned to the suffering of their peers, groaned again. A terrible descending chromatic slide laced with anxious tears.

Freddie came close to Anastasia and nuzzled against her cheek. From up close, her could see even more clearly that her eyes were red and swollen. He pushed his mouth close to her ear. "*This isn't you who you are, Anastasia.*"

There was a moment of silence that stretched on and on. She leaned against him. He felt a single dry sob move through her body and her warm tears on his fur. He kissed her forehead. She took a deep breath, held it, and exhaled slowly.

Then Anastasia turned and her gaze swept the crowd. "Is this what we're fighting for, to be like them?" She lifted her forepaw and flicked the Claw closed. "No. This betrayal has not shown us the worst in ourselves." She nodded at Wellbutrin, who ran forwards and screwed the jar lid back in place. "This betrayal has shown us *why we fight*."

Anastasia turned and walked away from the jar. Wellbutrin picked it up and carried it off to the sidelines. Freddie's head was swimming. He made his way back to his place by Nicodemus and crouched there, breathing hard.

"Enemies are everywhere," said Anastasia, steadying herself against a boulder. "A million generations of rabbits have brought us here. A million generations of mothers have had their hearts torn by fear of what will happen to their beloved baby bunnies, baby mice, baby squirrels, baby songbirds, and baby raccoons."

Nicodemus and Mabel raised a feeble call of ratification, followed by the crowd. Looking around, Freddie could see on the faces of the animals that they were relieved to be away from the terrible, dark vision of themselves.

Anastasia paced along the front of the assembly. "We fight to free not just ourselves, but a million generations to come."

A slow-building cheer rose up from the assembled animals, all hoping for a positive resolution. Freddie began a triple-thump, and a few others followed.

"Our battle with the killers is almost upon us," said Anastasia. "We cannot fail. Because now everyone knows what is possible." Her scent was bright and powerful.

The triple thump gained power.

"Even if we die, next month, next year, another Free

Army will rise." All the animals joined in the triple pulse of ratification with feet and voices. Freddie felt a wave of gratitude wash over him.

"It doesn't matter what we suffer. The world will change in a matter of days, and it will never be the same." The Loving Auntie leaped up on a boulder, paws outstretched. *"What are you fighting for?"*

"Freedom!" roared the assembly, home at last. *"Freedom!"*

GAETAN

The *Posse Comitatus* was just a couple of days above the Narrows now. The Summerday Clan had gathered for their nightly nuzzle. The wolves tussled and rolled and play-fought, gold wolf on gray wolf, their happy growls mixing together in a lavish display of family emotion. Even Micah Summerday, when he was not on stage, was often to be found rough-housing with the cubs, throwing himself down on his back to let the little ones play-bite him.

Gaetan stood, as he often did, at the edge of this rumpus, feeling awkward. Aliyah liked having him around the pack for some reason, even though he was clearly in the friend zone, but he didn't feel like that bought him a full entrée into the family. Also, like all the coyotes, he found the wolves a little embarrassing with their schmaltzy love and kisses. Coyotes didn't do that. Coyotes knew the world was a hard place, and acted accordingly.

Sephora trotted up out of the gloaming. "Any word of Alaric?"

Gaetan shook his head. "Sorry, no, Clan Mother."

Sephora frowned and bit her lip. "It's been almost a week. Where is that boy?"

The wolfy playtime broke up. Aliyah and Tennyson ran into the shadows under a nearby ombu tree, laughing. Gaetan watched them for a moment, then turned away. Micah came over to Sephora and nuzzled her. She licked his ears and he growled like a puppy and nudged her rib cage. Grammy Kark dropped in through the gathering night. "Golden children," she said, scratching at the dirt. "Always playing."

Gaetan had learned enough to know that when this old crow showed up, something important was likely to be discussed. He skulked around the edge of the conversation and casually lay down under a bush.

"Mother of my mother," said Sephora. "What have your wise old eyes seen this day?"

The ancient crow hopped a few times and looked at the golden wolf. "It's not what I have seen. It's what I have heard."

Micah lay down, exhaled in a way that he probably assumed did not sound irritated, and rested his aquamarine eyes on her. "Tell us, Grammy."

"The criminal rabbits are busy, clever little creatures," said the ancient crow to Sephora. "Just as you saw the other day with the armored weasels. Every time you counter them, they are one step ahead."

Micah cleared his throat. "We've cleared out most of the North Shandy," he said. "Almost nine hundred square miles. Every warren checked for contagion, criminal warrens killed. So far *one* warren has fought back against Aliyah's idea. I'd call that a win."

Grammy Kark fluttered her wings and kicked at the dry

earth. "Rumor has it that the criminals have new weapons that can kill from far away."

Gaetan's ears pricked up at this. Unlike most other canids, he had never had any difficulty believing the rabbits might do something new and dangerous.

The huge golden wolf scoffed and rolled onto his back. "Rumor also has it that rabbits can fly and breathe fire."

"Rumors from who?" asked Sephora.

"Songbird chatter," said the crow.

"Songbirds will repeat anything that rhymes," said Micah lazily. "I'd as soon get scuttlebutt from a waterbug."

Grammy Kark fluttered into the air and landed on Micah's muzzle. She stood looking down into his eyes. "Farkillers are real," she said. "The Dead Gods had them."

Micah locked his huge aquamarine eyes on her for a long moment. "When the Dead Gods come back, be sure to let me know." He rolled up onto his feet, sending her fluttering. "In the meantime, beloved Grammy, I hear your murder calling."

"Darling, tone," said Sephora. "Grammy Kark is one of our oldest friends."

"And any friend of your mother's is a friend of mine," said Micah. He stretched. "Now it's time to howl."

ANASTASIA

It was late at night and the air was cool. Anastasia and Wendy were walking along the southern edge of the Narrows, having a last-minute status meeting. Storm clouds rolled overhead.

"How is the new tactic working for Plan B?" asked Anastasia.

"Hard at first but practice making better," said Wendy. "Don't want go out. But..." She shrugged eloquently, ears flapping. "Will if needed."

"Good," said the Loving Auntie.

Wendy gestured along the line of bushes. "Put sharp sticks here."

Anastasia glanced toward her. "No."

Wendy stopped. "What?" she rumbled.

"We don't kill helpless animals," said Anastasia.

Wendy scoffed. "Last time I check, woof not helpless."

Anastasia looked up at the snippets of moon showing through the fast-moving clouds. "A falling animal is a helpless animal." She turned to look at Wendy. "No sharp sticks."

"We need defend our army," barked the Assault Leader.

"We're not going to act like the people we are fighting against," said Anastasia. "So, *no*."

Wendy stamped and came very close to the Loving Auntie. Her voice came out as a raspy hiss. "You said *no more rules*." The brief flashes of moon flickered in her dark eyes.

Anastasia stood still. "Turns out there are rules," she said evenly.

"Who make them?" shouted Wendy. "Who make this rule?"

Anastasia looked at her for a long time. "Me."

NICODEMUS

The morning sun shone brightly over the bunker. "We were hoping to get to thirty crossbows, but some are getting jammed. It looks like we'll be lucky to get maybe twenty-four fully functioning ones," said Nicodemus to Anastasia and Wendy as they lolloped through the practicing grounds. "When the history of the Known World is written, the raccoons and mice building a brand new kind of weapon in a few weeks will get a chapter in itself."

"If we live through this, there will be chapters for all," said Anastasia, "Starting with one on the sleepy old Reader who came out of retirement to build a war machine."

"I get a whole chapter?" said Nicodemus. "I was hoping for a footnote."

Soon, they were surrounded by the hubbub of the crossbow teams. The crossbows had now been modified to be used by squirrels. So there was a wide platform above the stock where the squirrels could stand, aiming by balancing and firing by tugging a cord.

Now the Ascending Squirrels were practicing leaping into their positions on the balancing platforms, just above the grooves where the quarrels lay, sharp-tipped and feathered.

They stopped for a moment to watch a squirrel, in a wide stance with the trigger cord held lightly in her hand, surf the crossbow sights into a dead lock on the target, a thick round gourd. Then the raccoon holding the gourd sent it rolling down a slight incline. The squirrel leaned left, and the crossbow's front sight drifted leftwards, tracking the rolling gourd.

"Now," said the raccoon, and the squirrel pulled the trigger cord. Instantly, the quarrel crossed the intervening thirty-five yards and buried itself in the gourd. The raccoon whistled appreciatively.

"The squirrels are scary good at this," said Nicodemus. "That Oga For Young Goats mumbo-jumbo that Dingus dreamed up gives them incredible focus." He groomed his shoulder. "But we won't have as many quarrels as we hoped. The craftmice have been working night and day, but it's taking longer than we thought to knap the arrowheads. Looks like we'll end up with around four hundred. That probably means about sixteen or seventeen quarrels per crossbow."

"Can't waste any," rumbled Wendy. "Killers *must* charge at Narrows. Must get close."

"I've been working on that," said Anastasia. "Death Rage learned a lot about the wolves on her trip. She's been telling me how they think."

Just then, a chunky bluebird dropped down near them, flanked by a finch and an oriole.

"Where are they, Stan?" asked Anastasia.

The bluebird hawked up a glob of phlegm and spat it out. "They're coming faster than we thought. They'll be at the north end of the Narrows tomorrow morning."

"Ouch," said Nicodemus. "We're going to have about fifteen quarrels apiece."

"We finish killer surprise tonight," rumbled Wendy.

"Can you dig that much?" asked Anastasia.

"Maybe not as wide as we wanted," growled Wendy. "But we rabbits. If we can't dig good, we deserve what we get."

POSSE COMITATUS

The *Posse Comitatus* was gathered near the north end of the Narrows. Late in the day, one of the coyotes from the North Shandy clan showed up with a travois of dirty apples from a nearby raccoon orchard that the wolves had overrun. It had dark smears down one side. As usual, after the Summerdays had eaten their fill, they let the other *Posse* members have the apples as part of the spoils of war.

"*Chasseurs!*"[26] shouted the coyote. "Who says we need raccoons to have a good time? Get your dirty apples here. All free. Courtesy of Clan *Bâtard.*"

The Summerdays did not often indulge in alcohol, but it didn't take long for the rest of the hunters nearby to belly up and pick out a dirty apple. Gaetan and Lilou each plucked out a plump Crimson Snap and went and sat on top of the cliffs that looked out over the ocean. The cliffs here were a hundred and twenty feet high, and the wind came racing in off the waves.

Gaetan took a big bite of his apple and put his face in the wind. "Rain's coming," he said.

Lilou took a small bite and chewed it thoroughly. "Haven't seen you in awhile. How's your girlfriend?"

"Shiny. Wolfy. Gorgeous." Gaetan crunched his apple bite. "Everything I'll never be. Plus, she's all huggy-kissy with an uplander."

Lilou stretched and adopted a sisterly mien. "She just needs to see the real you so she can see how impressive you are. Maybe you can play a word game or something."

Gaetan glared at her and then took a playful bite at her muzzle. She nipped him back and suddenly they were play-fighting again, just as when they were cubs three years ago.

Isadore and Juliette each got a dirty apple and sat under

---

[26] Hunters!

a red alder with other foxes in their squad. Foxes had a tendency to be finicky with dirty apples, but tonight they dove in with abandon.

"A toast," called Isadore after a few minutes.

"A toast!" cried the other foxes.

Isadore stood, the white scar on his face catching the last rays on the setting sun. "Tomorrow, we cross the Narrows," he said. "And then we'll be on the home turf of the thugs. Probably half the warrens will be criminal hotbeds."

"Clean 'em out!" shouted another fox, his chin wet with apple juice.

"That means we'll all be feasting every day after tomorrow. And nothing would give me greater pleasure than to see the vixen I love … fat and sassy again." He picked up what was left of his apple between his two front paws and held it up. "To love!"

"To love," roared the foxes.

Then Juliette stood, swaying a bit and leaning against the tree trunk. "You get attacked, out of the blue, by people who don't play by the rules…" She trailed off. Isadore rested his paw on her haunch. "Not gonna lie," said Juliette. "It changes you. Makes you afraid the world will never be safe again."

There was a sympathetic "Mmmmm," from the assembled foxes.

"So I'll just say this," said Juliette. "A weasel asked me the other day how it felt to be with all these foxes, because, you know, we're not *pack* animals." There was a mild titter at this classic fox joke, usually aimed at coyotes and wolves. "And I told him," said Juliette, "it feels *good*. If anyone wants to start a pack when this is over, hit me up." She looked at

Isadore. "We'll collect our cubs, be a real family again…" She trailed off, looking teary-eyed. There was a burst of gallant cheering from the other foxes, and Isadore gently helped her to a seated position.

The weasels favored mushrooms, but they would opportunistically eat any fermented fruits they came across, so they tucked into the apples with a will. Saskatoon had her back legs curled around a big brown Grammy Jones apple, and she was breaking off pieces with her hands and sucking on them. Another weasel, black from head to toe, sat next to her.

"Did you hear about that weasel thing that happened a few days ago?" asked the newcomer, whom she knew only slightly.

"The murders?" asked Saskatoon. "Yeah, I heard. I'll remind some bunnies of that when the time comes. It'll be a party." She shoved another piece of soft, crumbly apple into her mouth.

"But did you hear the whole story?" asked the other weasel, his eyes restless in the golden light of the sunset. "The wolves are keeping it quiet."

Saskatoon's paw full of apple stopped in midair. "What're you talking about, brother?" she asked.

"The criminals sent out a note," he said. "'*Run while you still can.*'"

A chill ran down Saskatoon's spine. Those were the words ringing in her ears when she had been driven out of Warren *Sans Gloire* in the South Shandy several months ago, running in fear from *rabbits*. It was a nasty memory.

"No," said Saskatoon. "That's not what it said."

"Pretty sure that's what I heard," said the black weasel, taking a big bite of apple.

Saskatoon felt her lips sliding back, exposing her teeth. "You lie," she hissed. "You *lie*!"

The other weasel looked at her in surprise. "Take it easy, sister. Just making conversation."

Saskatoon felt a hot wave of embarrassment wash over her, which was multiplied when she realized several other nearby weasels were looking at her. "Sorry," she mumbled. "Guess I've got … rabbit fever."

The black weasel chewed and swallowed. "There's a lot of that going around."

DEATH RAGE

It was dark and blustery as Death Rage sneaked into the alcove under the bunker where Bricabrac was being held in the gallon *Vegenaise* jar. She knew what she wanted to do, but she wasn't sure how she was going to do it. She had taken off her helmet so as to be a bit more incognito.

A single moonbeam shone through a scree of small branches and fell on the jar where it sat on the earthen floor. She could see Bricabrac curled in a circle on the fresh bedding of leaves and moss, with his back to the water gourd. His recent dinner of cherries and pecans lay scattered near him.

He lay still, his forepaw flung over his eyes. A conflicting roil of emotions seized her. She was about to do something very bad, but she could not stop herself.

She came close to the glass and tapped on it. Bricabrac did not respond. Her heart was in her throat. Was he still alive?

She tapped again, and Bricabrac woke and sat up groggily. Then he saw her and came to the glass. He put his front paws on it. She could see him talking, but she could only hear him faintly.

Death Rage looked up and saw that the wall had partly crumbled near the jar. She ran up the jumble of concrete pieces and managed to leap from there to the top of the jar. There were a dozen large air holes punched in the metal lid.

"Hey," she called quietly. "Bricabrac." She looked around nervously. The alcove was empty, but there were many animals around the bunker. It would not do to make too much noise.

Immediately, Bricabrac was standing on his toes, stretching upwards. "Who is that?"

"Shhh," said the mouse. "It's Death Rage. I'm here to help you escape."

Bricabrac looked astonished. "What?" He squinted up through the air holes. "By Rattus, it *is* you!" He put his hand on his head. "You … are a glorious angel."

"How can I get you out?" she asked. "I might be able to break the jar with a stone, but that's going to make a lot of noise and bring the rabbits."

"Right, right," said Bricabrac, rubbing his head.

"What else could I do?" asked Death Rage.

Bricabrac paced for a few moments. "Ummm, I think if you push the jar on its side, I might be able to unscrew the lid. I can use the air holes to get a grip."

Death Rage sat on the edge of the lid and put her feet against the wall. She took a deep breath and pushed as hard as she could. The jar leaned away from the wall very slightly.

She relaxed her legs to let the jar rock back into place, and then pushed again as it leaned outward. It moved a little further this time.

Bricabrac could feel what she was doing, so he threw his weight against the edge of the jar in time with her pushes. A few oscillations later, the jar leaned past the tipping point and fell onto the earth with a soft *thunk*.

Bricabrac rushed to the lid, gripped the airholes and started to unscrew it. Death Rage scampered down the broken wall and helped him, and in a few moments, the lid fell out onto the soft earth.

Bricabrac clambered out and knelt down before Death Rage. He seized her forepaw and kissed it. Hot tears fell from his eyes. And for once, he had no words to say. Death Rage gently stroked his forehead.

Finally, he gathered himself, and began to speak, earnestly, quickly. "I didn't mean for this to work out like it did. With you guys getting killed. I was just helping my family get work. I've never been part of a war effort because there's never *been* a war like this." He stopped to catch his breath. "Most jobs are just one-offs. They don't mean anything." He put his face in his paws. "I'm not a traitor."

"I believe you," said Death Rage.

Bricabrac took a deep breath. Then he stood up and collected himself, smoothing his fur. "If you are ever in dire need and a rat can help, say these words." Bricabrac leaned forward and whispered a phrase into her ear.

She nodded. "I'll remember that."

Bricabrac ran back into the jar for a moment and gathered his few belongings. When he came back out, he paused and looked at Death Rage closely. "I know your love for Anastasia is great, and she will be angry. So I have to ask, why?"

Death Rage looked into his dark eyes. "When you put that dime in my backpack before I went to wolf country, you saved my life," she said simply. "The debt that I owe you is worth more than honor." She paused. "I think."

Bricabrac could see the conflicting emotions on her face. He stepped forward and hugged her. "Don't think of it as being dishonorable," he said. "Think of it as becoming an honorary rat."

"Geh," Death Rage shook off his hug and stepped back, grimacing. But then she gave him a sidelong glance. "Thank you."

"Your servant," said Bricabrac. Then he bowed deeply and disappeared into the night.

Chapter 17

The greater one wins and the lesser one loses. This is not only a law, it is a good law. If you are born a hunter, be glad.

—Micah Summerday, solstice remarks

Aliyah

The night-before-battle jitters had everyone's nerves jangly. For the last few days, Aliyah had been feeling irritable and snappish, but now she felt fidgety and excited, although she did not really know why. Wolves usually enter estrus once a year, around February, to create a spring birth for the cubs. But stress can throw off this ancient cycle.

As Aliyah and Tennyson roamed through the large encampment of the *Posse Comitatus*, she sampled dirty apples freely as she went, unusually for her, and Tennyson followed her lead. Soon, she was pressing her flank against his as they strolled.

At one place they tippled, a skulk of foxes had been giving a series of long, emotional speeches about love and family, interspersed with lots of teary-eyed nuzzling. At another,
a boogle of weasels had set up some ancient xylophone bars
across two logs, and the matriarch was playing a sprightly
dance tune as the others undulated their long slender bodies
through a rather showy rendition of the *mambo*.

Aliyah was bright-eyed and giggly and felt like treading
new territory. She leaned into Tennyson, resting her chin on
him as they walked. "This is just like history in the making,
you know? Tomorrow we're going to clear out a criminal
gang that's been terrorizing our people. One day, wolves will
sing songs about this. So amazing to be here for it."

"We can tell our grand-cubs about it," chuckled Tennyson.
He struck a pose, "I was there when those bad rabbits came
rushing down the field ... with their noses wiggling *so hard*..."
He got up on his back feet and pranced, putting his two front
paws up to act as ears as he waggled his nose like a rabbit who
meant business.

Aliyah giggled and sat on her haunches. She noticed—
again—how cute he was. How free. Not like the local stick-
in-the-mud boys, who were so serious and never talked about
anything but clan business and hunting, and had never even
been to City of Oom.

Tennyson dropped onto all fours, his silver fur gleaming
in the moonlight. "The glorious apple crawl continueth," he
proclaimed. "Who shall we hit next? The coyotes for a little
visit to tufftown? Or maybe the crows for their mellifluous
cawing that just ... gets you right here." He slapped a paw
over his heart.

Aliyah giggled and leaned up against his side, moving him into some shadows under a copious stand of warm, sugary honeysuckle. Then she turned and backed into him. Her scent was fierce and musky.

"Let's," she said.

Tennyson slid his face close to hers, licking her ears and rubbing against the soft fur of her cheek. "Aren't your parents the breeding pair in your pack? They're not going to like this."

Her green eyes were smiling in the moonlight. "Oh, them," she scoffed. "They're love puppies. They already let a young mother with cubs join." She turned to face him. "And if we *do* get cubs, and they don't like it, we can move to the South Shandy. We'll be the new Summerday agents down there."

Tennyson grinned and nibbled her ear. "You've got it all figured out, haven't you?"

Aliyah looked up at the moon. "We can call it the Summerwinter Clan."

The silver wolf laughed and rested his chin on her back. "You almost make me forget that Micah Summerday might maul me for this."

"Don't be so squishy," said Aliyah. You're starting to make a girl feel … underappreciated."

"Well, we can't have that," said Tennyson.

"No, we can't," said Aliyah. She turned and batted him with her hip again. "So, *let's*."

Armée Libre

Of course, the crossbows weren't quite done, so the raccoons and craftmice labored over them furiously throughout the night, making sure the new balancing platforms for the squirrels were sturdy.

There was also worry about the possibility of rain, with the thunderclouds scudding in off the sea. Nicodemus looked at the sky over and over through the long night. Finally, he said, "I think there will be rain in the uplands, but not here."

"From your mouth to Pfizer's ear," rasped Adderall, as he squinted at the balancing platform that he was trying to keep locked in place with resin and shims.

Wendy had long ago picked out the best place to defend the Narrows. It was important that the killer army not know their preparations, so the fortifications, although thoroughly planned, could not be fully executed until the night before. So Wendy and the rest of the rabbit leadership had organized more than five hundred rabbits drawn from recent additions to the Free Warrens to execute a huge earthworks project in a single night. That way, the troops in the *Armée Libre* could rest up and be fresh in the morning.

"Dig!" growled Wendy as she strode through the vast excavation. "We dig or die." The rabbits worked at a frenzied pace, but in a grim silence, saving their breath. They all knew that the Narrows was the best place to stop the killer army. If they failed here, the rest of the Million Acre Wood would lay open to the scythe of death sweeping down from the north.

Stan was still drilling the songbirds on the tactics they had been practicing for weeks now. "Eyes, eyes, eyes!" barked the bluebird as a tornado of brightly colored flyers swarmed around him. "Get in fast. Get out fast. Live to fight another day." At moonrise, he sent them to their roosts.

Wellbutrin and Lorazepam got stuck with organizing a

crew of cantankerous raccoons on a dangerous mission, dragging a heavy, reeking load far out into the Narrows, to where one of the few trees grew.

Anastasia was out by the tops of the cliffs where the winds blew the fiercest, pacing, muttering, chewing her nails, and trying to come up with the words that would help give birth to a new world. *The word creates. Everything else follows.* Love Bug kept the Auntie's Guard distant and quiet. He knew she was struggling. And when he saw her start drawing circles around herself in the earth, his heart ached for her.

The Ascending Squirrels had scattered themselves in the trees above the earthworks and assumed the lotus position. In a state of mindfulness and receptivity, they opened their eyes to what would be tomorrow's battlefield and soaked up the details of every bush, tree, and blade of grass.

Mabel walked a little way out into the Narrows, knelt down, and quietly sang a new hymn to a new Yah, the revised god of rabbits.

Posse Comitatus

The *Posse* members were milling around at the north end of the Narrows. A small group of foxes and weasels came running down the line, playing leapfrog and laughing.

Gaetan stood looking out over the field they were about to cross. It was a stretch of grassy ground eighty yards wide and two hundred yards long, with scrubby woods at each end. On the eastern side, the Boreal Cliffs rose into the sky, the steep face peppered with scrub. On the western side was a sheer drop of a hundred and twenty feet down to the saltwater below.

"Why don't we just go?" asked Gaetan. "What are we waiting for?" Lilou shrugged, still hungover from the night before. So Gaetan set off at his brisk, limping trot to where the golden wolves were standing together in a knot. When he arrived, he could hear that creaky old crow who always seemed to hang around with the Summerdays. She was speaking in low, urgent tones.

"Beloved shiny cub and War Leader," said Grammy Kark. "You are great and powerful. *And* I am begging you not to run out across this open ground."

Micah Summerday was pacing. "Why haven't the raptors heard of these farkillers?"

"Raptors don't talk to songbirds," said Grammy Kark.

"Actually, they're kind of afraid of songbirds now," said Aliyah. "Ever since those mugging incidents started a few weeks ago."

"I am a servant of this community," said Micah. "It is my calling to act as War Leader. That means when it is time to go, *I go*."

"We don't even know that there's anything over there but rabbits and squirrels," said Tennyson. "Aren't we overreacting a little to a rumor?"

Sephora turned baleful eyes on him. Aliyah made a nervous "hush up" gesture and Tennyson fell silent.

Grammy Kark led Micah and Sephora a few steps away from the assembled *Posse*, until they were out of earshot.

"Dearest ones," she said, her voice soft and soothing. "I am the Oldest Mother. Far older than any wolf. I have seen much." She looked at Sephora. "I knew your great-grandmother, who died long before you came into this life. I chanted the birthing rite when your grandmother was born, when your mother was born, when you were born." She looked at Micah. "I have served the Summerday Clan since the day Kiskari Highsummer created it out of love and death. If ever you would hear me, hear me now."

The two golden apex killers stared at the ancient crow without speaking.

Grammy Kark came near to them. "This kind of flat ground breeds farkillers. Our Readers have seen this over and over again in the histories of the Dead Gods." She paused, black eyes glinting. "My Lord, you are almost certainly right. There's probably nothing out there. But the Summerdays are rare and precious. So just let this one bit of wisdom guide your path. Don't launch your first wave with the few, launch your first wave with the many." She stopped and looked over her shoulder at all the hunters milling around a few dozen yards away.

Sephora's eyes flicked over to the mass of animals and back. "You mean foxes," she said.

"Yes, daughter of my daughter," said the old crow.

"So I'm going to send in the fox where the wolf is afraid to go?" said Micah, disgust written on his face. "I don't do that."

Grammy Kark and Sephora shared a long look. Then the ancient crow stepped up to the glowering wolf and fixed him with her obsidian eye. "Golden boy," she said, her voice scraping out like a steel rasp across a dull blade. "Your life has always been easy. But this is not hunting, this is *war*. If you don't understand that, today will be your last day on Earth."

Armée Libre

Wendy had chosen the Free Peoples' line of defense well. In the dawn light, the crows and raptors flying over the Narrows could see that something was happening at the south end, but the heavy growth of bushes and scrub prevented them from seeing exactly what. And the rabbits, being rabbits, had put to use the skills earned by untold generations of warren-concealing does when they built their earthworks the night before. It could not be seen from more than a few yards away. And the songbirds rose in furious swarms to drive off any flying interloper coming down the field, so the aerial scouts of the killer army could not get close enough to see any details.

Still, there were problems.

"The earthworks isn't as wide as we wanted," said Nicodemus. "Some may get across."

"They ran out of time," said Mabel, biting her lip.

"Where crossbows?" demanded Wendy, double-bumping Lorazepam hard in the flank when she appeared suddenly, soaking wet, in the midst of the roiling crowd of rabbits, mice and squirrels making last-minute preparations.

Lorazepam spread her front paws in a gesture of helplessness, "That rain in the uplands last night is making the stream rise. We can still get the crossbows across but it's hella muddy. It's taking awhile." She shivered.

"How long?" growled Wendy.

"An hour, maybe two," said Lorazepam.

Wendy turned away, barking orders at lieutenants.

Anastasia was standing among the bushes, working out lines of fire with Dingus and the other Ascending Squirrels.

Her Kevlar jacket with the camo side out made her disappear among the scrubby branches and leaves.

She noticed a shiny flicker in the corner of her eye. It was an outcropping of rainbow quartz on a small grassy hill about eighty yards behind the *Armée Libre* fortifications. At this moment, with the battle rushing up at them, her anxiety was raging. So the shiny stone kept poking into her attention. *Here I am. Don't let the bad thing happen. Come and touch me. Now.*

The *thrum* pulling her toward the stone was strong, and already turning into an ache. Best just to do it now and get it over with. It only took a few minutes. And it was far from the killer army, so it was safe enough. She had already touched it several times in recent days. Usually the anxiety discharge lasted for many hours. The last couple of times, she had ducked her Guard and just run off quickly, but then Love Bug made her promise to stop doing that.

She took a deep breath, made eye contact with her Guard, and turned and ran for the outcropping.

GRAMMY KARK

The late autumn air was cool, and a light breeze was blowing. Grammy Kark was perched on the branch of an olive tree growing at the north end of the Narrows. A large osprey was sitting near her, preening his white breast feathers. The animals of the *Posse Comitatus* were milling about, talking excitedly about the day to come. Grammy Kark ignored the ruckus. Her keen eyes raked the swirl of activity at the far end of the field, two hundred yards away.

"Hey," she said to the osprey. "Look at that rabbit down there with that … thing wrapped around it."

She pointed with her right wing. The osprey looked. "Weird," he said, and went back to cleaning himself.

Grammy Kark watched the rabbit scamper toward a chunk of colorful quartz. "I've already seen this rabbit do this a couple of times," said the old crow. "Why is it doing that?"

"Who cares what the lunchmeat do?" asked the osprey. "Long as I get my share."

"Songbird chatter says the criminal leader has some kind of armor," mused Grammy Kark. "I thought it would be shiny but…"

"You listen to songbird chatter?" scoffed the osprey, yellow eyes rolling.

"Oh, yes," said Grammy Kark. "Our not-so-bright friends can't stop themselves from saying whatever's in their colorful little heads, so—" She broke off and leaned forward. "Look, there's a squad of rabbits moving with her. Keeping her in the middle of a circle. That's—" She reached out and grabbed the osprey's leg with her talons. "That's a guard formation if I've ever seen one." She turned to look at him. "That's a leader. Maybe it's *her*." She rocked back and forth on her perch. "Anastasia."

"Really?" said the osprey. He squinted down the field. "Seems scrawny for a war criminal."

Grammy Kark turned to the osprey. "You want to make a ten dollar bounty?" she said, her black eyes bright. "Just nip down there and snatch her. Drop down the cliff face and skim along the beach so no one sees you coming."

"What about their songbirds?" asked the osprey as he

cleaned his beak with his claw. "There's a ton of them. Nasty little creeps."

"They're all focused on the battlefield. They're looking at *us*, not her. You can be in and out before they know you're there."

"Mmmm," said the osprey, stretching his black and white wings that dwarfed the old crow. "I guess I could. Be good for my rep."

Now the rabbit was standing next to the shiny rock, her paw resting on it.

"She only does this for a couple of minutes," hissed Grammy Kark. "Go now! I promise you, Clan Summerday will be *grateful*."

"Righteous," chuckled the osprey. Then he spread his wide wings and glided toward the cliff edge.

LOVE BUG

Anastasia stood by the rainbow quartz boulder, her forepaw resting on its shiny surface. It looked like her lips were moving but Love Bug could not hear what she was saying. The Loving Auntie's Guard were holding a steady perimeter at twenty yards. After weeks of this, they were practiced and dependable.

A cold gust swept in off the ocean, bringing a trace of salt with it. Love Bug and the other members of the Guard turned their backs to the wind for a moment to keep the stinging spray out of their eyes. Even Anastasia hunched and turned to look away from the wind.

As Love Bug stood, eyes resting on the brilliant colors

drawn from the rainbow quartz by the low, slanting rays of the sun, a dark shape dropped into his field of view from above. Startled, he took a step back and then realized the shape was a raptor, dark wings spanning more than five feet, gliding toward Anastasia.

He leaped forward, yelling a warning to her, calling to the Guard. His heart banged against his chest as his claws tore the ground, and he fumbled his bite blade into his mouth. Around him, Guard rabbits were converging. Ahead he saw Anastasia turning as the curved black talons reached for her. Then she threw herself sideways, trying to flick out her Claw. But before the blade could appear, the dark talons were closing around her body, and the great wings beat the air like thunder as the osprey wheeled and headed for the edge of the cliff.

Aliyah

Aliyah was pacing at the *Posse Comitatus* headquarters knoll at the north end of the Narrows when an osprey dropped in at a steep angle. It held a wriggling brown rabbit. A moment later, Grammy Kark glided onto the knoll and folded her wings, looking intently at the squirming creature.

Aliyah ran over and sniffed. "Where'd you get this?"

"Just behind their line," said the osprey. "Grammy Kark says—"

"Hush, now," said the old crow as she examined the rabbit and its jacket, pecking at it. "Let me look first."

The rabbit was silent. The osprey shifted his grip. "This thing is weird," he said. "My talons won't go through it. And it has ribs, so I can't squeeze it."

"Maybe it found some old Dead Gods junk and crawled in and got stuck," said Aliyah. She turned away. "Just eat it."

"*No.*" It was Grammy Kark's creaky voice. She seized an edge of the fabric covering the rabbit's back and sides. "This is armor," she said finally.

Aliyah glanced down at her own golden chain mail with the Summerday crest on the front. "What? No it isn't."

"Can't be pierced. Can't be crushed," said Grammy Kark. "It's armor." She hopped around the rabbit. "So expensive. So hard to make. Who wears armor?" She looked at Aliyah. "The precious ones."

The osprey grinned and stretched his wings. "So that means…"

"Congratulations, Diveboy," said Grammy Kark, looking up into the osprey's bright yellow eyes. "You just won yourself a lovely bounty. This is Anastasia Bloody Thorn, queen of the rent rebellion."

FREDDIE

Freddie was supervising a squadron of rabbits firming up the packed earth firing positions prepped for the crossbows when he noticed a hubbub rising behind him. He turned and saw Love Bug racing toward the embankment, with the Loving Auntie's Guard strung out behind him.

As soon as he reached the first rabbits under the bushes, Love Bug started babbling, gesticulating, seemingly pointing in several directions at once. A swirl of rabbits grew around him. Something was wrong. Freddie left his team and moved toward the knot of rabbits and mice growing around Love Bug.

As Freddie got closer, he could hear Love Bug's voice, shrill and rapid, but could not make out what he was saying. Tears were streaming from Love Bug's eyes. He raked a claw across his own chest as he spoke, his sharpened claws tearing out chunks of fur. An outcry of alarm began to well up from the swirl of creatures around him.

Freddie's stomach felt like it was being squeezed by fist. *Where's Anastasia?* His eyes swept the area and came up with nothing. In a few more seconds, he was close enough to hear, and the words tore out a piece of his heart and threw it to the wolves.

"They got her!"

GAETAN

Anastasia was in a small pit, still wearing her camouflage jacket. Around the lip of the pit was a swirling mass of coyotes, weasels, foxes, and wolves, laughing and bantering. Every few seconds, a hunter would lunge forward in a half-playful killing strike, sending Anastasia bolting to the other side of the pit amid snarls and cheers.

Gaetan struggled to stay upright and push himself forward so he could see what was happening. Anastasia's eyes were wide and rimmed with white, and she was stumbling, clearly exhausted. Her cheeks were covered with dried tears.

"So this is the little *morveuse*[27] that started it all?" asked one of the North Shandy coyotes. "Hardly a mouthful."

"The doe who would be queen," hissed a white weasel,

---

[27] Brat.

leaning forward and taking a quick swipe at Anastasia's face with her claw. "Run while you still can, sssister." Anastasia stumbled away, a rivulet of blood running down her left cheek.

"She killed her own peoples' god," said one of the foxes. "That's why they went crazy."

Suddenly, there was a fox in the pit with the Anastasia. It was Juliette. Gaetan recognized her from the terrible scar across her neck. A twitchy growl ripped out of her throat as she lunged at Anastasia, bowling her over. Anastasia kicked wildly, with Juliette right on her, trying to close her jaws on the Kevlar armor. As she rolled back up onto her feet, a shining blade appeared by her right paw, and she immediately slashed the air in front of Juliette's face, which stopped the fox in her tracks.

There was an appreciative murmur from the audience of canids, "Ooh, she's a *féroce*[28] little minx," said the North Shandy coyote. "Just like I like 'em."

"All right, ladies," chuckled a large wolf as he stepped down into the pit. "Nobody's getting hurt today until Lord Summerday says so." He stepped in between Juliette and Anastasia and gently pushed Juliette out of the pit with his nose.

Gaetan stared at Anastasia. He knew what it was like to be the smallest, weakest animal in a crowd. She was alone, she was injured, and she was surrounded by enemies. Terrified and weepy, she would not give in. Canids don't fight from a position of weakness. Once they lose, they crawl and submit. This skinny brown rabbit had already lost everything, and

---

[28]   Fierce.

would certainly lose her life today, but she would not stop fighting. He could not take his eyes off her.

Suddenly, there was a raucous fanfare from the crows, a dotted rhythm in ascending fourths, and Micah and Sephora Summerday appeared, flanked by Aliyah and Tennyson, with Grammy Kark gliding overhead, and a whole retinue of creatures large and small trailing behind.

The animals around the pit parted in a wave, and Micah Summerday stepped forward, looking down at the enemy of all he stood for. Anastasia had sheathed her weapon. She wiped at the blood on her face and sat up tall. Her gaze traveled slowly up from the ground until she met his bright aquamarine eyes.

He looked at her for a long moment. "Thanks for taking this meeting," he rumbled. "Now, what are we doing here?" He blinked slowly. "Crime wave?" He looked around. "Some people want to call this *war*?" His eyes tracked back to Anastasia. "You tell me, little brown bunny."

She held his gaze. Gaetan could see her trembling. Finally, she said, "I just want to live."

Micah laid his chin down on his paws so that his head was on the same level as hers. "So do I," he said. "And you want to kill me."

Anastasia flinched as Micah's hot breath washed over her. She spread her front paws and everyone could see that they were shaking. "I have nothing against the Summerday Clan," she said.

A huge guffaw burst out of the assembled predators. Tennyson pretended to wipe his forehead as he looked at Aliyah and mouthed "Whew!" The white weasel strutted around like a game show host, milking the applause.

Micah held up his paw and there was immediate silence. Sephora tried to come close to his ear and whisper something and he waved her off.

He rested his aquamarine eyes on Anastasia. "Nonpayment of rent. Conspiracy to foment rebellion. Murdering an agent of lawful authority. And now you have come here to assault your Landlord. Why?"

Anastasia leaned toward him and tipped her ears forward in a gesture of intimacy. "Our weapons are poor. We are just small creatures who hope for a world where most of our children can live long enough to grow up."

Someone in the crowd scoffed. Micah's eyes flicked toward them and they were instantly silenced.

Anastasia continued. "We thought if we could make enough of a fuss to bring you here, maybe we could talk, just like we are now."

Sephora stepped forward again, and Gaetan was close enough to hear her whisper. "Why don't we let Grammy Kark talk to her? She's really good at this."

While Sephora was whispering, a small crew of weasels came forward, carrying a stout cage made of small branches reinforced with wire.

"*I'm* talking to her," said Micah.

A female rat with dark brown fur and a copper earring was clinging to the cage, adjusting a door hinge. Gaetan noticed that Anastasia stiffened when she saw her.

"Frippery." Anastasia spat the name out.

"I'm really sorry," whispered Frippery.

"Rats is for rats, right?" said Anastasia.

"I didn't think it would come to this," whispered the rat.

Sephora nuzzled in by Micah's ear. "Grammy Kark could get some information out of her," said Sephora. "She's clever. You know that."

Micah gave her a sidelong glance. "As Grammy Kark recently reminded me, this is war."

"Yes," said Sephora.

"And I am War Leader," said Micah.

"I know you are, my love," said Sephora.

"So I am speaking with the prisoner," said Micah.

"You have to get in the cage now," whispered Frippery apologetically.

Anastasia's gaze passed slowly over the crowd of killers. Gaetan was surprised to find that he wanted to be seen by her. He pushed forward so he was in her line of sight, standing awkwardly with his injured leg. Her eyes moved across him. Then she turned and crawled into the cage.

"Golden child, if I may," began Grammy Kark, as she hopped up beside him.

"You may not," said Micah. He lifted his massive paw and placed it on her wing, crushing it into the ground. His aquamarine eyes rested on her as he transferred more and more weight onto that paw. Her face creased with pain.

"I understand," she said. "Please accept my apology, Lord Summerday." Suddenly, there was a whine in her voice. "Please."

Micah picked up his paw and sat up. His eyes swept the crowd. "Friends," he said. "It's time."

Chapter 18

The moon's not full 'til the rabbit howls.
—Raccoon proverb

LOVE BUG

Love Bug could not sit still. A single question played over and over in his mind. *Why? Why did you let them take her? Why?* He ran this way and that along the edge of the meadow, his guilt clawing at him, as plan after plan of response occurred to him and was quickly thrown away. He was aware of the Auntie's Guard watching him with alarm, but he couldn't spare a thought for them.

The entire rabbit embankment was a swarm of frantic energy. Rabbits, mice, squirrels, raccoons, and songbirds swirled in a vortex around a lumpy brown shape. Wendy stood upright, her huge back feet rooted to the ground, while she was bombarded with questions, demands, and updates. She responded in rapid growls, scarcely moving as she stood in the center of the power vacuum created by Anastasia's loss, dispensing answers and orders in staccato bursts.

One of the songbirds rushed up and breathlessly announced that most of the crossbows were across the stream now, but they were being slowed down because some of the raccoons were fighting. Wendy's obsidian eyes flicked over to Nicodemus, and with a barely perceptible jerk of her head, she sent him off to deal with it.

In the next instant, Love Bug heard something he had never heard before. A low, throbbing moan that climbed a few notes and then dropped down and guttered into silence. It was the howl of Micah Summerday, and it shocked him out of his dithering. He looked across the flats and saw, two hundred yards away, a huge golden wolf step out in front of the assembled killer army.

"Renters!" called the golden wolf, "This is your Landlord. Your rent rebellion is illegal." He paused, then slowly rolled out his next words. "I have your queen."

The swirl around Wendy froze, with every eye looking down the field at the Summerday War Leader.

"Come forward, criminals," said Micah. "Or she's going straight into my belly."

A pitiful moan broke out of the hundreds of throats on the embankment. The one whom it had seemed might—just *might*—be able to change the old sad story of their lives was suddenly revealed to be just another scared little animal, her life hanging on the whim of a grasping overlord.

There was a long quiet moment. This was not how it was supposed to go. The plan had been all about the crossbows.

Get the killers to charge. Let the crossbows cut them to pieces from a distance as they ran. Let the earthworks take care of any killers who reached the free side. Then go out and mop up stragglers with spears and bite blades.

Everyone knew what it meant to go out there, leave the cover of the scrub and expose yourself to a thousand hungry jaws, now grinding with the killing joy. No one moved. No one looked into anyone else's eyes.

"Come forward, *now*," said Micah.

Wendy took a step forward and started to shoulder her way through the crowd. The people parted before her in a nervous wave. They were all silent. From a distance came the sound of the killer army hooting and laughing.

Love Bug knew what the animals around him were feeling. Their scent was rising and mingling into a sad gray of acquiescence. It was as every god had said, as everyone had always known: They were born to die. As needed.

They had done their best. It had been a good run. Now it was over. The ending was being written, as they had always known it would be, by the victors. The ones with the big teeth. And if you had ever thought it was going to end any differently, you were a fool.

Wendy stepped up onto a small rise and looked out over the sea of small animals. "I go," she said. The animals around her looked down at the ground. "Everyone stay here," she rumbled as she walked through the bushes toward the grasslands, toward the killers. "That's an order."

The mice near her began to kneel as she passed. The rabbits followed suit. Then the raccoons dropped their burly bodies onto their knees.

Love Bug, standing at the edge of the meadow, saw her coming toward him. A force of nature wrapped up in a blunt, hairy package. And also an ordinary person pushing through a cyclone of chemical alarm bells to walk into danger. For a friend. For a chance at a better world.

He was so proud to be her buck. This is what he had been born to do. This was the real meaning of love. To support her in this moment of crystalline clarity.

As she approached him, most of the animals were behind her. No one else could see her face. For just a moment, she let him see the terror in her eyes. The nakedness of her fear drew tears from him. He could not speak. He lifted his left paw, pads inward. *I will follow you.*

She saluted him with a gentle lift of her head. There was nothing else to be said. It is the one who will save your life that will also walk with you into death. Love Bug slipped under her huge ear, and he felt a peaceful warmth spreading through him.

They stood at the edge of the meadow, looking out across the killing field. Love Bug willed himself to take the next step. He shivered. Then he heard someone speaking behind him.

"I'm coming," said Freddie, his voice was high and trembling. "For her." Love Bug turned to look at him. Freddie sat up tall, and his eyes swept the crowd of animals. "For all of us." There was a muted breath of ratification from the crowd.

Death Rage leapt up onto small stone. "I was born a prey animal, but I will *not* die as one." She unsheathed the Kiss of Death and held it over her head. An early shaft of sunlight flicked through the gray clouds of morning and for a moment her steel rapier gleamed. Her voice pierced the misty scrub as she strode forward. "We are coming, Anastasia!"

Mabel lifted up her head and shouted, "*Vive les sans gloire!*"[29] Then she too stepped forward. The triple stamp of affirmation was slow in coming, and ragged, but it did come.

In the end, a little under three hundred rabbits and a little over three hundred mice marched out onto the field of battle, including most of the Loving Auntie's Guard. In addition to their own weapons, each one was dragging three additional spears, designed to be inserted into holes dug in the ground at an angle, creating a small forest of points leaning toward the enemy. It was the Plan B they had hoped they would never carry out.

It was a long march, made longer by the fact that they were walking into an onrushing torrent of fear that made each step a fight against an almost overpowering urge to flee.

Love Bug noticed more and more rabbits and mice trembling the further they got from the bushes. And he could not keep his forelegs from shaking. So when he found himself walking next to Mabel, he said, "Can you sing something? Something that makes us sound like … winners?"

Mabel looked at him for a long moment, and he could see in her eyes she was replaying the fling she'd had with the handsome little white bunny boy just a couple of months earlier. After a mist of sadness drifted across her face, she opened her throat and poured out a stream of soaring melody.

---

[29] Long live the inglorious ones!

> *"Half a yard, half a yard,*
> *Half a yard onward,*
> *Onto the Fields of Life*
> *   Marched the Six Hundred.*
> *Forward, inglorious*
> *This day, victorious*
> *Walking where Owners walk*
> *   Came the Six Hundred."*

POSSE COMITATUS

The Clan Father of the Summerdays, Landlord of the Million Acre Wood, roared with laughter as he watched the tiny line of lunchmeat march toward him. The mice were all invisible, since they were so small they ran mostly under the grass. So the army of predators stood and watched a few warren's worth of bunnies marching reluctantly across the greensward.

Soon, all the hunters were laughing, over a thousand strong, white teeth flashing in the morning sun. Saskatoon and a number of other weasels improvised a skit featuring trembling warriors who were stepping so reluctantly that they were actually moving backwards. The foxes all yipped at this.

A small team of weasels was carrying Anastasia's cage around on their shoulders, following Micah as he strolled along the front of the line. The animals in the *Posse* cheered whenever the cage came near them. The weasels blew kisses to the crowd.

Armée Libre

When the ragged line of rabbits and mice had advanced about fifty yards from their embankment, Wendy raised her paw and the *Armée Libre* slowed to a stop.

As she stood in the center of the line, a hundred terrified questions came at her from every direction. She shrugged them off, and raised her paws in the pre-arranged signal for *Dig spear holes now*. Her lieutenants, watching for the sign, immediately mirrored it, so in a few seconds it swept the Free Army.

The animals fell to with a will, leaning close to the ground, plunging their claws into the earth, tearing at the roots with their teeth. They knew what to do. Even though they had hoped they would never execute Plan B, they had practiced it many times. Wendy had insisted on it.

Soon after, the raptors floating in lazy circles above the north end of the Narrows began to drop. But as the first one, a northern goshawk, began to speed up and tighten his spirals, augering in toward Wendy, Stan unleashed a cloud of hundreds of songbirds. They rose out of the scrub and flew at the goshawk like a tiny colorful cyclone, trilling a rapidly rising aggressive melody with contrapuntal elements.

The reputation of the songbirds had apparently been well-established, because the goshawk sheared off and took a lengthy flight path out over the salt water.

Most of the *Armée Libre* animals had their first spear planted now. Two to go. They were digging holes several inches deep, and placing the spears so that the top three or four inches protruded from the earth, leaning slightly forward.

Now came a dozen fearsome raptors, flying in a group, a hundred feet above the battlefield. This time Stan sent the songbirds out in long whirling ribbons that did not close with any of the raptors but showed that they could at a moment's notice. So as soon as any raptor attacked a rabbit, they would be mobbed by a gang of songbirds and exposed to a death by a thousand cuts. The first raptor would certainly die. Maybe the second. The third might survive.

Another group of songbirds spun in an aggressive wheeling gyre just above where the rabbits and mice were digging. As brightly flickering spots of animated color, they prevented the raptors from looking past them and seeing clearly what was happening down on the earth below. For the moment, it was a draw. After a couple of minutes, the raptors peeled off.

Now most of the second spears were in place. On to the third. At any moment, the killer army might come charging down the field. The *Armée Libre* soldiers tore at the earth like demons. *Can we do this? Are we doing this?*

After the raptors cleared out, the crows came whipping down the field, flying low, attacking nothing, seeing and hearing everything. Wendy threw the paw sign, *Be silent,* and it raced throughout the *Armée Libre.* The songbirds flew at the eyes of the crows, sharp beaks darting in, two or three songbirds per crow. The crows' attempt at aggressive close surveillance quickly collapsed into an aerial brawl with the songbirds roaring their climbing attack melody and the crows shrieking their rage at being thwarted by these lesser flyers.

A rain of feathers, black, orange, blue, yellow, and red tumbled down onto the diggers as they finished burying their last spears. Now a tiny stealth forest of sharp points, forty feet wide, stretched across the Narrows, awaiting the fast-running feet of those who came to kill.

Wendy raised her forepaw and threw another sign. *Map your area now.*

The rabbits quickly dashed in expanding circles around their positions, seeing and noting the location of every point. They knew how to do this. They lived by it, their minds shaped by thousands of generations of scouting and remembering terrain, seeking the tiny advantages that might save their lives when running from a predator.

Finally, the last of the crows were driven off. The rabbits and mice hunkered down, breathing hard, covered in dirt, roots, leaves and bloody plumage. Had the crows seen anything? They would find that out when the killer army was upon them.

ANASTASIA

Anastasia, trapped in her cage and deafened by the jeers and laughter of the Blessed Army, yearned to see a single friendly face. The loneliness of her position was terrifying. Almost worse than the fear of oblivion was the knowledge that every person she could see wanted her dead. It was like an icy wind that sucked all the warmth from her heart.

Friends from *Sans Gloire* swam before her eyes, and she was surprised to find that Freddie's round, honest face offered the most comfort. If she could have just a moment to snuggle against his soft gray-and-black fur—to feel his sturdy, loyal heart beating—the freezing darkness that was threatening to engulf her might subside, just a bit.

But that was not to be. Anastasia pressed her paws over her eyes. All she could do for Freddie now, and for all the souls who had believed in her, was to bring forth the words that would spring her trap. *Make the Blessed charge those crossbows.*

This was their one chance to change the odds and cut the killer army to pieces from afar. Once the Blessed horde passed the Narrows, they would go back to their search-and-destroy tactics, sweeping like a golden blade through the warrens who had dared to dream. And the bright blossom that had briefly begun to unfurl in the Million Acre Wood would wither and die.

She dropped her paws and sat up straight. Time for her final act of love for the little ones. She would give it everything she had.

"Lord Summerday," called Anastasia. "My people are on the field of battle. How do you think the wolf singers will commemorate this moment in song?"

"It will be a funny sssong," hissed Saskatoon. "Some lunchmeat thought they could overthrow the world, and they found out—oops, no!—they were just sandwich fixings all along." The weasels holding up Anastasia's cage giggled.

Anastasia turned her head very slowly and fixed her big golden eyes on Saskatoon. "I saw you when you were in my warren," she said coolly. "You slinkied in a fine killer, and then my people came and buried their teeth in you, and you were *afraid*. When you turned and bolted for the door, you peed all over yourself."

"You lie!" shouted Saskatoon. The weasels holding the cage turned and looked at her.

Anastasia came close to her and pressed her face against the wood and wire. "Poor little wea-wea-weasel," she murmured in a kindly voice. "*Run while you ssstill can.*"

Saskatoon flew at the cage, unleashing a torrent of snarls and biting at the wires. Anastasia laughed and pretended to bite at the wires of the cage herself.

Micah, hearing the commotion, came over. "Are you bothering my weasels, little war criminal?"

Anastasia sat up. "My Lord Summerday," she said. "I want to address you in terms of the greatest respect." She paused to clean her left ear. "I want to, but … somehow, I can't." She pressed against the wire close to Micah. "There are creatures in the Million Acre Wood who eat sweet leaves and drink cool water. They sing and they dance and they tell stories and they hurt no one. They are welcome in the world and they are strong and proud and free. Do you know what they are called?" She fixed him with her golden eyes. "Rabbits."

"That's the best you have?" cooed Sephora, as she came up next to Micah. "I'm already bored with it."

"There are other creatures in the Million Acre Wood," said Anastasia. "All they do is murder other animals. They are hated by everyone and welcome nowhere. Do you know what they are called?" Her scent was bright and spiky. "*Parasites.*"

"Watch your mouth, little bunny," said Grammy Kark.

Anastasia rolled on her back. "You're the tiny lice crawling through our fur, drinking our blood and laying your little nits."

"Your death could be fast and easy or slow and terrible," said Grammy Kark. "Think twice, child."

"You're the tapeworms creeping through the guts of

bears," cooed Anastasia. "Just waiting to be shat out on the morning dew."

"Hush!" Grammy Kark flew at the cage and pecked at Anastasia's eyes, pushing her beak through the small spaces between the wires.

Anastasia laughed and retreated to the far side of the cage. "You're not big. You're *small*. Disgusting. Hated."

"No," said Micah. "The wolf is a creature of love."

"You love yourselves and your stooges," said Anastasia. "No one loves you."

"*Everyone* loves us," said Lord Summerday.

"The world was handed to you by some god hardly worth the name," said Anastasia. "But the world has changed and you're just starting to suspect it."

Sephora leaned over the weasels. "Open the cage. Shut her up."

"I know you're afraid of what's down at the end of the field," said Anastasia quickly as the weasels attacked the cage with many hands. "Do you know why?"

"Don't listen to her," said Sephora.

"It's not because we have magical weapons," said Anastasia.

Saskatoon hissed. "We don't know how to work the lock. Get that rat!"

Anastasia pressed her face against the wires, staring into Micah Summerday's swimming pool eyes. "You know what's down there in the bushes, my Lord? It's the future." Saskatoon and the other weasels bit savagely at the wires, spitting threats. Anastasia pulled back and kept talking. "It's a future filled with clever bunnies, and fierce mice, and crafty rats. And yakking squirrels, brilliant songbirds, and hard-working raccoons. But there are no Landlords in it. Because we don't *need* Landlords."

"Shut up!" shouted Sephora, kicking the cage and sending it tumbling.

Anastasia whirled around and around as the cage rolled but her voice was insistent, unstoppable. "*You need us but we don't need you.*"

The cage came to rest. "No," said Micah Summerday.

The whole Blessed Army was silent now, listening. Anastasia pressed on, relentless. "And now that everyone knows that, it doesn't matter whether you kill me or not, because all the lunchmeat who come after me will know it."

"You're insane!" croaked Grammy Kark. "K-k-kill her!"

"We will never lay down and pay you rent with our bodies again," said Anastasia. "And without us, you die." She pushed close to the wires, eyes bright. A thousand predators hung on her every word. She made them strain to hear, as she whispered in the terrifyingly slow cadences of a death march. "*Now ... we ... are ... Owners.*"

Micah Summerday came close to the cage, his eyes boring into her. His breath was hot and fast and washed over her with the stink of a thousand deaths, but he said nothing.

"Don't listen to this monster, my love," said Sephora. "Blood Father is looking far away. All is well."

A weasel ran up. "Can't find the rat anywhere."

"The sun is setting on you, but you're too old and stupid to realize it," said Anastasia. "So let me do you the last favor a rabbit will ever do for you. I'll show you." In the dead silence, she yelled, "Wendy! Now!"

A hundred and fifty yards away, Wendy just barely heard Anastasia's call, but she knew immediately what to do. She raised her paw and threw the pre-arranged signal. Then a team of raccoons who had lain all night in the tall grass near one of the few trees on the greensward began to haul on a rope. In a few seconds, they were lifting into the air the corpse of a golden wolf, strung up by the back feet. The carcass was surrounded by a cloud of flies.

It was the once-proud, once-beautiful Alaric. And a large, carefully lettered sign had been attached to the body. *"Run while you still can."*

Anastasia craned her neck to see what was happening with the wolves. Micah and Sephora Summerday appeared to be stupefied by this vision of their only son. For a few moments in the morning silence, the one sound that could be heard on the battlefield was the buzzing of the flies. After a few seconds, they turned to look at each other. A sob crept out from between Sephora's clenched teeth, and it turned into a roaring, tremolo groan as tears began to run from her hunter-green eyes.

Micah raised his head, opened his massive jaws, and rolled out a throbbing bass note that vibrated the head of every animal within half a mile. The other wolves joined in the howl, then the coyotes, then the foxes, and they beat their paws upon the ground. The crows and raptors opened their throats and poured out a mixture of rage and fear that tore at the air. And the weasels screeched out a pulsing cacophony of snarl while their paws lashed a frantic counterpoint on the earth.

ARMÉE LIBRE

"Oh Yah, they're coming," said Love Bug. He felt his teeth chattering as he tried to seize his bite blade. He took a quick step to the side to press his flank against Wendy. He slipped under her big ear. He tried to say something but no words came out.

Wendy turned and pressed her blunt muzzle against his ear. Her deep and comforting rumble flowed into him. "You very good boy." She licked his forehead. "You Goldkiller."

Death Rage ran to the top of a small stump and raised her rapier. Her bottlecap helmet gleamed. "Warmice!" called Death Rage. "After today, the wolf will fear the mouse. Are you ready?"

"*Timent muram!*"[30] roared the warmice.

There were no other speeches. Everyone was too scared for speeches. Most of the bunnies looked like it was all they could do to hold their weapons without running.

Wendy held up her paws in the sign announcing the new tactic they had been practicing. *Bink blade now.*

And then Micah Summerday ended his howl, and the killer army stopped with him. The sudden silence was shocking. The Free Army saw him rear up on his back legs, and then lunge forward onto the field of battle with the fourteen wolves of the Summerday Clan on either side of him. Several dozen coyotes fanned out on each side of the wolf line. And hundreds of foxes and weasels raced just behind, a scrambling horde of teeth and claws.

---

[30] Fear the mouse!

More than a thousand predators were racing down the greensward toward the line of six hundred mice and rabbits. They ran in silence, mouths open. It was shocking how fast they covered the ground.

The rabbits and mice all fell silent as many quiet prayers were muttered. In front of them was a forty-foot-wide strip of spikes, invisible under the grass. Even with that, the defenders felt naked and intensely vulnerable. No one knew where the crossbows were. Were they in place? Would they fire in time? Or maybe the Free Army would be revealed as just another tragic footnote in a long line of stories that all ended the same way. *Brave heroes, cut down on that terrible day.*

The animals charging down the field outweighed the defending animals by factor of more than a hundred. The spikes would slow them down, but unless the crossbows began firing, the confrontation between predators and prey would be nasty, brutish, and short.

As the wave of predators rolled toward them, time seemed to slow down for the defenders. The fear gripped them like an ice burn over their shoulders and down their spines. Every system carved into their bodies by a million years of evolution was screaming at them to flee. But they did not.

Freddie tasted bile in the back of his throat. A few feet from him, someone was throwing up. Several near him were sobbing with fear. He could smell hot urine.

The line of predators was growing more ragged as it got nearer. With all the killers running at full speed, some were getting out in front. A silvery wolf, with a lighter, more elegant build than the heavy Summerdays, was far in the lead.

He entered the spike field running at full tilt and passed harmlessly over the first row of points. Then the second. Then the third.

The rabbits in his direct line of travel began to back up.

Wendy shouted, "Hold!"

Then the wolf slapped a front paw down onto a pointed tip hidden in the grass. Instantly, his body was tumbling, rolling across the turf, a white-hot snarl coming out of his throat. He scrambled to his feet, shaking his injured paw, his eyes already scanning the rabbits twenty feet away, picking out his first target. As he gathered himself to make his killing leap, his motion was briefly slowed. In that moment, a brilliant red and green flicker of color hissed over the rabbits' heads like a malevolent hummingbird and slammed into his shoulder.

It was a quarrel fletched with the feathers of a painted bunting. The crossbows had arrived.

Dingus

Dingus saw the silver wolf backing up, eyes wide, batting at invisible enemies, confused by the pain in his shoulder caused by no animals he could see. Right behind him came the mass of alpha predators in the front line of the charge.

"Fire, fire, fire," chanted Dingus, as he stood in warrior pose on the crossbow firing platform, his front knee deeply bent, and his left hand outflung, holding the trigger cord. "Into the mass of them."

Boing and the other Ascending Squirrels took up the chant. *Fire, fire, fire*. Five more crossbows snapped, sending their quarrels flying, streaks of color penetrating the battlefield.

Then seven more crossbows fired. Flickers of blue, yellow, red, white, green, and black raced forward. And when the last ten fired, every color of feather in the songbird universe was hurtling toward the phalanx of killers, all guiding arrowheads of obsidian and flint.

On each side of Dingus, Wellbutrin and Lorazepam were laying on their backs, pushing against the thick part of the bow with their back feet as they pulled the bowstring up to their chests with their hands. Working together, they slipped the string over the catch-hook on the stock, and the crossbow was cocked. Wellbutrin grabbed a quarrel from the pile next to him and slapped it into place in the firing groove. Lorazepam pushed the quarrel up the groove until the nock snugged against the bowstring. Now the crossbow was reloaded and ready to fire. They rolled away from it quickly to make sure they didn't get hit by any fast-moving parts.

Dingus surfed his weapon back to neutral, using his body weight to control the angle and aim of the crossbow atop its coconut mounting. In truth, the horde of bodies just arriving at a point sixty yards away hardly required careful targeting. He centered the crossbow and jerked the trigger cord, sending another carefully napped stone point flying toward the killers.

ALIYAH

Aliyah, racing down the field with rest of the *Posse Comitatus*, was shocked to see Tennyson take a tumble just as he got near the line of rabbits. And even more surprised to watch him start flailing and snapping at empty space.

There were several young coyotes sprinting a few steps in

front of her, so she cut behind them and started to angle across the field as she ran, taking a trajectory that would bring her to where Tennyson was now biting at his own shoulder. She could not begin to imagine what was happening to him. A frisson of worry burned along the nape of her neck.

Then the young coyotes got near the rabbits, and one of them was abruptly rolling on the ground snarling, holding her foot strangely. Another yelped and whirled, wide eyes looking everywhere. Aliyah could see something like a blossom of blue and orange flowers sprouting from his chest. She shook her head and blinked. *Some kind of rabbit magic?*

The three remaining coyotes approached the line of rabbits, and slowed to engage with them. She thought, *this should be quick.*

FREDDIE

Freddie's heart was in his throat as the trio of coyotes came rushing at him. Then there was no more time for fear, just bink blading. *Don't stop. Don't fight. Don't think. Hit and move.* That's what Wendy had drilled them on.

He launched himself at the nearest coyote and struck a glancing blow across the shoulder with his bite blade. The coyote snarled and turned, snapping at the spot where Freddie had just been.

But Freddie was already gone, moving onto the second coyote, bite blade leading, looking for any target at all. A bit of hock presented itself as Freddie hit and rolled near the rear leg. Freddie slashed wildly with his blade, and without knowing whether he had connected, spun his body to hurl himself at the third coyote, who was behind him. By midleap, he was bringing his head around to the front and realizing he was about to crash-land against a wide sandy-gray flank. He clenched his teeth and stiffened his body as he made contact, driving his blade deep into the coyote's side.

The snarl of rage came out like a ripsaw, and the teeth were rushing toward him a moment later. He got one back leg against the furry flank and pushed off, sending himself on an awkward flailing trajectory out into space. Just as the jaws were about to close on his trailing leg, he saw Mabel come tumbling past him. She whipped her head sideways and dragged her blade across the coyote's forehead.

An instant later, the coyote was swinging its head back toward Mabel, and Freddie was hitting and rolling across the grass. He knew where all the points were, since he had just mapped this area, so he arched his back as he rolled over a buried spear. He cleared it just in time to see a gold-and-grey wolf loom over him, plant a heavy foot on the sharp point, and then go sprawling, a buzz-saw snarl erupting from its throat.

The memory of Wendy's voice barking orders during the drills was still playing in his head. It felt good. And for the first time all day, he didn't feel like throwing up. *Maybe we have a chance.*

Chapter 19

The wolf is already within you.

—Dingus Oakrunner

Posse Comitatus

The wolves and coyotes in the first rank of the *Posse Comitatus* arrived at the thin line of rabbits expecting to sweep through them and rush to the end of the field, destroying the criminal uprising in a matter of minutes. All the waiting around and rumors of farkillers seemed laughable.

It was only a few seconds since they had seen Tennyson and the two coyotes fall and go rolling across the turf, and there hadn't been time to even consider what that might mean. So when the line of sprinting canids entered the field of invisible spikes, and they saw first one, then two, then many on their left and right stumble and fall, snarling and yelping, they had no idea what was happening. And the flicks of color racing past their peripheral version were even more unfathomable.

A single *idée fixe*[31] drove them forward: *Get the rabbits.*

But when they arrived, the line of rabbits exploded into motion. These were not stunned and terrified creatures, already crippled by the Giving. These were not even soldiers holding a line against on oncoming force. As the heavy, galloping predators crashed into them, the rabbits became like water, flowing through and around the larger animals. They moved so quickly their bodies were a blur, bundles of muscle and fur attached to a gleaming blade. The *Posse* members thrust their jaws forward, here, there, side to side, snapping, snarling, unable to seize these will-o'-the-wisp fighters who struck them and moved on.

The warmice dialed up the chaos by on order of magnitude. Largely invisible under the grass, they rose from the turf to drive their spears into vulnerable parts, and then vanished when the mighty jaws came roaring at them for retribution. The injuries they inflicted were small but they were many. In short order, the predators who had had the good fortune not to step on a buried spear still found themselves limping, beset by more different points of pain than they could even be conscious of.

It was the swarm, the classic weapon of the littles against the bigs. The same asymmetrical tactic had permanently changed warfare among the Dead Gods in the mid-twenty-first century, when hordes of cheap and tiny drones piloted by

---

[31] Fixed idea.

nonstate actors destroyed the massive robowarriors fielded by the wealthiest nations.

And everywhere in this tumbling melee, the crossbow quarrels flew, seven-inch spikes arriving with a colorful, deadly flourish.

Dingus

After Wellbutrin and Lorazepam cocked and loaded his crossbow, Dingus spread his hands wide and leaned into a glide that swept the nose of his weapon across the wide scrum now stretching across the Narrows. He saw a golden wolf coming to assist the silver wolf he had hit earlier. The golden wolf had some kind of shimmery thing on its body. It sparkled in the sun almost like agouti fur.

Dingus leaned back and to the left to slow the crossbow's sweep and raise the nose a little. As the sight passed over the golden wolf's shimmering chest, he snapped his trigger string and sent a green and black quarrel flying. The shot was dead on, and Dingus was astonished to see the quarrel strike the golden wolf's chest and bounce off.

"Reload, reload, reload," he chanted. The golden wolf helped the silver wolf stand, and was now pressing against it, pushing it into a run, headed back north, away from the crossbows. Wellbutrin accidentally dropped the string on his side and Lorazepam's fingers got pinched against the stock. She snarled and then licked her fingers. Wellbutrin whined an apology.

"*Geh*," said Dingus. There was something special about that golden wolf. Best not waste any more quarrels there. His old, irritable voice surfaced for a moment. "Get the silver one."

"*Get the silver one,*" chanted the Ascending Squirrels. "*Get the silver one.*"

CROWS

Grammy Kark, flying about fifty feet above and behind the charging *Posse*, could see what was happening in a way the animals on the ground could not. The first wave of canids, dominated by the wolves and coyotes, was now stuck at the rabbit line, lunging this way and that, biting at every nearby movement, getting hurt, falling, not advancing. And the smaller foxes and weasels were bunching up behind them, a rolling wave turning on itself, almost completely ineffective.

And she could see, every few seconds, more flicks of color whipping down the field from the scrub and bushes at the southern edge. These were hitting mostly wolves and coyotes, causing significant pain and distraction. And, unlike most of the animals in the fight, she had the trichromat vision that enabled her to see the red streaks of blood beginning to appear.

"Farkillers!" she shouted. "The rabbits have them. Get to the far end of the field and destroy them. To the bushes! Spread the word!" All the crows around her took up the cry, "To the bushes! To the bushes!"

Soon, some of the larger canids were peeling off from the scrum and heading down the field. This loosened the pack so that the foxes and weasels could began to slip through. Some of them got caught up in the fight. Others followed the developing rush to the end of the meadow.

As Grammy Kark flew back and forth along the line of battle, she cast a quick glance upwards and saw the raptors circling high above, clearly disinclined to enter such an uncouth melee. They were killers, not fighters. *Diveboys too good for the dirty work, as usual.*

She dropped a little lower and considered putting her beak and claws into the fight, but thought better of it. Those rabbits looked dangerous.

WOLF & RABBITS

Micah Summerday, heavier and slower than the fastest runners, had ended up in the second line of the charge. So now he was entering the spike field and delivering the swath of destruction he was known for. As he seized rabbits and tossed them aside, the other rabbits in his path started to retreat from this onslaught, bounding away from the certain death in his murderous jaws.

Wendy recognized him by his aquamarine eyes. He was several yards away and coming fast.

He registered her as something strange, a lumpy brown shape, not elegant, not a rabbit. He started to lean his trajectory toward her, but his stride did not slow. This would be just another snatch-and-go, with the killing shake delivered on the run.

Wendy leaped sideways, her huge back feet tearing up turf. She was briefly airborne, then hit and rolled, trying to keep her razor sharp bite blade out of the dirt.

Micah's head tracked her leap, but partway through he decided she was not worth slowing down for. Not when there were magical rabbit weapons in need of destruction just fifty yards away. He continued on, claws raking the earth, driving forward.

Wendy shredded the ground with her back feet as she reversed course. And as the huge golden wolf passed in front of her, she leaped and went airborne, ears flapping, hurling herself toward his unprotected flank. Her blade tore a long gash in his side.

Micah roared at the unexpected jolt of pain, turning, jaws opening, ready to tear this bizarre hell-thing to pieces.

But as he curled into a circle, Love Bug, seeing the opportunity of the curved, exposed left side of his neck, lunged at him and plunged his bite blade into the beautiful expanse of golden fur. His blade sank in, and then he fell back, a trickle of crimson already beginning to show.

Micah felt the burn and turned automatically toward the new pain. But when he saw that Love Bug was already scrambling away, he tensed his back legs to continue his charge.

At that moment, Freddie shoved his bite blade up from beneath, just as Death Rage rose from the grass and drove her rapier into his forepaw.

Micah roared, leaping upwards away from the pain, then spun in a circle, jaws snapping wildly on empty space. The Landlord of the Million Acre Wood had never fought anything more complicated than a stag or wolf. Big animals are a single, obvious enemy. They attack you with their understandable weapons, and you always know where the threat is coming from. Multiple attacks from non-entities like rabbits and not-really-rabbits were something he had no plan for.

Nevertheless, he righted himself and plunged down the

field toward the unknown danger, bloody but unbowed, leader of his people.

STAN

Stan, hovering over the embankment with his reserve force of songbirds, quickly climbed to a hundred feet above the battlefield. From the moment Anastasia had been seized, one question had not left his mind: *Where is the godmother?* Now, emerging above the fray and looking down the battlefield, he could see the majority of crows engaged in an aerial scrum with the main force of songbirds, just above the ground combatants. High above, the raptors were wheeling slowly.

Then his sharp eyes picked out something else: the glint of sunshine on *aluminum d'or* wire two hundred yards away at the north end of the Narrows. He didn't know what it was exactly, but the shine of metal was rare in the Million Acre Wood. *Could be her.*

Things started to click. Crows busy. Far side open. Raptors looking the other way. This was a moment of opportunity that his aerial cavalry was made for. It was worth taking his reserve of a hundred songbirds and making a dash for it.

"*Paisanos!*"[32] he trilled as he sliced through the leaf layer and then caromed through the small tree branches toward the cliffs, just clearing the heads of the squirrels piloting their crossbows. "Follow me and your names will be sung forever."

---

[32] Compatriots.

The reserve songbirds swirled behind him, winding into their warcry.

"*Piano, piano,*"[33] called Stan. "This is a surprise party."

The songbirds became hushed and followed Stan over the edge of the cliff, flowing like brightly colored liquid. Stan led them closely along the cliff wall, out of sight of the crows, and the orderly cyclone of confetti shadowed his every move.

After two hundred yards of fast and silent flight, Stan left his reserve near a large outcropping and surreptitiously popped his head over the edge of the cliff. They were at the north end of the Narrows. The area was now mostly clear of hunters. There were just a few injured fighters who were limping away from the battle. Then he saw, a few dozen yards away, a small cage made of stout twigs and golden wire.

Anastasia was in the cage, chewing though the wood but defeated by the metal. A brown rat was clinging to the cage, fumbling with the lock.

Stan trilled to the songbirds and they came swooping up past the cliff edge, following him toward Anastasia, moving in a tight group. A moment later, they swarmed the cage, covering every square inch of it and seizing it with their feet. Several nearby foxes looked up, startled, and then started to move toward the colorful swirl. But just as they were getting close, the songbirds took to the air, with the rat still hanging on. Within seconds, they were dropping over the lip of the cliff.

---

[33] Softly, softly.

DINGUS

"Large targets, large targets," chanted Dingus, as he surfed the sights of his weapon across the battlefield. "You and your quarrel are one."

"I and my quarrel are one," sang the Ascending Squirrels.

The sound of crossbows firing rapped out a steady cadence.

"*Lokah samastha sukhino bhavanthu,*"[34] chanted Dingus, briefly entering tree pose while Lorazepam and Wellbutrin cocked and loaded his crossbow.

"*May my thoughts, words, and actions contribute to worldwide joy,*" responded the rest of the Ascending Squirrels, droning a fifth above him.

Dingus saw a golden wolf with aquamarine eyes coming down the field. He stretched out his left hand, and his crossbow began to drift along a path of intersection. His voice lifted on a relaxed melodic line. "Golden one," he crooned. "Focus, focus, focus."

He pulled the trigger cord and sent the obsidian arrowhead flying. A moment later, he saw the wolf twitch, then turn his head to bite at a cluster of feathers buried in his flank.

In his peripheral vision, Dingus saw Wellbutrin and Lorazepam exchange a glance across the crossbow stock, their dark eyes unreadable within their masks.

Dingus fell forward into downward dog pose as the raccoons quickly reloaded his crossbow. "It is not the way that is mindful," he murmured. "It is mindfulness that is the way."

---

[34] May all beings everywhere be happy and free.

SASKATOON

Saskatoon came gliding up toward the frenetic turmoil of the spike field. Weasels are not fast runners, so she was on the lagging edge of the *Posse Comitatus,* ready to kill and in no hurry to move on. She saw a mouse rise out of the grass with a rapier in her hand and a handsome flat helmet with scalloped edges strapped to her head.

"Hello, Missy," she said relaxing into the killing patter she was comfortable with, trying to forget that very uncivil, unfunny, unlikeable rabbit in the cage. "Well, aren't you dressed to kill."

"I came to slay," said the mouse, and the rapier flicked into *en garde* position.

Saskatoon smirked and raised her head up high above the mouse on her long slender neck. Then she grinned her mouthful of white spikes into existence. "You are so precious," she said, and cocked her head back for the death strike.

"I only have one thing to say to you," said the mouse.

Saskatoon smiled, luxuriating in the hot, murderous energy swirling around her. "What is that, pooh bug?" she cooed. Then she settled in and waited for a really good answer.

"Here be dragons," said the mouse.

A small horde of warmice rose out of the grass around Saskatoon, each armed with a spear. She was just working up something exceptionally clever to say when suddenly, they were on her.

SEPHORA

Sephora Summerday was in the first wave of the *Posse Comitatus* to reach the embankment. She hadn't seen Micah get waylaid by rabbits, and she had missed all the points in the spike field, so she was just running, her strong muscles powering her sleek form, feeling the killing joy. Flicks of color were speeding past her, but she had as yet no awareness of what they were, so she was unconcerned.

She didn't notice that there were hardly any wolves, and just a few coyotes. She was surrounded mostly by a wave of foxes, since they were small enough to slip through the melee unengaged. They were just arriving at the area right in front of the bushes, with her a few steps behind.

Then something unbelievable happened. Just as the canids were about to rush in among the bushes and decimate the farkiller teams, the earth fell away beneath their feet. Instead of being solid ground, it was revealed to be flimsy lattice work of branches and twigs, with a light covering of dirt. And below, there was dark, empty space. Sephora was already slowing down when she heard the cries begin. She skidded to a stop at the edge of what she realized was a long pit, and saw foxes tumbling and yipping below, some leaping haplessly upwards and falling back. She blanched under her golden fur. *What is this trickery?*

The pit was several yards wide and spanned the width of the Narrows. She might be able to jump it, but she could just as easily fall. Most of the *Posse* would be held back. A quarrel whizzed by her like a mosquito the size of a sparrow, cutting a small notch in her ear. She flinched from the sudden, sharp bite of pain, shaking her head, trying to collect her thoughts. Then she was backing away, unable to comprehend what this had to do with rabbits. She was just turning and starting to run when she saw Micah stumbling toward her, bleeding from quarrels embedded in his throat and chest.

ISADORE & JULIETTE

Isadore and Juliette were loping along easy-peasy at the back of the *Posse Comitatus* charge. Juliette couldn't run very well with her injuries because they had not healed perfectly. So even though her rage was great, her pace was casual.

What they didn't realize was that by now all the wolves and most of the coyotes had been hit at least once, which left the twenty-four Ascending Squirrels surfing their crossbows and scanning the field for new, smaller marks. And two slow-moving foxes at sixty yards were an inviting target.

So just as Isadore was about to say, "Let's make this a fine, foxy day, babe," a quarrel suddenly skimmed past his neck, leaving a gash that quickly turned red. He yelped and leaped to the side, turning round and round, looking for the source of the attack.

Most of the *Posse Comitatus* members had no real idea what the rumored farkillers were, so Juliette had no inkling that the flicker of brightly colored feathers that had just passed by was actually a spike with a sharpened blade for a tip.

What she did know was this: rabbits were bad, rabbits had magic, and now these monsters were threatening her family again. With the scars they already bore, she didn't need a second warning.

Juliette pushed into Isadore's confused whirl and caught him on the third spin. "We're leaving," she said. "Let the wolves fight their own battles." He was a little dazed from his panicky spinning, so she pushed him back toward the north end of the battle field. He took a few steps, looking uncertain.

Then a green and black crossbow quarrel skimmed up

Juliette's back. She yelped in fear, then nipped Isadore's haunches to make him run. "Go!"

STAN

The reserve songbirds rose over the edge of the cliff at the southern end of the Narrows to find the embankment area in chaos. Crows were everywhere, shrieking and diving at the squirrels, raking them with their talons, and driving them off the crossbows. The raccoons were flailing blindly, forced to keep one foreleg over their faces to protect their eyes from the crows' darting beaks.

Stan grimaced. *Must have noticed us leaving.* The songbirds set the cage down and hurled themselves toward the attacking corvids. Within seconds, the scrub above the embankment was a maelstrom of flickering hues as the brightly colored songbirds closed with the dark flyers and engaged in aerial slugfests as they whipped through the complex tracery of low-hanging branches.

Out of the corner of his eye, Stan noticed the rat fumbling the lock off the door of the cage, then bracing its back legs against the wire as it pulled the door open. An instant later, Anastasia was pushing her way out and taking a great gulp of the free air.

ANASTASIA

Anastasia stood, staring, her mind awhirl. Three minutes ago, she had been caged among enemies, with death very close at hand. Now she was back in the bosom of her own people, and her life once again stretched out before her. The whiplash of this sudden transition left her feeling stunned and wobbly, but she was determined to make the most of it.

Since the songbirds had flown her back below the edge of the cliff, she had not been able to see what was happening on the battlefield. And a quick glance northward now showed a fantastic jumble of creatures in motion. The long open pit in front of the crossbows revealed that the deadfall trap had been sprung. Beyond that, it was hard to see how the battle was faring. The best thing for her to focus on now was what was right in front of her.

Many of the squirrels were hiding from the crow onslaught, even though the songbirds were now pulling most of the crows into defensive action. And most of the raccoons were scattered through the brush with their paws over their eyes.

Anastasia ran down the line of crossbows. Only a few still had functioning fire teams. Where was Dingus? She raked the area with her golden eyes as she ran. At last, she found him laying dazed under an ivy leaf with a bleeding injury behind his left ear, his tail laying limp beside him.

She knelt next him, nuzzling his cheek and licking his injury. It looked like a puncture from a crow's beak had torn his scalp. And the blow to the head had left him a little stunned. "Are you okay, old friend?" she asked, her mouth next to his ear.

He looked at her and touched his head. "Crow got me from behind," he said dreamily. "Who let them in here?"

"Don't know," said Anastasia. She bumped him with her nose. "Want to show these hooligans what an Ascending Squirrel can do?"

Dingus looked at the blood on his hand and said nothing.

"Your people need you," said the Loving Auntie, giving him another friendly nudge. "This is your time." Dingus shook his head. It looked like he was trying to focus his eyes. Anastasia felt a chill descend on her.

She moved in front of him and fixed him with her golden eyes. "Who's the Squirrel Without Antecedents?" she asked. "Who is He of the Most Excellent Equanimity Which Cannot Be Trifled With by Blessed Thugs?"

At the sound of these familiar phrases, Dingus raised his head and looked at her for a long moment. His tail twitched and he clambered to his feet. "Me."

Sephora

Sephora ran to Micah and knelt by him. He was bleeding badly from both bite blade and crossbow wounds. The area around him was only grass. There was no cover.

The buzzing death messengers coming from the murderers in the bushes seemed to have slowed down in the last minute or two, so she seized this moment of opportunity. She gripped a nearby dead coyote by the scruff of his neck and dragged it in front of her mate. Then she grabbed a dead fox in her mouth and pulled it over. Not far away was a dead rabbit. Sephora picked it up and placed the body on top of the coyote.

In a few moments, she built a wall of dead and dying animals to protect her and Micah from the murderous spikes flying out of the wall of scrub.

She lay as flat as she could and nuzzled the neck of the

War Leader of the Summerday Clan. His breathing was ragged. "My love, my love," she whispered. "Stay with me."

The dropping eyelids opened and the aquamarine eyes looked at her. "I thought we were honorable. Why is Blood Father looking at us?"

"I don't know, Micah." Tears filled her eyes. "But we can make it out of this. We're survivors."

She saw something out of the corner of her eye. It was Aliyah, crawling up to her. She was bleeding from a gash in her left foreleg, but otherwise her armor had protected her. "Mummy," she whined. Then she caught sight of Micah's half-closed eyes. "Daddy," she groaned, then nuzzled his side, panting. "What should we do, Mother?"

Sephora rolled over and looked in her maple-leaf green eyes. "You are a good daughter," she said. "You were the smart one. You saw all this coming."

"No," groaned Aliyah. "I didn't want this."

Sephora licked her face for a few moments. Then she said. "You are the future of the Summerday Clan. I *love* you." She nuzzled her daughter's cheek. "Do you hear me?"

"Yes," sobbed Aliyah, her tears turning the dust around her face into mud.

"I'm going to ask you to do one thing now," said Sephora. "Are you ready, Goldybug?"

"Yes, mummy," said Aliyah, her breath fast and ragged. "How can I help?"

Sephora pushed her head down by Aliyah's face so she could make eye contact with her. She held her gaze for a long moment. Then she said, "*Run.*"

Aliyah stared at her, teary-eyed. "What?"

"Run back," said Sephora. "Start again. Make us proud."

"But what about you and Daddy?"

"We'll be fine," said Sephora. Her breath was fast and shallow. "Just going to rest here for a minute."

"But what—"

"*Go*. Now," said Sephora, and nipped her. Aliyah scrambled away from her mother's teeth and sprinted toward the north end of the battlefield. Sephora watched her go for a few moments, then turned back to her mate. He had started to thrash, like he was trying to get up. "Just rest, my love," she whispered. "Our little girl is safe."

"They need me," said Micah.

Sephora licked his muzzle. "You're safe now. Stay and rest."

Micah fought his way up onto his elbows, blood running from the quarrels buried in his flank, his chest, his neck. "They need their War Leader."

"Shhh. Who needs you?" asked Sephora, trying to get him to lie down.

Micah looked at her kindly and licked her forehead. "The animals," he said simply, and stood up.

ANASTASIA

Anastasia saw the golden wolf with aquamarine eyes stand up from behind the makeshift shelter of animal bodies and begin to walk forward. Immediately, the other wolf jumped up and seized a dead coyote, trying to shield them both with the carcass.

"There," she said to Dingus, who was standing on his

crossbow, arms outflung for balance, trigger cord laying lightly across his palm. "Micah. Sephora. Both of them."

She heard Anima Mundi's voice in her ear. *Every death is cause for sadness.* She pushed it away. *You're nobody. You're just me.*

Dingus nodded. "Fellow seekers," he called out to the Ascending Squirrels, now all standing balanced and ready, their crossbows cocked. "Let us lay down these golden angels, so their blessings may run free."

There was a mass hum of ratification from the other squirrels.

"Now," said the Loving Auntie.

"Welcome to the eternal zero," said Dingus.

Then the crossbows snapped, and the stone blades of twenty-four quarrels sent the Lord and Lady of the Million Acre Wood to the Forever Forest.

Dingus's bright silver voice floated out over the battle field. "*May your hunting always be fine.*"

FREDDIE

The battle was winding down. The fifty yards from the spike zone to the crossbow embankment had been the scene of much fierce fighting, and many had lost their lives. Most of the remaining hunters were fleeing northward.

Freddie walked through the chaotic landscape as though in a trance, his unsheathed bite blade dragging in the dirt. He had fought bravely, and he was glad to be alive, but he could not bear to be in the presence of any more death. When he passed the golden forms of Micah and Sephora Summerday, he averted his eyes.

I guess we won. This thought, which would have been titanic in its impact only a few hours ago, now called forth no response from him. A gash in his left shoulder and a tear on his right flank generated a dull pain. He should find something to stop the bleeding, but his limbs were leaden. He felt as though he had nothing left to give. Finally, he just pulled some fur from his own belly and used it to matte his injuries.

Then he saw a stream of small animals carefully crossing the deadfall trap on one of the few large branches that had been placed there for just that reason. Among them was a lean brown bunny with golden eyes.

Anastasia. His heart leaped. She was safe. He didn't know how, but that didn't matter. As the Loving Auntie stepped out onto the battlefield, she was immediately mobbed by joyful animals. She sat up tall, buffeted by the crowd, scanning anxiously for someone. When she saw Freddie, she immediately ran toward him.

She pressed her face against the fur of his cheek. Her breathing was fast and ragged. Her scent was urgent. "When I was in that cage, and the killers were all around me, I—" she broke off, shuddering. "I wanted so much to see just one … friendly face. And the person I wanted to see most"—she pulled back to look at him—"was *you*, Freddie."

Freddie was astonished and struck dumb. The crowd of animals swirled around them, trying to see what was happening.

Anastasia pressed against him. He could feel her lean, hard body shivering. "I just wanted to see … my friend. The one who looks out … for *me*…" Her eyes swept over the press of animals around them. "For *us*."

Freddie felt a warm glow begin at his shoulders and

spread across his body. He absorbed the tension coming from her taut, ropy muscles and let it run out through his feet into the earth. It felt so good to be doing something for her, when he had thought he would never see her again.

She nestled against him. He trembled and kissed her forehead tenderly. She allowed it, and then kissed his.

The hubbub around them was raucous and joyful, but Freddie had no trouble hearing her when she put her mouth close to his ear and said, "I love you."

He caught his breath. Tears came to his eyes and shone like newborn diamonds. He thought his heart might burst with joy.

Anastasia

It was late on the day of the battle. There was much celebrating going on among the Free Peoples, and also much grieving. Many rabbits, warmice, and songbirds had given their lives to make this victory possible.

Nicodemus had organized the raccoons and squirrels to collect the dead, respectfully carrying the bodies off the battlefield and laying them out in a small grassy sward where loved ones could cover them with flowers and kisses and say their last farewells. This in itself was new. Previous memorial services had been for friends whose bodies had been taken by predators. Now, for the first time, they were able to honor the bodies of warriors who had fallen in battle.

Mabel and her acolytes walked among the exalted dead, singing a sweetly intertwining descant, anointing their foreheads with cedar resin and white rose nectar. Anastasia followed after, sprinkling fresh lavender over their still forms, placing her forepaw on their hearts, and kissing them one by one.

After they were done, Wendy, along with Love Bug, Death Rage, Stan, and her other top captains, walked among those who had offered their lives so bravely. They were carrying bits of bloodied fur and red-stained quarrels they brought from the battlefield. They surrounded each fallen friend and knelt down. "You *gaisgeach*."[35] said Wendy. "You *curaidh*."[36] The fighters touched their foreheads and extended their paws. *Respect*. Wendy stood by the head of each of the fallen and spread her forepaws wide. "Today you *win*. You trample your enemies even in *death*." Then they rubbed the blood of the dead predators on the footpads of the heroes.

After much discussion, it was decided to raise a great earthwork and place the bodies inside, so there would be a permanent memorial to the victors of the Battle of the Narrows. The rabbits would move the earth. The raccoons would bring stones. And the mice would create an intricate mosaic representing the spirit of freedom.

The leadership of the Free Peoples had also been talking all day about what to do with the foxes, weasels, and coyotes who had fallen into their deadfall trap. There were well over a hundred, pacing and yipping. The rabbits had no solid plan for what to do next, which made it clear to everyone how no one had really believed they would ever get this far.

What should they do? With the Free Peoples dead and

---

[35]   Warrior.

[36]   Champion.

wounded foremost on their minds, many animals were in favor of killing the captured hunters. Anastasia faced down these grieving friends and family of the martyred dead and said, "We do not kill defenseless animals. That is not who we are."

There was much angry murmuring, so Nicodemus stood and said, "If we are ever going to be a sovereign nation, and speak as peers with other nations, we *must* have rule of law."

So it was that Anastasia and her retinue came to be walking along the edge of the long pit and looking down at the hunters below. A cacophony of snarls and whines rose up.

Memory of their cruelty to her when she had been in their hands washed over her. There was a bitter taste in her mouth. She found herself rethinking the definition of "defenseless" and then managed to push it aside.

"Hunters," she said. "You fought for a way of life that no longer exists. You were born an Owner. I was born a Renter. You were born a killer. I was born a victim." Two raccoons carrying injured rabbits off the meadow on a litter crossed her field of vision. "Was it brave of you to attack rabbits and mice? No." She scratched at the earth. "But you fought under the old law. And we will respect that. You will not be harmed." Her gaze flicked from face to face. A mix of growls and whimpers came forth.

"Now there is a new law. Killing any member of the Free Peoples in the Million Acre Wood is punishable by death." A confused groan rose from the pit. She reached for the ancient rabbit legal formula and spoke over the rising noise. "This law will stand until mountains walk, rain falls upward, or there are two suns in the sky."

She looked over the gathered predators who all stood staring up at her, still wearing shocked and wounded expressions, stunned that a rabbit was dictating terms. *How much law did you give me when I was in the pit?*

"We are going to set you free," said the Loving Auntie. Surprised gasps sounded from every group. "I know you need to eat. That is not my problem. The lives of my people are my problem. You may go anywhere in the wide world. You may kill whosoever you can. But you may not do it here." She stood tall. For the first time, her gaze took in the little animals around the edge of the pit as well as the killers below. "In *our* land, if you violate *our* law, you will be hunted, you will be killed." She shook out her Claw and raised it high. "I, Anastasia Bloody Thorn, Rabbit Without Antecedents, Leader of the Free Peoples, command it."

Then she turned away, exhausted by the battle. And the forbearance.

Chapter 20

The Sun kissed the Earth like her own child on the day Newly Beloved came home.

—Book of Secrets, 12:37

Aliyah

It was now three days since the proclamation of Anastasia Bloody Thorn had been carried throughout the Million Acre Wood by the songbirds, fierce and joyful in their new capacity as messengers for the Free Peoples.

Aliyah kept moving north. Not running, it was more like sleepwalking. The bright new day for the little animals was for her the end of the world. All the family she had ever known had gone to the Forever Forest on that dark day on the Narrows. And her shiny new love, Tennyson, had also fallen and lay still.

She ate nothing. Drank the barest sips of water. And kept drifting away from the scene of destruction, moving toward her home among the Spires.

When she arrived, she walked through the empty spaces between the stone pillars, feeling the vast emptiness. The Summerday Clan was over. The cubs were gone. The crows were scattered, their nests empty. The fearsome wrath of the rabbits drove all before it. No one wanted to risk being here when the new lords of the Wood arrived. A pall of fear overlaid everything. Even in the bright autumn days, to her everything seemed gray.

Aliyah visited her personal spaces and nosed among her things. She shook off her chain mail and dropped it into her old backpack, along with a few personal items, mostly gifts from Micah and Sephora.

She knew she could not stay, so her plodding feet eventually led her to the foot of the Midsummer Path, the long and winding series of switchbacks that slowly climbed the Boreal Cliffs and led to the uplands.

As she drew near the foot of the Path, she saw a dark smudge skulking under an old apple tree. As she got closer, she could see it was a sandy-gray coyote, fearful, limping. *Gaetan.*

She ran to him and they touched noses. Then they nuzzled each other's faces. She could find no words, but she did, finally, feel her tears began to flow. Under a brilliant sun, the shiny golden wolf and the small scruffy coyote stood and wept together.

At last, they turned and took their first steps onto the Midsummer Path and up into a new world.

FREE PEOPLES

A month after the battle, it was now late autumn, and the foliage was in full flame. Of course, the rabbits paid no attention. To them, the cool-weather color splash had been the same since time immemorial. What was different about the air was not the newly arrived fine nip, but rather that it was free. Because *they* were free.

You don't cast off the habits that have kept your people alive for millennia in the space of a few weeks, so everyone was still behaving very carefully. The long shadow of the Blessed Ones still lay over the Million Acre Wood, long after they had been exposed as malevolent grifters and driven from office. But in the hearts that beat in the chests of tens of thousands of little animals, something was waking up, little by little, every day.

This is ours.

They had never known—never dreamed of—any story that did not center on the Landlords, with themselves as hapless short-lived walk-ons. Their definition of a good day used to be *I survived,* with elaborate thanks due to every god it was possible to remember. Now it was simply *I woke up, I had breakfast, and nothing happened.* And the *nothing* was so very, very good.

The opportunity to create a new world was dazzling in its sweetness and rarity. Anastasia and her team threw themselves into the work of governance with joy and fervor. They did a census and discovered there were more than a thousand warrens in the Million Acre Wood. They used these as the headquarters of administrative districts and set up an Assembly, with representatives of all the songbirds, mice, racoons, and rabbits living in these areas.

There was much to be done. Even though this moment was bright, dangers lurked around every corner, and Anastasia was determined that the Free Peoples would have a vigorous defense. Yasmin, as Captain of the Home Guard, she put in charge of the militias fielded by each warren, making sure the defensive posture stayed strong even as it relaxed. And Holly, the Home Steward, continued as the operations chief of the Free Peoples, putting her mixture of empathy and situational awareness to good use. She also had plans to set up permanent trade routes for craft items and special foods, building on their *ad hoc* trade routes set up to move sharpstone north for the Battle of the Narrows.

After the dust had settled, the two young mothers began bunking together, sharing a burrow and raising their kittens as a team. Under their leadership, council meetings became more kit-friendly, often including afternoon dill tips and plenty of breaks for a fresh air romp.

Wendy had a long talk with Anastasia about claiming what she had earned by leading the *Armée Libre* to victory: an all-expenses-paid trip back to her home island. Now, a few months into her snuggly relationship with Love Bug, and luxuriating in the hero's welcome she received everywhere in the Wood, she decided to stay awhile longer. The ride home could wait. The *Armée Libre* was evolving into a new role. She was enjoying the challenge of refitting her victorious army into a rapid response team, patrolling the common areas as well as points of entrance from the uplands.

Wendy asked Love Bug to be her second in command. He was happy to take the post, especially since it promised easy access to his favorite position, tucked in under her big ear. And he was making noises about accompanying her on a trip to her island one of these days. The *Sans Gloire* does were still marveling at Love Bug's transition from teen Romeo to boyfriend material, but the kits adored his endless stream of cheesy jokes. And he wore his title of Goldkiller lightly.

Freddie, who continued to talk up peace even while he dreamed up new weapons, was free to putter among his tools and ideas. He was glad to turn his engineer's mind to a wide variety of projects, starting with refining the crossbows. And he spent all day looking forward to Anastasia lying next to him on their bed of moss and leaves in the evenings, feeling her lean, muscled body slowly relax as they snacked on blueberries and talked about their days.

Death Rage continued with the school for acrobatic pugilistic arts she had started earlier. And students came from far and wide to learn from the only mouse in the world who had been inside both a coyote's mouth and the fortress of the once-mighty Summerdays, and come out alive each time.

At first, Anastasia had been furious with Death Rage for setting Bricabrac free, but after many long talks with the earnest mouse, she had come to see her side of the story. Bricabrac's sister Frippery had not been seen since she unlocked Anastasia's cage on the day of the battle. After it became clear that she had saved Anastasia's life by making herself scarce when the Summerdays wanted her to open the cage, her *rats is for rats* transgressions were overlooked. Now both rats were safely back in City of Oom.

Nicodemus was thinking hard about connecting the libraries in all the warrens. He also wanted to try and set up an expedition to the Spires to find some of the original written pages containing the Word of Yah written down by crows centuries before. He said future historians would never forgive him if he failed to add these priceless artifacts to the Library *Sans Gloire* permanent collection.

Stan decided to stay on and become the official leader of

the aerial squadron of the *Armée Libre*. He was also carrying on studying with Dingus with an eye to becoming an Oga For Young Goats adept.

Dingus and the Ascending Squirrels, still seeking the perfect balance between attachment and renunciation, had decided to keep a toehold in the outcomes-based community. So they agreed for the moment to continue as crossbow surfers.

Wellbutrin stayed in the North Shandy for awhile to help the raccoons there reclaim and rebuild their apple orchards, while Lorazepam came back south to manage their burgeoning dirty apple business.

Grégoire and Juniper were talking about setting up a school for Healers. And Juniper was becoming an expert at hunting medicinal herbs and wanted to have a trained herbalist in every warren.

Mabel was pursuing her goal of creating a new mythology out of the old Word of Yah, delivering them as stories in the Book of Secrets about Newly Beloved. As the Rememberers in general became unmoored in this new world, some followed her ideas. Others drifted away from Yah entirely. Some took up Oga For Young Goats. One or two even inquired with Wendy about the teachings of the god of fierce lops, Elsie McGowan.

Sunbeam said nothing about what Olympia had asked her to do, but she was seen often wandering widely through the territories along the south bank of the Shandy. Something seemed to make her uncomfortable at both *Sans Gloire* and Bloody Thorn. Finally, Mabel came across her in a wood by the river and took the dreamy adolescent bunny to live with her at Tumble Stone Warren. "Here's a little quiet space for you," she had whispered in Sunbeam's ear as she found the young doe a sleeping nook next to her own. Slowly, the 'Y'-shaped scar on her forehead began to fade from pink to white.

Tobias, the sometime Lord Harmonizer, made himself scarce. Indeed all the ecclesiastical worthies of the Known World Symposium made it their business to fade into the background, all the better to avoid any mob justice that might otherwise be coming their way.

Aiden did show up one day, not long after that Battle of the Narrows, and humbly knelt before Anastasia. He wept as he told her how wrong he had been and how much regret he had for the ideas he had put in the service of Olympia. He announced that he wished to go to the uplands and evangelize there among the heathen rabbits, spreading the good news of Newly Beloved that he had been learning from Mabel.

Anastasia, bemused, let him go. Even now, as the unquestioned leader of the Million Acre Wood, she was dreading the conversation she would have to have with her mother.

ANASTASIA

It was late afternoon on a sunny fall day when Anastasia went to see Olympia. Nicodemus, Freddie, and others offered to come with her, but she had declined. She was not sure what she would say, and not at all certain that the event would leave her covered in glory.

She did bring her Guard, and she simply walked the mile or so to Bloody Thorn Warren and sat down in front of the main entrance. It was the very hole she had been pushed out of seven months ago. Her heartbeat was fast and thready, but she sat very still. Her Guard fanned out around her and stood silently, flanking her with gleaming bite blades and spears.

She could hear some whispered commotion coming from inside the warren, and in a few moments, a handsome gray doe with a slash of white across her face and down her back came out. It was Olympia.

Her ocean-blue eyes were very wide and beautiful. She came toward Anastasia and kissed her forehead. Then she made herself small, looking up at her daughter.

"You know what I have done," she said. "I was wrong about the world. You were right."

Anastasia stared at her without speaking. The slanting rays of the sun made Olympia's gray fur look warm and soft. The Loving Auntie's Guard stood like statues, their burnished weapons a symbol of Anastasia's plenary power.

After a long moment, Anastasia spoke. "You sent children out to be killed by our enemies." A silent grimace passed over her face, and for a moment, her lips rose off her teeth. "Coriander died because of you."

"The Yah bunnies told me I had to do something," said Olympia. Her gaze flitted across the armed warriors gazing at her with unblinking eyes. "I deeply regret my choices."

"You tried to have me killed," said Anastasia. Her scent was a storm of whirling knives. "I could have died because of you."

"I tried to save our family. I made the hard decisions to protect as many as I could."

Anastasia felt a familiar burn start along her back. Somehow, when calculations were made on behalf of the family, she was always the disposable one.

Her mother spoke again, her voice warm and reasonable. "But none of this matters. You were right. You won. You can choose to forgive me. Or you can send me to the Lucky Fields. I await your decision." Her blue eyes were huge and shining.

"For you, I think 'forgiveness' ... has no meaning," said Anastasia. She flicked out her Dragon Claw, and the amber light bathed it in a golden glow. It hovered in the space between them. Olympia looked at the shining blade. She was still as a statue.

"I don't want to be the kind of person who ends lives because it's convenient," said Anastasia. "I believe that you were trying to help your family." She ran her left paw pad along the flat of her Claw. "I want to help you remember who your family is." She took hold of Olympia's forepaw and rested the tip of her blade on it.

Olympia did not resist. A tiny cry escaped her as the tip of the Claw slipped into her pad.

"You are not my mother," said Anastasia. She punctured her own left forepaw with her weapon, and then pressed their paws together. As their blood mingled, she said, "You are a killer. I am a killer. We are blood sisters. We are *family*. The tightest kind of *family*. Do you hear me, sister?"

Olympia looked astonished. She nodded slowly. Anastasia released her sticky paw.

"Now go out to the ocean, where the bitter marram grass grows," said Anastasia. "Dig yourself a burrow. And stay." Her eyes flicked over to her Guard. "Don't make us come looking for you."

Olympia nodded slowly, without speaking.

"If I have need of a slippery killer, I will send for you,"

said Anastasia. "Bring your gifts when called for and earn your place in the history of the Free Peoples."

Olympia came near to her and kissed her forehead. Her blue eyes were shiny with tears. She spoke in a whisper. "I understand, dear sister."

FREE NATION

It was the day of the first Assembly. The Million Acre Wood was about to become a nation. Thousands of animals from all over the Million Acre Wood were gathered in the meadow at the foot of the high hill near *Sans Gloire*. What kind of nation would it be? That was still undetermined.

Anastasia and Freddie were sitting side by side near a stand of marigolds growing in the grassy area at the crown of the high hill, soaking up the warmth of the autumn sun and watching the animals gathering on the wide grassy area below.

She was wearing her Kevlar jacket with the golden side out, and the *aluminum d'or* circlet on her forehead shone brightly in the sun.

Nearby, a bevy of young kittens tumbled about among the flowers. Watching the kits made her feel warm and happy and sad, all at the same time. Born just a month earlier, they had never lived in a world where raptors might fall from the sky at any moment, so they played with a carefree abandon that Anastasia could never have imagined.

Freddie noticed her looking misty-eyed at the kittens. He kissed her forehead tenderly, avoiding the side of her face where her wounds had mostly healed but were still tender.

"We did it," he said, smiling.

"I still can't believe it," she said, and nuzzled into the soft gray fur of his neck.

They were silent for a long moment.

She blew out a long, slow breath. "So many kits now," she said. "It's wonderful."

"Yes," said Freddie.

"Soon there will be more kits in the Million Acre Wood than ever before."

Freddie's eyes flicked toward her. "Mmm," he said, and groomed his forepaw. "It's a problem that I don't think any rabbits have ever had."

"It's a beautiful, beautiful problem," said Anastasia. "I'm grateful to have it."

"Me, too," said Freddie. "There's also one that's not so beautiful. Crows from City of Oom have been seen flying along the Boreal Cliffs. Stan thinks they're scouting."

"Of course they're scouting," Anastasia. She almost began to draw a complex design in the earth, but stopped herself. "The bears in City of Oom can't be happy there's a free nation of small animals right next door. That's going to give their own small animals ideas. And of course, the hunters we pushed out are probably all in Oom right now, telling them we're dangerous monsters."

"We *are* dangerous," said Freddie, as he raised himself into a ferocious stance. "We will nibble the carrot tops right out from under you."

They caught sight of a messenger approaching. Anastasia rubbed Freddie's soft grey ear tip with her long brown ear. "Plenty of problems," she said. "But they're problems for tomorrow, not today."

A yearling bunny wearing a band of gold agave cord around the base of her right ear hopped up to them. She was one of the messengers in the new communications network Yasmin had started. "Loving Auntie," she said, smiling. "It's almost time. They're all so excited to see you."

Anastasia scoffed. Freddie leaned into her, his mouth close to her ear. "Oh, let them love you," he said. "They deserve it." He pulled away to look her in the eyes. "And so do you."

"Shall I tell them you're on your way?" asked the messenger. "Sorry to be so pushy."

"Yes. And don't be sorry," said Anastasia. "You're just doing your job." She got up and licked the messenger bunny's forehead. The messenger was clearly a little flustered by this gesture of respect from such a great personage, and *binked* as she bounded off, singing a little song.

Then Anastasia and Freddie strolled down the scrubby hillside toward the waiting animals. The meadow at the base of the hill was filled with thousands of rabbits, mice, and raccoons, delegates from the districts centered on all the warrens in the Million Acre Wood. The branches of the oak trees ringing the meadow were alive with the multicolor twinkle of songbirds and the flicker and zip of squirrels. There had never been a gathering like this.

Anastasia approached the dais the rabbits had built as an earthwork on the side of the hill. As she emerged from the bushes, the animals caught sight of her, and they began to chant. "*Long live the Queen! Long live the Queen!*"

Anastasia waved her paws in a shushing motion. "No, no," she said.

The sea of animals looked up at her expectantly, so hope-ful, so joyful. The scent that rose from them was relaxed, happy, pointy, and bouncy, all at the same time.

Anastasia took a deep breath and called over the excited chatter. "*I will never be your Queen.*"

A vast *awww* swept over the crowd. Would there be no wonderful golden goddess handing out treats for the rest of their days? It was not what they had hoped for. There was also some vigorous cheering from the Readers interspersed among them who had a better idea what actual queens are really like.

Anastasia shook her head and smiled, then stood tall. "*I will never be your Landlord,*" she shouted.

A vast cheer erupted at this, as these little animals, thou-sands strong, felt the history-making import of this moment. It was as though a great weight had been lifted, and animals throughout the crowd began to leap into the air, making joyful noises, and clapping their paws together. Hundreds of rabbits went full *binky*. It was *bink* upon *bink* upon *bink*, until the meadow looked like a popcorn extravaganza. Raccoons rolled on their backs and trilled as they shook their broad bellies. In the trees, the squirrels rattled their bean pod noisemakers and the songbirds burst forth in marvelously complex call-and-response fanfares to celebrate their new nation.

Anastasia rocked back a bit under the weight of all this hoopla coming at her. Then she spread her paws wide and stepped to the edge of the dais. "*For as long as you want me, I will be your Loving Auntie.*"

A vast wordless cry of love burst from thousands of little throats. Most of them had never met or even seen Anastasia before this day, but they knew she had changed their lives forever. She glanced back at Freddie and heard his words again in her ear. *Let them love you.*

She reached out toward them in a gesture of wide embrace, and in return, they lifted their forepaws to her, eyes filled with tears of joy and yearning and hope that this amazing new life could somehow keep going, world without end.

The inchoate cry of deep affection gradually coalesced into a chant that shook the hills, underpinned by a deeply affirming triple thump that took hold among all the animals, and then went on and on. "*Auntie, yay!*" they roared. "*Auntie, yay! Auntie, yay!*"

Thank you

Thank you so much for reading *Summerday*! Please let me know what you think of it by leaving a rating or review on your favorite online sites for discussing or buying books.

Summerday is the second book in the *War Bunny Chronicles*.

The first book, *War Bunny*, is available now at your favorite online bookstore. The third book in the series, *City of Oom*, is currently in development.

Please join the email list to:

- Get the scoop on sequels, audiobooks, and other developments
- Hear about freebies and special deals

You can sign up at www.christopherstjohn.com.

If you'd like to reach me with any questions, please email me at sansgloire@gmail.com.

Thanks again!
Christopher St. John

Acknowledgements

I would like to thank the animals who served as models for some of these characters. Rescue bunnies all, they've come to have a profound impact on my understanding of who counts as a "person." Anastasia and Freddie came from SaveABunny in Mill Valley, California. Love Bug and Wendy came from RabbitEARS in Oakland, California. Mabel was rescued from a California fur farm and lives with a friend.

I'd like to thank my sisters, Catherine McKenzie and Julia Singer Presar, who have spent many hours talking through ideas with me.

I'd like to thank the beta readers who provided wonderful and astute feedback, pointing out lots of ways *Summerday* could be better, greatly enriching the story. A heartfelt thank you to Teryl Mandel, Hannah Niklaus, Nancy Gage, Chantal Comeau, Caitlin Throckmorton, Julia Singer Presar, Adrian Frost, and Cee.

The team at Harvest Oak Press has spared no effort to make *Summerday* the best it can be. It was wonderful working with editor Laurel McKenzie, and Belle McClain's evocative cover art is the perfect match for this story. Thanks for all your hard work!

And I must offer oodles of thanks to my wife, Gayle Paul, who this year, and every year, wins the Grand Slam Award for Being The Super Duperest Number One Very Tiptoppy Most Bestest Of All Da Bunniez.

Made in the USA
Monee, IL
09 April 2023